Linden Hills

'I think your folks got a great home,' Norman said, staring into space. 'I've been telling Ruth that soon as we get on our feet, I'm applying for a house in Linden Hills.'

'And you'll live in it alone.' Ruth went to the back window that looked down on Linden Hills. 'You know, wherever you go, I'm game – Spring Vale, Park Heights, even out of state. But I'm never going back down there again. I've had that life, Norm, and I lasted six months. Those folks just aren't real – excuse me, Lester. I'm not trying to talk about your mother.'

'No, talk about her,' Lester said. 'It's true. I was just telling Willie this morning, those are a bunch of the saddest niggers you'll ever wanna meet. They eat, sleep, and breathe for one thing – making it. And making it where?'

'Up.' Ruth shrugged her shoulders and sighed. 'Everybody wants to make it up there.'

Also by Gloria Naylor

The Women of Brewster Place

Gloria Naylor
Linden Hills

METHUEN

A Methuen Paperback

LINDEN HILLS

British Library Cataloguing in Publication Data

Naylor, Gloria
    Linden Hills.
    I. Title
    813'.54[F]   PS3564.A895
    ISBN 0–413–59230–8

First published in Great Britain 1985
by Hodder and Stoughton Limited
Copyright © 1985 by Gloria Naylor

This edition published 1986
by Methuen London Ltd
11 New Fetter Lane, London EC4P 4EE

Printed and bound in Great Britain
by Richard Clay (The Chaucer Press) Ltd,
Bungay, Suffolk

This book is sold subject to the condition
that it shall not, by way of trade or otherwise,
be lent, resold, hired out, or otherwise circulated
without the publisher's prior consent in any form
of binding or cover other than that in which
it is published and without a similar condition
including this condition being imposed
on the subsequent purchaser.

For my parents —
Roosevelt and Alberta Naylor

Grandma Tilson, I'm afraid of hell.
Ain't nothing to fear, there's hell on earth.
I mean the real hell where you can go when you die.
You ain't gotta die to go to the real hell.
No?
Uh uh, you just gotta sell that silver mirror God
propped up in your soul.
Sell it to who — the devil?
Naw, just to the highest bidder, child. The
highest bidder.

There had been a dispute for years over the exact location of Linden Hills. Everyone associated with Wayne County had taken part in it: the U.S. Post Office, census takers, city surveyors, real estate brokers, and the menagerie of blacks and whites who had lived along its fringes for a hundred and sixty years. The original 1820 surveys that Luther Nedeed kept locked in his safe-deposit box stated that it was a V-shaped section of land with the boundaries running south for one and a half miles from the stream that bordered Putney Wayne's high grazing fields down a steep, rocky incline of brier bush and linden trees before curving through the town's burial ground and ending in a sharp point at the road in front of Patterson's apple orchard. It wasn't a set of hills, or even a whole hill — just the worthless northern face of a rich plateau. But it patiently bore the designation of Linden Hills as its boundaries contracted and expanded over the years to include no one, and then practically everyone in Wayne County.

The fact never disputed by anyone was that the Nedeeds have

always lived there. Luther's double great-grandfather bought the entire northern face of the plateau, descending from what is now First Crescent Drive to Tupelo Drive — which is really the last three of a series of eight curved roads that ring themselves around the hill. But Luther's double great-grandfather, coming from Tupelo, Mississippi, where it was rumored that he'd actually sold his octoroon wife and six children for the money that he used to come North and obtain the hilly land, named that section Tupelo Drive. And at the time none of the white farmers gave a flying squat what he called it, 'cause if some crazy nigger wanted to lay out solid gold eagles for hard sod only good enough to support linden trees that barely got you ten cents on the dollar for a cord of oak or birch — let him. And the entire bottom of the land is hemmed in by the town cemetery. Had to be half-witted — who'd want to own land near a graveyard, especially a darky who is known to be scared pantless of haints and such? They pocketed Nedeed's money and had a good laugh: first full moon on All Hallows would send them spirits walking and him running to beg them to buy the property back. That is, if he didn't starve to death first. Couldn't eat linden trees, and Lord knows he wasn't gonna raise spit on that land. Would raise a lot of sand, though. Knees were slapped and throats choked on tobacco juice. Yup, he'd raise plenty of sand while trying to get a team and wagon down through that bush to fetch supplies.

But Nedeed didn't try to farm Linden Hills. He built a two-room cabin at the bottom of the slope — dead center — with its door and windows facing the steep incline. After the cabin was finished, they could see him sitting in front of it for an hour at dawn, high noon, and dusk — his dark, immobile face rotating slowly amid the lime tombstones, the tangled brier, and the high stretch of murky forest. He sat there every day for exactly seven days — his thick, puffed lids raising, lowering, and narrowing over eyes that seemed to be measuring precisely the depth and length of light that the sun allowed his wedge of their world.

"Guess he's trying to *think* a living out of that land." But their victory had been replaced by a question as they watched Nedeed watching the path of the sun. No one admitted that they lacked the courage just to walk over and demand to know what he was doing. There was something in Luther Nedeed's short, squat body that stopped those men from treating him like a nigger — and something in his eyes that soon stopped them from even thinking the word. It was said that his protruding eyes could change color at will, and over the course of his life, they would be assigned every color except red. They were actually dark brown — a flat brown — but since no man ever had the moral stamina to do more than glance at his face, because those huge, bottomless globes could spell out a starer's midnight thoughts, black men looked at his feet or hands and white men looked over his shoulder at the horizon.

As the sun disappeared on the seventh day of his vigil, Luther Nedeed closed his eyes slowly and smiled. Patterson said he was hauling his apples away from the field and the sight of Nedeed sitting there grinning like one of them heathen E-jip mummies scared him out of a year's growth, and when he got home, all the bushels facing Nedeed's side of the road had fruit worms in them. He claimed that as the justification for the eight-foot fence he erected on the northern border of his orchard. It might have been closer to the truth to admit that he just couldn't stomach the sight of Nedeed dragging all those dead bodies into his yard. Because the day after Patterson's alleged plague of worms, Nedeed went and bought a team of horses, a box-shaped wagon, and began an undertaker's business in the back room of his cabin. His proximity to the town cemetery put little strain on the horses and funeral hearse, and Nedeed knew that, unlike the South, the North didn't care if blacks and whites were buried together so long as they didn't live together. Appalled by the reports of the evils that lay below the Mason-Dixon and the cry that "the only good nigger is a dead nigger," Wayne County let it be known that any of their sable brothers who were good and dead were welcome to a Christian burial right next to a white person — Tuesdays, Thursdays, and Saturdays, the days assigned for colored funerals.

Nedeed then built wooden shacks up on the hill, from what is now First Crescent Drive down to Fifth Crescent Drive, and rented them out to local blacks who were too poor to farm and earned their living from the sawmills or tar pit. He also wanted to rent out shacks along Tupelo Drive, but no one wanted any part of the cemetery land. It was bad enough they were down on their luck and had to resort to living in the hills, but they didn't have to live near that strange Nedeed by a graveyard. News that someone had moved into the hills was always rebuffed: They lived *up* from Linden Hills; only Nedeed lived down on Linden Hills. And the white farmer who owned the grazing land over the stream at the crest of the hill would fight over being told that he had land in Linden Hills: That was coon town and he didn't have a blade of grass there; he was *across* from Linden Hills.

The fact that no one wanted to be associated with his land didn't bother Luther Nedeed. The nature of things being what they are, his business thrived. And over the years he was able to build a large, white clapboard house with a full veranda and a concrete morgue in the basement. He went away for a while in the spring of 1837 and brought back an octoroon wife. Rumor had it that he had returned to Mississippi and bought back the wife he had sold to a Cajun saloonkeeper. But the girl who set up housekeeping in the undertaker's home couldn't have been more than twenty years old, and Nedeed had owned Linden Hills for almost seventeen years by then. She gave him a son the following winter — short, squat, dark, and with an immobile face, even from birth. He grew up to carry his father's first name, broad chest, and bowlegs. Big frog and little frog, the town whispered behind their backs.

Luther left his land and business to this only son, who everyone was betting would sell it before the old man was cold, since little Luther had been sent to one of them fancy boarding schools and surely had more sense than old crazy Luther to hold on to worthless hill land. But the son came back to the land and the undertaking business and carried the butt of the jokes about his father's property on his quiet back. It seemed that when old Luther died in 1879, he hadn't died at all, especially when they spoke to his son and especially when they glanced at those puffed eyelids and around those bottomless eyes. He, too, brought an octoroon woman into his home who gave him only one son — another Luther Nedeed.

Nothing was changing in the white clapboard house at the bottom of Linden Hills. There was another generation of big frog and little frog going through the hills together every first of the month to collect rent. What was changing slowly — very slowly — was the face of Wayne County. Farms were dwindling and small townships were growing in the place of cornfields and fruit groves. Putney Wayne's son had sold a quarter of his pasture to a shoe factory and the smoky cinders blew over the entire field, settling in the sheep's wool and turning the grass an ashy blue. This caused Wayne's grandson to think that the price a Welsh developer offered him for the land was a miracle, and he grabbed the money and headed for New York City at the miraculous speed of thirty-five mph on the new railroad lines and never came back. The second wealthiest man in Wayne County bought a curved-dash Oldsmobile, proudly announcing that he now had the power of three horses that he could feed for a tenth the cost of grain.

But the wealthiest man in Wayne County sat at the bottom of Linden Hills and still carried wooden coffins to the cemetery with a horse and wagon. Old Luther's son had sent away to England for the circulars from a new locomotive company called Rolls-Royce that was willing to custom design and ship him a funeral hearse with a mahogany dashboard and pure silver handles. He locked the circulars up in his desk, went to the second wealthiest man, and bought his team of Cleveland Bays at an incredibly low price. Nedeed knew he would have to wait until almost the poorest white family in Wayne County owned an automobile before even dead blacks rode in mahogany and silver.

Old Luther's son was finally able to rent shacks along Tupelo Drive. These tenants didn't seem to mind that they were surrounded by a cemetery. Talk had it that they had been murderers, root doctors, carpetbaggers, and bootleg preachers who were thrown out of the South and needed the short memory of the dead and the long shadows of the lindens for their left-of-center carryings-on. Nedeed didn't care how they were able to pay their rent so long as they did it promptly on the first of the month. When the area within five acres of his funeral home became populated, he constructed an artificial lake (really a moat), a full twenty yards across, totally around his house and grounds. He filled it with marsh weeds, catfish, and ducks. Now the only entrance to his veranda was at the back, through a wood-and-brick drawbridge that he always kept down, but his neighbors saw the pulleys on the bridge and took immediate offense. Seemed as if he wanted to make out he was better than other folks — yeah, separate himself from the scum. Well, everybody knew that he'd been able to make them fancy changes on his house — building extra rooms and a *third* level — 'cause years ago he'd financed gunrunners to the Confederacy. A rebel-loving nigger and now he was putting on airs with his blood money. They secretly nicknamed the lake Wart's Pond — a fitting place for him and his frog-eyed son to squat on.

But they kept paying him rent and letting him bury their dead. And as the faces on the hill changed and the old town became a young city as the last farmlands gave way to housing developments, Nedeed sat on his porch swing and watched the sun move as it always had over his world. He remembered his father and was thankful that he had lived long enough to watch his words engraved in the scarred landscape of the county: Let 'em think as they want; let 'em say as they want — black or white. Just sit right here and they'll make you a rich man through the two things they'll all *have* to do: live and die. Nedeed watched the sun, the twentieth century, and the value of his hard, sod hill creep upward as slowly and concretely as the last laugh from a dead man's grave.

The young municipal government soon took an interest in Linden Hills and tried to buy it from old Luther's son, who was now very old himself. His refusal to sell provided months of employment for title searchers, city surveyors, and public works assessors. The location of Linden Hills made confiscation for the purpose of a bridge, tunnel, or some other "public good" ludicrous. Nedeed told the assessors that if they could come up with a blueprint for any type of municipal project, he'd *give* them the land — root to leaf. But set one brick on his property for some high-blown private development and — he pointed a gnarled finger at the squat carbon copy beside him — he would personally drag Wayne County all the way to the Supreme Court. The title searchers and surveyors were then sent to unearth crumbling state statutes and fading deeds, looking for some clause that either invalidated or whittled down Nedeed's claim to the hill. Finally, an ambitious young lawyer found a seventeenth-century mandate forbidding Negroes to own, lease, or transfer property in Wayne County — regrettably, the same law that prohibited Hebrews, Catholics, and Devil worshipers from holding public office. Mayor Kilpatrick called an emergency meeting of the city council and they voted six to nothing to revoke the mandate. The mayor thanked them for convening on such short notice; then, after strongly advising the young lawyer to seek employment outside of Wayne County, he decided to let the matter of Linden Hills rest.

Nedeed, seeing that the government and real estate developers wanted his land so badly, decided to insure that they'd never be able to get their hands on it. So he went throughout the hill with his son beside him and, starting with First Crescent Drive all the way down through Fifth Crescent Drive, sold the land practically for air to the blacks who were shacking there. He gave them a thousand-year-and-a-day lease — provided only that they passed their property on to their children. And if they wanted to sell it, they had to sell it to another black family or the rights would revert back to the Nedeeds. And it seemed as if there were always going to be Nedeeds, because his son's pale-skinned bride was bloated with child. It surprised no one when the baby was male and had the father's complexion, protruding eyes, and first name — by now it had come to be expected.

Nedeed gave the same thousand-year-and-a-day option to the tenants who rented along Tupelo Drive, but he didn't have to worry about them. They couldn't move because only he would tolerate them on his land. Linden Hills was puzzled over Nedeed's behavior. Why was he up and being so nice to colored folks when his daddy had been a slave dealer and he himself had sold guns to the Confederacy? Probably trying to make good with his kind before the Lord called him home. "God bless you," an old woman breathed over her parchment of paper. Let him bless *you* — you'll need it, Nedeed thought as he stonily turned his back.

Like his father, he saw where the future of Wayne County — the future of America — was heading. It was going to be white: white money backing wars for white power because the very earth was white — look at it — white gold, white silver, white coal running white railroads and steamships, white oil fueling white automotives. Under the earth — across the earth — and one day, *over* the earth. Yes, the very sky would be white. He didn't know exactly how, but it was the only place left to go. And when they got there, they weren't taking anyone black with them — and why should they? These people, his people, were always out of step, a step behind or a step ahead, still griping and crying about slavery, hanging up portraits of Abraham Lincoln in those lousy shacks. They couldn't do nothing because they *were* slaves or because they *will be* in heaven. Praying and singing about what lay beyond the sky — "God bless you" — open your damned Bible, woman, and you'll see that even the pictures of your god are white. Well, keep trying to make your peace with that white god, keep moaning and giving the Nedeeds over half a year's wages to send a hunk of rotting flesh off to heaven in style instead of putting that money into bonds or land or even the bank at one-and-a-half-percent interest. Yes, make your peace with that white god who lived beyond the sky — he was going to deal with the white god who would one day *own* that sky. And you and yours would help him.

Sure, they thought him a fool — look at the fools that he had to claim as his own. When they laughed at them, they laughed at him. Well, he would show them. This wedge of earth was his — he couldn't rule but he sure as hell could ruin. He could be a fly in that ointment, a spot on that bleached sheet, and Linden Hills would prove it. He had given his people some of the most expensive property in the county. They had the land for a millennium. Now just let them sit on it and do what they do best: digging another man's coal, cleaning another man's home, rocking another man's baby. And let them learn to count enough to keep paying monthly insurance, because they could read enough to believe that heaven was still waiting while they wrote just enough to sign those insurance premiums over to him. Nedeed's last vision when he closed his puffy eyelids, with his image bending over him, was of Wayne County forced to drive past Linden Hills and being waved at by the maids, mammies, and mules who were bringing the price of that sweat back to his land and his hands. A wad of spit — a beautiful, black wad of spit right in the white eye of America.

But Nedeed hadn't foreseen the Great Depression that his grandson was to live through. Those years brought another pale-skinned bride to the clapboard house, the construction of a separate mortuary and chapel, a triple garage, and the first set of automated hearses. They also brought a wave of rumors that Nedeed managed to come through so well because he'd sold all his stocks and bonds just a day before Black Friday and kept his money in a coffin, where it grew like a dead man's toenails because he sprinkled it with the dust he gathered from the graves of babies.

Luther Nedeed didn't care where Linden Hills thought he had gotten his money, but he spent several years deciding where it should go. Watching America's nervous breakdown during the thirties, he realized that nothing was closer to the spleen and guts of the country than success. The Sunday papers now told him what the sun had told his dead fathers about the cycles of men: Life is in the material — anything high, wide, deep. Success is being able to stick an "er" on it. And death is watching someone else have it. His grandfather's dream was still possible — the fact that they had this land was a blister to the community, but to make that sore fester and pus over, Linden Hills had to be a showcase. He had to turn it into a jewel — an ebony jewel that reflected the soul of Wayne County but reflected it black. Let them see the marble and brick, the fast and sleek, yes, and all those crumbs of power they uniformed their sons to die for, magnified tenfold and shining bright — so bright that it would spawn dreams of dark kings with dark counselors leading dark armies against the white god and toward a retribution all feared would not be just, but long overdue. Yes, a brilliance that would force a waking nightmare of what the Nedeeds were capable. And the fools would never realize — he looked down at his son playing with a toy dragon — that it was nothing but light from a hill of carbon paper dolls.

There would be no problem in financing his vision. It took exactly three phone calls and one letter to acquire the state charter the new Tupelo Realty Corporation needed to finance, construct, and sell private developments. Nedeed never doubted that he'd be able to build the houses; the real problem was deciding who in Linden Hills should own them. This was something that he couldn't leave to his lawyers, so with his son beside him Luther Nedeed visited every shack on the hill and talked to his tenants. He walked through Linden Hills as it would be — along smooth curved roads, up long sloping lawns and manicured meridians. He stood under the door fronts of imitation Swiss chalets, British Tudors, and Georgian town houses flanked by arbors choked with morning glories, wisteria, and honeysuckle. Driveways were lined with mimosas, and gazebos sat in the shadow of elms and tulip oaks while lavender and marigolds outlined the bases of marble fountains and aviaries. He trod quietly amid his vision, knowing that he must take extreme care to weed out anyone who threatened to produce seeds that would block the light from his community. And empty goblets let through the most light, Nedeed thought as he began knocking on doors down along Tupelo Drive.

He started with the ones who would be the most eager to work with him on the future of Linden Hills. The children of the parasites and outcasts from the South, who could find a welcome only from the dead that bordered their homes, wanted nothing better than a way to forget and make the world forget their past. Many had already taken the ample income from their families and built frame houses on their land, with wire fences surrounding the neat front yards and backyard gardens. Beyond the money they had received from their parents, they had no use for the clouded inheritance of incense, blood, and distilled alcohol that had built the walls which they were constantly painting and whitewashing as if to remove a stench. Yes, they would gladly match dollar for dollar the investment from the Tupelo Realty Corporation to build up a community for their children to be proud of. So when their grandchildren thought back, it would be to Linden Hills. When they needed to journey back, it would be to the brick and marble they would erect with this man's help. Strong, solid walls and heavy, marble steps — the finest in the new community — strong enough, solid enough to bury permanently any outside reflections about other beginnings. The Tupelo Realty Corporation offered them all this, and a memory was a small price to pay.

Nedeed's work was done quickly in Tupelo Drive, but now he had to tread more carefully as he made his way up the rest of the slope. Most of these people were proud of the lousy quarters and dimes, damp with their parents' sweat, that had been invested in their thousand-year-and-a-day leases. The painted walls, additional bedrooms, and raked dirt yards were the labor of people who had hopes of building on, not over, their past. These were the fools who could do the most damage if he let them stay. There were some up there who had rooted themselves in the beliefs that Africa could be more than a word; slavery hadn't run its course; there was salvation in Jesus and salve in the blues. Sure, Nedeed could tell them that you spelled real progress in white capital letters, but their parents hadn't been able to read and here they sat as living proof that you could survive anyway. No, people like that looked back a millennium, and if they could sit on Linden Hills for a millennium they'd produce children who would dream of a true black power that spread beyond the Nedeeds; children who would take this wedge of earth and try to turn it into a real weapon against the white god. He'd cultivate no madmen like Nat Turner or Marcus Garvey in Linden Hills — that would only get them all crushed back into the dust.

He knew how to stop that before it began. Even a goblet filled with the darkest liquid will let through light — if it's diluted enough, Nedeed thought as he carefully dressed himself and his son before they visited the rest of Linden Hills. As he placed his polished wing-tip shoes on their sagging front porches, he watched them watching the crisp lines in his linen suit, counting the links in his gold watch chain, and measuring the grade of his son's gabardine knickers. He made a note of the eyes that returned to his dark face carrying respect and not suspicion, and silently chose the ones who then found some pretense to make their playing children come up from the road or out of the house to stand quietly and listen while he talked about everything from the weather to the price of soap. He could now safely tell these about the Tupelo Realty Corporation with its low-interest mortgage and scholarship funds to Fisk and Howard, because he knew they were calling their children to watch a wizard: Come, look, listen and perhaps you will learn how to turn the memory of our iron chains into gold chains. The cotton fields that broke your grandparents' backs can cover yours in gabardine. See, the road to salvation can be walked in leather shoes and sung about in linen choir robes. Nedeed almost smiled at their simplicity. Yes, they would invest their past and apprentice their children to the future of Linden Hills, forgetting that a magician's supreme art is not in transformation but in making things disappear.

Nedeed got rid of the unwanted tenants by either buying or tricking them out of their leases. He finally managed to clear out most of the upper slope, but when he reached First Crescent Drive, he ran into a problem with Grandma Tilson.

"I used to fish with your daddy down in that there pond, Luther, and he gave me this land and I ain't giving it up. So take your frog-eyed self and your frog-eyed son out of here. And I know your evil ways — all of you. So if you plan to try something like burning my house down while I just happen to be in it, I got this here deed *and* my will registered at the courthouse. Your daddy weren't no fool and he didn't fish with fools either."

Mamie Tilson's grown children hadn't made her a grandmother yet, but she had carried that nickname from a young girl because she was born with an old face, the color of oiled cheese-cloth. Her clear skin allowed people to see the firmness of character that it covered. She had never minded staring down a Nedeed, because she liked what she read about herself in their bottomless eyes. So when Nedeed put his foot up on the top step of her porch and in a slow whisper asked if she wanted to think her position over, she paused for a moment and then sent a wad of tobacco spit near his wing-tips. That said she had thought it over and hoped he finally understood her answer.

Nedeed took his son's hand and left her yard. Let the hateful old hag just sit up there and rot. She'd die one day and then his son would deal with her children. The Tupelo Realty Corporation would build around her, and even over her if need be. He'd bury that one flaw deep in the middle of his jewel and no one would know the difference.

Nedeed didn't live long enough to have the pleasure of actually burying Grandma Tilson, who shuffled past his grave for ten winters. But he did see the outlines of his dream crystallize into a zoned district of eight circular drives that held some of the finest homes — and eventually the wealthiest black families — in the county. When the city first zoned its districts, the grazing land that once belonged to the sheep farmer, Putney Wayne, became Wayne Avenue. And after two white children drowned in the stream that separated Linden Hills from the avenue, a marble banister was erected along both its sides. The eight circular roads that curved around the three faces of the plateau were designated as First Crescent Drive, Second Crescent Drive, Third Crescent Drive, and the city commissioner wanted to continue it all the way down to Eighth Crescent Drive. But the families in the newly slated Sixth, Seventh, and Eighth Crescent drives of the Linden Hills section went to the commissioner and protested. Their area had always been known as Tupelo Drive and should stay that way, and besides, the old town cemetery cut them off from the other side of the plateau, so he didn't have eight whole crescents anyway. The city commissioner reared back in his tweed swivel chair and told them in so many words that he was keeping it just like it was and if they didn't like it,

they could go to hell. They went to Nedeed, instead, who went
to Washington, D.C., and had the town cemetery and Tupelo
Drive designated as a historical landmark.

News of this sent the Wayne County Citizens Alliance, headed
by Patterson's great-granddaughter, to the commissioner's office,
to question why their side of the plateau wasn't a historical
landmark as well. Their families had owned land there long before the Nedeeds. Patterson even dragged in her family Bible
with dates and names that went back to the Revolutionary War.
The disgruntled commissioner told them that there was nothing
he could do. It seemed that Washington thought the site where
some ex-slave's cabin had been more American than the sheep
dung that had sat on her parents' land. And as long as that socialist with his nigger-loving wife was in office, that was the way
it had to be. And no, they could *not* start calling their foot of the
plateau Tupelo Drive. Weren't his street plans messed up
enough already?

That didn't stop the white families on the other side of the
plateau from telling stray tourists that, of course, they lived in
Linden Hills — the *real* Linden Hills. And even after both Nedeed and Grandma Tilson had died, some of them were still
putting LINDEN HILLS on their mail. This only added to the confusion of the post office that had to deal with the poor black families across Wayne Avenue in the Putney Wayne section who
were also addressing their mail LINDEN HILLS. The Putney
Wayne residents were telling census takers, school superinten-
dents, and anyone else who cared to listen, that since Linden
Road ran up the side of Linden Hills, crossed Wayne Avenue,
and continued northward for three miles through *their* neighborhood, they lived in Linden Hills too. Weren't both areas full of
nothing but black folks? And trying to call their section Putney
Wayne was just another example of the way all those lousy racists in Wayne County tried to keep black people down.

Because the cemetery stopped Linden Road at Fifth Crescent
Drive, Tupelo Drive could only be entered through the center of
Fifth Crescent, and the Tupelo residents built a private road
with a flower-trimmed meridian headed by two twelve-foot

brick pillars. They then put up a bronze plaque on the pillars and had the words LINDEN HILLS engraved in deep Roman type. This caused the residents on First through Fifth Crescent drives immediately to erect a wooden sign — WELCOME TO LINDEN HILLS — behind the marble banister and the stream, separating them from the avenue. They didn't know what those people down in Tupelo Drive were trying to pull; maybe their homes weren't as large and fancy as those down there, but they definitely knew that they also lived in Linden Hills. They had the papers — actual deeds — that said this land was theirs as long as they sat on it, and sit they would.

So now practically every black in Wayne County wanted to be a part of Linden Hills. While it did have homes that had brought a photographer out from *Life* magazine for pictures of the Japanese gardens and marble swimming pools on Tupelo Drive, that wasn't the only reason they wanted to live there. There were other black communities with showcase homes, but somehow making it into Linden Hills meant "making it." The Tupelo Realty Corporation was terribly selective about the types of families who received its mortgages. Entrance obviously didn't depend upon your profession, because there was a high school janitor living right next to a municipal judge on Third Crescent Drive. And even your income wasn't a problem, because didn't the realty corporation subsidize that family of Jamaicans on Tupelo Drive who were practically starving to put two of their kids through Harvard? No, only "certain" people got to live in Linden Hills, and the blacks in Wayne County didn't know what that certain something was that qualified them, but they kept sending in applications to the Tupelo Realty Corporation — and hoping. Hoping for the moment they could move in, because then it was possible to move down toward Tupelo Drive and Luther Nedeed.

Yes, Linden Hills. The name had spread beyond Wayne County, and applicants were coming from all over the country and even the Caribbean. Linden Hills — a place where people had worked hard, fought hard, and saved hard for the privilege to rest in the soft shadows of those heart-shaped trees. In Linden

Hills they could forget that the world said you spelled black with
a capital nothing. Well, they were something and there was
everything around them to show it. The world hadn't given
them anything but the chance to fail — and they hadn't failed,
because they were in Linden Hills. They had a thousand years
and a day to sit right there and forget what it meant to be black,
because it meant working yourself to death just to stand still.
Well, they had the chance to move down in Linden Hills — as
far as Luther Nedeed, sitting at the foot of the hill behind a lake
and a whole line of men who had shown Wayne County what it
was possible to do with a little patience and a lot of work. They
wanted what Luther Nedeed had, and he had shown them how
to get it: Just stay right here; you step outside Linden Hills and
you've stepped into history — someone else's history about what
you couldn't ever do. The Nedeeds had made a history there and
it spoke loudly of what blacks could do. They were never leaving
Linden Hills. There was so much to be gotten. Surely, in a millennium their children could move down or even marry down
the hill toward Tupelo Drive and Luther Nedeed.

Tupelo Drive and Luther Nedeed: it became one cry of dark
victory for blacks outside or inside Linden Hills. And the ultimate dark victor sat in front of his home and behind his lake and
looked up at the Nedeed dream. It had finally crystallized into
that jewel, but he wore it like a weighted stone around his neck.
Something had gone terribly wrong with Linden Hills. He knew
what his dead fathers had wanted to do with this land and the
people who lived on it. These people were to reflect the Nedeeds
in a hundred facets and then the Nedeeds could take those
splintered mirrors and form a mirage of power to torment a
world that dared think them stupid — or worse, totally impo-
tent. But there was no torment in Linden Hills for the white god
his fathers had shaken their fists at, because there was no white
god, and there never had been.

They looked at the earth, the sea, and the sky, Luther thought
sadly, and mistook those who were owned by it as the owners.
They looked only at the products and thought they saw God —
they should have looked at the process. If they could have sat

with him in front of a television that now spanned their tiny planet and universe to universes beyond the sun and moments that had guided their hand, they would have known the futility of their vengeance. Because when men begin to claw men for the rights to a vacuum that stretches into eternity, then it becomes so painfully clear that the omnipresent, omnipotent, Almighty Divine is simply the *will* to possess. It had chained the earth to the names of a few and it would chain the cosmos as well.

A white god? Luther shook his head. How could it be any color when it stripped the skin, sex, and soul of any who offered themselves at its altar before it decided to bless? His fathers had made a fatal mistake: they had given Linden Hills the will to possess and so had lost it to the very god they sought to defy. How could these people ever reflect the Nedeeds? Linden Hills wasn't black; it was successful. The shining surface of their careers, brass railings, and cars hurt his eyes because it only reflected the bright nothing that was inside of them. Of course Wayne County had lived in peace with Linden Hills for the last two decades, since it now understood that they were both serving the same god. Wayne County had watched his wedge of earth become practically invisible — indistinguishable from their own pathetic souls.

The only ones who didn't seem to know what was happening in Linden Hills were the thousands of blacks who sent him applications every year. And since there was nowhere left to go with his land and nothing left to build, he would just let the fools keep coming. Let them think that he held some ultimate prize down there. Let them think that they were proving something to the world, to themselves, or to him about their worth. Unlike his fathers, he welcomed those who thought they had personal convictions and deep ties to their past, because then he had the pleasure of watching their bewilderment as it all melted away the farther they came down. Applications from any future Baptist ministers, political activists, and Ivy League graduates were now given first priority, since their kind seemed to reach the bottom faster than the others, leaving more room at the top. And whenever anyone reached the Tupelo area, they eventually disappeared. Finally, devoured by their own drives, there just wasn't enough humanity left to fill the rooms of a real home, and the property went up for sale. Luther often wondered why none of the applicants ever questioned the fact that there was always space in Linden Hills.

But they were too busy to question — they were so busy coming. And the one consuming purpose in Luther's life was to keep them doing that. Get them in, give them their deeds, and watch them come down. The plans and visions of his fathers might have been misdirected, but the Nedeeds could still live as a force to be reckoned with — if only within Linden Hills. His dark face at the bottom of the hill served as a beacon to draw the blacks needed as fuel for that continually dying dream. And it could go on forever through his son. But whenever Luther was forced to look at his son, his heart tightened.

Luther had not followed the pattern of his fathers and married a pale-skinned woman. He knew those wives had been chosen for the color of their spirits, not their faces. They had been brought to Tupelo Drive to fade against the whitewashed boards of the Nedeed home after conceiving and giving over a son to the stamp and will of the father. He actually had to pause a moment in order to remember his mother's first name, because everyone — including his father — had called her nothing but Mrs. Nedeed. And that's all she had called herself. Luther's wife was better than pale — a dull, brown shadow who had given him a son, but a white son. The same squat bowlegs, the same protruding eyes and puffed lips, but a ghostly presence that mocked everything his fathers had built. How could Luther die and leave this with the future of Linden Hills? He looked at this whiteness and saw the destruction of five generations. The child went unnamed and avoided by his father for the first five years of his life and Luther tried to discover what had brought such havoc into his home.

He took out the journals and charts that were locked in the ancient rolltop desk in his den. Weeks were spent tracing the dates and times of penetrations, conceptions, and births for every Nedeed in Linden Hills. He then matched all of this with

the position   earth's axis at those moments
and it all   passed down to him about the
facts of   days of penetration at the ap-
pearan   born when the sun has died."
   Lut   ut. He had done that — it was
follo   Nedeed before him, his seed
was   uinox so the child would come
d   en the winter's light was the
                      for generations, so what was
                      miliation of seeing a doctor to
                      bnormal with his reproductive
                      s returned positive and healthy,
                      e for what he had felt all along
                      hat this child could be his son.
                      against the clapboards of Tu-
                      on the shadow floating through
                      take form in front of his face. He
                      walked and sat down. He heard
                      e. He distinguished between the
                      frame and smelled the perfumed
ta   see the amber flecks in the heavily   the right side of the lips. The
long neck, small breasts, thick waist. Woman. She became a
constant irritant to Luther, who now turned her presence over in
his mind several times a day. Somewhere inside of her must be a
deep flaw or she wouldn't have been capable of such treachery.
Everything she owned he had given her — even her name —
and she had thanked him with this? The irritation began to fester in his mind and he knew he had to remove it or go insane. He
could throw her out tomorrow; there wasn't a court in this country that would deny him that right, but no one in his family had
ever gotten divorced. And she had to learn why she was brought
to Tupelo Drive. Obviously, he had allowed a whore into his
home but he would turn her into a wife.
   It was then that Luther reopened the old morgue in his basement. He worked alone and in a methodical fury, connecting
plumbing and lighting, stacking trunks and boxes against the

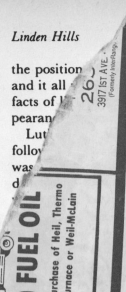

damp walls. A grimy sweat stung his eyes as he erected metal
shelving and wired an intercom. He brought down clumsy cartons of powdered milk and dry cereal, and finally, trembling
from exhaustion, he dragged two small cots down the twelve
concrete steps. He stood in the middle of the basement and surveyed his work.

Now, let her stay down here with her bastard and think about
what she'd done. Think about who she was playing with. He
climbed the steps and checked the iron bolt on the door. Did she
really think she could pass her lie off as his son? His fathers
slaved to build Linden Hills and the very home she had tried to
destroy. It took over a hundred and fifty years to build what he
now had and it would be a cold day in hell before he saw some
woman tear it down.

It was cold. In fact, it was the coldest week of the year when
White Willie and Shit slapped five on Wayne Avenue and began
their journey down Linden Hills.

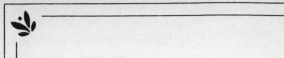

December
19th

The business district of Wayne Avenue was contained within five blocks on the northern side of the street. It had one library, one dry cleaner, one supermarket, and two delicatessens (one of which sold a better grade of marijuana than of olive loaf and took numbers when the taxi stand was closed). There were three liquor stores and three storefront churches — the Tabernacle of the Saints and Harry's Cut Rate Winery standing side by side. A host of small real estate offices were sprinkled amid all this, and their dusty windows held crayoned placards advertising garden apartments in Linden Hills. But the apartments they actually leased sat directly across Wayne Avenue — minus the gardens and the careful maintenance that existed when white families had lived there. These apartment buildings were the enclave of the hopeful who had fled from the crowded sections of Putney Wayne and the alleys of Brewster Place. They now felt terribly suburban because they had two scarred trees at each end of the block and could actually look down into Linden Hills from their back windows. Wayne Junior

High School with its large asphalt yard, handball courts, and
basketball rings took up one whole block on this side of the avenue.

Willie and Lester approached each other on the side of the
school yard. Willie had just crossed the avenue from one of the
liquor stores, his small brown package tucked into the pocket of
his light pea jacket.

"Hey, Shit."

"Hey, White."

Willie held out his left hand, palm up, and grinned at Lester.
"Take it to the left."

Lester grinned back, smacked a gloved hand down on Willie's,
and held out his right palm. "Take it to the right."

The ritual was finished with Willie's right hand. Then arms
up — "Take it all if it's good and tight" — four hands making
two fists. And the boys laughed.

They had greeted each other like that since the time they had
attended the school they now stood in front of. Both had graduated — Lester to Spring Vale High and Willie to the streets.
But they had been inseparable in junior high school, and it was
there they had picked up their nicknames and their desires to be
poets. Willie K. Mason was so black that the kids said if he
turned just a shade darker, there was nothing he could do but
start going the other way. Didn't ice get so cold it turned hot?
And when you burned coal, it turned to ash; so if Willie got any
darker, he'd just have to turn white. Willie believed this for a
while and went around in the summer wearing long-sleeved
shirts and a huge panama hat. He dreaded the thought of waking up white one day because then his mother would kick him
out of the house and none of the really fine sisters would let him
kiss them. So the darkest boy in Wayne Junior High was tagged
White Willie. He became friends with Lester Tilson in the seventh grade after helping him fight a ninth grader who had called
Lester "Baby Shit" because of the milky-yellow tone in his skin.
The boy was twice their size and welcomed Willie's intrusion
because he was able to save his knuckles and use Willie's head
against Lester's jaw. When Lester and Willie got up from the
ground with their bloody noses soaking their shirtfronts, Willie

told the boy, "There's more where that came from if you call him Baby Shit again. He ain't no baby."

"Well, he look like baby shit. Tell him to put a diaper on his face."

Lester was ready to fight again, but Willie felt it was time for a compromise. "Look, I don't want my man to kill you now. Just call him Shit, and we'll leave it at that."

He convinced Lester that was a cool name. Imagine — Shit. A real cuss word and nobody could get into trouble from the principal or anything for saying it: if it's his name, it's his name, so what could the teachers do about it? Lester wasn't too sure about Willie's logic, but he knew he'd be in for it if he kept bringing a torn and dirty shirt home every day. And since his mama was known to have a right hook worse than any boy at Wayne — even the ninth graders — he let matters lie.

They went through the eighth and ninth grades together, swapping baseball cards, Smokey Robinson 45's, and lies about their conquests over the tight-hipped girls at Wayne who were notorious at the time for not giving it up until they were married — or at least in college, because if they got pregnant, then it was by a man with a degree. Willie had shown Lester his first condom. He hoped that if only half of the stories Lester told him were just halfway true, Lester would be able to teach him how to manage the secret of that small disc of rubber so expertly that Willie could then convince the other guys that maybe some of his own stories weren't lies.

"Come on, Shit, put it on."

Lester stared at the limp, elastic nipple as mystified as his friend. "Naw, man."

"Aw, please. Just show me once. See, I've got this girl really ready. But she's scared of getting banged up. And all the other times I did it, I just went natural, ya know. But this particular one won't do it unless I use this."

Lester took the condom with his heart pounding and tried to keep his hands from shaking. He examined it slowly while Willie waited, his eyes intent on each of his movements. Lester finally shook his head with disgust and flipped it back at Willie.

"Man, that's too small. It'll never fit me."

"Yeah?" Willie looked at his friend with new respect. "But it stretches."

"I don't care — you got the wrong size for me. No point in breaking a good rubber."

"God," Willie said as he slowly uncurled the elastic tube to its full nine inches, "you must be really *something.*"

And Lester had shown Willie his first poems. They were studying for a geometry exam at Lester's home on First Crescent Drive. Lester looked up several times at Willie's dark, knotty head bent over a smudged looseleaf of triangles and lines. He nervously fingered the loose papers crammed in the back of his textbook, hoping that today would be the time he could summon up enough courage to pull them out.

"White?"

"Yeah."

"Nothing." Lester sighed and put his head back down into his book. Writing poems was sissy stuff in the crowd he and Willie hung with — unless it was something about Miss Thatcher's umbrella-shaped behind, or just maybe on Valentine's Day you could get away with it if the sister who was receiving them was fine enough. But crap like this about sunsets and flowers, and how sometimes he still got a little afraid in the dark, or how he wanted to grow up and be like Malcolm X, his favorite person in all history. Or the way it felt looking at the strong, muscular body of Hank Aaron twist around when he swung a bat — damn. He didn't want Willie to think he was a fruit or something.

"White?"

"Shit, don't keep bothering me if it isn't important. I think I got old Thatcher licked on this one. I can take that test tomorrow and prove that the shortest distance between two points ain't no straight line."

"Here." Lester stuck the papers in his face. "Read this." His suspended breath burned him while Willie smoothed out the crumpled sheets and began to read. Then he saw the edges of his friend's mouth turn up just a flicker.

"If you laugh, so help me God, I'll jump up from here and

kick you right in the butt. And if you tell anybody at school, I'll call you a liar, White Willie — and, and, I'll kick you in the butt again. I can beat you and practically every other guy there except Spoon and that's 'cause he fights dirty. Give me my stuff!"

Willie held the poems out of Lester's reach. "Hey, lay light, man. You know, these are really good."

Lester flushed with pleasure but it would be unthinkable to show it. Then he'd really be a fruit. He sucked his teeth. "Aw, they're nothing."

"No joke, Shit. You must have put a lot of time into these."

"Two seconds — that's all. Less time than you need to take a leak."

"Well, it sure takes me a lot longer than that to do mine, and they ain't this good."

"Yeah?" Lester felt the muscles in his face relax but he checked himself. "Come off it. I never saw you writing no poems, not even about Miss Thatcher."

"I never saw you neither, but you got 'em right here."

Lester wasn't going to be trapped that easily. "Okay, where are they? Come on, let's go to your place right now and let me read them."

"You can't read them, Shit."

"Yeah, I thought so."

"No, they're not on paper. They're all up here." Willie pointed to his head. "You know how my house is; I don't have a room all to myself like you. If my brothers saw me writing poems, they'd call me a queer and then it'd be all over school and I'd have to fight my way home every day. You know, most guys think you're a sissy if you like this stuff."

"Yeah." Lester nodded. "I know. But you can't worry about those losers. What are yours about?"

So Willie began to recite to Lester. Crude, choppy verses about a place called Bedford-Stuyvesant in New York, which Lester guessed must be a lot like Putney Wayne. Garbage can hide-and-go-seek. Winos who spoke wisdom. And Willie went on — about how it felt to hear your father beating your mother and what the tears looked like on your face. Willie hadn't grown up around too many sunsets and flowers, but he too was still afraid in the dark sometimes. And once he had gotten the same crazy feelings from staring at the thighs of a Knicks center that he got from touching pretty Janie Benson.

Lester then went under his mattress and dug out more crumpled papers that he said he had to hide from his older sister, who was lower than a snake and once had read his diary, which was mostly lies anyway but it got him a whipping from his mother. Geometry forgotten, they sat in Lester's room for hours, reciting to each other the lines that helped to harness the chaos and confusions in their fourteen-year-old worlds. Bloody noses had made them friends, but giving sound to the bruised places in their hearts made them brothers.

Willie had left school after the ninth grade. He said there was really nothing more they could teach him. He knew how to read and write and reason. And from here on in, it was all propaganda. He was now free to read the books that were important to him, not to some rusty-minded teacher. And if you wanted to write about life, you had to go where life was, among the people.

Lester went on to high school and graduated because his mother swore she'd see him dead before she saw him a dropout since, in the end, it would amount to the same thing. But he came to the conclusion that Willie had been right, although Lester could put his poetry in the school literary magazine. So all of his mother's tears, threats, and stony silences couldn't convince him to enroll at the university. Didn't he want to be more than a bum like his dead father? He'd be the only kid in Linden Hills not going to college. Lester told her that Kiswana Browne hadn't finished college and her father was hardly a bum — they had the best house on First Crescent Drive, didn't they? That Browne girl was mentally disturbed — everybody knew that — putting holes in her nose, taking some heathen name, and going to live in the slums of Brewster Place. But Lester had all of his faculties. Didn't he want to go to the university and come out a great poet? Lester had his mother there. Exactly — he was going to be a poet, and to write great poetry you had to be out among the people, not locked away behind a twenty-foot stone wall.

Mrs. Tilson threw up her hands. He was his father's son and she might as well accept it. His grandmother — that scheming Mamie Tilson — should have died a lot sooner before she'd corrupted his brain like she corrupted his father's. And Mrs. Tilson would never forgive herself for letting that scum, Willie Mason, come into her home and influence her son while she was probably the only one in Linden Hills who treated him like a person. Lester hardly remembered her treatment of Willie in the same light as she did, but it seemed that she had decided to stop nagging him about school and that was good enough for the present.

So Lester then joined Willie in giving poetry readings in coffeehouses, bookstores, and the city park. They supported themselves with odd jobs because they couldn't make a living from their work. And Willie couldn't even pick up the occasional five dollars that Lester got from getting a poem into a local newspaper because he never wrote them down. Willie continued the habit of creating stanzas in his mind and eventually had a repertoire in the hundreds. He said his aim was to be like the great slave poet, Jupiter Hammon, who memorized thousands of verses because he couldn't read. Willie considered it a terrible drawback that he had even gone as far as junior high and so could read very well. The written word dulls the mind, and since most of what's written is by white men, it's positively poisonous.

Willie sought out fewer and fewer jobs over the years. He became a regular on Wayne Avenue, where he'd rented a room, and could be seen sipping wine and smoking pot with other young black men who were either tired of looking for work or tired of finding it. When he got drunk enough he dropped his street language and totally bewildered them with long recitations in perfect iambic pentameter about the state of American society. So Willie gained the respect of Wayne Avenue because he was a "deep" dude. But it was getting toward the end of the year and the icy winds had driven Willie's audience into their separate homes. He was now forced to talk to himself, and his reflections disturbed him. He was twenty years old and the last job he had he worked side by side with a twelve year old who came in after school. Would that be his fate at thirty and forty?

What difference did it make that he could arrange the ingredients on a cereal box into heroic couplets while he shoved it
into a bag and carried it out to someone's car? With jobs like
that, he saw himself frozen in time, never becoming a man, just a
very gray-haired boy. He'd think about Linden Hills and all
that it offered, and wonder if perhaps there might have been another way.

Willie thought about this now, looking at Lester, who had at
least finished high school and would inherit a home on First
Crescent Drive.

"Hey, man, what you know good?" Willie said.

"It's good and cold, bro — I'll tell you that. Saw you coming
out the Tabernacle. You been praying?"

"Ah." Willie stamped his feet to keep the ice from seeping into
the soles of his shoes. "You know I was in Harry's, getting a little
liquid fire for my coffee. This time of year brandy's all you can
get to keep you warm. The babes don't wanna hang with nobody around Christmas who can't shell up for a gift."

"Know what ya mean."

"Do you, Shit?" Willie looked at him closely.

"Sure I do." Lester frowned. "Hey, I don't have no job either.
They lay off at the factory this time of year."

"Them's some nice threads you sporting on your hands and
feet." Willie nodded at Lester's thick suede gloves and Western
boots.

"These?" Lester threw out his hands and stamped his feet as if
wanting to fling the things off. "It's an early Christmas present
from my mom and sister. Said they might as well give it to me
now since it's so bitter and I'm too damned trifling to buy myself
something to keep away frostbite. A nice way to say Happy Holiday to a fella — huh?"

"Least you got someone to care about whether you freeze or
not. It must be nice to have a family in Linden Hills who can afford that kind of stuff."

Lester started for a moment and then stared at Willie. "Hey,
baby — come out of it. Is this my main man talking? That ain't
caring, White, that's showing off. See what we gave you? Now
what you gonna give us, you no-good bum, you. They gave me

this stuff and prayed it would burn my ass every time I wore it. And believe me, if I was a better man and it wasn't so damned cold, I would've left this crap right under their Jesus-tripping, tinseled tree."

Willie was silent and crammed his cracked hands deeper into his pockets.

"I know you're saying, sure, I'm standing here trembling in a pea jacket and thin-soled shoes and this mother's talking about turning up his nose at gloves and boots. But I'm telling ya, Willie, it's torment every time I have to wear this, 'cause it's less than a week till Christmas and I ain't got the money to buy them something expensive. You know those type of broads. I'd better not bring in no Woolworth's perfume and powder set. It's Chanel or nothing. And I ain't got no Chanel money, so it's nothing. And then I'm nothing and they've made their point *again* for another year. Merry Christmas, baby."

Willie sighed. "Yeah, I guess you're right."

"Guess nothing, why —"

"It's not cold enough for you two? You just gotta be out here reciting poetry, even if it's only to each other." The man who called to them came up with a young woman pressed against his arm, her body turned slightly in toward his for warmth because the thin beige coat afforded her very little.

"Hey, Norm, tell it right, baby."

"Hiya, Ruth." Willie was always awed in front of Ruth. He had never seen a woman whose beauty seemed to go down to the bare bone. He saw it pushing out from under her skin to highlight the bronze tinge that the wind put on her smooth, round face, a face like smoky caramel. And her oval eyes, narrowed against the wind, didn't look squinty like most people's but positively sexy, as if she was doing that just to make his heart stop. He often dreamed about his friend's wife, and it was always the same. She was lying on his bed with that golden-brown glow on her face coating her entire body. And he was standing over her, just looking. There was no desire or need within him to touch her, just a heady contentment in watching her nipples and pubic hair all golden and glowing like her face. Then there would be a knock on his door and his mouth would go dry because he knew it was Norman. And Norman would, somehow, manage to come in through the locked door and Willie would say, "I was just looking, Norm, just looking." And Norman would say, turning toward the golden goddess on the bed, "Yeah, she's really something, huh, man?" Willie would wake up and wonder why he never wanted to do anything to Ruth while she lay on his bed — just look, as he was contented to do now, a little tongue-tied in front of her.

"Norm," Lester said, "if I had a woman like that this morning, I wouldn't be out here freezing her to death — I'd be at home squeezing her to death."

Norman and Ruth laughed, and Willie was disgusted by the cheap rhyme that Lester dared apply to Ruth. She deserved at least a sonnet.

"Les, it's all in your mind," Norman said. "It's not that cold."

"Not cold? Man, it's cold as a witch's tit."

"Why do you men always apply something bad to a woman? Why can't it be cold as the devil's balls?"

"Aw, don't come off with none of that women's lib stuff," Norman teased her. "How do you know if the devil's got cold balls, you ever slept with him?"

"No, but Les has never slept with a witch either."

"He did if he scored with that disaster he was dating last month." Willie found his tongue and was thrilled to see that he had made Ruth laugh, her voice floating high and translucent above their heavier ones.

"Look, why don't you joy monkeys come on up to the house and have a little something hot?" Norman offered.

Lester counted their heads dramatically. "But there's four of us here. Since when you got more than two cups?"

The Anderson's poverty was a standing joke on Wayne Avenue. People said that if Norman brought home air, Ruth would make gravy, pour it over it, and tell him not to bring so much the next time.

"I'd like you to know that we have *three* cups." Ruth smiled. "One each for you and Willie, and Norman and I can share the other one. And we've even got the coffee to put in them, too."

"And I got the cream." Willie pulled his brandy out of his pocket.

"Aw right!" Norman slapped him on the back.

They crossed Lindèn Road and entered one of the dilapidated garden-apartment buildings. It was difficult to notice what wasn't in the Anderson's apartment because so much care seemed to have gone into what was there. Visitors found themselves thinking, What a nice feeling to be allowed into a home. And it *was* a home with its bare wood floors, dusted and polished, and with the three pieces of furniture that sat in three large rooms: one sofa in the living room, one kitchenette set with plastic-bottomed chairs on uncertain chrome legs, one bed. Two towels hung in the bathroom side by side with two washcloths folded neatly over them. In all the rooms there were matching colored shades that served for curtains or draperies. Norman took the boys' coats and hung them over his and Ruth's on the only two hangers in the guest closet.

"Wooh, it's good to be inside. You folks sure get great heat in here." Willie rubbed his cracked hands together and saw the steam misting on the windows.

"It's a wonderful apartment in the winter," Ruth said. "There's always plenty of heat. And in the summer when the windows are open, the cross-ventilation is better than air-conditioning, isn't it, Norm?"

"You're right about that." And Norman went to the stove to put on water for the coffee. The Andersons looked around their apartment as if the warm and cool air that filled up the empty rooms were all that mattered.

Ruth put three Styrofoam cups on the table, setting the ones in front of Lester and Willie as carefully as she would china. And she gave them each a plastic spoon with a paper napkin folded underneath. Norman poured the coffee and made such a ceremony of unwrapping Willie's cheap blackberry brandy and adding it to their cups, you might have thought it a rare cognac. And when the two boys raised the steaming coffee to their lips, that's exactly what it tasted like.

Their hosts sat there, talking and laughing with such ease that

Willie had a hard time figuring out how Ruth and Norman were both drinking from the same cup. Norman would take a sip and talk, and then she'd take a sip. It soon appeared unthinkable that there should be more than one cup between them since they never reached for it at the same time.

Lester and Willie were careful not to bite into the rims of the soft Styrofoam. They knew the cups were to be washed and used repeatedly. They would be made to last until Norman got the pinks, when they would be destroyed. Ruth had bought hard plastic cups once, but Norman had managed to splinter those and stick the edges into his wrists. Now there could be no danger of that happening next year — if it was the year for the pinks.

Looking at him, it was difficult to imagine that this square-jawed man with the gentle, sloping lips was the same one who every other spring went up and down Wayne Avenue, screaming and tearing at his face and hair with his fingernails, trying to scrape off the pinks. He resorted to his teeth and bare nails only after everything else had failed — jagged sections of plates and glasses, wire hangers, curtain rods, splinters of wood once part of a dresser, coffee table, or her grandmother's antique music box. Up and down Wayne Avenue — in a frantic search for untried edges and textures to dig into his skin — until he was taken away, arms forced and laced to his side, and sent into a twilight that dimmed the shades of his nightmare.

People wondered why Ruth stayed. They knew she was used to better since she'd once had a husband down on Fifth Crescent Drive. And Norman could never keep a job for more than a year and nine months. And she'd certainly keep no furniture for longer than that. He'd come out of the hospital after three months and usually get a new job within a week, or at the most two. But then a year and nine months later, it would happen again.

She didn't stay because every dime he did earn, when he could earn it, was brought home to her; or because he would take her swollen feet out of her waitress loafers, put them in his lap, and rub them patiently for hours; or because the music in his laughter had a way of rounding off the missing notes in her soul. No, none of that would have kept her there. Because Ruth was a woman who wanted children and that anchor of security which comes with the weight of accumulated things: good brocade chairs, linens, a set of company silverplate. And she came to realize after their fourth summer that she could have none of that with Norman. He would manage to destroy everything that was painfully gathered for almost two years and then awaken from his twilight cry, promise to take his medication, see the psychiatrist, and he would — for each of the seven seasons before the return of the pinks.

Ruth had gotten tired, past bone-tired, of hurting from being crushed between her hatred and love of this man. Tired of being afraid to have children and of thinking that one spring he just might kill her. Tired of looking into his beaten eyes when he came back from the hospital and saw his life shredded on the floor of their home. She was leaving six winters ago. That year had started off badly anyway. Her ovaries became seriously inflamed, and since there was just no money to treat them, she lost her job at the restaurant, no longer able to lift those heavy trays of food. And the pinks were due again by spring. She phoned her mother who said Hallelujah and loaned her a set of luggage.

Ruth packed early one afternoon, but the burning in her side forced her to lie down and rest. As soon as the pain lessened, she'd get the rest of her things, call a cab, and go. But Norman came home at two o'clock, eyes red-rimmed and threatening to roll back into his head. He told her that he felt the pinks were coming, and he was lucky this time, he'd been able to leave the plant before the guys saw them clinging to his flesh. God, he was so relieved to have made it home to her.

Contempt mates well with pity. So Ruth raised herself up in the bed and lashed out against what was driving her from everything that she loved. She was through, did he hear her, through. Because he was a maniac — a fucking, crazy maniac. And she hoped to God that this time he would drive a piece of broken glass through his heart. Then a sharp pain bent her over at the waist.

Norman saw with concern the tight lines around her eyes and

mouth as she dug her fingers into her side and shivered on the bed. Gently, he pulled the sheet over her knotted body, and just as he went to stroke her forehead, he was thrown into another dimension. A wad of pink slime hit him on the back of the hand and moved up his wrist in wet, sucking motions. He cried out and beat his arm savagely against the air. The slime fell to the floor and curled up into a soft ball, but then it began to inch its way back toward his leg. Norman turned to the bed and reached out for her like a bewildered child. "Ruth?"

She curled up in the bed and moaned.

Oh, Christ, she was sick. Ruth was sick and those bastards were on their way. He turned to run toward the bathroom and a clammy weight slammed into his neck and slowly clawed its way up to his ears. His skin crawled toward his scalp, trying to escape the consuming mass, as he threw himself against the bathroom sink. His brain screamed, Scrape them off. But Ruth was sick, and he could never stop, he knew he could never stop. The glass of water he'd run splashed over his knuckles and soaked the front of his shirt when he stumbled back to the bedroom. He could smell his flesh dissolving under the pinkish slime that now clung to his chin and throat. The glass tumbled to the bed and what was left of the water seeped into the pillow and sheets. The aspirin poured out of the plastic vial, rolling over his fingers and falling on Ruth's hair and shoulders. The jellied mucus was now biting into his chest and gnawing at his thighs and groin. The screaming now came from his very being. Scrape. But he could never stop, never stop, so just please, Ruth, take your aspirin.

Norman rocked by the edge of the bed with his arms clasped around his middle, trying to hold the pieces of his dissolving body together. Large, oily tears rolled down the side of his mouth and dripped from his chin. Did she need another pillow? He could get another pillow. But when he tried, his knees had been eaten away and he only got as far as the dresser and began to sag toward the floor. The screaming was now coming from the bed.

"Norman!" It was the wail of a woman embracing a nightmare. "Scrape. Them. Off."

So Ruth stayed. She let the neighbors wonder, and she offered a mute face to a frustrated and berating mother. She knew it served no purpose to answer those silent or shrill questions — no one would ever believe that she was still there because of some aspirin and a glass of water. And quietly she just didn't replace the furniture that Norman had destroyed. She removed the glasses and silverware from the apartment. The hangers went next and the metal curtain rods. The smashed television and stereo set were succeeded by a cheap transistor radio since she insisted that she had no use for the clutter of new things; and besides, they were saving for a home. Then every other spring she went to the bank and emptied their account to pay for his hospital bills, medication, and therapy sessions. They filled the vacant spaces in the apartment with the memories from long walks in the park, bus outings to the beach, and window-shopping for that new home; with Norman massaging her back, and her clipping his toenails, with plans for adopting a baby — with a whole, safe year and then that summer, fall, and winter before the next pink spring.

"So after the dude tells me that, I said, 'Man, you don't know how to handle a woman.'" Norman cut his eyes at Ruth. "You gotta put your foot on their necks and let 'em know who's boss."

Ruth sucked her teeth. "Why don't you stop it?"

"And then if that don't work, you put the *other* foot on it, too."

Lester and Willie burst out laughing and looked at Ruth, who was smiling and shaking her head.

"Now why you sitting here, telling these boys that nonsense?"

"What nonsense? A man's gotta be the boss in his home!" And he brought his palm down on the table and winked at Lester.

"Hey, boss, you forgot to get all the corners when you waxed the floor yesterday. Don't let it happen again."

Lester and Willie hooted through their hands, "Wooh, Norm! She got you cleaning floors?"

"That's right." Ruth got up, went behind Norman's chair, and put her arm across his chest. "And we take turns making the bed and scrubbing the toilet, don't we, baby?"

"Aw, I don't know about all that," Norman mumbled.

Ruth brought her arm up to his neck and forced his head back gently. "Don't we, baby?"

"Well . . ."

Lester and Willie howled.

"Because what rules in this house, Norm?"

"*I* rule in . . ." He laughed and tried to bring his palm down again, but she tightened her grip on his neck and forced his head back until he was looking up into her eyes.

"What rules in this house?"

Norman stared for a moment into the smoky ovals above him. "Love rules in this house, Ruth."

She pecked him quickly on the forehead. "You got that right, sucker."

Willie's forehead burned as though it were him she had kissed. And his fingertips tingled at the way her voice lilted up at the word "sucker" and surrounded it with music, the way iridescent bubbles would sound if solidified and bounced against each other. And Norman had that voice all to himself, every day, to call him Daddy or Sweet Bits, or even bastard. What he wouldn't give to have Ruth just call him bastard, all encased in bubbles like that. He bet Ruth could even say "motherfucker" and make it sound like a prayer. And it seemed so unjust for that voice to belong to a man who ran through the streets tearing at his flesh.

"See how she pushes me around?" Norman stroked the hand on his chest and appealed to Willie, who only nodded curtly. Suddenly, he didn't feel like clowning anymore. "She's even got me painting this apartment twice a year. I told her that the paint's gonna get so thick on these walls it'll push us out of here."

"I like change." Ruth looked around at the walls. "I'm already thinking about something new for January."

"Why don't you try pink?" slipped out of Willie's mouth, and the look Ruth gave him over Norman's shoulders crumbled his heart. Norman looked down into his coffee cup, and Willie glanced at Lester for help, but his friend seemed to have disowned him.

"No," Ruth said, looking straight at Willie. "That's a good color for bathrooms, but I had something more like a pale green in mind for the kitchen."

"If you do that, Ruth, I'm never coming back in here," Lester said. "My mom's got that whole damned house done up in green. I asked her what she's trying to do — get that guy on the can of peas to marry Roxanne 'cause it looks like nobody else will?"

Everyone laughed but Willie, who found that it now even hurt to smile. He wanted to crawl across the floor to Ruth on his knees, bury his head in her lap, and beg her to forgive him. She hated him now, he knew it. She would never smile at him again or even talk to him. He was doomed to go through life without hearing the smallest of music from that throat.

"I think your folks got a great home," Norman said, staring into space. "I've been telling Ruth that soon as we get on our feet, I'm applying for a house in Linden Hills."

"And you'll live in it alone." Ruth went to the back window that looked down on Linden Hills. "You know, wherever you go, I'm game — Spring Vale, Park Heights, even out of state. But I'm never going back down there again. I've had that life, Norm, and I lasted six months. Those folks just aren't real — excuse me, Lester. I'm not trying to talk about your mother."

"No, talk about her," Lester said. "It's true. I was just telling Willie this morning, those are a bunch of the saddest niggers you'll ever wanna meet. They eat, sleep, and breathe for one thing — making it. And making it where?"

"Up." Ruth shrugged her shoulders and sighed. "Everybody wants to make it up there."

"Yeah," Lester said, "and up means down in the Hills. Ain't that a bust? Down toward Tupelo Drive. They're scraping and clawing to move closer to that weirdo, Nedeed, and his damn funeral parlor. You know, my mom's got her heart set on Roxanne marrying some turd who's come around a few times, just because he lives down on Third Crescent Drive. Never comes in the house, mind you. Sits outside in his Porsche and blows the horn as if he'd be contaminated by walking on First Crescent."

"Who's that?" Ruth asked.

"Xavier something or other — a real fruit name."

"Yeah, Xavier Donnell. So he's still driving that 1950 Porsche. I told you about him, Norm — the one who has his horn rigged up to play 'God Bless the Child.' "

Norman laughed. "Aren't you two being a little hard on those folks?"

"No, we're not." Ruth frowned. "You know his aunt had the gall to call me last week and say she was looking for someone to do her windows for the holidays. And if *I* wasn't available — since I'm moving in that sort of crowd now — I might know someone who is. I told her that I not only didn't do windows, I didn't have to do housework because my husband provides for me very nicely, thank you. Then I slammed down the phone. The old bitch — imagine!"

Willie cringed when Ruth spit out the word "bitch." So she could talk with fire in her voice. And that's how she would talk about him from now on. "Came into my house and had the gall to insult my husband — the black bastard." Oh God, why couldn't he just die?

"You know what my mom is always telling Roxanne? 'Make sure you let Xavier know that your grandmother was *very close* to Luther Nedeed's grandfather.' God, Grandma Tilson would piss in the grave to hear that one. She hated those Nedeeds. She said Nedeed would pay her five dollars to catfish with him 'cause the fish would run from his hook." Everyone laughed but Willie. "No, really. And she said he'd pay double that just for her catfish heads. She promised when I got old enough to understand, she'd tell me what he did with those fish heads. But before she died, she had other stories about them to make your balls curl."

"I can imagine," Ruth said. "A man who looks like that is capable of anything. Willie, you're awful quiet. Do you want more coffee?"

He didn't feel worthy of talking to her and just shook his head.

"Willie's a little down 'cause it's Christmas and he's short on cash," Lester said.

"Join the club." Norman smiled at Willie.

"I'm telling you, man, I should be president of that club,"

Lester said. "I've been racking my brains about what to do for presents for Mom and Roxanne. And it's hard as hell to pick up work around this time of year 'cause people hold on to their jobs."

"You know," Ruth said while staring out the back window, "I was just thinking — you guys might not want to do it, but there's plenty of spare jobs around Linden Hills right now. There's lots of people like Mrs. Donnell looking for someone to do heavy cleaning and clearing up extra bedrooms for guests. And they know you, Lester, so you could take Willie along. Ah, but why would you want to be bothered with them?"

"Look," Lester said, "a buck's a buck. And they'd get a real charge out of seeing me doing their dirty work. They could bring their kids to the window, point, and say, 'See how far you'll fall if you don't keep kissing ass and get a dah-gree?' "

Even Willie laughed at the way Lester curled his top lip under and spoke through his nose.

"And my mom would have a shit-fit knowing I was doing that to buy her a present. That alone would be worth it."

"What do you think, Willie?" Ruth went and put her hand on his shoulder. "It's not much of an idea, but I hate to see you looking so sad just because of money."

Not much of an idea? It was a wonderful idea — colossal. Anything that put the music back in Ruth's voice as she spoke to him. He would go into Linden Hills and work his butt off. Then he'd take the money and buy her and Norm a great gift — maybe even a turkey, too. Ruth wanted him to go into Linden Hills and he would go. He was just sorry that she hadn't asked him to go into hell for her so he could really prove himself. "Sounds ace-boon-coon to me." Willie swallowed to dissolve the joy in his throat from her touch.

"Great," Lester said. "Now you'll see what I was telling you before: all that glitters ain't gold, baby."

"And all that shakes ain't Jell-O," Norman added.

"Norm, leave the poetry to the boys and just do what you do best. Don't ask me what it is, but when I figure it out, I'll let you know." He went to throw an empty cup at Ruth, and she started to duck behind Willie's chair but stopped suddenly. "What's that sound?" She tilted her head and went toward the back window.

"I don't hear nothing but the steam pipes," Norman said.

Ruth frowned deeply and stared through the pane. Then she lifted up the window.

"Ruth, are you crazy? It's three degrees out there."

"Shh, listen."

The cold wind blew into the kitchen, and they didn't know if it was the freezing air or the long, thin howl it carried with it into the kitchen that made the hair stand up on their arms.

"Christ, what's that?" Norman's jaws were trembling. "A sick animal?"

Ruth closed the window and stared down the hill. "That wasn't an animal. I don't know what it was, but God, it wasn't an animal. Sometimes when the leaves are off the trees, sound can be carried like that all the way up the hill. When I was on Fifth Crescent Drive, even in the summer you could hear organ music coming all the way up from the funeral chapel. That lake acts as some sort of springboard for sound."

"Maybe old Nedeed's down there embalming someone who wasn't quite ready." But Lester's joke died under the icy echoes that remained in the room.

"Lester, when you guys go down looking for work, be careful."

"Careful of what, Ruth?"

"Well, Lester, you know, they're very security conscious. Someone might not recognize you, think you're prowlers, and call the cops. And there are Dobermans and wired fences and . . ." Ruth stared back at the window. "And things like that. Just be careful, that's all. Look, humor an old lady."

"Since when did you get old?" Norman patted her on the hip.

"Two days after I became Mrs. Anderson." She slapped his hand gently. "Didn't your mama ever tell you not to touch things that don't belong to you?"

"It belongs to me." Norman gave her hip a squeeze.

Ruth shook her head. "God help you, Mr. Anderson, it sure does."

* * *

"Now, them are some nice folks." Lester closed the collar of his coat to block the first shock of the wind.

"Shit, I could kick myself for what I said. I wouldn't hurt Ruth for nothing in the world."

"Ah, don't worry about it. I bet they've already forgotten the whole thing. She's not like my mom. Man, she can tell you things somebody said to her in 1958 and she's still waiting to get 'em back. So all's well, blood, your baby still loves you."

"Cut that crap out."

"Cut what out? You've got a crush on her a blind man can see."

"That's a lie."

"She's a looker though, huh?"

"She's all right."

"And them tits," Lester said, cutting his eyes at Willie. "Wouldn't I just love to stick a hand down that blouse and grab one of them monsters."

"Chill it, Shit."

"And Lord, them thighs. I could spread those winners and ride all the way to Alaska."

"I said, lay off!"

"Why?" Lester shrugged. "She's nothing but a broad."

"You know what your problem is?" Willie narrowed his eyes at Lester. "You been hanging with these whores on Wayne Avenue so long you don't know class when you see it. That's a *lady*, dammit! And she's too good for you to be wiping your greasy mind all over her body. You ain't worth six inches of her toenails. She's a saint . . . She's a —"

"Yesss?" Lester lowered his voice and pulled his right eyelid down with his finger.

Willie stopped. "Why, you . . . son of a . . ." And he swung at Lester, who ducked and ran across Linden Road toward the school yard. Willie chased him. "Come back here, you turkey. I owe you one for that!"

He caught up to Lester by the fence and pinned him against it by the collar. "Now say, 'Long live Uncle Tom,' six times."

"Aw, Willie, that's kid shit." Lester laughed.

Willie banged him hard against the fence. "Go on, say it. 'Long live Uncle Tom.' "

"No!"

Willie bounced him again. "You know I could always beat you, Les, even though I'm shorter. Say it!"

"Okay. Long live Uncle Tom." Willie released him and Lester backed away a few steps and shouted, "So he can marry your mama!"

Willie laughed and tried to kick at him, but slipped on the ice. Lester came back and helped him up. "You all right?"

"Yeah." Willie looked through the chain-link fence. "Man, we sure had some good times here."

They walked along the front of the school and passed the main entrance. There were three bronze plaques over the triple doors.

> I am the way out of the city of woe
> I am the way to a prosperous people
> I am the way from eternal sorrow

Chico and the Raiders had spray-painted their insignia over the middle plaque:

> Sacred justice moved my architect
> I was raised here by divine omnipotence
> Primordial love and ultimate intellect

"You know, Shit," Willie said, looking up at the last bronze plaque —

> Only the elements time cannot wear
> Were made before me, and beyond time I stand
> Abandon ignorance, ye who enter here

— then down toward Linden Hills, "I could have done all right if I had gone on to school."

"You're doing all right now."

"Naw, I mean I could have been a doctor or something. You know I have six hundred and sixty-five poems memorized up here — six hundred and sixty-five, and lots of 'em ain't mine. I have all of Baraka, Soyinka, Hughes, and most of Coleridge. And Whitman — that was one together dude. My mom says with a memory like that, I could have breezed through med school."

Lester didn't say anything for a moment, but then he stopped walking and pulled at the chain fence. "Ya ever wonder why they put fences around these schools, White?"

"Huh?" Willie had been lost in thought.

"I mean, you can see it with an elementary school 'cause the little kids might run out in the street without thinking or something, but why around a junior high and high school? It's not to keep people out, 'cause the gate's always open and sometimes even stray dogs wander in. Remember the time that mutt came in and we tied Miss Thatcher's math book to its tail and ran all over the school yelling, 'Yeah, Miss Thatcher's finally gone to the dogs'?"

Willie smiled. "What ya getting at, Shit?"

"Fences, White, fences. Even at the university: big, stone fences — and why? The gates are open, so it's not to keep anybody out or in. Why fences?" He looked at his friend's blank face. "To get you used to the idea that what they have in there is different, special. Something to be separated from the rest of the world. They get you thinking fences, man, don't you see it? Then when they've fenced you in from six years old till you're twenty-six, they can let you out because you're ready to believe that what they've given you up here, their version of life, is special. And you fence your own self in after that, protecting it from everybody else *out there*.

"You wanna be a doctor? All the books are in the library. Why can't you just go and read them, sit for an exam, and get an internship? No way, right? Why? 'Cause they gotta get you inside that fence. You gotta get that mark on your forehead and that print in the palm of your hand that you've sat through the philosophy and history and crap that goes along with it. They gotta be sure that when you go out among real people, your fences are all intact. Then when you move to Linden Hills, or wherever, you're gonna stay put and help vote out radicals and heave a sigh of relief when you read that a Panther got it in the back from an L.A. cop."

They walked on in silence and finally reached the marble banister that separated First Crescent Drive from Wayne J.H.S. "Okay, good buddy." Willie slapped Lester on the back. "What time do you want me to meet you tomorrow so we can start hustling a little change?"

"Hey, White, look. Why don't you come home with me and spend the night, and then we can get up early and head right out?"

"Ah, man, I don't know. Your mom has never been too keen on me."

"Look, it's my house, too. And if I wanted to pull rank, Grandma Tilson really willed it to me anyway. She said she knew I'd do the right thing after my mom dies, and burn it to the ground."

Willie still looked hesitant.

"And see, what we can do is take it drive by drive and work our way down from Second Crescent to Tupelo. That way you won't miss a thing and you can see what I was telling you about these people. And remember, Ruth thinks it's a good idea for you to do it, too."

"Ruth ain't got nothing to do with me doing this."

"Yeah, I know, but since she's going out of her way to call people for us and all — even though she doesn't mean anything to you — it would just be human to meet her halfway and get an early start. I mean, not that you give two shits about what Ruth —"

"What y'all having for dinner, Les?"

Lester smiled broadly. "Whatever it is, it won't taste good. The only woman in the world who cooks worse than my mother is my sister. And tonight is a toss-up between them two."

Willie looked over the marble banister. "Hey, can you still jump this stream?"

"Probably not. My legs are longer now, but somehow they've gotten stiffer."

"We could probably walk over it today — the water's frozen solid."

"Thank God for that. In the summer that water stinks so you wake up with the taste in your mouth. And these folks refuse to get this stream filled up, but they'll spend money to keep this banister repaired."

"Well, because of the school. I heard two white kids drowned here once."

"Willie, they don't give a damn about them kids. None of their children go to that school now. It's what I was telling you before — it's a them-and-us thing — it's a fence, man. Just another fence. Hey, why don't you jump it?"

"You kidding? I'm walking right down Linden Road to your house."

"What happened? You used to think you were the world's greatest athlete."

"Yeah, I also used to think that you were big enough to break a rubber. But reality sets in after a while, don't it?"

Lester laughed. "You're right about that."

It was impossible to see the bottom of Linden Hills from where they were standing on Linden Road. The land didn't slope down on a smooth incline — it was steep and jagged, so even with the trees bare only the housetops on Second Crescent Drive were visible. The hill seemed to slope for about three hundred feet and then fall into an abyss. They were about to turn left into First Crescent Drive when Willie grabbed Lester's arm.

"Hey, listen, there it is again."

Lester stopped but he only heard the wind whipping through the naked branches. "Aw, don't tell me Ruth's got you spooked. It's nothing but the wind."

"No, I swear, Les. I heard something weird."

They waited a moment longer and Lester's chin began to tremble. "White, the only sound out here is my teeth chattering. Come on inside before I freeze."

The Tilson home was the first one just off Linden Road. It was the smallest house on a street of brick ranch houses with iron picket fences. Its two-story wooden frame had been covered with

light green aluminum siding, and three brick steps led up to a
dark green door. Going inside, Willie noticed that Lester had
been right about one thing: his mother loved green. Willow-
green print furniture sat on jade carpeting and there were
green-and-white Japanese porcelain vases arranged on the tables
in the living room. The curtains in the hallway and living room
had avocado stripes and fern prints, and with the light coming
through them, they gave a whisper-green tint to the white walls.
He had expected the dark green Christmas tree, but it was decorated entirely with emerald satin balls that reflected onto the
tinsel.

"Les-ter, is that you?" A twittering voice came from the
kitchen followed by mincing footsteps and the appearance of a
petite woman. There was something quick and nervous in Mrs.
Tilson's movements that always reminded Willie of a bird. And
she did have the milky skin of a canary, but coming through the
hall beside the curtains even that shade seemed to have turned
green.

She stopped suddenly when she saw the two boys. "Why, William, how nice." She gave him a smile composed of several jerky
motions with her closed mouth. "I haven't seen you in ages. It
was sweet of you to drop by today."

"Evening, Mrs. Tilson." Willie always felt big and awkward
and black around this delicate, yellow woman.

"He didn't *drop by* today — he's spending the night." Lester
took their coats and hung them up. "What's for dinner, Mom?"

Mrs. Tilson followed his movements intently with her tiny,
darting eyes. "Well, I guess we can always find more, and especially for such a good friend of Lester's."

"Look, I know you didn't plan on me being here." Willie had
difficulty finding something to do with his hands. "It's sort of
short notice and I'm not very hungry anyway. I —"

"Non-sense." Mrs. Tilson patted his hand lightly and rapidly.
"There's always something for company. But we're eating like
peasants tonight — just fried chicken. But I'm trying something
a bit daring with the potatoes. A cheese and wine sauce I saw in
the papers."

"I love fried chicken," Willie volunteered eagerly.

"Like I said — common food, but filling. Come in and sit down, and tell me what you've been doing with yourself, William."

"Don't you have to watch your sauce or something?" Lester took Willie's arm. "I thought we'd go to my room and play some tapes till dinner."

Mrs. Tilson took Willie's other arm, and he was amazed at the powerful grip of her thin fingers as she firmly guided him into the living room. "Lester has always been so selfish, William. Now he knows I want to have a few minutes to catch up on your life and he's trying to herd you off to himself."

She patted a cushion on the sofa and Willie sat down gingerly on the edge and put his hands over his closed knees. Lester followed them and bounced down on a chair in the corner, sprawling his feet out.

"Lester, must you abuse the furniture that way?" She turned her head to Willie quickly. "Upholstering is so dear these days and he's going to ruin my springs. I just had the set redone this year; what do you think, William?"

"It's really lovely, ma'am." Willie gave an obligatory survey of the room.

"Mom, his name is Willie, not William. A thousand times I've told you, it's *Willie.*"

"Willie is a derivative of William, Lester. Surely his birth certificate doesn't have Willie on it, and I like calling people by their proper names."

"Yes, it does, ma'am. My mother named me Willie K. Mason."

"Oh." She darted her eyes over his body. "And what does the *K* stand for?"

"Nothing, just a *K*. I guess she liked the sound of it."

"How ... different." She gave him another serialized smile.

"It's not different at all," Lester said. "Southern people often give their kids initials for names — and your mom's from Alabama, right, Willie? — you know, like TJ or LC."

"I know that, Lester, but I always thought those initials stood for something. It just never occurred to me that people lacked such imagination they had to resort to giving a child a letter for a name."

Willie cringed and Lester narrowed his eyes. "Well, I guess there are two ways of looking at that, Mom. Some people wonder why someone would be stupid enough to give a child three multisyllable names that he never learns to spell and is going to drop as soon as he's old enough to realize that nobody gives a damn about any of it anyway." He turned to Willie innocently. "Did you know my full name is Lesterfield Walcott Montgomery Tilson, Willie? Or is it Lester *Field*walcott Montgomery Tilson, Mom? They had to type those letters so close together on my birth certificate it's hard to make them out now."

Mrs. Tilson's mouth tightened. "I gave you a name that I thought would fit the heights I hoped you'd climb. It was a great name for what I dreamed would be a great man. Needless to say —"

Lester cut her off. "Mom, even the president of the United States doesn't have a desk large enough for a nameplate like Lesterfield Walcott Montgomery Tilson. I'd have to become a pimp to afford a desk that big."

Willie couldn't hold on any longer and started coughing and patting his chest. Mrs. Tilson looked at him sharply. "Is there something wrong, Willie?"

"I don't know, Mrs. Tilson." He coughed again. "I seem to have a catch in my throat."

She turned to Lester coldly. "Get him a glass of water. And don't forget to bring a coaster." She watched Lester leave the room, then put her hands lightly on Willie's arm. "I don't know why he likes to plague me — do you, Willie?" Willie knew he was damned if he did and damned if he didn't. But fortunately she had no intentions of waiting for his reply. "If you listen to him, you'd think it was a crime for me to want a better life for my children than I had." She gave a long sigh and looked down at her hands. "Life wasn't easy with Mr. Tilson. I never went to college because I got married early and started having children. And then I felt it was my place to be at home and help them to become decent human beings. I only wanted them to have things — to be able to make it in the world alone. You know how hard it is for black people, Willie, and especially black men — everyone wants to hold them down. I didn't want that to happen to my son. Is that so wrong?"

Willie had to agree that there was really nothing wrong with that. He planned to shake his head sympathetically at Mrs. Tilson, but she had already gone on, her light voice pecking at his ears.

"I had to live in this house almost on the charity of other people. My husband's mother never liked me, and all because I wanted to make something of this place. I was never one for keeping up with the Joneses, but it's pretty embarrassing to have the worst house on the block and to just settle for that."

Willie started to say that he thought she had a lovely home, but before he could clear his throat she had forged ahead.

"Do you think I like being laughed at by my neighbors because my husband never wanted anything nice? Everything you see here I had to scrape and quarrel and beg for, and it's not that much. There are homes across Wayne Avenue that are better than this one, and we live in Linden Hills." She gave another long sigh.

Lester called from the kitchen, "I can't find no coasters among all this mess! I'm bringing the water without one."

"Did you hear that English? 'I can't find no coasters.' And he knows better, Willie. He just does that to plague me. He's decided to be nothing and do nothing with his life, and he never lets a day go by without reminding me of it in some way."

Willie mumbled something about Lester being a poet.

"Yes. His poetry." Mrs. Tilson sighed and looked down at her hands again. "Some of the finest men of our race were poets, but does Lester ever get any of his published? You can't live off little bits of looseleaf that you hide under your mattress. And what's to happen twenty, thirty years from now when I'm dead and gone? Can he ever hope to support a family from reading in coffeehouses? I know what will happen. He'll let my home run down and then sell it for anything to just about anybody. My grandchildren will be ragged and homeless. You have a mother, Willie. Does she want that for you? Is that the way you get this black pride that Lester's always writing about?"

Lester came back into the room and set Willie's water glass down on a folded paper towel. Mrs. Tilson looked at the paper towel with disgust and shook her head. And Willie almost found himself doing the same thing. She wasn't such a bad woman — a little prissy, but hell, every mother wanted her kids to do something with their lives if she was any kind of mother at all.

"Willie and I have been having a nice, long chat."

"I'll bet." Lester slouched back into the chair. "Did she get to the part yet about her naked grandchildren begging in the subways?"

Mrs. Tilson nodded at Willie as if to say, See what I was talking about? and then she got up. "I'm going to set the table. We'll eat as soon as Roxanne gets in." She patted Willie on the shoulder and gave a final sigh before leaving the room.

"Why don't you lay light on her, Les? She means well."

"Sure she does, White. She meant well when she killed my father, too. That's one well-meaning woman. It took a crowbar to pry her out of his casket after she had him working two jobs with a heart condition. Two fucking jobs, and for what? Because so-and-so had a finished basement, and so-and-so sent their daughter to Brandeis. And didn't he want his kids to have *something?* What in the hell was that something she kept talking about? So it was always, 'Lester, your father's too tired to play catch with you,' or 'Don't wake him up with your nonsense, remember his heart.' But she'd wake him up in time to catch the bus for that midnight job. And when he refused to do it anymore, he was a failure, a bum. Every time she tells me I'm going to be like my father, I think about him sleeping four hours a day for ten years and want to choke her. She's wrong, I'll never be like my old man. No woman's gonna hound me into the grave so she can weep over it in imported handkerchiefs."

Lester's tense jaw muscles had deep red lines along them, so Willie knew it wasn't wise to disagree with him at the moment. For the second time since he'd come into that house he was at a loss for words, and the slamming of the front door mercifully broke the silence in the room.

Roxanne Tilson called out from the front hall, "Mom, I'm home," and put her brown suede coat away. She insisted on wearing calf-length knit dresses that didn't quite complement her full curves. Her body gave the impression that it was just one good meal away from being labeled fat. And Roxanne was constantly on guard never to have that meal. So her life consisted of nibbles: bits of lettuce and cucumber, dabs of fish and cottage cheese. She never lost weight because periodic depressions would send her nibbling potato chips, French chocolates, and Hostess Twinkies — only to start the cycle over again. She had her mother's canary coloring, but Roxanne groomed her life and body with a hawklike determination to marry black, marry well — or not at all. And at twenty-seven, with a decade's worth of bleaching creams and hair relaxers, coupled with a Wellesley B.A. and a job in an ad agency, she was still waiting. She remained at home because a Linden Hills address was far better than any she could afford on her own salary, and as the girls at the office said, you don't get a Park Avenue husband with a Harlem zip code.

Roxanne felt comfortable with the fact that she had paid her dues to the Civil Rights Movement by wearing an Afro for six months and enrolling in black history courses in college. These courses supplied her with the statistical proof that black men were further behind white men than ever before, and that the gap would keep widening. It was only a minority of that minority who were ever going somewhere and she was determined that one of them take her along on that ride. She knew the competition was stiff. Besides a multitude of other sisters like herself, she had to outrun an ego, a career, and desperate white women to snatch the heart of such a prize. But she was confident that a formula for success lay somewhere in a cross between her two heroines — Eleanor Roosevelt and Diana Ross — and she was constantly juggling the mixture. Looking at her brother only reminded her of the statistics she was up against; if he turned out that way with his background, what hope was there for other black men and the 100 to 88 ratio of black women who had to pick among them?

Roxanne sailed past the living room and turned her head. "I see Lester is into his favorite activity. And Willie? Haven't seen you in ages — I thought you were in jail." She laughed and kept on going.

"We love you, too," Lester called behind her and stuck up his middle finger. He gave a long sigh. "Well, blood, now that the zoo's assembled, let's go eat."

Mrs. Tilson had set the dining room table with china, silverware, and linen napkins in honor of Willie, whom she said she'd always loved, and she emphasized her devotion by sitting beside him and patting his hand. Willie wished she hadn't gone to so much trouble, because the starched linen kept slipping off his lap, and he spent the evening cringing every time his heavy knife hit the thin plate or his teeth clinked against the fragile Norwegian crystal. Lester didn't have those problems because he picked up his chicken with his hands and tore off huge chunks with his teeth. Any juice that dripped on his fingers was wiped off with a slice of bread before he stuffed it into his mouth. Between the two bites of chicken and teaspoon of potatoes that Roxanne consumed during the entire meal, she dominated the conversation with the importance of her new promotion, the various slights she endured at the office, and at least five references to the fact that she had a date that night. She was mentioning Xavier for the sixth time when Lester threw down the thigh bone he was sucking. "If I hear that fruit's name one more time, I'm throwing up this half-done chicken all over the table!"

Roxanne glanced calmly over her shoulder. "That would surprise no one. You've been sitting there eating like a pig all evening. You might as well finish the meal in character."

"Well, some of us in this family eat like pigs and some of us look like pigs, so I guess it all evens up," Lester said and braced himself for a fight.

Roxanne flushed deeply and addressed her mother. "Do I have to take this? After working all day, am I to be subjected to this type of abuse by someone who didn't even pay for the toothpicks on this table?"

"Lester, Roxanne, please, not in front of company." Mrs. Tilson gave Willie a nervous smile, showing her small teeth.

"Company?" Roxanne's empty fork clattered against her plate. "We don't have any company tonight. All we have is a carbon copy of the nothing that Lester's determined to make of his life."

"Hey, wait a minute," Willie said. "I didn't *beg* to come here, you know. My luck's not so hard I gotta listen to this for a few potatoes and a —"

"You've gotta lot of damn nerve insulting my friend," Lester cut him off. "And who have you ever brought here? That fag with the pink silk ties won't even set a foot in this door. He sits out there and blows his horn like he's picking up someone from a whorehouse. Now, you wanna talk about nothing — that's nothing, baby."

"You wouldn't know a real man if he was jammed down your throat." Roxanne swung around to face Lester. "Xavier is the vice president of minority marketing at General Motors. And what have you ever done except scrape a plate clean?"

"Don't you worry about it, I've done plenty. I'm working for immortality, but that's something you'll never understand."

"Im-mor-tal-ity!" Roxanne's voice was steadily climbing, leaving her Wellesley accent behind. "That crap you write? That's an excuse for freeloading and not getting a real job. I've read your junk. 'Up with the nation, down with whitey.' How you gonna get rid of 'em, Lester? Like you did that chicken — chew 'em to death?"

"E-nough!" Mrs. Tilson banged her fork on the tabletop.

"You're right about that." Lester got up from his chair. "Come on, Willie."

"No, wait." Mrs. Tilson grabbed Willie's arm. "Now Willie's going to think we're a group of barbarians in this house. Roxanne, I want you to apologize."

"Why? I meant every word I said."

"No — to Willie. What you and Lester think about each other

is one thing, but Willie is our guest. And only the crudest of people are rude to their dinner guests."

Willie felt a flood of regret for every bad thought he'd ever had about Mrs. Tilson.

"All right, I'm sorry," Roxanne mumbled. "When I'm angry I talk too quickly. My remarks were uncalled for — to *you.*" She looked straight at Willie.

"Aw, forget it," Willie said. "And thank you, Mrs. Tilson. The meal was excellent."

"Not at all, Willie. You're welcome here anytime."

Willie followed Lester up the stairs, thinking it was a pity he had disrupted his mother's dinner like that. She had been trying so hard to have things nice. He glanced back over his shoulder to take a final look at the table setting and saw Mrs. Tilson mouthing something behind her hand to Roxanne.

Lester's bedroom window faced the front of the house so it overlooked Linden Hills. Its southern exposure provided the perfect light for growing plants, but he refused to have anything green in his room. A four-foot poster of Malcolm X was taped over a dresser littered with old newspapers, Classic Comic books, and half a set of the Arno Press black history series. A pair of brown silk briefs hung over the portable television screen and under the television stand was his stereo and tape deck. Three-foot stacks of Malcolm X's taped speeches and Aretha Franklin and Earth Wind & Fire albums and cassettes were piled at the foot of the stand. Willie was lying on the king-sized bed with his legs crossed up in the air while Lester dug through his tapes.

"You've gotta hear this one, White — 'Message to the Grass Roots' — where Malcolm talks about those Toms who sold out the March on Washington in 'sixty-three."

A horn blew outside. "There goes the prick." Lester sighed.

Roxanne stuck her head inside his door. "Excuse me, Lester, do you have the twenty dollars I loaned you last week?"

"Why? Is it your turn to pay for the hotel?"

"Look, I don't have all evening. If you have my money, would you please give it to me?"

"I've only got ten." Lester kept sorting through his tapes.

"That'll be fine — I never like going anywhere without my own money." Roxanne was practicing her Eleanor Roosevelt profile and spoke very patiently. She watched him for a few more seconds. "And I'm in a hurry!"

Lester got up and gave her the money. "Can't Mr. General Motors come off a few bucks for you? I thought your first commandment was never give it up for free?"

Roxanne put the money in her bag. "Thank you, very much," she enunciated slowly. The horn blew again. "And if you're looking for your Malcolm X tape, it's in my room." She closed the door and ran down the stairs.

"Couldn't get a rise out of her, huh?" Willie said, staring at the ceiling.

"Now, what would she want with my tape? She knows it pisses me off to have her touch my stuff."

"Maybe she likes listening to him — that's one heavy dude. And you said she studied black history in college."

"Yeah, and what good did it do her? You know, when Kiswana Browne came around collecting clothes for the Liberation Front in Zimbabwe, Roxanne told her — and I quote — that after careful consideration, she'd reached the conclusion that the people of Zimbabwe weren't ready for independence. You got that one? I guess that's why Grandma Tilson said Nedeed's great-grandfather backed the Confederacy — we weren't ready to get out of slavery. And he went to one of those fancy Eastern schools, too. She's a true prodigy of the Hills, that one. Man, Kiswana took one look at the lot of us and got the hell out of this house. And for a looker like that, I was ready to pull off my jocks for Zimbabwe and hand 'em right to her, but she wanted nothing to do with us after that. And that two-faced porky's got the balls to play my tapes? The X would turn over in his grave to know that."

"He might be turning over in it when you play 'em too, Les." Willie was still staring at the ceiling. Then he turned over on his elbow to face the hurt and confusion he expected in his friend's eyes. "I mean," he began slowly, "I've been listening to you make speeches all day about how fucked up the people in this neighborhood are and how hopeless your mom and your sister are, but to paraphrase another heavy dude — methinks the nigger doth protest too much. 'Cause you still live here, Shit. You still live here, with all your hollering and screaming Uncle Tom at other folks, and I think you like living here. And all I'm saying is call a spade a spade and leave it at that."

"Hey, wait a minute, Willie."

"No, you wait a minute." Willie sat up on the edge of the bed. "I've heard you out, now it's my turn." He sat there quietly for a moment. "I grew up with five brothers and sisters in three rooms, three *small* rooms. And when we came out here on Wayne Avenue and had four rooms and a tree in front of our building, we thought that was moving up in the world. My mom got beat up every night after payday by a man who couldn't bear the thought of bringing home a paycheck only large enough for three people and making it stretch over eight people, so he drank up half of it. And she stayed, Les. She stayed because a bruised face and half a paycheck was better than welfare, and that's the only place she had left to go with no education and six kids. You think people should live like that, Shit? Because these folks in Linden Hills didn't want that kind of life doesn't make them freaks. You wouldn't want it. I don't think you'd trade this big bedroom for the third of a studio couch I had most of my life. And I don't think that playing Malcolm's tapes and calling your sister's old man names makes up for that, either."

Lester went and sat on the bed beside Willie. His eyes followed the pattern in the rust carpeting and he began to trace it with his toe. Then he sighed and looked up. "You're right, Willie. I've never had to live that way and I wouldn't want it now."

"Because this is your *home,* man," Willie said gently, "and that's why you're still here."

"Yup, that's why I'm still here — this is home." Lester sighed again. "This is home, a house with a thousand-year-and-a-day lease. I hate it, but I eat well and my laundry's done for me and my TV's fixed when the color fades . . ." Lester frowned into the carpet. "Willie, I never meant that having an education and a comfortable life was wrong. Malcolm believed in education."

"I know. The Muslims even set up their own schools, and they ran businesses. They still do."

"Yeah, but these people have gone beyond that — I can't really explain it. You know, my grandmother called it selling the mirror in your soul."

Willie tapped his chest. "Since when did we get one?"

"A soul?"

"No, a mirror." Willie smiled.

"Well, I guess she meant giving up that part of you that lets you know who you are. She would often say, 'Child, there's gonna come a time when you'll look at the world and not know what the blazes is going on. Somebody'll be calling you their father, their husband, their boss — whatever. And it can get confusing, trying to sort all that out, and you can lose yourself in other people's minds. You can forget what you really want and believe. So you keep that mirror and when it's crazy *outside*, you look inside and you'll always know exactly where you are and what you are. And you call that peace.' Ya know, White?"

"No, Les, not really."

"Well, anyway." Lester sucked his teeth. "These people have lost that, Willie. They've lost all touch with what it is to be *them*. Because there's not a damned thing inside anymore to let them know. And if that's what a degree or a five-syllable job title is going to cost you, then you don't want it, believe me, Willie. But you're right, I'm probably not much better than the rest of Linden Hills. I haven't gone all the way, but I've sold myself for a pair of clean socks and a chicken dinner."

Lester looked so dejected that Willie wanted to put his arm around his shoulder, but he punched him lightly instead.

"Hey, blood, look at it this way — if it's any consolation, your mom says she's laying five to one that you'll die without a pot to piss in. And you know, even though we hate to admit it, our moms are usually pretty much on target when they predict stuff like that."

Lester brightened. "You know, I think you've got something there."

"Sure." Willie nodded. "There's hope for you yet." And they laughed.

"You wanna split a joint?" Lester asked.

"Great. I think a little light entertainment is what we need after all this heavy bullshitting. Let 'er rip."

Lester went into the back of his closet and brought out a brown envelope.

"You got any incense?"

"Naw, my mom's too hip for that. We gotta crack the window."

They cut off the lights and sat on Lester's bed with their backs resting against the headboard, silently passing the reefer between them and watching the luminescent circles cast by the street lamps mellow and expand on the windowsill and floor. A cold burst of wind shot in through the cracked window and brought with it a long, thin wail as it trailed along the floor and gently shook the edges of the bedspread.

"Jesus, there it is again!" Willie's mouth went dry.

They sat frozen on the bed, waiting for it to come again, and when it snaked in through the open window, Lester and Willie forced themselves not to reach out and touch each other. They each sat alone in the dark, trying to link some sort of human emotion to that sound because an ancient instinct told them it wasn't an animal sending out that cry into the world. They knew it didn't sound like someone in pain or danger. And it didn't echo the heightened edges of despair. Lester and Willie were totally confused, since there was really nothing that had touched their twenty years to help them locate its cause — they had not lived long enough to recognize a plea for lost time. Up from the bottom of Linden Hills, winding between bare branches, it came sliding into Lester's room again, clear and distinct now that they had even stopped breathing to await its arrival. This time it moved across their chests, up the far wall, and over the ceiling before dying at the base of the window.

Lester's bladder loosened and he jumped up. "I've gotta take a leak." He almost ran to the door and went into the hallway.

Willie went to the window, slammed it shut, and then turned

on the lamp at the nightstand, telling himself the cold air in the room was making him tremble. The lighted room reassured him that nothing had changed. The books, the poster, the television — the world he understood was still intact. He went back to the window and cupped his hands against the cold glass and peered down the slope. The streetlights threw the shadows of the naked tree branches onto the roofs in Second Crescent Drive and then Linden Hills dropped off into a dead void.

The wind brought the cry again, but it went unheard by Willie as it rattled against the closed window and then returned back over the treetops and houses below. Back through the brick pillars on Tupelo Drive and along its shrubbed meridian. Back across the frozen lake in front of the white clapboard house. Then down through a basement air vent. Down to die in the aching throat of a woman who was crouching over the shrunken body of her son.

December
20th

The clock on the morgue wall ticked for the sixtieth time past midnight. She sat on the edge of the cot with her son's head resting on her shoulder. The limp body was hugged to her chest while the pale, shriveled arms and legs dangled behind her back. She could taste the blood in her raw throat and her jaw muscles ached from the strain of clamping her lips together. Hours ago she had decided that she would scream no more. So she closed her eyes and let her mind swing with each movement of the clock's rusty gears . . . *Sec-onds* . . . *Sec-onds* . . . She knew how to die. Just let the mind swing out — and bring it back a little less. Swing out — then back a little less. Let it slip. Slip. Toward the edge. Toward sleep.

Time. You let time take your son, now let it take you. She had only wanted those last few seconds — was that asking so much? She begged them to come back — and they would not come back. She knew the days were gone. So many days ago when she could have taken her body, pressed it across his face and put her baby to sleep. But she waited for the door to open. Surely Luther would unlock the door since the child was sick. He was testing her, that's all. He wanted to see how long she could endure. So she had feared something more than the dying eyes of her son. She feared releasing him and then hearing the bolt slide back from the door. Hearing the intercom click on and say she could come up now — it was over — only a breath after killing her son.

Sec-onds . . . She was so terrified of those seconds, looming white and huge in that eternity of space between the numbers on the clock. They kept her listening to the heaving chest, enduring the fevered touch. Mama, help me. And she did not. She waited — in fear of those seconds. But she begged them to come back. Just one. Give her one so she could help her child. Time. She would scream no more for time. No. Just let the mind swing out — she could never leave this basement alive now. Because Luther knows that he's a dead man. Swing out — he knows that she would rest, eat, grow strong. And wait. Yes, she was doomed here. So put your mind on the clock. Right there. On the clock. And let it swing you to death.

Luther fixed himself his nightly brandy and soda, and then sank his head back into his leather recliner. It had been a difficult day and tomorrow would be even busier. There was the Parker funeral in two days, so the body had to be dressed for the wake to-morrow. And then he had to squeeze in a few hours to act as an usher at Winston Alcott's wedding tomorrow morning. Why did he keep thinking tomorrow? He looked at his watch. It was a quarter past midnight, so all of that had to be done *today* — dammit. And he was so keyed up he knew he wouldn't be able to sleep for hours. He pressed the tired lines on his forehead and sighed. Nothing had gone smoothly since his wife had been downstairs. It annoyed him that her absence was much more in-trusive than her presence had ever been. It had an irritating way of showing up in his dwindling supply of clean laundry, the ac-cumulating dishes, and the light film of dust on his desk. Where was he supposed to find the time to take care of all that? He wanted to have a fire in his den. Burning logs gave a nice atmo-sphere to the room around the holiday season, but he couldn't spare the effort now — and with Mrs. Thomas away until the beginning of the year . . . He sighed again. Not that he truly regretted the necessity of dismissing their housekeeper. She never made his eggs like his wife had. Three minutes — every morning it was the same damned argument — no more and no less than three minutes, and you start with tepid eggs so they don't crack in the boiling water.

He took another sip of his drink and grimaced. He always managed to add too much brandy. Now her absence even lay at the base of his burning throat. Six years of a decent brandy and soda weren't going to wash down the drain because of one problem. His father was right: breaking in a wife is like breaking in a good pair of slippers. Once you'd gotten used to them, you'd wear them until they fell apart, rather than go to the trouble of buying a new pair. Well, in a few weeks she would have learned her lesson. And then next spring, she'd conceive again and he'd get the son he should have had in the first place. God, it would have taken him seven years. But the world had changed so much since his father's time — women had changed dreadfully. Ideally, he should have married a woman who was the age of his fathers' wives — sixteen, seventeen at the most. But today, that was impossible because they were pampered and irresponsible. Now women that young were nothing but empty-headed children, totally incapable of managing a household like this. And he didn't dare marry any of the ones he met during his college days. The black women on that campus had an arrogance about them, an overinflated sense of their uniqueness in getting that far. Sure, they had wanted a husband but not at the cost of their future — a sullen, discontented lot — it was too much to ask them to share *your* future and legally own half of what they've never worked for. But he had known when the moment was right to pick the perfect woman for Tupelo Drive.

At his tenth college reunion, he'd moved carefully among the ones who had never managed to marry at all by that time. And he noticed those who had lost that hopeful, arrogant strut. There was a certain edge of bewilderment in their voices when they spoke about their advanced degrees, their apartments, and their jobs, because obviously none of that had made them desirable

enough. And tipping the scale at thirty, the only thing they en-
visioned for their future was dying alone. Marriage was a sigh of
relief at that age. She had been a teacher, an accountant, a
chemist — but now she could be a woman. And she'd quickly
forget the foolish dreams that she'd had for a mate ten years ago.
She was more than willing to join the life and rhythms of almost
any man — and for a man like himself, she'd bend over backward. So he had lived alone for many years and waited to choose
such a woman at that college reunion and bring her to Tupelo
Drive.

But he couldn't understand what had gone wrong. He had
never been cruel or abusive to her. He must have given her at
least six lines of credit in his name, never questioning what she
bought or why. And he asked so little of her in return. Just come
into his home and respect him and the routines of his household.
Work along with him to continue the tradition of several generations. Simply honor what his family had done, just as he
honored it. And she couldn't bring herself to do even that.
Through some sort of twisted willfulness, she had not only
disrupted his home but almost managed to destroy lifetimes of
work, to erase the labor of those proud, strong men. And then
she had expected him to accept that without a murmur. No, he
was definitely not his father's son. His father would have let her
rot down there. But he was trying so hard to adjust to the new
world around him, and nothing could be served by going to
those extremes. And besides — he looked at his drink — she did
have some qualities worth saving.

He tapped his glass thoughtfully. She probably thinks that she
wants to poison me. If he let her up now, she would — or put a
knife through his back. It's too soon after the child's death —
that was certainly regrettable. But it had been an expedient turn
of events, for he hadn't really thought about what to do with it
once she was allowed to come back upstairs. It certainly couldn't
have stayed in his home. But it was a pity the child had to suffer
that way because of its mother's ingratitude. By now she understood that he controlled her food and water and light. Whatever
she had been allowed — upstairs or down — was hers not by

right, but as a gift. And she had only herself to blame for the child's death. She wouldn't have been down there in the first place if she hadn't tried to make a fool of him. With all her willfulness, she now saw that she couldn't save her bastard — but she'll want to save herself. Yes, Luther nodded, she'll want to save herself.

He had seen enough people with their dead to understand the course of grief. At first, there is always the overwhelming sense of despair and some even think of joining the dead. But then as time increases in minutes, hours, days — the survivors are eventually surrounded with enough of it to be awed by the privilege that separates them from that coffin. And they begin to see that they aren't mourning that shell of flesh; they are mourning the loss of life itself. Yes, if he let her sit down there with that body long enough then she'd realize that she didn't really want to kill him. No, she only wanted what she had wanted so badly when she married him. He was no fool; he knew she would never have looked at him if it weren't for the feel of the name *Mrs. Luther Nedeed* as she slipped on that white satin and brocade, the cold smooth rings. The touch of the name in her silver, mahogany, and velvet. The smell of it in her imported colognes. The sight of it on thick, embossed invitations to the best homes in town. And the sound of the name — yes, the sound of the name on the tongues of the idiots who were panting and pushing to be somewhere in the corner of her memory. And to have those things, you had to be alive. And she wanted to live. She wanted to live so badly that if she thought there was no more food coming, she would even look upon that body alongside her as a way to stay alive. Having thought that, she would come upstairs and think no more of killing him than she had thought of saving her own life. He would give her a chance at life.

Luther went to the water valves under the kitchen sink and turned them on. Then he clicked on the intercom: "Mrs. Nedeed, I'm giving you some water now. There will be no more food. Please catch as much as you can quickly because it won't be on all night."

He left the valves open and went back to sit down. He started to fix himself another drink, but changed his mind. He didn't want a headache tomorrow; there was too much to do and he would have to drink at least one toast at Winston's reception. Winston had him worried for a while: he thought Linden Hills was going to lose him. But it seems to have only taken that one letter to his father to straighten things out. Old man Alcott had brought him around in no time. Yes, they all come around. He sighed, got up, and turned off the lamps in his den. The huge, lighted fish tank in the corner cast whirling shadows on the carpet as the dark, bloated catfish slithered through the long weeds, their thin whiskers undulating slowly among the smooth blades of grass.

Luther watched them for a moment, feeling the tension in his body relax. Maybe tonight. He was really too tired to sleep. He could begin preparing the Parker body for the wake; the powder and rouge and dressing shouldn't take more than an hour. That would save him some time when he woke up. Yes, that's what he needed to do; a little work would put him to sleep. He took the net hanging on the side of the tank and caught one of the catfish. In the kitchen, he hacked off the head of the struggling body and put it in a plastic bag. Then, before carrying it out the back door to his mortuary and the body of Lycentia S. Parker, he shut off the valves under the kitchen sink.

The thunder from the metal sink in the corner washed over her brain and her mind was flushed from the clock by the rush of sound through the open faucet. She groaned, pressed her chin into the child's shoulder, and gasped the air like a drowning fish. Would this torture never end? Oh God, please stop that noise — she couldn't hear the clock. Painfully, she took a deep breath, concentrated, and tried to go on without it. But the spraying water forced different rhythms into her brain — Iwantyoutolive . . . Iwantyouto-live . . . Iwantyouto . . . Once that sound had meant a salvation that was prayed for and bargained for with the same promises offered any god. And it came as an answer from that untouchable region, sending her in flight across the basement hurriedly to catch what was needed for bathing and drinking. And then to wet the dry cereal after the milk was gone. But then even the cereal had gone. So it became a frantic flight from rest or sleep because she never knew — it might be a redemption that only lasted minutes, or once it had gone on for days until she thought the noise would drive her mad as she cursed and then feared the cursing of their one source of life.

But she didn't move now. There was no longer any need. Send water. Send light. Send food. A day or an eternity — it didn't matter. Any possibility of salvation lay withered in her arms. She would have to die down here now. And she would die in her own way.

The whining receiver on the wall announced the coming. And the stale basement air filled up with the voice: *Mrs. Nedeed, I'm giving you some water now. There will be no more food. Please catch as much as you can quickly because it won't be on all night.*

She listened numbly. There was no meaning to those patterns of empty noises. The words didn't connect inside of her to any history or emotion. She was past being moved to disbelief, frustration, or anger. The power of that voice was gone. It didn't demand that she fear or hope — or hate. No, she did not even hate now. She sat there calmly and irrevocably immersed in the simple fact that had become part of her being: Luther was a dead man if she left that basement alive. And so she knew she could never be allowed to leave. So she waited patiently for the voice to cease, for it to withdraw the thunder. Still holding the child, she lay down on the cot. Now she must wait until it was quiet again. A euphoric weakness spread through her body and she drifted off to sleep.

Lester woke up and found himself bound in a respectable half nelson that had his neck fixed firmly under Willie's chin and his right ear at the mercy of long, gravelly columns of air. He tried to wriggle free without waking Willie up, but finally had to resort to thrusting his one free elbow into his friend's stomach.

"Hey, White, wake up!"

Willie's eyes flew open blindly. "Yeah, right. Morning." And he buried his chin deeper into Lester's neck and went back to sleep.

Lester jabbed him again. "Let me up, will ya. You hugging me worse than a woman."

When Willie forced his mind to focus behind his open eyes, he finally saw their position in the bed. "And they said it wouldn't last." He hugged Lester and let out a deep yawn.

"You sick bastard." Lester laughed while untangling himself. He went to the window and began a series of arm push-ups against the frame.

"You gotta be kidding me." Willie buried himself deeper into the covers.

"Nope, every morning — fifty of these and then fifty deep knee bends. I owe it to the daughters of America to keep this body in shape. I don't want the ones waiting at the end of the line to be disappointed when their turn comes."

Willie watched for a while through one eye. "You don't have a bad ass, though."

Lester looked over his shoulder. "Keep that up and you're not sleeping here anymore."

Willie grinned and pulled the covers over his cold nose. His mind wanted to catch the fading ends of the night images that had driven him toward the security of his friend's body. But the flashes of a huge clock with snakes and spiders for hands and numbers were quickly dismissed as he sought a more comfortable reason. "Now I know what it is — why is it so damned cold in here?"

"We Tilsons are loyal Americans." Lester continued his push-ups. "She drops that thermostat to fifty-five degrees every night. Gotta save the nation's energy so we'll have enough left to fuel those tanks and missiles that are keeping us safe from commies and gooks and possible sneak attacks from Harlem." Then he saw a black limousine turn out of Second Crescent Drive and head up Linden Road toward Wayne Avenue. He watched it until it was cut off from his view. "Now, here's something for you." Lester turned to Willie. "I coulda sworn that guy was gay and now he's getting married today."

"Who?"

"Winston Alcott from Second Crescent Drive. Mom and Roxanne bitched for a week when they realized they weren't getting an invitation to that gig. But they should know the game by now. Your scorecard's rated by how many folks you can get who live below you to show up at whatever shit you have going on. Now, if the Nedeeds are there today, that'll really be something. Ol' Winston reached way down the hill to fill up his guest list. Jesus, all the screeching that went on in here about some fag's wedding."

"Well, looks like he's not if he's getting married."

"Yeah." Lester frowned slightly. "But I wondered for a while. He was always hanging around with this tall, dark-skinned dude —"

"And you hang around with a short, dark-skinned dude. That don't mean that you're a fruit."

"But you *never* saw him with a woman and then — bam — he's engaged."

"I never saw you with a woman, either." Willie sat up in bed. "A coupla chimpanzees, maybe. And then last month, that flat-chested thing you shoulda run out and bought a leash for, but never —"

The thick paperback that flew across the room barely missed Willie's head, and he covered up his face with the quilt to block the other books that came right behind it. "All right, truce!" He stuck his arm up from the covers. "I'll admit it — I've had to keep a few cans of Alpo around the house in my time, too. And if you don't let me up, I'm going to leak on this mattress."

"Christ, don't do that." Lester came and gathered up his books. "We gotta get going anyway. I figure we could check out Mike, he's the janitor of those town-house apartments on the next street. With Winston's wedding going on today, maybe there's something to do around the reception hall."

"Probably waiting on tables."

"Man, are you kidding? This is going to be one of them classy, catered affairs. They'd only want *white* waiters for that. The best we can hope for is washing some dishes or hauling garbage."

"You mean I can't put on a monkey suit and pour the vichyssoise?" Willie's mouth dropped in mock horror.

"Don't let it crush you, blood. Before the day's over, you'll have your fill of monkeys — and they'll all be in suits." Lester shook his head slowly. "Oh, yeah, suited to the hilt."

Winston Alcott smoothed the sleeve on his tuxedo and pulled at the cuff needlessly — it was perfectly straight. It was as straight as his shoes were polished as the top hat on his lap was brushed as the striped ascot was knotted, as straight as his walking cane piled in the back window of the limousine along with the canes of his three ushers and best man. He rode in the back seat, between his cousin and David, his best man. His brother's stiff back in the front seat told him that the others were as uncomfortable as he was. They were making the stilted movements of people who were afraid of the clothes they wore, dreading that the slightest imperfection would reveal that it wasn't their usual mode of dress. The only one in the car apparently at ease was the driver, Luther Nedeed. It seemed as if he'd been born wearing the Edwardian costumes that hung like dead weight on the other men.

"Gentlemen, why so gloomy?" Luther glanced in the rearview mirror at the three in the back. "I've seen happier faces at my funerals."

They all laughed obediently and Winston forced himself to keep smiling as he desperately sought for something light to say. "Even on the corpses, Mr. Nedeed?" It hurt to keep his mouth turned upward when it wanted to join the rest of his spirit slowly caving in around the dull throbbing in his center.

Luther looked straight into Winston's eyes in the mirror. "That's an interesting analogy, Winston. I guess every young man feels a bit like that on his wedding day. You're burying one way of life for another. But if you'll suffer me a further metaphor, after every death is a resurrection, Winston — hopefully, one to paradise."

"Or Pampers." His brother looked over his shoulder and winked.

"Or paper rollers on your pillow." His cousin took up the joke.

David said nothing.

"Don't let them bait you, Winston. Their turn will come soon enough. And all you bachelors can take it from a seasoned married man — in spite of occasional drawbacks, it can be a fulfilling way of life."

"But not the only way of life, Mr. Nedeed." David spoke for the first time and the sound of his voice caused the ache in Winston's middle to flare up.

I won't be your whore ——

"No, I'll grant you that, David." Luther's eyes continually sought Winston's in the mirror and he was forced to meet them, not wanting to turn his head toward David. "But it's the only way if a man wants to get somewhere in Linden Hills."

"I know plenty of *single* men who've done just that." David stared out the side window.

"Ummm." Luther took a sharp left turn and Winston tightened his body to keep from swinging against David's knees. His leg and thigh muscles ached from resisting the motion that pulled him toward the left window. Oh God, just let them get there. It's only twelve damn blocks. Were they driving in circles?

"But where are they living, David? In those small apartments on Second Crescent Drive. And who would want to spend the rest of their lives there? No one's been able to make it down to Tupelo Drive without a stable life and a family. Besides, Winston didn't want to stay single, did you, son? You didn't want to go it alone."

"No." The limousine pulled up to a red light and Winston finally saw the gray stone church three blocks away. "David and I were just talking about that last week." He looked at David's averted head. "About how I didn't want to be alone."

I won't be your whore ——

"About how difficult it is for a man to do the things he's got to do — alone." Winston's saliva tasted bitter as he swallowed. Shut up, he thought, you're almost there. You can't reach him in three blocks. What can you do in three blocks that you couldn't do in the last three months. There's nothing you can say to make him hurt with you. Winston knew he would have to sink his teeth into David's throat and tear the jugular vein, smash his head against the car window until it was splintered and smeared with blood to have him hurt as he hurt, to force him to share this moment as he'd shared so many others. He could never do it with words. Winston squirmed forward in his seat. "Isn't that light taking a long time? It's probably broken — just run the damn thing." The anger in his voice startled everyone but Luther, who smoothly turned his dark face around to the back.

"Don't worry, Winston." His mouth was the only part of his face that smiled. *"Cassandra will still be there."*

"But she doesn't count and you know it." Winston took the lighter off the coffee table and lit his cigarette.

"She's got to count a hell of a lot if you're marrying her." David looked out the living-room window with his hands wedged deeply into his jeans pockets.

"Why?" Winston blew the smoke noisily between his tight jaws. "She wanted a husband — I needed a wife. It's straight out of a soap opera. And they lived happily ever after until the next floor-wax commercial."

David shook his head slowly. "If that's your attitude, then I feel sorry for that girl. She's got some life waiting for her."

"What other attitude am I supposed to have?" He savagely crushed the freshly lit cigarette into the tray. "I didn't want this — *they* did. And I'd think you'd save a little of that pity you're so generous with for me. What kind of life am I gonna have, goddammit!"

"It's the kind you want, Winston."

"That's a lie."

"Then if it's a lie, son, I guess you'll be thinking about marriage soon." Mr. Alcott narrowed his eyes as he spoke, and he tapped the envelope in his hand gently on the top of his desk. "I assume you're seeing someone now. A young man with your looks and future must be beating them off with a stick." He smiled slowly.

"Sure, I date a lot." Winston's throat was dry. "But I don't see any need to rush into something serious. For God's sake, I'm only thirty, Dad."

"Well, I'd already had two children by the time I was your age." He continued to stare at his son.

"The world's a lot different now." Winston hated the tone creeping into his voice; it was too defensive. And in spite of the air-conditioning in the office, he felt himself sweating. "Some men aren't settling down until their forties. I figured once I'm thirty-five or so I'd start thinking about it. By then my career should be —"

"By then . . ." Mr. Alcott's voice suddenly shed its soft covering. "You might not have a career. Whoever sent me this letter threatened to send one to the senior partner in your firm. And they said that the next one would be accompanied by pictures."

"Pictures of what?" Winston leaned forward in his chair. "Of me having lunch with David? Of us walking down the street or sailing out at the lake? Those are the only type of pictures that anyone could have. And they can send them to be printed up in the damn newspaper for all I care." He was horrified because he couldn't control the rising hysteria in his voice. "Or maybe that sick creep will clip out the picture from our college yearbook, where David has his arm across my shoulder at graduation — yeah, that's certainly hard-core evidence to condemn me with."

"It just might be." Mr. Alcott frowned at the envelope in his hand. "Remember who you are and where you are. A law firm like Farragut and Conway would kick you out tomorrow if you sneezed wrong. So do you think a black man can afford to have these types of rumors hanging over his head?"

"I'm telling you, they're a lot of filthy lies." Winston was trembling visibly. "But if you want to believe them, go ahead."

"Lies or not" — Mr. Alcott came from around the desk and put his hand on Winston's shoulder — "filthy or not" — he squeezed the narrow back — "they'll make you hang for it, son. I didn't invent this world, Winston. But I broke my ass so you and your brother could have it a lot easier than I did. And you've done me proud. Your life's barely begun and you're already living in Linden Hills. I could never dream of that when I was your age. Sure, worse comes to worst, you could come here and work for me. But in ten years, twenty years, would you be happy as a lousy insurance broker? You're brilliant, boy. Don't throw away a chance to be a corporate lawyer with a firm like that because of ... well, because you're young and can't really see what it might mean later. And since you say you're planning to think about marriage, now is as good a time as any, isn't it?"

There was a long silence.

"Well, isn't it?" Mr. Alcott repeated himself, but Winston knew it was no longer an open question. It was a final challenge to confirm or deny that letter.

"Yes, I suppose so."

"Good." Mr. Alcott patted his back. "No one's asking you to rush out and marry the first woman you see outside today. But mull it over and I think, with all things considered, you'll realize that it's the kind of life you want, Winston."

"If it's not the life you really want" — David turned away from the living-room window — "remember, I offered you another." And his round, brown eyes melted slowly into his words. They melted for Winston like the mist on his steamed bathroom mirror as he stood before it clean and wet with the memory of the hot, beaded water still caressing his back and shoulders. And him reaching out with his hand to clear it away — first from the face that stared back so like his own. The firm even jaw, the damp wiry beard that could be traced down into the chest if he were careful and gentle enough to move aside the stray hairs that grew into the smooth plane of the neck. The mist sliding down the neck toward the chest under his slowly circling hand, revealing the silvery image of his waist, his hips, his lean and woven thighs. The wetness slipping across the sweating glass over the fine down on the testicles and collecting there like crystal welts. Palm following palm, breath meeting breath through the blurred mirror — complete.

Winston tore his eyes from David's face and they followed his voice into his hands. "I can't live with you. Not in Linden Hills. That would be suicide, and you know it."

"There are other places to live."

"Not like this — and my future is here. My career . . ."

"Fine!" David threw up his hands. "I don't need a thousand replays of that tune — I've heard it all before. I understand where you're coming from, believe me. And all this new development means is that you've chosen to live without me. It's really sort of simple, isn't it?"

Winston looked up at him with narrowing eyes. "Why are you doing this to me? We've been through so much together. Why do you want to try and hurt me now? You know she can't touch what we have between us. If you really understood, you wouldn't be standing there trying to make me choose when there's really no choice about it."

"For Christ's sake!" David's fist came down on the windowsill. "No one is making you do anything. You have chosen, brother. So just act like a man and admit it. Have enough backbone for once in your life to accept responsibility for what you really want. Not your father, not your law firm — *you*, Winston. Because I'm man enough to know what I want. And it's not playing second fiddle in anybody's life."

"So because I have to do this, you're telling me that it's over."

"That's right."

"I don't believe you." Winston shook his head. "I don't believe that you can turn your back on eight years just like that. People don't give up friends that way."

"Sure, we can still be friends. And as your *best* friend, I'm standing up with you as your *best* man next week, aren't I? It would look sort of strange if I didn't. But that's not what we're talking about now, so don't play games with me."

Winston looked down into his hands again. No, that's not what they were talking about. And they weren't even talking about remaining lovers; they had moved beyond that years ago. Because when two people still held on like he and David, after all the illusions had died, and accepted the other's lacks and ugliness and irritating rhythms — when they had known the joys of a communion that far outstripped the flesh — they could hardly just be lovers. No, this man gave him his center, but the world had given him no words — and ultimately no way — with which to cherish that. He smiled bitterly and looked up. "Don't you see what I'm up against? How am I going to live with you when they haven't even made up the right words for what we are to each other?"

"Oh, they've made up plenty of words and you can read them on any public bathroom wall. And that's what you can't face. You want the world to turn inside out and *make up* a nice, neat title that you can put on your desk. And that's not about to happen. You can't handle anything less than that because you're a made man, Winston. They made you a good son, a promising young lawyer, and now they've made you ashamed of what you are. You can go ahead and run from it. But don't expect me to run with you."

"I'm not running from anything." Winston forced his voice through his closing throat. "I've accepted that I can't live without you. And I've been trying to tell you that all afternoon in every way I can. Do you want to make me beg now, is that it?"

David sighed and went over to the couch and lifted Winston's face gently. "The only thing I want you to do is finally to try and start *making yourself.* Make yourself happy with that girl — please, do that." He took his hand away. "Because she's all you've got now."

Winston's face slowly crumbled and he reached for a cigarette, but his hands were trembling so badly he brought them back to his lap ashamed.

David watched him with a sharp tenderness in his stomach, and before he could stop the words, they burst out of his mouth. "But you remember, I was willing to do anything for you."

Winston's smile was almost cruel. "You can't walk into Sinai Baptist next week and marry me."

David pressed his lips together as if he'd been slapped.

"Right." He nodded his head slowly. "You got me there. And since I can't be your wife, I won't be your whore."

The limousine pulled up in front of the church, with the pink and white crepe paper wrapped around the antenna and fenders beating a dull tempo in the December wind. The men got out, and just as Winston saw the billowing edge of the bridal gown in the door, it exploded into a dozen white flashes of light that would freeze his image for the wedding album.

"Now I want you boys to try and stay out the way of them folks carrying the trays." The stoop-shouldered old man led Willie and Lester to a corner of the large utility kitchen. He pointed to a pair of double swinging doors. "They gonna be coming through there like greased lightning 'cause they'll be over two hundred folks to serve. And don't want no accidents with all them high muckety-mucks out there."

"Don't worry, Mike, we'll be careful," Lester said.

"Good. I appreciate your help 'cause, fact is, I should be scraping them platters and hauling the garbage myself, but I don't know how they expect me to do all that alone with my rheumatism."

"They should have the waiters pitch in and give you a hand," Willie said. "That's what they're getting paid for."

"Naw suh." Mike threw up his hands. "The office come talking to me about some union — it ain't in they contract to scrape no plates and dump garbage. White folks got it good, don't they — even them waiting on tables. The realty company never worried 'bout me having no union, and I got six of these buildings to tend. Bad enough I get run ragged all during the week with a thousand fix-this and do-thats, they even wants me here on my day off to clean up after 'em. The least drip in the faucet, they banging on my door talking 'bout they nerves. A stray piece of paper and they calling the office on me — I'm letting the neighborhood run down. I never saw such a bunch of finicky niggers in all my life."

"As if they really cared about Second Crescent Drive," Lester said. "Everybody knows they come here and pay all those fancy rents, hoping for the first chance to beat it out of here and get into a home down the hill."

"That's just it, son. With the realty office sitting at the end of the street, they gotta show how good they take care of these here premises so they get a shot at something better later on. So they wear me to the bone. Pure slavery's all it is."

The old man kept complaining to Lester, and Willie went to

the swinging doors and looked through the oval glass. The reception hall was beginning to fill up and the sixteen-piece band was playing soft background music. Large round tables, holding huge silver centerpieces of carnations and poinsettias, lined both sides of the room. The unoccupied bridal table sat on a raised and carpeted platform facing Willie across the long polished floor. Reflections from the crystal-tiered chandeliers glimmered on the silver patterns in the wallpaper, the sprays from the champagne fountain, the brass buttons of the waiters as they moved between the tables and the bar.

"Some setup, huh?" Lester stood behind Willie.

"I'm telling you." Willie nodded. "Look at the size of that cake."

The four-foot wedding cake held miniatures of the bridal party on two sets of golden stairways that ran up each of its sides. A tiny spray of liquid sugar rose mysteriously from its center and sprinkled the small bride and groom at regulated intervals.

Lester sucked his teeth. "It's disgusting."

Willie didn't think so. He secretly felt a bit proud that someone black could afford all this. That cake alone must have cost a small fortune — and then all this other getup. Even if they had to go into hock for this reception, it must really be something to be in a position to make that kind of debt. This was definitely no fried-chicken-and-potato-salad affair. The waiters were coming into the kitchen and unwrapping trays of marinated shrimp, stuffed artichokes, caviar, and some kind of cheese that Willie didn't recognize, so he knew it must be expensive.

And the clothes on those sisters. Willie couldn't tell the difference between the Halston minks and Saint Laurent fox capes out there, but the way those black women floated into the banquet hall like glittering birds of paradise spelled sable to him, sable beauty. The impeccable makeup, the manicured hands and custom-made hairdos were only rivaled by the sculptured attire of their male escorts. At first he watched in awe as the room filled and the waves of people mingled and separated into variegated patterns of silk, cashmere, and brocade. But even as glass after glass was refilled from the champagne fountain and the talk and laughter took on a flushed energy, Willie couldn't help feeling that something was missing from the jeweled sparkle in the air. Then he happened to notice a woman sitting to his left in a pink satin suit. She had bent her head forward to listen to a pepper-haired man across the table. And just as she went to throw her head back in a smooth arc of laughter, the white fur on the back of her chair slipped toward the floor. Her hand shot out to retrieve it, halted a fraction of a second, and then made an uninterrupted swing to come to rest on her bosom as her head finally lay back on her shoulders. The laughing woman with the apparently ignored fur trailing on the floor now told Willie what he'd missed from that room: spontaneity. His eyes flew around the long hall again over lifted glasses, backslaps, and nibbling mouths. And he could see that he hadn't been alone in his awe of all that splendor. He was actually watching them watch themselves having this type of affair. The soft strains of a slow waltz drifted through the doors and Willie made a mental bet that they'd dance to nothing more exciting than that the entire afternoon. These niggers would be afraid to sweat.

The music suddenly stopped and there was a slow drum roll and the far doors were swung open for the wedding party. Each couple was announced over the microphone by the maître d'. Each was greeted with a round of applause, and the announcement of Mr. Luther Nedeed escorting Miss Rosalyn Tyler brought a sustained ovation and some guests even stood up to clap.

"So that's Nedeed." Willie peered through the glass panel. "Pretty, ain't he?"

"Yeah," Lester said. "That face would stop a clock."

Willie felt an inexplicable twinge at those words and found himself asking aloud, "I wonder what his old lady looks like?"

"You know, it's funny. I've seen her a couple of times but I couldn't pick her out in that room right now. She's got the kind of face that wouldn't stand out in your mind — sorta average."

The bride and groom finally entered, bowed to the cheers of their guests, and went to the center of the floor officially to begin the first dance. The waiters began to stream back into the kitchen with their trays. But Willie and Lester had nothing to do except remove a few loose toothpicks and crumpled napkins. As the trays kept returning completely empty, Willie felt his stomach growling and sighed. They might look like birds of paradise, but they sure ate like vultures. So he and Lester went back to the door to watch the dancers.

"Well, ol' Winston did all right by himself," Lester said as the couple waltzed around the room. "She's not bad-looking."

"Nice eyes, but too skinny for me." Willie shook his head. "I like my women with some padding on 'em so when you go in for a landing, you don't get stuck on a pelvis bone."

"It's not bothering Winston none — he's just grinning away."

Willie's head followed the circling couple and he imagined himself and Ruth gliding out there on the polished oak floor. She would be looking up into his eyes just like that woman was, all dewy and covered with cream lace. And he would hold her around the waist and smile down at her just like that guy was doing now. But no — something about Winston's face didn't quite fit into Willie's daydream. No, he could never imagine himself smiling at Ruth like that. Why, that guy looks like someone had punched him in the stomach and his lips sorta froze up that way.

When the dancers left the floor, Lester poked Willie in the side. "Hey, get that, over in the corner. It's that douche bag, Xavier."

A tall man, with a face the shape and color of a brown egg, sat with his arm thrown over the chair of a young, blond woman. He playfully offered her a bit of cheese and she ate it from his fingers. Then he bent over and whispered in her ear and they laughed.

"That mother," Lester spit out. "He told Roxanne he wasn't invited to this shit and now he shows up with that pink job. I oughta go out there and smash him in his face."

"Shit, lay light." Willie pulled at his arm. "It's none of your business."

"It is my business." Lester pulled his arm away. "He came

slobbering over my sister just last night, but she's not good enough to come here with him when it's broad daylight. I just wanna go out there and let him see me. Then he'll know his game is up."

The waiters hurried back through the swinging doors and Lester started to go out, but Willie grabbed his arm again. "You wanna get Mike in trouble? You know we ain't supposed to be here," he whispered. "You start something and that nice old guy loses his job for trying to help us."

That stopped Lester for a moment. "But why would he *do* that, Willie?"

Willie saw the hurt in his eyes. "I don't know. Some guys just like to go that way, I guess. And you don't know, it might have nothing to do with Roxanne. Maybe that woman's one of his business friends or something," he offered hopefully, but not believing it.

"Yeah, sure." Lester sighed.

Willie looked at his friend's face, which would probably be lighter than that blond woman's when she was suntanned. "Les, you ever been with one?"

"Why would you ask me that?" There was a defensive edge in his voice.

"I don't know." Willie shrugged. "I was just wondering."

"Well, yeah, a coupla times." Then he went into an exaggerated whisper. "But never in broad daylight." They smiled at each other. "When I used to read my stuff at the coffeehouses in the city, they'd come up to me afterward and we'd start talking, ya know?"

"Well, I never have. But I always sorta wondered —" Willie glanced at the waiters pouring soup into silver tureens at the other end of the kitchen. "Are they really different?"

"Nah." Lester shook his head. "But I'll tell you something, they're easier."

"Yeah?" Willie's eyes widened. "Ya know, I've heard guys say that."

"It's true. They don't put you through the rain dance that the sisters do. I use to think that was really something. It made me feel special, you know what I mean? But then once . . ." Lester's voice dropped off. "I never told you this, but . . ." He looked at the floor. "I met this girl once — after reading at this jazz session — and then we went to her place and got stoned. God, she had some good weed in that fancy pad. And then after the whole thing had gone down, she rolled over in the bed and started stroking my arms and stuff and said, 'That was nice, so I can imagine how great it would have been if you were really *black.*' "

"Christ!" Willie whistled.

"I swear to you, White." Lester stared off in space. "That was the first time in my life that I wanted to hit a woman."

They heard another slow drum roll, and a crash of cymbals brought the reception hall to a muted hum. The maître d' stuck his head in the kitchen and told the waiters to hold the soup until after the toasts. Lester and Willie went back to the door and Luther Nedeed was mounting the bandstand. The room was totally still as he adjusted the microphone and delicately cleared his throat.

"Gentlewomen, gentlemen. Before we settle into the marvelous repast that is awaiting us, pray bear with me as I extend our warmest regards to the nuptial union of Mr. and Mrs. Winston Alcott."

"God," Willie whispered, "does he always talk like that?"

"Yup, straight out of a gothic novel. He spoke at my high school graduation and you know what he called black folks? 'We denizens of the darker hue.' Made it sound like a disease. That nigger's unreal."

Luther had taken two small velvet cases out of his jacket pocket. "As an old friend of the Alcotts, I was honored to be an intimate part of this wedding party. And as the president of the Tupelo Realty Corporation, this occasion gives me unspeakable joy because Winston Alcott has been an outstanding member of this community, doing it great pride and showering it with his talents and vitality. And now today, he has taken the step which will insure the stability and growth of Linden Hills. I applaud you, Winston Alcott. We all applaud you."

There was a healthy response from the room.

"For somebody who is so full of *unspeakable* joy, he's sure got a lot to say," Lester said.

"Shhh," Willie said.

"But I feel that a moment like this requires more than applause. Yes, much more. So it does me great pleasure to announce that after you return from your nuptial retreat, you will not be bringing the new Mrs. Alcott back to Second Crescent Drive. You have proven your dedication to Linden Hills, and now Linden Hills will open its arms to you." Luther unsnapped the velvet cases and held them up. "The Tupelo Realty Corporation has decided to give you a mortgage on Tupelo Drive."

There was a loud gasp from the room and then wild and thunderous applause as Luther turned full circle on the bandstand, with his arms lifted high above his head, displaying the contents of the cases. There was a platinum-and-diamond key-shaped necklace in one and matching cuff links in the other.

"Well, I'll be damned!" Lester whistled. "Winston must be pissing happy over that one."

But Willie noticed that Winston hadn't changed the expression he'd been wearing all afternoon. The frozen grimace that was passing for a smile held while he watched Luther put the necklace around his bride's neck and then shake his hand. In fact, it never melted an inch until a handsome young man followed Nedeed onto the bandstand. The room slowly settled down again for the best man's toast.

David's smooth voice was relaxed and pleasant. "Well, I see that I have a tough act to follow." He smiled, showing his firm white teeth as the guests laughed. "But I don't think that my words will be any less sincere than Mr. Nedeed's when I offer my congratulations to the new couple."

He turned to face the wedding table and spoke directly to it. "Mr. Nedeed addressed Mr. Alcott and so I would like to direct my remarks to the other half — and as some would say, the *better* half — Mrs. Alcott." David waited for the laughter to cease and Willie waited for Winston to keel over in a dead faint, because that's exactly how tight his face had become. "Cassandra, I've never been very fancy with words. And so when I knew I wanted

something very special for this occasion, I went to a man who
devoted his life to words and found something that I feel fits this
day perfectly. Since this poem will speak about the trials that are
ahead of you in marriage — and the joys — I want you to imagine that your new husband is saying these words to you."

David took a folded sheet of paper out of his jacket and began
to recite in a clear and steady voice:

> "Whoever you are, holding me now in hand,
> Without one thing, all will be useless,
> I give you fair warning, before you attempt me further,
> I am not what you supposed, but far different."

"Hey," Willie said, "that's Whitman. But why would he be
reading that one? It's —"

> "Who is she that would become my follower?
> Who would sign herself a candidate for my affections?"

"Holy shit," Willie whispered and turned to Lester. "He's
changed the words. It should be, Who is *he* that would become
my follower? Who would sign *himself* a candidate for my affec-
tions?' Les, Whitman wrote that poem for a man."

> "The way is suspicious — the result uncertain, perhaps destruc-
>   tive;
> You would have to give up all else — I alone would expect to
>   be your God, sole and exclusive,
> Your novitiate would even then be long and exhausting,
> The whole past theory of your life, and all conformity
>   to the lives around you, would have to be abandon'd;
> Therefore release me now, before troubling yourself any fur-
>   ther —
>   Let go your hand from my shoulders,
> Put me down and depart on your way.

> "Or else, by stealth, in some wood, for trial,
> Or back of a rock, in the open air,
> (For in any roof'd room of a house I emerge not — nor in com-
>   pany,
> And in libraries I lie as one dumb, a gawk, or unborn, or dead)

But just possibly with you on a high hill — first watching
   lest any person, for miles around, approach unawares,
Or possibly with you sailing at sea, or on the beach of the
   sea, or some quiet island,
Here to put your lips upon mine I permit you,
With the comrade's long-dwelling kiss, or the new husband's kiss,
For I am the new husband, and I am the comrade."

"Will you listen to that?" Lester said. "He's making a fool of
the whole lot of them."

But Willie knew that the guy reading that poem wasn't aware
of anyone else in that room but the dude behind the bridal
table. There was something strange going on between that
bandstand and bridal table.

"Or, if you will, thrusting me beneath your clothing,
Where I may feel the throbs of your heart, or rest upon your hip,
Carry me when you go forth over land or sea;
For thus, merely touching you, is enough — is best,
And thus, touching you, would I silently sleep and be carried
   eternally."

Willie was thoroughly perplexed. Those words spoke of something pretty deep just between two people. But what could have
driven that guy to stand up there and broadcast those things before the world? And how could there have been anything like
that between them in the first place? It gave him a queasy feeling in the pit of his stomach to think that one man could feel
about another as he felt about Ruth.

David had put the paper back into his pocket and picked up
his glass for the toast. But Willie knew he hadn't finished reading the entire poem. And he wondered if Winston knew what
the rest of it said. Did he know that that guy was standing up
there and telling the whole world that he was kissing him off for
good?

But these leaves conning, you con at peril,
For these leaves, and me, you will not understand,
They will elude you at first, and still more afterward — I will certainly
   elude you,

Even while you should think you had unquestionably caught me, behold!
    Already you see I have escaped from you.

But yes, he had to know, because Willie saw that room dissolve into a molten vat of air that Winston was having trouble
breathing. That dude was sitting out there among all those folks
and no one could see that he was drowning. And when he finally
raised his glass to return the salute of the guy on the bandstand,
he was no longer wearing that pasted-up smile. It had been replaced by a mouth that looked like it was shaping itself to drink
poison.

Willie shuddered as he saw them finally drink the champagne.
If they had meant that much to each other, why in God's name
was he getting married? Willie frowned deeply and turned to
Lester. He wanted to say so much about what was out there. To
have his friend help him sort out this troubling confusion over
the charade he had just witnessed. But all those feelings only
came out as "Les, he didn't finish it. There's much more to that
poem."

"Well, I've heard enough anyway. I told ya I had a feeling
about them two — queer."

Yes, Willie thought, turning back to the oval window, there
was definitely something very queer about that cake, that champagne fountain — the diamond key glittering on that woman's
neck.

. . . Nor will my poems do good only — they will do just as much evil, per-
    haps more;
For all is useless without that which you may guess at many times and not
    hit — that which I hinted at;
Therefore release me, and depart on your way.

But whatever had gone down between those two guys must
have been something very special.

The ring of pale women wrapped in lace bridal veils danced around
the cot in her dream and gently threw flowers on the stale blanket.
They faded quickly as she opened her eyes but their chant still
echoed in the space between her sleeping and waking breath:

Mourn our son. Mourn our son. She blinked her mucus-caked eyes rapidly in the dim light and looked at the dead weight on her chest, her chilled body actually feeling warm against the coldness and rigidity of the flesh she held. She eased the child from her; its muscles had stiffened around the shape of her body, so that the limbs were permanently spooned toward her. She heard the clock ticking and closed her eyes with relief. It was quiet now. Taking a deep breath, she looked around the room at the cold shadows falling on the child's pale skin, the concrete walls, their pile of rancid clothing, the metal shelving, the stacked trunks and boxes, the dry sink in the corner. She would leave it all very soon, but there should be somebody to pity this. And there would be no one. Their bodies would be carried away, dumped somewhere, and left unmourned because no one would know. But didn't she know?

She put her elbows on her knees and sank her hands into her hair. No, she couldn't pity that shell behind her because it wasn't her son. She had assisted at enough funerals, stood in the shadows of enough chapels to realize that grief was only attached to memories. Her real son was now in the cradle of her mind and to mourn she would have to remember. That alone would be enough to kill her. The thought sat in her lap and she stared at it. Then slowly she began to smile and her lips started trembling from silent waves of laughter. Why, she was afraid that a few memories would kill her. Her laughter finally broke in hard, dry heaves as her fingers dug into her scalp. She bent farther over her knees and coughed up phlegm and blood but she couldn't stop, so she laughed and spit. Laughed and spit, her raw throat pulsating. It would be enough to kill her. She threw her head back and screamed with laughter, small tears running down her temples. Her stiff sides ached terribly as she fought for control and managed to silence, but not stop, her heaving chest. Still smiling, she reached up to wipe the tears away. Yes, it would kill her. Her breathing was still deep but evenly spaced as she wiped the mucus from her nose with her sweater sleeve. Always taking the easy way out. Always. You're a coward even up to the end, aren't you?

She sighed and stared off vacantly into the shadows. Her weight on the mattress was gradually pulling the child's body toward her and a hand touched her back.

— Daddy doesn't like me.

She leaped up from the cot, but the memory seared through her mind before she could shut it out.

— Don't be foolish, your father loves you.

— He doesn't play with me. He doesn't talk to me.

— Well, he's a very busy man and he's tired when he's home. Hey, I bet *you* don't love Mama.

— Yes, I do.

— Oh yeah, how much?

— Well . . . more than I love Spiderman.

— Will you love me when I'm an old, old lady?

— Uh huh, even when you're forty.

She paced by the cot, pressing her temples so tightly the skull bone threatened to give way. But the memory had already splintered into blinding needles of white light that burned so badly she knew if it didn't stop, she would have to bash her head against the concrete floor. It was just a shell, just a shell. The wetness from the tears that couldn't fall through her clenched eyes helped to smolder the burning fires in her head. She sat down on the other cot trembling. I'm so sorry but I can't mourn you. It hurts too much to die that way.

She could hear the clock again ticking loudly in the basement. Before she died, there must be something that she could do to let them know that she cared. She couldn't mourn her son, but she could bury him. Luther didn't have to know the truth. When he walked down those steps and found the body dressed for a burial he would think that in spite of what she had allowed him to do, she had at least found the courage to mourn.

She started to wrap the body in the blanket it lay under but it was coarse and cheap, smelling of weeks of sickness and fever. She couldn't leave him in that. She went to the corner and opened a trunk of old clothes, remembering silk dresses and brocades in her search for extra blankets weeks ago. Her hand touched a gauzy film and she pulled out the end of a long bridal veil trimmed in yellowing lace. It smelled of mildew and dust, but when she pressed a corner to her nose, there was a faint scent of lavender. She could wrap him in this — yards and yards of finely tatted lace and pearls. She kept pulling the material and it seemed to unravel forever so she dug into the trunk and extracted the folded veil. It was wrapped around a leather- and gold-bound Bible. LUWANA PACKERVILLE 1837 was etched in fading gold on the bottom border. She held the book stoically in her hand — There can be no God — and pressed her lips together. Then opening the cover, there in a delicate, curled scroll were those very words. She stared at the page, slowly flipping it over and finding nothing else, turned it back and tilted the Bible toward the light. ''There can be no God'' remained. Yes, whoever you were, Luwana Packerville, you were right about that. This house couldn't still be standing if there were a God.

She threw the Bible on the cot and began to wrap the lace veiling around the child's body. How strange; what must that woman have seen or lived to be moved to leave such a message buried in her wedding veil? Tupelo, Mississippi. She was probably this child's great-grandmother or one of the many mothers that Luther never talked about. The lace now hung loosely from the child's feet to its neck, but she hesitated before wrapping the face. Go ahead, nothing can hurt him now — it's just a shell. But she still bent down and kissed the white forehead before she could bring herself to drape the small face.

— Why don't I look like Daddy?

She balled the material up in her fist. Don't remember. But a silver frame came searing into her mind.

— Do you see this picture? Well, that's your grandmother and you look like her.

— But I'm a boy. She's a girl.

— So, boys can look like girls. And don't you think she's a pretty lady?

She kneeled slowly by the cot with the veil bunched up toward her mouth and pressed her wrenching head on the covered body. But this time the pale scent of lavender somehow helped to lessen the pain. Yes, you looked like your grandmother. And the mother before that. And the mother before that. Oh, my baby, what have I done to you? With horror she saw the answers forming through image after image strung out by white hot links webbing themselves among the crevices in her brain. Her hand clawed around the Bible and she buried her head deeper into the lace-covered body, but it was too late to block them out. Her mourning had begun.

December
21st

Xavier Donnell was falling in love with a black woman. It was one of the most terrifying experiences of his life. He was trying to remember when he had ever been this afraid. Why, it was worse than that summer at boy scout camp when he'd gotten his fly caught in the motor of the garbage compactor. And far worse than the report last year from the auto clinic that two of his transmission valves might be irreplaceable. At least he had been able to scream his way or buy his way out of those situations because he could pinpoint exactly where the danger lay. He had seen the iron gears chewing up the front of his shorts, smelled the oily teeth as they pulled him into the back of the machine. But when he looked at Roxanne Tilson, all he saw was a woman, no better or worse than the dozens of others who had flowed into and out of his life — soft where she should be, curved where he'd expect it, sweet behind the ears, mellow between the breasts, and pungent in that mystifying zone where the thighs joined the center of her body. She had flowed in that way but something was terribly wrong: she wasn't flowing out.

Somehow she had frozen around his liver, on the walls of his stomach, and in the cavities of his intestines; and she was dripping out much too slowly. When he found that it had become cold enough inside to affect his heart and cause a chill that made it shiver when he touched her, he tried to build up a series of heated arguments to melt her away: she's too fat, too loud, too slow, and he always hated being kept waiting for anyone, especially a woman. But those fiery complaints didn't help when he kneaded the full flesh on her thighs and stomach, or when the waiting became anticipation of the first, piercing note of her "sorry" that would engulf him in a symphony for the rest of the evening. Those damn shivers would return, leap on him unexpectedly over a plate of fettuccine or in a darkened theater, to remind him that something was happening inside that was beyond his control. Something that kept drawing him much too quickly into a center that held his first memory of love and fear: the dark, mellow texture of her female being. White chocolate, he'd think, burying his nose into her soft neck and nibbling upward toward the dimpled chin, seeking the hidden essence of cocoa that was embedded in the deep-yellow cream of her skin, that he could taste on his tongue, smell on his hands and arms. The colors and tints from the thighs that brought him into the world, the breasts that kept him alive and warm. The mindless plunge and search for the eternal circle that would let him die over and over in the cavity that gave him life.

But Xavier had come a long way from the womb. At thirty-one, he knew he'd come a long way, period. Graduating from the University of Nowhere, through a mixture of patience, hard work, and premeditated luck he had managed to move up in a place like General Motors, where it was so easy to get lost among the myriad Ivy League and ivory-skinned credentials of men who were just as sharp and hardworking as he was. While his rise had been meteoric and his cashmere suits managed to withstand the change of altitude, that tenth-floor office with its shag carpet and oak panels housed a fragile god. Because Xavier was forced to see his exploits as much more than those of some superman, he had to join the rest of General Motors and worship the rise of a Super Nigger. So he found himself as only a high priest perched in a temple and burdened with the care of this image. And like all fragile gods, it demanded constant attention and surveillance for any telltale cracks in the clay feet, a softening around the knees, a dulling of the luster.

He was holding down two full-time jobs, and he had to carry one home with him all the time. He took it on vacations and to the gym and to visits with his grandmother. It went to bars and ball games and to bed with him. There wasn't a moment of his life that Xavier could afford to forget his duties as high priest, because if the image ever crumbled, his own fate wasn't too far behind. He didn't dare question the validity of this worship, or even the power of this hollow god, because one reality was clear: that was all they had given him to serve; and somehow in serving, he had become. So he feared this rapid descent into the essence of Roxanne while knowing no other way to be complete. Could his god survive in the arms and between the thighs of the first flesh that knew his true mortality? Or would it crack under the echoes of those eyes that put ice packs on his bruised genitals when he was sent home early from boy scout camp?

Xavier needed time to think this present situation out — lots of time — but he didn't trust himself. His insides were out of control and he knew that if he didn't take some sort of drastic action, he would ask Roxanne Tilson to marry him. And the only thing that frightened him more than that was the thought that she would say yes. He had tried everything to discourage her so she'd take the matter out of his hands. He didn't call when promised, he broke dates, confused himself and her with excessive warmth and then excessive coldness. He'd even committed the unforgivable sin in a black woman's canon by openly dating white women and seeming to enjoy it. Surely, that was enough to have her discount him as a piece of garbage, a lost soul. But after taking that empty-headed receptionist to Winston's wedding and making a complete fool of himself, hoping Roxanne would hear about it and jump to all sorts of conclusions, the phone remained silent all morning. That really pissed him off. Here he was all day yesterday thinking about her, and in a few weak moments even wishing that she was the one beside him; and now today she was on his mind, wearing him out well beyond the true importance she held in his life — and no call. It was impossible that she hadn't heard; half the neighborhood had been at that reception. No, she was just waiting him out like she always did. The woman was definitely manipulative, never complaining or asking where he'd been from week to week. Pushy and conniving is all it was. Pushing herself into his head so he'd have to start caring about why she didn't care.

He knew he just had to do something, and as a last resort, he called his friend Maxwell. He admired Maxwell's total control of any situation. They were the only two black men on the tenth floor at GM, and Maxwell's office was even closer to the executive director's than his. Xavier had watched him closely at board meetings, regional conferences, and even in the executive washroom, for the fine seam that held him together, but it was invisible. He knew that might be easy enough to cover up in a boardroom but never in the bathroom. Maxwell could sit in his huge, glass-enclosed office without a hair or paper clip out of place. Xavier had been proud when Maxwell befriended him because it showed that he had proven himself. He became Xavier's mentor in office and latrine politics, and Xavier valued his advice, which all boiled down to a constant maxim: "Keep it all inside and when it just has to come out, *you* decide where and how much." So he had to be extremely careful when he made that phone call. How could you retain the respect of a man who was able to sever a sprig of parsley from its stem as easily as some people cut the meat from around a T-bone, if you were in a panic over some woman? No, just drop by for a quick drink, a chance to shoot the breeze about the latest Mailer essay in *Penthouse,* and just maybe he could find the courage to bring up what might be one of the most important issues of his life.

Just as Xavier saw the silvery Stingray pull into Third Crescent Drive, his aunt came into the living room.

"Xavier, the Tilson boy and his friend are cleaning out the garage. And when they're through you're going to have to pay them, because I'm going out now."

"Who?" Xavier had been looking for the perfect spot in the room to position himself. Now, just where and how would he be sitting if there were only something trivial on his mind?

"The Tilson boy, Xavier — Lester." Mrs. Donnell pulled on her coat impatiently. "I need all that junk out of the garage, and I don't have time to stay here and watch them. Millicent and her whole brood up and decided that they're going to fly in from Cincinnati to spend Christmas with us, and I've got to run out and buy them gifts. So just check up on them and pay them when they're through. Fifteen apiece should be enough."

"The garage? Look, I have company coming over and I can't be running out there every two seconds; can't they do it another time? I don't want those guys messing around my Porsche."

"No, they can't. And how are they going to hurt that car, it's buried under a padded quilt!"

Since his aunt had refused to install a heating system in the garage, Xavier kept his Porsche under a down-filled tarpaulin to protect the engine from extreme changes in temperature.

"Well, they might throw a box or something on it without thinking. Do you know what it costs to get a scratch or dent out of that hood?"

Mrs. Donnell buttoned up her leather gloves. "Look, I'm not going to stand here and argue with you. I have a million things to do this afternoon, and then I have to rush back here to get to Lycentia Parker's wake tonight since you refused to go and pay your respects for the family."

"Why should I go when you hated her guts, and I didn't even know her?"

She narrowed her eyes. "Young man, you have a lot to learn, but have it your way. I'm going outside and tell them to go away, and later on you can get out there and clear it out yourself, but it has to be done *today*. Millicent is coming in tomorrow afternoon and she'd just love to see that we live in a pigsty. Not that it would matter to you, but I hope you know that all that rubbish in the garage is a fire hazard and you might just wake up one night and find it and your precious Porsche in flames. Then what would you —"

"All right, all right. Just tell them to be careful, that's all."

"Yeah, I thought so." She headed for the back door. "And don't let them in here on my carpet, because they'll be full of grime. Pay them in the kitchen."

Xavier watched her retreating back, making his daily wish for the speedy appearance of the day when the house would be all his while conveniently forgetting that it could only dawn after the night of her death. He rushed back to the front window and peered anxiously through the Venetian blinds. He took a deep breath to compose himself as Maxwell's car finally pulled up to the curb. Now Roxanne was rising to torment him through her brother at a time when he needed all of his faculties together. He sat down and waited for the doorbell to ring.

Maxwell Smyth turned off the engine of his Stingray with a smooth forty-five-degree turn of his wrist, waited exactly three seconds, and pulled out the ignition key. When he swung his long legs over the low door frame, his silk scarf was arranged around his neck so that the wind could disarray the gold fringe just enough to let it stray casually on the brown and tan tweed of his open jacket, which complemented his light wool pants and matching brown turtleneck. He neither shivered nor hurried in the December air. His tropical gait in the frigid wind was as awe-inspiring as a magician breathing under water. But Maxwell's powers lay in the micro-thin weave of his thermal long-johns and in his knowledge that slow, deep breaths raise the body temperature without noticeably altering the rhythm of the chest. To even the most careful observer, this man seemed to have made the very elements disappear, while it was no more than the psychological sleight-of-hand that he used to make his blackness disappear.

Maxwell had discovered long ago that he doubled the odds of finishing first if he didn't carry the weight of that milligram of pigment in his skin. There was no feasible reason why it should have slowed him down since in mass it weighed so little, and even that was consistently distributed over his six-foot frame. But the handicap had been set centuries before it was his turn at the gate. And since he knew no tract of ground but the planet earth and no competition but the human race, he had to use the rules as written and find a way to turn a consequence into an inconsequence in his struggle to reach the finish line as a man.

He lucked onto the magic formula for this very early in life by being blessed with an uncommon spelling of a very common name. He remembered the slate-blue eyes of his first grade teacher flying back to his small dark face when she handed him a name tag reading MAXWELL SMITH and he told her no — S-M-Y-T-H, and this time the eyes actually focused him into existence. Whether it was impatience, embarrassment, or faint amusement, it was still recognition. For that moment, he counted because he had upset an assumption. And Maxwell Smyth learned to drag that moment out by not aiding the clumsy attempts of receptionists, clerks, and arrogant booking agents as they grappled with reordering their ingrained expectations of his name and his being. He relished the feelings of power and control as his blackness momentarily diminished in front of their faces — an ordinary name had turned into the extraordinary and taken its owner with it in the transformation.

The trick was now to juggle other feats that would continually minimize his handicap to nothing more than a nervous tic. In college he found that his blackness began to disappear behind his straight A average, and his reputation for never sweating or getting cold. He trained himself to survive on three hours of sleep while never appearing tired during classes, heading the student government, editing the school newspaper and the yearbook. Always immaculate and controlled, he kept them all wondering how it was done, so there was little time to think about who was doing it. His twenty-one-hour days even gave him time to socialize, and although most of his friends were white, that wasn't a conscious choice on his part. Maxwell neither courted nor shunned the other black students; he liked to think of himself as gravitating toward humans who shared his *inner* temperament, and anyone — black or otherwise — who he thought wanted to be around him because of something as inconsequential as the pigment of his skin he dismissed as shallow. So the black women he wanted to date found him strange and the white women strangely comforting.

He tackled General Motors in the same way he had the campus of Dartmouth, quietly disappearing behind his extraordinary record as regional sales representative, business manager, vice president for consumer affairs, and finally assistant to the executive director. But the stakes were a lot higher there, with no room for error; any break in his stride, any telltale mannerism or slip of the tongue might shatter the illusion he was standing behind. Because Maxwell knew they would never have dreamed of allowing a black man next to the executive director, it had to be the best man. And this delicate balancing of reality demanded perfect control over his work and his subordinates. He allowed nothing to happen at the office that didn't put him at the best advantage or that he couldn't manipulate to make it seem so. He weighed the decision of whether or not to smile at his secretary with the same gravity as that with which he considered the advisability of a new line of sedans.

There was never any danger of his breaking down: sanity lies in consistency. And Maxwell retained his mental health by exercising the same type of control over every aspect of his being. Since he couldn't manipulate the weather outside his home, he adjusted his body accordingly; but once inside his carefully appointed duplex, an elaborate series of humidifiers and thermostats enabled him to determine the exact conditions under which he would eat, sleep, or sit. He found the erratic rhythms and temperatures that normally accompany sex a problem, so he rarely slept with a woman. He didn't consider it a great deprivation because before he was even thirty, an erection had become almost as difficult to achieve as an orgasm, and hence he would save himself the trouble until he was married and just had to. In short, his entire life became a race against the natural — and he was winning.

The pinnacle of his success lay in his French-tiled blue and white bathroom. It was one of the most beautiful rooms in his home, with Italian marble fixtures: an imported toilet and matching bidet that sat on a plush white carpet. Lemonweed and wintergreen flourished in the windows and in tiered chrome planters that hooked on the shower rod. Over the towel racks he'd installed a hidden speaker that was connected to his stereo system. The only thing his bathroom lacked was toilet paper, which he kept in the closet and brought out for rare guests since he never needed it. Through a careful selection of solids and liquids, he was able to control not only the moment but the exact nature of the matter that had to bring him daily to the blue and white tiled room. His stomach and intestines were purified by large quantities of spring water and camomile tea. He found variety in clear juices — apple, strained cranberry, and, on rare occasions, small sips of Chardonnay, preferably from the vineyards of Pouilly, where no yeast was added to the fermentation. He learned that the very tips of broccoli florets, asparagus, and even parsley moved less noticeably through his system than the stems. Young animal flesh — baby scallops, calves' liver, and breasts of squab were the purest to digest. This was supplemented with dried kelp from the waters around New Zealand, ground bone meal, and wheat germ. He would have put a forkful of cabbage, a slice of onion, or a single bean into his mouth with the same enthusiasm as a tablespoon of cyanide. Because when Maxwell sat each morning, on his Italian marble — his head erect, his ankles disappearing into the thick carpet, and his fingers drumming the tempo of a violin quartet on his knees with his eyes closed, before moving straight to the bidet, where he was sprayed with perfumed and sudsy water, and then on to the shower — except for the fact that he was totally naked, those first five minutes could have taken place on the seat of a theater or concert hall, with absolutely no clues to tip off even the nearest party about his true nature.

After the success of this daily ritual, Maxwell was more than ready for any challenge at General Motors. And when he made his way into the lobby, up in the elevators, and past the file clerks, stenographers, and small offices of his subordinates, he drew the inevitable mixture of awe, envy, and hatred that is the lot of exceptional achievers. And, of course, he was misunderstood. He would have found the comments that he was trying to

be white totally bizarre. Being white was the furthest thing from
his mind, since he spent every waking moment trying to be no
color at all. The charges of "ball-buster" or "slave-driver" were
only levied because he required from his staff what he was willing to give himself. But he might have been faintly pleased had
he overhead a frequent whisper in the typing pool, "Ya know,
Smyth acts like his ---- don't smell" — because it didn't. And
having conquered the last frontier, there was nothing that stood
between Maxwell and the ultimate finish line but time. When
the executive chair became vacant, the board of trustees
wouldn't think twice about giving the best man the job. And
that's the only kind of man he was.

Xavier heard the first set of chimes and decided to let the bell
ring again before he answered. But Maxwell had no intention of
ringing twice. After one depression of exactly two seconds, he
stood there calmly waiting for the door to be opened. He knew
he was expected, made sure he had been heard, and so the only
logical sequence would now be admittance into the house.
Xavier sat nervously in the lengthening silence, finally realizing
that Maxwell wasn't going to ring again. If he opened it now, he
needed some excuse for not answering immediately, but if he
waited much longer he gambled on Maxwell's leaving. It was a
play of wills on each side of the oak door, and Maxwell won out.

"Hey, sorry I took so long. I was upstairs when you first rang
and I was waiting for the second ring to be sure that it was the
bell."

"No sweat, mon ami." Maxwell's scarf glided off and was held
out to Xavier. "What's shakin'?"

His greeting told Xavier that he considered this a very intimate visit because he was willing to engage in French and ghetto
dialect, the two pet passions he reserved for close friends. He
walked toward the couch, intently surveying the room. The few
times Maxwell had been there before he had glanced around,
seeming to sniff the air in case some new addition or omission
might call for him to realign his opinion of Xavier.

"Can I fix you a drink?"

"If you have Chardonnay — with just a *kiss* of a chill."

Xavier shrugged his shoulders. "Well, it's cold."

He poured himself a double shot of bourbon and Maxwell allowed him to talk about the weather, car repairs, and the company's annual meeting for what he deemed an appropriate amount of time, and then choosing a place in the conversation where he knew Xavier would least expect it — "So what really brings me here, mon copain? I know about the cold; I've just driven through it with my rebuilt carburetor after interrupting the outline for my brilliant presentation for the spring convention, but what I still don't know is *why?*" He leaned back on the velvet cushions and smiled, enjoying the flicker of consternation in Xavier's eyes. He had heard the suppressed panic in his voice over the phone and a true curiosity had brought him out of his house to see what could be so important that Xavier had to try so hard to make it sound trivial.

"Well, I thought it might be nice to have you over. Except for a few hurried lunches at work, we never really get a chance to relax and just be friends."

Maxwell knew that Xavier fully understood that sparing the time to lunch with a subordinate at work was an act of friendship, so he remained silent and waited for a real answer to his question.

Xavier took a deep swallow of his bourbon. "And, uh, I wanted a little feedback on some longer-range plans. The thought had occurred to me that I might want to start to think about thinking about marrying Roxanne Tilson."

"Sacré Dieu, blood. Why?"

Xavier panicked; that wasn't what he had really meant to say and now he didn't have a ready answer that would retain Maxwell's respect. How many times had he heard him say that love was for teenagers and fools? He sought desperately for a reply, wishing that he smoked. "I know this may sound bizarre" — he took another swallow of his drink — "but there are times when she reminds me of Eleanor Roosevelt."

Maxwell frowned and thought a moment. "Well, my cleaning lady bears a striking resemblance to Indira Gandhi, but that's no reason for me to drag her down to City Hall. Are you sure that's the only reason?"

"There's nothing to be sure or unsure about." Xavier got up and went over to the bar. "It was just an idea I thought about playing with, that's all. And she was just one of the many women who came to mind. To be honest, she's not even a serious contender. I mean, the real issue is whether or not this is the time for me to settle down. But I'm not too sure that I should rush into anything, you know?"

"Oh, I know perfectly well what you mean. A decision like that is loaded with disaster — even if you could find 'a serious contender,' as you put it. And I don't hold out much hope for your doing that."

"Really?"

Maxwell shook his head and sighed, turning his wineglass gently between his fingers. "Now, let's be reasonable. I know that, for whatever reasons, you're only into black women. I'm not knocking it, mind you. But you're going to have to face some hard, cold facts: there just aren't enough decent ones to choose from. They're either out there on welfare and waiting to bring you a string of somebody else's kids to support, or they've become so prominent that they're brainwashed into thinking that you aren't good enough for them. The few who just might be up to your standards, who've distinguished themselves in the world, are into white men. Name me one black woman who's making a name for herself in the arts or entertainment and I'll name you two who have white husbands. Don't we see it every day in the magazines and newspapers, or right downtown? The best and the brightest are going that way, so what's left for you? The Roxanne Tilsons of this world."

Xavier winced. "I don't really see anything wrong with her," he mumbled.

"Well now, of course she's been to the right schools — Wellesley, wasn't it? And you're from the same neighborhood — even though she's up there on the border, it's still Linden Hills."

"Of course." Xavier's voice was slightly impatient. "How could I have even looked at her if that wasn't the case?"

"And she's pretty enough, although there's a bit too much avoirdupois."

"I wouldn't call her fat." Xavier narrowed his eyes. "She's full."

"Yes, she's full *now*, but you know that most black women have a tendency to let themselves go. Look in any spa or gym and they're outnumbered ten to one. And believe me, it's not Roxanne's fault. It's an old throwback to the jungle days when they had to store up food like camels because the women did most of the hauling. So what they do now is starve themselves until they get you and then gain ten pounds before the reception's over. And from then on in . . .." Maxwell shook his head slowly and shuddered. "But the real question is not whether you can find one who'll fit into your Porsche, but who'll fit, period."

Xavier stared off into space and thought, But we read the same books, like the same music. We both want to travel. He found himself wishing that Maxwell would shut up and go home. He hadn't called him here to listen to all this. He had done nothing but cause him to think of all the reasons why he should run out tomorrow and buy an engagement ring, but somehow he didn't want that. And what he needed desperately to know was why.

"Look, Maxwell, I find that just a little hard to buy. They're out there in all shapes and sizes once I'm ready. But maybe I'm just not ready now, you know?"

"Oh, you're ready. Ready and raring to go. But the sad thing is that there isn't a mother's daughter out there ready for you. And you want to know why?" Maxwell sat on the edge of the sofa. "Because Roxanne Tilson is only the clone of a whole mass that are coming out of these colleges with their hot little fists clenched around those diplomas and they aren't ready to hear nothing from nobody, least of all you. When they've done that four- or six-year stint at the Yales, Stanfords, or Brandeises, they no longer think they're women, but walking miracles. They're ready to ask a hell of a lot from the world then and a hell of a lot from you. They're hungry and they're climbers, Xavier, with an advanced degree in expectations. Hook up with one of them and whatever you're doing isn't good enough, and you're doing damned good as it is."

Maxwell's knuckles tightened around the stem of his glass. "I'm going to make a confession." He leaned toward Xavier. "I once thought about marrying a woman like Roxanne and she wasn't half so attractive, but she had a Ph.D. from Princeton and I was much younger then and could have forced myself to overlook a lot of other things. But when it came right down to the line, I realized that she just didn't understand me. She just didn't appreciate the problems I was going through. And if a woman can't do that, at least she should be quiet and stay out of your way. Remember, a man only lives two places — at work and at home. You and I both know the sacrifices we made and are still making to walk that tightrope out there; it takes every ounce of strength we've got. So, can you afford to be drained when you come in here?" He stabbed his finger toward the ground. "Can you afford to be reminded — in five-syllable vocabularies no less — that the rope's a lot thinner than you think and it's a lot farther to the ground?" Maxwell's voice had risen a quarter of an octave, which was his equivalent of hysteria, and it stunned Xavier.

"But if you feel that way about it," Xavier almost whispered, "I don't understand why you were willing to weather all that flack when you promoted Mabel Thompson."

"Of course I promoted her." Maxwell leaned back and smiled, taking a split second to regulate his breathing. "Any fool could see from her résumé that she was overqualified for that lousy job in the bookkeeping department. I brought her into my office and now I have one of the most efficient cost analysts in the eastern division. While all those other clowns were busy looking at her color and sex, I looked at her personnel file. And I knew that any woman who managed to support herself and two younger brothers while getting through accounting school with straight A's would have to be a tiger. But you know what happens when you try to bed down with one? You get your balls clawed off. And that's the bottom line, isn't it?"

Yes, that was the bottom line. Xavier could never see himself with any woman who wasn't determined to go somewhere with her life. But he knew that the road was a lot more cluttered for a black woman and a successful journey meant sharpening her spirits to grind away all the garbage that stood in her way. And just maybe when that switch was turned on, it couldn't tell the difference between his living flesh and anything else. If he needed anything more than Roxanne, he needed those constant reminders hung on him healthy and intact that he could still hang on.

"Mabel probably needed those claws to survive." Xavier frowned into his bourbon.

"I'm sure she did. And I thank her, and my twenty percent reduction in marketing costs thanks her. But let somebody else marry her."

Xavier sighed and watched his ice cubes melt away into the amber fluid. He knew that if he watched them long enough, the frozen crystals would lose their shape and edges, become indistinguishable from the mahogany sea that was keeping them afloat. We read the same books, like the same . . . Just concentrate on the brown liquid that's dissolving the ice. He didn't have to get up and find a stirrer, or even rotate the glass. Just sit there and soon, very soon, there would be nothing but a mouthful of watery bourbon that could be gotten rid of in a single swallow with no harm to his throat or stomach, and definitely no chance of heartburn.

"I understand what you're saying, Maxwell. But that doesn't leave much for me, and I've no intention of spending the rest of my life alone."

"You don't have to — and it leaves quite a bit for you. And I'm hardly talking about only white women; this whole planet is full of women to choose from if you're willing to branch out."

"Well, I guess I could ask to be transferred to one of the offices overseas — there's no telling who I might meet on the plane."

"Laugh if you want to, but it won't be a laughing matter when —"

They were startled by a sharp rap on the back door. Oh God,

he'd forgotten all about Lester being out in the garage. Xavier opened the kitchen door on two sweaty and grimy faces.

"Your aunt said you'd pay us when we were through," Lester greeted him curtly. "Well, we're through."

"That was pretty quick." Xavier started to smile at Lester but was stopped with, "Well, there was two of us, so what's the problem?"

"No, no problem. I'm just amazed at how efficient you were, because I know how cluttered that garage was."

"You can go out there and check if you don't believe me. The newspapers are bundled and stacked beside the garbage bags and the boxes she left for all that other crap. And it's all on the side of the house for the trash collectors."

"I believe you, Lester." He turned to the darker boy. "I'm sure you fellas did a great job. I hope the car didn't get in your way. Please, come in and I'll go upstairs and get my wallet." At that moment, Xavier's conscience called for a great deal of generosity toward anything associated with Roxanne, even her arrogant kid brother.

"We'd rather wait out here."

"Well, I could stand to use your bathroom." Willie put his foot up on the back step.

"Sure, come on in."

"You know the cold has a way of working on your bladder."

"Yes, I know what you mean." Xavier held out his hand to Willie. "Xavier Donnell."

"Willie Mason, but I don't think we should shake." Willie turned his palms over. "My hands are pretty grubby."

"That's okay, a little honest dirt won't hurt me."

Lester stuck his hands in his pockets and rolled his eyes.

Willie was amazed at the softness of Xavier's skin. It felt like a woman's hand against his rough knuckles and calloused palm. This guy probably never lifted anything heavier than a ball-point pen.

Maxwell, feeling that he had been left alone for more than an appropriate time, appeared in the kitchen door. "Xavier, I'll have to be going."

Xavier turned toward him quickly. "Yes, let me get your scarf." He didn't really want to introduce the boys, but felt it would be rude not to. "This is Lester Tilson, Roxanne's brother, and his friend, Willie — Maxwell Smyth."

"Hiya." Willie smiled.

Maxwell nodded silently as he looked directly at Xavier. "It seems that this is your day for company."

"They're not company," he said a bit too quickly, and then turned back to them apologetically. "They're doing some work for my aunt outside."

"That's industrious." Maxwell's eyes swept over them.

"No, that's poverty." Lester leaned against the sink.

Maxwell seemed surprised — as if a parrot had been trained to answer him back. "Well, I suppose that poverty leads to industry," intending his remark to be the final word in a useless exchange.

Willie watched Maxwell's face and had the strange feeling that this man's words weren't really meant to reach across the kitchen toward them. His eyes seemed to stop at the green tiles on the floor in front of their feet. Why, it was the same feeling that you got talking to some white people. He suddenly felt very invisible to this tall, impeccable man and needed to hear his own voice to prove that he was in the kitchen.

"No, poverty just seems to lead to more poverty if you're black," Willie said loudly, and stared directly at Maxwell.

Xavier looked nervously from Willie to Maxwell. "I'll get your scarf. You can use the bathroom in the basement," he said over his shoulder to Willie and started for the door.

"No, wait." Maxwell held up his finger. Willie saw his linty pea jacket, frayed jeans, and cheap shoes materialize in Maxwell's eyes as they made their way slowly down his body. "You know, it's that sort of an attitude that will keep some people cleaning out garages for the rest of their lives. Being black has nothing to do with being poor. And being poor doesn't mean that you have to stay that way."

"Then I guess it's just a coincidence" — Willie felt his heart pounding — "that the majority of black folks in this country are poor, have been poor, and will be poor for a long time to come."

"Well, I see that you can conjugate verbs." Maxwell brushed an invisible speck off his jacket sleeve. "And a difficult verb at that. So it's probably not too much for you to understand that the only reason so many black people are still nothing is because they keep their eyes turned backward toward the times when they could be little else, and are still crying about what they could never do while what they can do is swiftly passing them by. And so, in that case, you're absolutely right — that type will always be nothing."

"First of all, I didn't say that poor black people were nothing. And second —"

"You might as well have," Maxwell cut him off. "Because that's just what it amounts to. It amounts to a blind, senseless existence due to an inability to take advantage of the progress that's continually going on."

"Bullshit!" Lester's voice startled everyone in the kitchen. "Man, you're the one who has blinders on. You wanna know why most black people aren't gonna move anywhere? Because this man's government is ruled by the few for the few. And I don't know how they taught you to spell progress in the school you went to, but on the streets you spell it W-H-I-T-E."

"I'm the living proof that that's a lie," Maxwell said softly. "And Xavier proves it too. And there are thousands just like us."

"Yeah, there are thousands," Lester said, "in a community of tens of millions which is surrounded by a white community of hundreds of millions. And you know what your thousands boil down to? A handful of raisins in the sun, a coupla jigaboos by the door — and that's it."

"But Lester, don't you understand?" Xavier frowned. "Those doors are opening — slowly it's true — but they *are* opening. And we have to be ready to take advantage of it."

"He's right," Maxwell said. "And a perfect example is this month's edition of *Penthouse*. You have it, don't you, Xavier? Would you bring it here?"

Xavier left the kitchen.

"Now," Maxwell said, "I'm a socially conscious man. And if we look at the scale of opportunities, who would really be at the bottom? Why, the black woman. If there were any doors to be shut, there would be more shut for her. I recently promoted a black woman in my office to an executive position and I was proud of that move because she deserved it. But that story is repeating itself all over this country. And you can't tell me that if black women are moving up, the rest of the black community can't."

Xavier handed Maxwell the magazine. "Now, just look at this." Maxwell flipped through the pages. "There was a time when you couldn't find a picture of one black woman in a magazine like *Penthouse*. And see what the centerfold is this month?"

Lester and Willie moved toward the kitchen door to look at the pages Maxwell was pointing to. There was an eight-page spread of a lush, tropical forest and a very dark-skinned model with a short Afro. Her airbrushed body glistened between the thin leopard strips that crisscrossed under her high, pointed breasts and fastened behind her back. She wore a pair of high, leopard-skin boots that stopped just below her knees, and she was posed to pull against an iron chain that was wrapped around her clenched fists. Each page offered the reader a different view of her perfectly formed pelvis, hips, and hints of her manicured pubic hair as she wrestled with the chain held by an invisible hand off camera.

The faces in the kitchen were close and quiet as the four heads followed the camera's skillful blending of light and shadow that subtly changed female beauty into breathless body. Willie was the first to take his eyes away, and the blood that throbbed in his temples wasn't desire but a whisper of shame.

"You call this progress?" Lester's head was still bent over the photograph. "They're trying to tell you that black people still belong in the jungle."

"But look." Maxwell flipped to the last page of the spread. The model had snatched the chain and brought its mysterious holder to her feet. One leg was raised in victory on the shoulder of a scrawny white man in a safari outfit, and his thick bifocals had slipped below the bridge of his nose. "That's the message." He pressed his finger on the photo, leaving behind a damp smudge. "And I don't have to spell it out, this picture is worth a thousand words." He closed the magazine dramatically. "Today *Penthouse*, my friends, and tomorrow the world."

Willie cringed inside when Maxwell called him "friend." And suddenly he wanted to be invisible to this man again; it had felt much more comfortable. But still something had happened in the last five minutes that seemed to bring the four of them together over more than a magazine. Willie knew he had to leave that room before someone asked him about that picture.

"Where did you say the bathroom was?" He turned to Xavier.

"Just down these steps." Xavier went to the basement door and switched on the light. "You could use the one upstairs" — he glanced at Willie's grimy shoes — "but the whole place is carpeted."

"No problem, I'd rather go down here."

Xavier followed Maxwell out of the kitchen. "I'll be right back, Lester."

"Don't rush, I'm not planning to cop your toaster."

Maxwell adjusted his scarf at the front door. "So that's Roxanne's brother. I can see why you said she wasn't a serious contender. That family has one foot in the ghetto and the other on a watermelon rind. There's no question of your marrying into something like that — you wouldn't have a snowball's chance in hell."

Xavier watched Maxwell through the window as he sauntered toward his car. There were still plenty of questions left about Roxanne, but he didn't have to answer them today. Or even tomorrow. He turned and picked up their glasses from the coffee table. The ice had melted completely into his bourbon and he swallowed it quickly before heading back to the kitchen.

As Willie climbed back up the narrow basement steps, it came to him why that photograph had troubled him, and it was more than just the heavy, iron chains. With her dark face, full lips, and high cheekbones, that woman was a dead ringer for his baby sister.

She sat on the cot across from the shrouded body of her child with Luwana Packerville's Bible resting open, face down on her lap. Her eyes were watery from trying to decipher the fine, webbed scrawl that was crammed onto the gold-edged tissue paper that separated one book of the Bible from another. Except for the date, 1837, stamped on the cover, there were no dates heading the various entries and no apparent order to the aging fragments of this woman's mind. Many of the tissued dividers had been left blank while others held entries that were evidently months or even years apart. She had reached the page between Jeremiah and Lamentations when she put her head back against the wall and closed her aching eyes.

> Luther told me today that I have no rights to my son. He owns the child as he owns me. He grew terribly enraged when I ventured a mild protest, and showed me the papers that were signed over to his agent in Tupelo. Foolish creature that I am, I thought my sale to him was only a formality. I thought in the name of decency my husband would have destroyed the evidence of my cursed bondage. But he keeps those documents securely locked away. O Blessed Saviour, can it be that I have only exchanged one master for another? Can it be that the innocent scribblings I sought only to hide from a husband's amused contempt are now the diary of a slave?

She thought her marriage would set her free, and it should have. It should have. She massaged her throbbing forehead. There must have been some law in this country that made that so. He was just being cruel and trying to frighten her. And she was so happy about that wedding. Finally free. Freed from those endless luncheons with other lonely women who could well afford the pewter-and-fern atmosphere that accompanied the piano bar and stuffed sole as they talked about all the right things while the real things would have to wait until the second carafe was ordered. Because they could ill afford the reflections waiting at the bottom of their empty wineglasses, that something must be missing if they only had each other across the table week after week. Freed from the burden of that mental question mark on her left ring finger — What's wrong with you if no one's wanted you by now? — since she could wear a metal band in its place. And so she had been free to marry a man that she didn't love because there was no question of asking for love in return. It had been enough that he needed her. Enough to

keep her silent when he brought her the gown and veil he had chosen. He wanted her all in white. And she put away the pale blue silk
with silver netting and wore his heavy satin with loose brocade
panels that hid her breasts and the outline of her waist and hips;
the cloudy veil so dense and folded she could barely see out and
surely no one could see in. All in white — even her hands were
covered with thick kidskin gloves as she carried the ivory roses
and baby's breath. She shuddered at the ghostly image — a
strange beginning.

Her eyes flew open and she stared down at the Bible in her lap.
Trembling, she went back to reread the entry between the books of
Genesis and Exodus.

> Luther has given me a strange ring. I am not partial to the pale metal
> because it is barely visible against my skin. In jest I told him that
> people will think he could not afford gold and so had welded our
> bond with silver. I was going to amend his peculiar reply that nothing
> welds our bond but his will, but something in his eyes hindered me.
> Surely he understands that our marriage is bonded in heaven
> through God's grace. I suspect I will grow accustomed to this color,
> but truly in the full sunlight, it is as if I wear no ring. We are going
> north in a fortnight to a place called Linden Hills. I leave this state
> with rejoicing. A new land. A new life.

It was becoming painfully clear. Her two wedding bands. The
one she wore was red gold with a deep antique finish that almost
matched the color of the finger it had been slipped on. But the
other had been platinum. *Tradition,* he had said. *It belonged to my
mother. Keep it where you will, but never wear it.* And she hadn't,
thinking it was so precious to him he was afraid she might lose it.
She couldn't see her wedding ring in the shadow that her body
cast on her hand: "It is as if I wear no ring." Then what had happened six years ago? Was she so busy being needed that it never
dawned on her she wasn't being married?

She now had the key to Luwana Packerville's buried memories.
Using these ancient records as signposts, the woman had found at
least one place that could offer an anchor of validity to the inner
flow of her life. Her bewilderment over the rules he had given her
about housekeeping and his diet before Leviticus; the sorrows of
never knowing her own mother next to the Book of Ruth; her fears

of being a new bride before the Song of Solomon. She had read and known this Bible well. And so the entry carefully placed between First Kings and Second Kings had been no accident:

> The child was weaned last month. He was well past two and could now take solid food without harm. Now Luther has taken him to the solicitor today. There is the matter of his will and other documents to be settled. He told me to prepare a special supper because, when he returns, he wants to celebrate his son's manumission. Since the law decrees that a child must follow the condition of its mother, I know he has gone to have the solicitor draw up free papers for the baby. This is the final humiliation. But I have enough pride not to beg him to manumit me as well. It is a small matter since I could go nowhere and would go nowhere — this is my home. Yet it still bears on me grievously. And if the love of God and all that is right cannot move this man, how can I hope to? So it is a bitter meal that I must cook to help celebrate the fact that I am now to be owned by my own son.

All of the tissued dividers between the long line of Hebrew prophets from Ezekiel to Malachai were left untouched. There seemed to be nothing that Luwana Packerville could find to guide her in almost four hundred years of proclamations by these iron men of God. She found the fading handwriting again on the page before the New Testament:

> There has been a sharp turn of events. This week a new housekeeper came to cook for us and do the washing. I was pressed beyond endurance to voice a protest. After ten years, I do not wish a strange woman preparing my meals and handling my things. I have little enough to do as it is — the child is constantly with his father, and with no friends or relatives to visit me, the days drag on so. Luther told me that I was foolish and should be proud that he was now set enough to afford such services for me. But I know it is not for me, because last week the papers told of a woman in Tennessee who was hanged for poisoning her master's soup, and Luther seemed much agitated over the account. When declaring that I would refuse to eat whatever this despicable woman seasoned in my kitchen, I was told that was my choice, but he and the child would eat from her hands. Yesterday I baked some molasses cakes. They were always my son's favorites; but he refused to touch them, though I saw he was sorely tempted. And when I labored to press them on him, the look he finally cast me chilled my blood. I know

what is behind all this and it breaks my heart. I have heard him and his father whispering.

There was silence throughout the four gospels and it was impossible to tell how many years had passed before the entry in front of the Acts of the Apostles.

I wish I had learned to sew when my mistress in Tupelo pressed me. But I found sitting still with nothing but scraps and threads to entertain my mind overbearing. I persisted in hunting up new dewberry patches and wandering the fields in search of fresh mint. The warm, buttered cobblers that sprang from my sojourns always softened her irritation over my neglected needle, but now I am paying for my obstinacy. Without my garden, the long winter months are intolerable here, and reading is now my sole pleasure. It seems so unjust that I am barred from having friends among the white wives because of my husband's color and among the colored because of his wealth. If there were only something to do or someone to receive my thoughts so they won't fester within me. God forgive me, but I am so envious of the holy apostles. They all had each other and whole congregations to write to. And it must have been wonderful to know that someone was awaiting their messages and that if they did not write, they would be missed. I write to no one and am missed by no one on this earth. Since I was brought from a place where I had no mother or father, no sister to call my own, to whom could I send my blessings for good heath, God's faith, love — and from whom could I receive them? I am just being foolish again. Here, preserved for all time, are the wonderful letters of our holy men trumpeting their joy and faith in our Saviour for thirsty hearts throughout the ages. I should drink of them and rejoice. But sometimes I do indeed wonder what it is like to have someone to care about what you will say.

My Dear Luwana,
    I am writing to you, my sister, because I must have someone to help me bear these trials. Is it a sin to wish for death when there are so many who would long to have all that I do? I know you must think that I am an ungrateful creature. For fifteen years I have never had to worry about hunger or nakedness or cold like so many of our brethren. I am free to come and go as I please and no one cares. But that is the problem, my dear — I feel as if I could leave this world tomorrow and no one in this house would miss me. With each year, the housekeeper takes on more and more of my responsibilities and I was so tired of my entreaties falling on deaf ears, I let Luther have his way.

I only managed to save my garden from the hands of some vile outsider by flinging myself on the ground in the yard and refusing to be moved. Yes, I screamed like a banshee at the feet of Luther and the new gardener, threatening to water the soil with my blood if I could no longer tend the flowers in it. I am sure you understand that I was driven to such disgraceful conduct because once my roses are taken away, I would have absolutely nothing since my son has become a stranger to me. And there are to be no more children as my bed belongs only to me. The child I had hoped to be a refuge for all the love I have to give grows more like his father with each breath and the two are now inseparable. And what is worse, they are becoming inseparable in my mind. I thus live with two Luthers in truth, and so I live alone.

Please tell me if there is something that I can do to shed these horrible shadows on my soul. I want so badly to rejoice in my blessings. I know I have neglected you shamefully over these years but if it is not asking too much, perhaps you can take a few moments and just remind me of all I have to be grateful for.

God's Speed,
Luwana

The tears that now stood in her eyes weren't from the strain of trying to decipher the fine scrawl. She could feel more of them gathering at the pit of her stomach and ebbing up toward her throat and the back of her eyes in gentle waves for the answers she would never get to the letters that hadn't been sent, the phone calls that hadn't been made. She had tried at first but there was less and less to talk about: their new job — her new baby. Their problems with finding a decent landlord — her problems with finding decent silverplate. What they heard the governor say about new tax shelters — what Luther said about it. What they heard Congress say about automobile regulations — what Luther said about it. What they heard the president say about the ERA — what Luther said about it. I called you to see how you were — oh, *we're* doing fine. Yes, all those lonely luncheon partners would never miss her now since she had been dead to them for years.

And she wouldn't have had the courage to send a letter like this to anyone. They would have pitied her and she had tolerated their pity long enough before she became Mrs. Luther Nedeed. And how could they ever believe that she was lonely when we just had a baby, and we were going to the Cape for a week, and we were about to renovate the attic? And how could she have even believed it herself — and she hadn't until she realized that Luwana Packerville could never get an answer to that letter. But there was an answer waiting on the page before the book of Romans.

My Dearest Luwana,

    Your words grieved me sorely, my sister, and I am trying to understand what you are going through. But there must be great consolation in the fact that you are at last mistress of your own home. Remember how vexed you would be when Mistress Packerville kept you trotting hour by hour on such trivial errands while she sat on her divan. And she would even call you from the pantry while your hands were smeared with dough to hand her a thimble that was barely two feet away. Well, now you have that luxury, so rejoice.

    I know you are disturbed by the papers your husband still keeps after all these years, but in truth you are no longer a servant. And since this man asks nothing of you, I cannot imagine what is pressing you so. I can understand that it is difficult to watch a child grow up and finally away from a mother's arms. But all children must grow.

    Of course I shall be more than happy to receive letters from you. It is lonely for me as well. Take heart, together we can weather these tiny tempests that blow through a woman's world.

Fondly,
Luwana

My Dear Luwana,

    Thank you for being so prompt in your reply. It was gratifying finally to receive a little encouragement from someone who has known me as long and as well as you. You are truly a gift from the God I was beginning to doubt. I tend to forget the small vexations that I suffered under Mistress Packerville because they pale in the light of the good she rendered me. You know I would not have learned to read or have knowledge of the grace of our Saviour were it not for her. I have not set foot in a church since I was a new bride. There is only one church in this county for the colored people, and Luther had a quarrel with the minister in the first month of our marriage and I have not been able to attend since. That may have given me some source of comfort. I could have talked to my God and my fellow Christians because you well know I cannot talk to this man. Mistress Packerville consulted me about everything that came or left that house. There was not an egg or a sack of flour that passed over that threshold without my knowledge. I am consulted about nothing that matters here. I know it is only contempt which prompts him to question me of my days when he knows they are those of a corpse. So when I think of Mistress Packerville, I think only of this Bible she gave me and the tears she shed when I had to leave her home. I have already left this house and believe me, there are no tears.

And I truly don't think you fully understood what I meant about my child. I know that all children must grow up and away from us. But you see, the papers that declare I never owned my child only confirm what I have always felt in my heart. From his birth, he has been his father's son in flesh and now in spirit. But I tremble daily, for I fear it is even more than that. For fifteen years I have watched them both walk and talk and eat. Believe me, I am not losing my mind but it is not just that he is Luther's son, he *is* Luther. And I fear that I have been the innocent vessel for some sort of unspeakable evil. It is clear to me that I have now outlived my usefulness to them, and they are trying to push me out of this house by making me a stranger to my husband and a stranger to my son. And the true horror is that I am becoming, sister, a stranger to myself. You would not recognize the girl you once knew in Tupelo.

Forgive me, I have gone on too long. I close with affection.

Luwana

My Dearest Luwana,

Pray, take hold of yourself. This senseless prattle about evil is unhealthy for your soul. There is nothing — do you hear me — nothing that is going on in your home that is not repeated in countless other homes around you. Please, venture out and make friends with the other wives. I alone am not enough for you. I know you feel it is impossible because you are despised by the farmers' wives around you and distrusted by the colored women up on the hill, but for the love of God, try. Go visit and take them flowers and vegetables from your garden this spring. Do something, my dear, because I fear for your sanity.

Always,
Luwana

My Dear Luwana,

I have not written in a year because I could see that you were growing impatient with me. I knew that to continue in that vein would cause you to tire of writing to me and so I needed to find some way to prove to you that what I said were not the delirious fantasies of a foolish woman. I was determined to do everything within my power to hold your trust. To lose you is to lose the only friend I have.

Now listen well. I have passed one full year without talking to my husband and my son. I sit with them and take my breakfast in silence, and then I get up from the table and sit in my rocker with my hands folded until we all assemble again at the evening meal. They communicate all their needs to our housekeeper and she fulfills them. Since I have asked for no new clothes or books, it is assumed that I need nothing. At the evening meal, I am always asked the same question: "Has your day gone well, Mrs. Nedeed?" and that only requires a nod of my head. Since I am never questioned any further, I need offer no information. And there has been much talk between them at our supper table this past year. They have made all the arrangements for the boy's college in Massachusetts, the construction of new cabins on Linden Hills, and it seems as if there is a war threatening between the states which may free all the slaves. But my opinions are never solicited on any of these matters and I volunteered none as I would have in the past. One full year, my sister, I have taken my meals in this manner, spent my days, and retired to my bed at night.

To the day it is exactly 665 times that I needed to open my mouth to speak — 332 times to answer their good morning's and 333 times to do the same in the evening. It would have been 720 times but this was not a leap year and they were both traveling for a little over a month — 32 days in exact reckoning — viewing different schools for the boy. When they returned on the evening of the 33rd day, that gave me the additional good evening.

I suppose you wonder how I can be so exact. Well, you know the silver hat pin that I keep next to my mirror? I use it to carve a line on my chest and stomach, which I then rub with black ink until the bleeding stops, for each time I am called upon to speak throughout the year. Once the wound has healed, the mark is permanently affixed and there is no danger of it washing off during my toilet. And I have carefully counted them all just before I sat down to write you.

Now I ask you, are these the rantings of an insane woman? Would their lives be any different if I had spared myself the breath it took to speak at all? Would the boy be considering another school? Would one more or one less cabin be built up on Linden Hills? At this moment, I can tear open my bodice to show you and the world that it would not.

The boy leaves for school on the morning train and I am sure that he will wish me good-bye. His father has trained him to be extremely polite. That will be the 666th time that I will be called upon to open my mouth. I shall let you know if he offers more than the "Good-bye, Mother" that I am prepared for. But I warn you not to anticipate it. I plan to place my wrapper on the back of the rocker and hide behind the draperies in the sitting room to see if he will just address the shawl and go on his way. He probably shall. So Luther will leave and I am still left with Luther. Need I say any more, my sister? Just that I fall on my knees and thank God in heaven for sending me you.

Luwana

There was no answer to that letter. And the remainder of the gold-edged dividers were blank. Even though she leafed all the way through to the Book of Revelations, there was no record of what happened to Luwana Packerville on the morning she made her six hundred and sixty-sixth utterance. The gentle ebbings of grief were building into a flood as she turned the blank pages over again and again, searching for that lost day. That just couldn't be all. She went back to Luwana Packerville's last words — "Just that I fall on my knees and thank God in heaven for sending me you." But it couldn't end there, and it hadn't. She had found the end in the beginning: "There can be no God."

And the flood finally broke for all those silent mornings filled with the deceptive hum of a thousand conversations that only amounted to pantomime. She put down the Bible, went over to touch the edges of the lace covering her son's body, and she began to cry. She cried because her beautician knew the shape of the mole behind her ear, because the grocer knew that she hated the taste of lamb, and the mailman could tell anyone that her favorite color of stationery was coral. She sat down in that basement crying as if her life depended on it, because if her life depended on it, the man she had lived with for the last six years wouldn't be able to tell the executioner as much as that.

The sun was just beginning to set when Willie and Lester turned into Fourth Cresent Drive. They walked up the flagstone path at the rear of the Parkers' home and Willie stumbled on his loosened shoelace in the fading light. He bent down to retie it. "Ya know, we've been going in through back doors all day. I thought Martin Luther King did something about all that."

"Yeah, but this guy really apologized over the phone. Said he was having a whole house full of people because of his wife's funeral tomorrow. He's not out to insult us like that dishrag, Xavier, was."

"Aw, he wasn't so bad. But I can't see why he hangs with that other guy — Christ, was he out to lunch."

"Yup, and vultures of a feather nest together. Donnell was just trying to hide his slimy wings."

"He gave us fifty eagles though."

Lester sucked his teeth. "Vulture money."

"It still spends."

"Anyway, I'd rather go around back here. I don't want to chance running into my mom 'cause she's probably in there with the rest, giving her respects to the dead and all."

"I've always wondered why folks say that. You can't really give the dead nothing. It's more like giving your respects to the living. Ya know what I mean?"

"It's more like a whole lot of nonsense as far as I'm concerned." Lester rang the bell. "This poor guy probably wants to be alone tonight instead of having a crowd of losers in here, eating up his food and trying to figure out how much he got from her life insurance."

The door surprised them when it opened, because they didn't hear the tumbler click. The hinges moved with a whisper and the presence of the short, balding man holding the knob seemed to do the same. "Ah, I'm glad you could come, Lester." His eyes were huge and distorted through the rimless bifocals.

"Sure thing, Mr. Parker. I brought along my friend, Willie Mason, to help."

"Of course, of course. Please, come in. I'm sorry you had to use the back way, you could have come in through the front because no one's arrived yet. And the caterers have set up and left long ago."

"Naw, it's all right. We understand."

"No, I didn't want you to think that I was sneaking you into the house or something." His eyes blinked rapidly as he spoke in a fierce whisper. "There's nothing shameful in what I'm doing, nothing at all."

They looked at each other over his head and frowned.

"Why would we think that, Mr. Parker?" Lester glanced uneasily around the huge, barn-shaped kitchen.

"No, not you. But some people wouldn't understand. And they just didn't know Lycentia. Mrs. Parker would want me to have you here. She'd want me to do what I'm doing tonight. And she'd know that I couldn't without your help."

Willie cleared his throat. "But what exactly do you want us to do?"

"Of course. I haven't said, have I?" Parker's false teeth gleamed in the dark room. "Well, come, come." He beckoned them out of the kitchen.

The only thing Willie knew was that Lester had said something about eight dollars an hour and they had been so excited, they hadn't thought about what it could be. But maybe they should have.

They followed Parker up a set of double stairs that led from the kitchen to the second floor. And since the house was a shrunken replica of a Victorian mansion, there was a second set of steps leading up from the front hall. Its curved mahogany banister continued along the open hallway, turning it into a balcony that overlooked the living and dining rooms. The tread of Parker's tiny feet was muffled by the thick carpeting that covered the upstairs hallway. He would tip along in the dark for two feet or so and then stop to look back over his shoulder. "Come, come." He finally came to an oak door at the end of the hall and paused to smile at them again before turning the handle.

Willie quickly gauged the size and age of the man. If he tried something weird, he and Lester could take this guy on with no trouble.

Parker turned on the lights in the room. All of the furniture had been pushed to the middle of the floor and covered with sheets. The rest of the room was completely bare except for a rolled-up carpet, a pile of newspapers, and a steam machine in the corner. The huge irises turned to them triumphantly. "Now you see what I mean?"

They didn't, but felt they should nod. Maybe his wife's death had sent him over the edge or something.

"The paperhangers, you know. With them coming tomorrow, there won't be enough time to strip the walls and redo them before I return from the burial. They can put the new furniture in place but there's just no time for steaming off the old paper, so I rented the steamer myself." He began to tremble as a sense of urgency crept into his voice. "But the wake's tonight and it must be off tonight. And I'm offering you almost as much as it would cost me if they did it. Sure, they're twenty dollars an hour but you aren't unionized or anything, are you?"

They both shook their heads.

"Well, I didn't want you to think that I was trying to take advantage of you. If you insist on more, I can arrange that, too."

"No. You want us to steam off the wallpaper, right?" Lester spoke slowly as you would to a child.

"Of course, of course." Parker nodded his head impatiently. "But do it quietly because I'll have guests soon."

Willie wondered how noisy he thought steam could be.

"And I don't see why I should have to explain, do you?"

They shook their heads again.

"I have a perfect right to redo her room."

"Oh, this is your wife's room?" Willie said.

"Of course!" Parker frowned at him. "And they'll probably wonder just like you why I'm doing it now."

Willie mumbled quickly that he wasn't wondering at all.

"But they didn't know Lycentia like I did. She would want it just this way. She would want me to walk back into this house with a new bedroom. She was a very determined woman, you know, with her own ideas about everything. And she often said, 'Chester, if I should be the shortest-liver, I don't want you to be moaning and groaning like a fool. Life marches on' — that was Lycentia tooth and nail — 'I want you to start new, do you hear me?' " Parker's shrunken face almost glowed as he surveyed the room. "And so I'm doing what she wants, what she told me to do." He turned back to Lester and Willie sharply. "And I don't see anything to be ashamed of — do you?"

They agreed that they didn't either. He should be proud that he had respected his wife's wishes this promptly.

"Of course, of course. I'm very proud. And I'm going to that service tomorrow with a clear conscience. But I'm not up to explaining all that to other people right now, so just be quiet, huh, fellas?"

When he left the room, shutting the door firmly but gently behind him, they turned to each other and grinned broadly. Then Lester tiptoed cartoon-fashion to the covered furniture and held the sheet in his hand. "I'll give you even odds that it's already under there."

"You think I got this old, this healthy, by taking sucker bets like that? Man, I *know* it's under there, but two to one it's psychedelic pink with vinyl cushions 'cause she's probably under thirty."

"Naw, that wouldn't be his style of under thirty. It's brass with purple velvet cushions."

"Okay, you're on."

He yanked the dustcover off the bedroom furniture, and the vanity set they were betting on was chrome with a white leather seat.

"Everybody loses." Willie laughed.

"Except old Parker." Lester covered up the furniture. "I wonder if he'll have the minister marry them right after the funeral. No point in wasting all those flowers."

"Of course, of course," Willie whispered hoarsely, "because Lycentia would have wanted it just that way."

Lester crouched and tiptoed over to plug in the steamer. "She said, 'Chester, don't throw your money away. Have it all done in one day and get a discount from that preacher, do you hear me?' "

"Well, he sure got a discount from us." Willie ran his hands along the peeled and aging paper. "This mess will take half the night. No wonder you said he was so eager to run you down today. A lousy eight dollars an hour between the two of us."

"What do you mean *between* the two of us? Shouldn't it be eight dollars for *each* of us?"

"Hey, you're right." Willie snapped his fingers. "And that'll still be a lot less than he was gonna pay those paperhangers. But I don't think he's gonna buy that."

"He'll have to," Lester said, "if we only do half this room and then call him back up here. 'You see, Mr. Parker, my buddy and I were just having a little dispute here. I thought you told me eight dollars an hour for each of us, and now he's saying you said eight dollars between us. And I know that couldn't be what Lycentia told you she wanted since she wanted this here room done before the engines warmed up on her hearse, now could it, sir?' "

Willie smiled. "I see you don't live in Linden Hills for nothing, Shit."

"Hey, look, the name of the game is break or be broken when dealing with these folks." The head of the steamer hit the wall with a dull hiss. "Now, get ready to scrape."

By the time they had finished stripping half of the room, the downstairs foyer was full of neighbors. People were moving slowly between the living room and dining room, forming quiet clusters of conversations that kept breaking and shifting as someone left to greet a newcomer, refill a coffee cup, or help themselves to the cold buffet that was laid out on a sideboard in the dining room. Willie and Lester walked along the banister in the darkened upstairs hallway, trying to locate Parker in the crowd. Lester recognized quite a few faces from First Crescent Drive, and his mother was sitting in the corner of the living room with a plate balanced on her lap. They finally spotted Parker seated quietly in the dining room at the head of a large oval table with a glass top and a centerpiece of white tea roses. The twelve chairs around the table were continually changing occupants. As soon as someone finished eating, another person would take his place, carrying one of the clear glass plates, which were stacked on the sideboard. From the second floor, the brass chandelier reflected the changing faces bent over the tabletop as clearly as a mirror.

Lester tried to get Parker's attention without calling out, but he sat with his eyes lowered to his lap and his plate untouched. Mrs. Donnell sat beside him and occasionally she would lean over, pat his arm, and urge him to eat.

"Oh Christ, how are we gonna get him up here?" Lester whispered. "He's down there playing the grieving husband."

"He won't have to play soon when we tell him we ain't finishing that room. Maybe we could throw a note down into his lap or something."

"Well, let's just wait a minute. Maybe his neck will get tired and he'll change expressions. And when he moves into one of those anguished appeals to heaven and rolls his eyes up here, we'll signal him."

But for the next five minutes all they could see was the light bouncing off Parker's smooth bald spot and occasional reflections from his rimless bifocals in the glass tabletop. Then a bloated hum started at the other end of the table and rose above the quiet murmurs in the rest of the room before a woman's sharp voice cut into it.

"Bob, this isn't the time or place to bring that up."

"Well, I still think it's a damned shame," the man beside her almost shouted.

Parker's head swung up toward that end of the table. "What? What's a shame?" His whisper, carrying the import of the bereaved, silenced the others. "Now don't be too hasty, Bob. Believe me, Lycentia would have wanted it that way, she was always saying —"

"Lycentia was the first one to bring it to my attention, Chester — God rest her soul — and she was dead set against it."

Parker began to tremble, little rings of moisture forming on his bifocals. "Why, that's not possible. She —"

"Chester, just last month she told me she had all the petitions in to the city commissioner and she was sure the council was going to impose that zoning restriction. Now I get the news today that they overturned our petition. And I think it's a damned shame, that's all. Because all that aggravation is probably what killed her — excuse me, Chester — this may not be the time for all this. But with all that woman's hard work, the city's still going to erect that housing project."

Forks clattered all around the table. "What?"

"There has to be some mistake."

"Mistake, my eye. Where's Bryan?" Bob twisted around in his chair toward the dining room door. "Bryan, you're the council-

man for this district, so I know you've got the inside dope. Didn't
the planning commission use our petitions for toilet paper last
week?"

"Now, Bob, it wasn't quite like that." The champagne-colored
man cleared his throat. "There was a lot of time spent considering all the issues involved. And certainly the feelings of this
community were given quite a bit of weight. Why, I personally
made a vehement appeal and used every ounce of influence I
could to be sure that your views were given a fair hearing — just
as I did for the new sewage plant and the renovation of those
vacant lots across —"

"Cut the mumbo-jumbo," Bob interrupted him. "We heard
all that when we elected you. All we want to know is did they or
did they not approve of building those low-income projects."

"Yes, but —"

"See!" Bob turned back to the table.

"But by a *small* margin." Bryan tried to raise his voice above
the scattered outbursts. "Bob, you and the others have got to
understand that there has been a lot of pressure on the mayor to
do something about the living conditions in Putney Wayne.
People are over there in tenements that should have been con-
demned years ago. There's no heat in most of them and at times
no water. The health department reported three cases of diph-
theria within six months — and it's no wonder, the way they
live. And one of the kids who caught it last year died recently, so
your petition was just bad timing, that's all. It's not my fault.
People were starting to talk epidemic."

"Well, you can't help but feel sorry for those mothers," one of
the women said, "but the city should just renovate the housing
that's already there. God knows they milk us enough as it is for
services we'll never use — all that welfare and food stamps. You
know what it costs just to print up those stamps — it's scandal-
ous."

"It's not that simple, Mildred. The city has to apply for federal funds to undertake any building plans and there are regulations about size and number of units. It's really less expensive for
you if they build an entirely new complex."

"Yeah, sure," Bob said. "And then they've got to *fill* those units and that means you're doubling the size of Putney Wayne in half the space. Then we get a whole army of them right across Wayne Avenue. Practically in our backyards. So you can kiss your safe streets good-bye."

"And just about everything else in our homes. You fill up the neighborhood with people like that, the next thing you know your TV's and stereos are walking out the door."

"Well, crime is everywhere. If worse comes to worst, you can always get extra security for your homes. But what about our children? The local schools are overcrowded as it is. We've managed to maintain a pretty decent standard of education so far, but this is just going to swing the ratio too far over. And I refuse to have my child suffer because the teachers will be overloaded with a lot of remedial cases and troublemakers."

"Thank God I don't have to send my Ernestine to these public schools."

"Well, if the council gets their way, we'll all have to take our children out of these schools — for their own sakes."

"Yeah, or the next thing you know, they'll be coming home with drugs and knives."

Upstairs, Lester touched Willie's arm. "Just listen to them," he whispered. "Any minute, someone's gonna say, 'The next thing you know, they'll be marrying your daughter.' Let's get out of here before I throw up."

Willie motioned for Lester to wait. He hadn't really been listening so much as looking down into the faces that were looking up through the clear dinner plates from the glass-topped table. And something was haunting him about the rhythm of the knives and forks that cut into the slices of roast beef. Click-scrape. Click-scrape. Click-scrape. Click-scrape. Now, where had he heard that before? *Click-scrape. Click-scrape . . . These days-of dis-inheritance.* Yeah, that was it. *These days of disinheritance, we feast on human heads . . .* The plates never seemed empty of the brown and bloody meat. The utensils worked their way from center to edge, exposing an ear here, a chin there. Parts of a mouth, a set of almond-shaped eyes.

The church bells clap one night in the week.
But that's all done. It is what used to be,
As they used to lie in the grass, in the heat,
Men on green buds and women half of sun.
The words are written, though not yet said.

Willie knew it was just an illusion. Those plates were actually being emptied, so the clicking and scraping couldn't go on forever. They had to stop in spite of what he was seeing. They had to put those forks down.

But the voices were beginning to circle the dining room in a fevered crescendo accompanied by a steady metallic tempo from the table.

"I hope they don't expect us to take this lying down."

"What is this — South Africa? As decent citizens and taxpayers, we should have something to say about what these officials do."

"Does Nedeed know about this?"

"Bryan, what should be our next move?" Bob asked. "We can't let it end here."

"Well, your community isn't the only one that's upset about the proposal. I was talking to Phil Mackelberg, the councilman who represents Spring Vale, and he'd just met with an ad hoc committee from the Wayne County Citizens Alliance, and it seems that they've been working to place this proposal on a referendum in the next election. It could be stopped in November." He cleared his throat nervously and glanced around the room. "But it would mean that Linden Hills would have to form a coalition with Spring Vale and the Wayne County Citizens Alliance in order to get enough support to defeat it."

"I'm for it," Bob said.

Willie whispered, "But I thought that Alliance was the Ku Klux Klan without a Southern accent?"

Lester shook his head. "Naw, just without the sheets."

There was an uneasy stirring downstairs.

"I don't know, we've had our differences with that group in the past."

"Yeah, but you have to sweep all that junk under the carpet."

"We've never needed them before — I don't see why we can't fight our own battles."

"It's not just *our* battle. Linden Hills has got to realize that we're part of a whole city. And if we don't hang with the Citizens Alliance then we'll hang separately."

"Well, I think this entire conversation is a disgrace!" Mrs. Donnell shouted. "Here we are turning this man's home into a public forum and his wife's funeral is tomorrow." She pressed Parker's arm. "Chester, you haven't heard a word we've said. I can imagine all the things on your mind right now."

"Oh, no, no." Parker looked up from his lap and focused on his guests. "Bob was right. Lycentia spent her last days working on that petition. She would often say to me, 'Chester, I'm going to do everything in my power to keep those dirty niggers out of our community.' And this evening is in her honor." He smiled weakly around the table. "So please, there's more roast beef, folks."

There was total silence for a moment. Gradually the people who were standing drifted out of the dining room, and the twelve seated around the table bent their hands over their plates in rapt attention to the music of their cutlery on the transparent surfaces.

> It is like the season when, after summer,
> It is summer and it is not, it is autumn
> And it is not, it is day and it is not,
> As if last night's lamp continued to burn,
> As if yesterday's people continued to watch
> The sky, half porcelain, preferring that
> To shaking out heavy bodies in the glares
> Of this present, this science, this unrecognized.

Willie sighed. "You're right, I've heard enough. Let's do what we have to and get out of here."

Lester went back into the bedroom and Willie was about to follow him when the doorbell rang and seemed to echo from every glass surface in the room. The crystal balls on the chandelier even tinkled. Luther Nedeed came into the dining room, carrying a cellophane-wrapped cake. He was the only guest Willie had seen bringing food that night, and it surprised him. He knew that his family always fried chicken and baked stuff for a wake and so it was the last thing he expected to see done in Linden Hills. Willie lingered in the upstairs hall a moment and watched Luther as he hesitated in front of the buffet. There was no space for his bundle next to the ornate array of catered food.

"Nice of you to come, Luther." Parker got up and took the cake from him.

"I guess I have to become accustomed to these modern ways." Luther seemed embarrassed. "In my time, friends and neighbors always supplied the food for these types of occasion."

"Of course, of course." Parker blinked at him. "But I didn't want folks going to a lot of trouble."

"It was no trouble, my wife baked it. She sends her regards, Chester, but she's not up to coming out tonight. And although I've been able to serve you in an official capacity in your time of loss, I felt I should come tonight in my unofficial capacity as a neighbor."

"Yes, haven't seen your missus in ages. Lycentia had mentioned something about a cruise, wasn't it? Did she enjoy it?"

"Immensely, but it's left her somewhat drained, so we've decided that she spend Christmas with relatives to save her the strain of entertaining. We're planning something for the spring."

"Well, I must give her a call as soon as the holidays are over," one of the women said. "This has been a dreadfully busy season with the Alcott wedding and poor Lycentia passing."

"Yes, yes." Parker nodded. "Everything is all up in the air. When I think about the plans that Lycentia and I had. But she always said to me, 'Chester —' "

"I'm sure, Chester," Luther said as he stared straight into his eyes, "that whatever plans you may still have won't be terribly disrupted." Parker almost cringed under his gaze. "Because," Luther continued slowly, "Lycentia would have wanted it that way."

"Oh, yes, Luther." Parker began to chatter. "Yes, she would

have. Why, just before you came in we were all talking about —"

"I know what everyone in this house was talking about." Luther took in the entire room with his dark, immobile face, and Willie felt the urge to move back into the shadowed hallway upstairs. "The same thing that's been discussed every time two or three people from Linden Hills have gotten together lately. And I can tell you that it's all been taken care of. The Tupelo Realty board met with the Wayne County Citizens Alliance today and there's little doubt that the referendum on the housing project will be put on the ballot next November. Now, the only thing left is to vote on it, and with our combined efforts there's no chance of it getting through."

"Now, there's a man who's talking sense," Bob said. "Luther, I've been trying to tell these folks that we all have a responsibility to the welfare of this county, and if the Alliance can see through that and work with us, then we should work with them. It's not about black or white, it's about our civic duty."

"It's nothing of the kind." Luther's voice was soft and low, but it carried throughout the room. "You know, Bob, my father often said, 'Lie to everyone in this man's world if need be, but never lie to yourself, because that's the quickest road to destruction.' The Wayne County Citizens Alliance is full of some of the most despicable racists on this side of the continent. And there isn't a soul in this room that doesn't know that." Luther almost smiled at the expression on their faces. "And you're only saved from being beneath their contempt because your education and professional status are above reproach and, more often than not, above theirs. But the people who would move into that new development don't have that saving grace, so the Alliance is free to engage in myths about inferior schools and deteriorating neighborhoods while all they're really fearing is the word *nigger*. And they've no intention of letting this county finance a breeding ground for their nightmares.

"We must give them credit for one thing: they've become civilized enough by now to recognize that there are two types — the safe ones that they feel they can control and trust not to spill tea

on their carpets while they use a dozen euphemisms to form a coalition to keep the other type from moving too close. And I suppose that since I've just spent an entire afternoon listening to all
that, I'm a bit reluctant to hear it all again tonight from you."

"Now, Luther, that's a bit harsh." Bob pushed the meat
around on his plate. "If you really thought that, you wouldn't
have been able to meet with those people."

"I met with them and I'll vote with them." And this time he
did smile. "Because I know that their nightmares are real
enough to send them running from the other side of the hill.
Real enough to get this entire district red-lined through the
banks, and my realty company wouldn't be able to finance another mortgage, and I'd have to watch the property values of
Linden Hills go plunging into an abyss. And do you think I'm
going to let that happen because a handful of fools can't stomach the thought of living next to another group of people that
happen to look like me?"

Willie wanted to applaud Nedeed. He had said all the things
that Willie had wanted to hang over that banister and shout:
Yeah, you turkeys, I'm one of those people in Putney Wayne you
didn't want near you. Maybe I don't carry a wallet full of credit
cards, but I've never carried a switchblade, either. Lester should
have been out here for this. At least Nedeed was honest — Willie
looked down at the suffocated room — deadly honest.

No one at the table was eating. Wineglasses were turned, napkins wiped clean mouths, and coffee cups were stirred. One
woman got up and left the table without a word, but no one's
head followed her out of the room. Luther picked up a clean
plate, filled it, and took her seat, completing the circle of twelve.
His knife and fork caught the rays from the chandelier as he delicately sliced into the tender meat. He chewed slowly and looked
around the table.

"Is everyone else finished as well? I hope not, since I've
brought dessert — and I hate eating alone."

One by one, the other knives and forks were lifted as the meal
continued with the pathetic motions of children being forced to
eat. The rhythm of the utensils was much fainter now, but Willie

could still hear it plainly upstairs because it went unchallenged by any conversation. They cut. They chewed. They swallowed.

> *This outpost, this douce, this dumb, this dead, in which*
> *We feast on human heads, brought in on leaves,*
> *Crowned with the first, cold buds. On these we live,*
> *No longer on the ancient cake of seed,*
> *The almond and deep fruit. This bitter meat*
> *Sustains us . . . Who, then, are they, seated here?*
> *Is the table a mirror in which they sit and look?*
> *Are they men eating reflections of themselves?*

Realizing that no one else was going to speak, Willie went into the bedroom. Lester was carrying fresh water out of the bathroom for the steamer.

"Hey, White, I was just about to come get you. I thought you got lost."

"Naw, Nedeed came in and I wanted to get a better look at him."

"Christ, I bet they're down there bending his ears with their gripes."

"No," Willie said. "As a matter of fact, they all shut up. Now they're just eating."

She was on her knees, surrounded by piles of dusty, yellowing cookbooks. She had hoped to find some other records left by Luwana Packerville, but the woman seemed to have disappeared. The damp concrete bit into her knees as she tore open the third cardboard box and found another stack of wire-bound recipes. She knew that these also belonged to the same woman, Evelyn Creton Nedeed; there was no need to open the covers and see that name written again in large block letters on the inside. And reading the carefully printed instructions for breads, stews, roasted meats, and puddings only knotted her stomach, reminding her that she hadn't eaten in days. But she still dug into the box, enduring the dust that entered her nose and dried her throat, hoping that something of Luwana Packerville's was wedged in between the thick, heavy cookbooks.

Her heart quickened when she saw a wad of papers but she unfolded them only to find columns and columns of canning dates: Thirty quarts of snap beans, May 1892. Twelve quarts of pickled tomatoes, September 1893. Twenty pints of blackberry jam, August 1896. The papers were thrown down in disgust. She was wasting her time. Forty years were gone. These recipes were from another lifetime. Evelyn Creton probably never knew Luwana Packerville. As she roasted her meats and canned her apple butter year after year, she didn't know that a woman had gone insane because she was barred from the very kitchen that Evelyn Creton later filled with her damned cookbooks. Even at that moment, on her knees, she could visualize the shelves she had kept them on. The same cherrywood cabinet that now held her own paperback guides for countless diets and nutrition plans, her encyclopedia of international cuisine, three hundred ways to a better quiche, and a hardcover edition of the modern woman's Bible, *The Joy of Cooking*. Evelyn Creton had obviously found joy in that kitchen as she filled her shelves with these recipes. And she didn't seem content to stop with just that. With a fanatical precision, the woman had even recorded the dates on which she purchased and used the ingredients for each recipe.

Potato Casserole

June 5th — Purchased: 50 pounds of potatoes, 12 pounds of cheese, 10 pounds of onions, 16 pints of cream.
June 5th — Used: 37 pounds of potatoes, 9½ pounds of cheese, 10 pounds of onions, 12 pints of cream.

She baked continually and in equally huge amounts.

Walnut Bread

June 6th — Purchased: 20 pounds of flour, 15 pounds of sugar, 2½ quarts of butter, ½ bushel of walnuts, 10 quarts of milk.
June 6th — Used: 15 pounds of flour, 7 pounds of sugar, 2½ quarts of butter, ½ bushel of walnuts, 8 quarts of milk.

But none of it made any sense because on June 7 she'd started all over again, adding two bushels of raisins to the same recipe. June 8, she substituted pecans for the walnuts. June 9, quarts of sour cream for the milk.

The woman cooked as if she were possessed. What drove her to make that kitchen her whole world? Between the buying, baking, and recording she had to be in that kitchen all day — and probably all night. There were only three of them in this house, so they couldn't have eaten all of that food. Maybe she was selling those things. But how could you sell gravy? In one day she had made forty quarts of chicken gravy, and the next day, turned around and made another forty with onions instead of mushrooms. She used a lot of onions in her recipes. And there were no food processors in those days, so Evelyn Creton must have done a lot of crying.

She sighed, knowing her search was futile, but she still emptied the box. At the bottom were two slim volumes covered in black silk. They were also recipe books, but their thickness and width set them apart from the others. There was no name printed on the inside cover but the block letters and the method of recording date by date the amounts purchased and used for each recipe marked them as belonging to the same woman. At first the contents confused her. Now most of the ingredients were measured in ounces and pinches, and the dates were crammed together so tightly they were almost a blur.

Her knees were becoming numb as she read, and her fingers tightened around the silk covers as she began to make sense out of the pages. She needed more light. She stood up too quickly. Her head swayed drunkenly and her eyes went dim. She reached for the railing on the cot, clutching the books to her side. She prayed that Luther wouldn't choose this moment to cut off the lights. She needed to sit down and rest for a while and then take her time to read through these two books very carefully.

Because there was no way that Evelyn Creton could have kept this set of recipes up on those cherrywood shelves.

December
22nd

Willie, eat it ... Eat it ... Willie opened another glass door and ran down the dark corridor, his knees pulling the bed covers from his shoulders and chin as he tried to escape the hands that shot out from the long row of erect coffins on his right side. But each step materialized another casket, another pale hand with bright red fingernails growing and curling like snakes around the cake that was offered in a shrill echo emerging from those open depths. Willie, eat it ... Eat it ... He pressed his hands over his ears and ran faster, trying to avert his eyes from the ghostly fingers, bloody snakes, and crumbling brown sweets that seemed to stretch ahead of him into eternity. His sneakers pounded down the narrow hallway and his body was soaked with sweat. He could feel the perspiration moving slowly down the insides of his thighs as his shirt clung to his back, armpits, and chest. But, oh God, he was so cold. Willie, eat it ... Eat it ... The screaming now replaced the sound of his heart, so the faster he ran, the louder it became.

And the faster he ran, the longer and more frantic the hands with their crushed gifts. To close his eyes was to risk stumbling, and moving to the left was to meet instant death in a huge vacuum. His legs were tightening, his chest burning, but there was nowhere to go but straight ahead. Any moment now they would touch him. A glass door miraculously sprang up in front of him and with a shriek of triumph Willie burst through it and landed awake on his bed.

The screaming echoes followed him into his room as he watched the lights from the passing fire engines streak across the ceiling. When the sirens moved off into the distance somewhere down in the streets of Putney Wayne, Willie could hear his heart beating again. Trembling, he reached to gather the blankets and sheets tangled under his feet. He knew he would have to shake like this until he got warm again. And once he was warm, he could go back to sleep. But, Christ, did he really want to sleep? What if that dream wasn't finished? He stuck his icy hands between his thighs and buried his nose under the blanket. He never should have eaten all that stuff Parker wrapped up for them. It was too late at night to have pigged out that way, but the roast beef was so tender he could have cut it with his breath. And that cake . . . His saliva still held the flavor from the rum, butter, and raisins. He should have left well enough alone and stopped after the second piece, but he hardly had to chew since it was whipped so finely it slipped down his throat like liquid. Nothing like the cakes he had eaten at home. Willie's mind snapped around that last thought. In fact, it was nothing like the cakes he had ever eaten in anyone's home.

He settled himself deeper into the covers with a slight frown over his closed eyes. But Nedeed said his wife made it. Willie could visualize the curve of his mouth, the exact placement of light and shadows on his lips as he formed the words, "It was no trouble, my wife baked it. She sends her regards, Chester . . ." He knew that the kitchen in Nedeed's house didn't look anything like his mother's. There was no way that his wife had to jam a piece of cardboard into the top of the oven door to keep it from flying open. She probably had one of those kitchens straight out of an ad in *Good Housekeeping:* microwave, dishwasher, and all kinds of shiny gadgets. But no matter what type of bowls or stove you have, milk is still milk, flour is flour, and sugar, sugar. And there's always something different about food when it's straight out of someone's home. That cake was too perfect. And the way the butter, rum, and raisins went down all smooth and easy, it didn't give him much time to think about it — he had almost missed tasting her absence. Willie curled himself tighter into the warm spot that his body had finally made under the blankets. He must remember to mention all this to Lester in the morning. Why would Nedeed lie? Just as Willie released his last conscious breath, the sirens began to scream again in the distance. He turned over in his sleep and shuddered.

Will he eat it? Her trembling hands smoothed down the yellowing page. Will this be the one to make the difference? Refusing to succumb to the deadening cold and sleep, she pulled the two blankets tightly around her shoulders and tried to concentrate on the page in her lap. She had gone through six months of the same weekly recipe for tea loaves, so she quickly skimmed over the records of new wheat flour, eggs, milk, and honey to the end, where she would find the additional ingredients that Evelyn Creton hoped would make the crucial difference.

> June 14th — Add: 2 pinches powdered dove's heart
> 6 amaranth seeds
> 1 pinch snakeroot

So this time it would be the snakeroot and dove's heart with the amaranth seeds. On June 7, it had been ground ivory-root. On May 31, three pinches of shame-weed.

It was the shame-weed that told her pages ago what Evelyn Creton was actually doing. Shame-weed. The name was so odd it had stuck after all these years. And she remembered being so ashamed of her great-aunt, Miranda Day, when she pulled up in that cab each summer, calling from the curb at the top of her voice, "Y'all better be home. Mama Day done come to visit a spell with her Northern folks." Coming with her cardboard suitcases, loose-fitting shoes, and sticky jars of canned whatever. Toothless but ready with a broad grin; almost illiterate but determined to give her very loud opinion regardless of the subject or the company. "Child, y'all sittin' there complainin' 'bout them wayward boys. Ain't never seen an onery man yet who didn't come round if you get yo'self a little shame-weed and bake it up in somethin' sweet." And perhaps if she hadn't been so eager to quiet the old woman, to move her out of the room away from the amused and contemptuous eyes of her teenaged friends, she would have also heard about ivory-root, white pepper, and sassafras. The amaranth seeds, snakeroot, and dove's heart that Evelyn Creton kept mixing and measuring page after page, month after month. A little more of this, a little less of that. His coldness and distance, the feeling that things weren't the way they should be must lie in something that she just wasn't doing right. If she hung in there long enough, he would change. It just took a lot of patience with a little reasoning. Then a lot of reasoning with a lot of patience. You talk more, you talk less — and you're patient. You cling, you rage — and you're patient. You just shut up for weeks on end — and you're patient. Wasn't that the advice, the very literate advice that she unearthed from sorting through all those books and articles? And there was nowhere else to turn except to her piles of *Cosmopolitans* and *Ladies Home Journals*. She wasn't going out into the woods like Evelyn Creton or Mama Day to dig up shame-weed.

Yes, she was so certain she could make "it" change, forgetting that it had started long before she walked into Tupelo Drive. No toilet articles on the dresser in that exquisite room she was taken to. No extra pillow on the canopied bed. No clothes in her closet. *The way it's always been done here,* he'd said. He needed his private space. But then he would come at night. Enter and leave her body with the same quiet precision that she saw when he balanced his accounts, read his newspaper, or dissected his steak. That entrance and exit from her bedroom and her body became part of a natural flow of motion that was Luther. If spontaneity and passion didn't exist in the rooms they ate in, entertained in, and sat in, how could she expect it in the room she slept in? How could she tell him that she knew from the men before her marriage that it could be — should be — different from this?

Yet she never thought the word *unnatural*. It hung in the air around her now, sending up the smell of mildew and dust from the pages in her lap. But wasn't it natural that she accepted his total absence at night after she conceived, since her days were filled with his growing concern about her health and diet? His keeping track of her visits to the doctor and the punctuality with which she took her vitamins and exercise. His being ready to satisfy her simplest or most extravagant demands during her pregnancy. His telling her with and without words that he would give her whatever she needed. Perhaps it was natural to feel that, somehow, she was being unreasonable for thinking she needed more than that. What else could explain his shrinking away, his look of injured bewilderment when she suggested that he still wasn't doing enough?

And then after the baby came, she got so caught up in the natural rhythms that filled her own days. The changes of diapers, the fluctuations of temperatures, the meticulous care of a new human being and an old house. It was so easy to keep busy while she waited for "it" to change. So easy to put faith in the fact that she could well afford that biannual trip to New York and that walk down miracle mile. Looking through the glass-and-chrome counters at the fragrant prophecies extracted from flowers, herbals, fruit, and wood. Picking up the tiny crystal vials that she had only to unstop to "steal a little thunder from a rose," or have "paradise regained." The round silver wands that promised that the colored wax they contained would let her lips "say it without a word." Closing her eyes to "imagine the possibilities" that would come from dusting Silversea, Twilight Skies, or Surefire on her lids. Those bewitchingly beautiful women leaning over the counters chanting the names of Lanvin, Jean Patou, Nina Ricci. She didn't have the time or desperation for recording, like Evelyn Creton, the number of bruised rose petals and jasmines set to soak in spring water; for pounding musk and civet into orris root and mint; for watching sandalwood and myrrh, sugar and ambergris dry into cakes of incense. She had just enough time to fly back from New York and throw her purchases on the dresser before picking up the natural rhythms of her day, confident that Lancôme had told her to "believe in magic," so that change was definitely on the way.

Page after page, the woman labored on her hair with the familiar lemon juice and olive oil, and the unfamiliar ragweed, nettle tea, and maidenhair fern. The records were so exact she could almost see her slender fingers massaging that pale face with glycerin, almond paste, and pigeon fat. She had often imagined that the cream-and-ivory women who slept in that canopied bed were incredibly beautiful. She was now haunted by the stinging memories that she could never hope to compete with skin that demanded beige powder and peach rouge. Page after page, until slowly the ingredients began to change.

September 26th — 3 parts lanolin
                    1 part henna
                    1 part beeswax
November 12th — 5 parts mineral oil
                    1 part raw umber
                    1 part lanolin

She went back to the top of the book. No, she hadn't misread these recipes for face cream. Henna. Umber. Henna-umber. Hennaumber — the words began to spin in her mind. It was horribly funny. But the cold kept her shoulders hunched under the blankets and her dry throat made even swallowing difficult, so inside she laughed. Inside, she threw her head back toward the ceiling and howled. Small icy tears formed at the corners of her eyes as the silent laughter pierced through the basement, reaching all the way up to that bedroom for all those nights she went to sleep, her face coated with bleaching cream while she dreamed of being Evelyn Creton in the same canopied bed that Evelyn Creton dreamed of being her.

Unnatural. The word hung on stubbornly as the cold began to deaden her mind. Half of the book was left, but she couldn't think anymore. She rolled her stiffened body onto the cot and curled into a fetal position under the blankets, cradling the slender volumes next to her chest as she closed her eyes. *Unnatural.* Did Evelyn Creton ever think that word? Or did she, too, form elaborate visions of afternoon registrations in hotels, morning rendezvous in the back room of his realty office? Tracing his appointment books for the missing hours that could be given to another woman during the day. Because she knew he spent all of his nights at home. She could account for every minute of his evenings. There was dinner, the seven-o'clock news, and then he went out to the mortuary.

Snow was threatening as Willie walked slowly along the wide sidewalk, checking the house numbers against the slip of paper in his hand. He wondered if Lester had made a mistake on the note he'd left at his house: "Meet me at the preecher's, 000 Fifth Crescent Drive." He had never heard of an address like that — which didn't mean much in this neighborhood. He was through being surprised about anything in Linden Hills. At first he expected 000 to be the house back at the corner, which would have made some sense in a way, but now he was almost in the middle of the block and the numbers kept going up. Did Lester mean 1000 Fifth Crescent Drive? But the number on this ranch house was 528 and there was no way it could jump to a thousand by the end of the street. Willie looked at the note and walked a bit faster. He felt uneasy being out there by himself. No one ever walked in Linden Hills, and he didn't want to be mistaken for a prowler. Somehow, when he was with Lester, that thought had never occurred to him. He glanced up at the sky; it was a milkish gray and the air had taken on the damp warmth that precedes snow.

"Hey, White. Over here!"

Willie had almost gone past the pickup truck. It was backed into a two-car garage large enough to be a small cottage, but it was dwarfed by the brick Colonial next to it. As he walked up the long driveway, he saw that the hinged signpost on the lawn did read "000."

"Man, I was heading for the end of the street. I figured you meant one thousand."

"Nope, this is it." Lester was carrying boxes marked *Xmas* from the corner of the garage to the truck.

"What kinda number is 0-0-0?"

"My exact question when he called. But you gotta hear the answer to that one from the Rev himself, and, man, it's a winner." He shoved the box into the back of the truck. "I tried to

wait for you as long as I could, but he called twice this morning
all freaked out about the Parker funeral and getting this stuff
over to the church for their Christmas party tomorrow."

"Yeah, sorry I held you up but I overslept."

"I figured that's what happened. I could have called you, but
you haven't broken down and gotten a phone."

"Once they break down that seventy-five dollar installation
fee, I'll be glad to. Until then, my friends gotta write me letters."

"Except me — I can't afford the stamps."

"Why don't you tell the truth — you can't write." Willie un-
balled the paper in his hand. "You misspelled 'preacher.' It has
an 'a' in it."

"Well, everybody can't be a genius with words like you. That's
why we depend on a phone."

Willie followed him to the corner and picked up a box. "Ya
know, I was thinking about that this morning."

"About being a genius?"

"Aw, cut it out. About having no phone. What if I'm lying up
there sick and need to call an ambulance or something. And I
was sorta sick last night. That stuff Parker gave us upset my
stomach." He paused a moment. "Did you get a chance to eat
any of that cake Nedeed brought?"

"Naw, I was too tired when I got in. I shoved it in the refrigerator, but Roxanne was still up playing some draggy music, so I
knew she was in one of her moods and I'd never see it again. And
sure enough, about three pounds of roast beef and almost half
the cake was gone when I woke up. She's got this real funny idea
about a diet: you don't get fat if no one sees you eating. I didn't
care about the meat, but I was gonna have the cake this morning
with a cup of coffee. And I knew better than to say a word about
it, 'cause she'd just start screeching."

"I'm sorry you didn't get a chance to taste it, 'cause I was
gonna ask you about that. There was something strange about
that cake."

"You said Nedeed brought it — that should explain it."

"No, I mean strange because he said his wife made it, but it
didn't taste like she did. I mean, it didn't taste homemade, ya
know?"

"Maybe it wasn't. He bought it at a bakery or something."

"But why would he lie about it? He went out of his way to say that his wife baked it. I remember that."

"Look, he was probably too ashamed to say that she wouldn't do it for him." Lester leaned on the box he had just shoved into the truck. "He probably came home at the last minute and said, 'Woman, fix me a cake to take to the Parkers.' And she told him to go embalm himself. He's not gonna stand up in a roomful of people and admit that, not a man like him."

"Yeah, I guess so." Willie frowned. "But if he was lying about that, maybe he was lying when he said she wasn't well enough to come out of the house."

"Maybe so." Lester shrugged his shoulders. "Hey, maybe he's got her roped to his bed for safekeeping. Now, let's face it. If you were as ugly as Nedeed, wouldn't you have to chain a woman to your mattress in order to get a little action? So give the poor guy a break."

They both laughed, Willie not quite as freely as Lester. He remembered the way Nedeed had taken on a whole room of people just the night before — and won. Sure, it was a bit too crazy to think of him chaining a woman to his bed. But he was definitely capable of it.

Willie picked up three boxes and balanced them in one hand. "Hey, you didn't need any help. This stuff is nothing."

"Yeah? Just wait till you get to those stacked up in the next corner. This is probably just the tinsel and balls and crap, but those others are full of cans and they've gotta weigh fifty pounds each. When Mount Sinai has a food drive, it has a food drive. But I don't know why he couldn't have had people drop it all off at the church."

"You mean this is for the Sinai Christmas party? So this must be Reverend Hollis's place."

"Yeah, you know him?"

"Sure, his church has been giving that party for years. My mom always took us when we were small. We went to Sunday school at Caanan Baptist, but when Christmas came all you got was a coupla candy canes and a Bible verse pasted on a tree-shaped card. But over at Sinai, man, they went all the way out:

sandwiches, cookies, punch — and *real* toys. They even had them wrapped up in silver and red paper and piled under this huge tree that seemed to touch the ceiling. And Reverend Hollis always dressed up in this Santa Claus suit and gave them out." Willie laughed. "Ya know, for years I thought the real Santa Claus was black because of that, and they were just lying to us in those picture books at school."

"Well, for years I thought he should have been black," Lester said. "Even though this white guy was sitting me on his knee and asking me what I wanted for Christmas, I knew my dad was the one hauling his ass to get it. And that always confused me. God, you're dumb when you're a kid."

"I guess if my mom could have taken us downtown to one of those stores, I would have had the same problem." Willie shrugged. "But I always thought Christmas was exciting and a lot of that had to do with Reverend Hollis and Mount Sinai. It's weird how much I can remember looking forward to that silly party." He smiled to himself. "But maybe it wasn't so silly. Ya know, after it was over they drew numbers for turkeys and hams, and one year we even got one. But everybody who came took away an armload of stuff: canned soup, pork and beans, tuna fish. Things you wouldn't eat for Christmas, but it came in handy later on. I guess his name's stuck with me because he'd lead us to the main chapel for some kind of blessing before we went home, and he'd stand there in the pulpit with his Santa Claus suit and always end up by saying, 'Remember, Christ gave you Christmas but Reverend Hollis gave you the cranberry sauce.' "

"You've gotta be putting me on."

"Naw." Willie shook his head. "It may sound stupid now, but it made good sense when you were a kid because sometimes there would be a can of cranberries in our bag. And, man, that was some beautiful church. Nothing like Canaan Baptist. Double balconies, big brass organ pipes, and even a grand piano. You could almost be swallowed up in the red cushions on those seats. And carpet — they even had carpeting in the recreation room, where the party was. And these long, stained-glass windows that made the walls look like rainbows. It sorta made you understand what people meant when they said, house of God. That was some place to be at Christmas."

"I wouldn't know, Reverend Mason." Lester shoved a box into Willie's arms.

"How would you?" Willie turned and pushed the box roughly into the truck. "That party wasn't for the kids in Linden Hills."

"I mean, we were Episcopalians, Willie. And I never had a reason to go to Sinai Baptist any time of the year. Not that I went anywhere much after I got past the Sunday-school age. I just had a hard time accepting all those things they were supposed to be doing in the name of God. The name of which God? The God of the U.S. Treasury if you look at this place. And you can hate me if you want, but I just can't get all choked up over some joker giving a kid a Tonka truck once a year when his garage is almost as large as my house. That's an LTD over there, Willie — did you notice? The only thing I can remember them telling me Jesus ever rode was a donkey."

"Well, our minister at Canaan only drove an old Buick. And it's a wonder that he got enough out of that collection plate for the gas and oil."

"I hear Hollis's church is so slick they don't depend on no collection plates. They have this con game called 'tithing.' Roxanne thought about converting once when she was into her nationalist fever. Said it was more black to be Baptist. But when she found out that all the members of Sinai were expected to give a tenth of their incomes to the church — before taxes — she decided to stay an Episcopalian and just grow an Afro."

"Maybe that's why we never joined. I used to ask my mom why she only took us there for the party and she said the services at Mount Sinai were too dry; the folks at Canaan had more spirit. But thinking about it now, I guess she figured there was no point in trying to compete with folks whose ten percent could outfit a place like that when our hundred percent could barely clothe us. Ya know, I never thought about how she must have felt taking us to that party each year and having to sit in those pews." Willie stared off into space. "Anyway, it's water under

the bridge. And I don't care what you say, it did make
Christmas seem special, so I always thought that Reverend
Hollis was a special man."

The Right Reverend Michael T. Hollis stepped out of his bathtub. He groped around blindly for a towel and, realizing that
the rack was empty, stumbled to the clothes hamper and pulled
out a used one. Trying to focus despite his throbbing forehead,
he decided that the monogrammed side was the least soiled and
dried himself with that. Satan was always busy. Now, he knew
there were at least three sets of towels on that rack last night —
or was it the night before? See that, he couldn't remember and
he certainly wasn't going to waste time thinking about it. He
had a funeral to preach and he hadn't been late for a sermon in
twenty years. Devil or no devil, he was getting dressed for work.
A sudden pain flared up in his middle and stopped him at the
sink. He gripped its edge, belching up the taste of Scotch and
bile from his sour stomach. Bending well beneath the mirror, he
turned and gargled his mouth again. He needed to take something to coat his stomach and there was just no time for breakfast. Imagining his ulcer reddening and spreading because he
had to push himself through a service without eating was
strangely gratifying. He could add this to a growing list of sacrifices his job demanded.

Walking into the bedroom naked and opening his mahogany-
and-brass armoire, he thrust his hand toward the right and
pulled out a suit. His winter suits were arranged in gradation of
shades from the tans, brown, blues, and on toward the blacks. So
he knew a right-angle plunge should give him the appropriate
color for a funeral. He grunted at the charcoal tweed he found in
his hand and hung it on his silent valet. He should have been a
lawyer, like his brother. He knew where Gabriel was at this very
minute: in Aruba, his toes buried in the sand and his fingers
wrapped around a Mai Tai or the waist of some shapely tour
guide. Sure, *his* phone could be ringing off the hook right now
because someone decided to get born, get married, or drop dead.
You want to set up a trust fund, buy a house, or see a will? Some

secretary pushed a button and put them on hold. They'd have to wait until her boss ran out of money at the casino and came home. But when his congregation needed him, he was at their mercy. In just this one week someone had already decided to get married and to die, so what was he to do? And you couldn't put Sunday on hold. No, it rolled around every week in spite of what plans he had. No wonder Gabriel was always asking him if he was crazy. No, he wasn't crazy, he was called.

Michael didn't know it then, but that moment had come when he was twelve years old, sitting in the fifth row of his grandmother's weather-beaten church. The rough floorboards threatening to give way under the weight of those pounding feet. The sagging walls miraculously held up by the Tennessee heat pushing in and the body heat pushing out. The stale air, the clapping and swaying, put him to sleep, his eyes flying open whenever an unpredictable explosion of sound shattered the rhythm of his stupor. Was it the same man or a series of men behind that plywood podium? They all sounded and looked the same to him. The faces disfigured and melting from the moisture in his eyes and on their foreheads and temples. One of a hundred evenings he had to endure in one of a dozen vacations to the country.

There was nothing particularly memorable about that evening, except that he was more tired than usual after running with his cousins in the woods all day, and there was a huge mosquito bite on his left knee that kept itching. And definitely nothing outstanding about the minister on whom he couldn't focus through his heavy eyelids. But somewhere in his sleep, in the region where sound can live without words and words without sound, just as the vibrations were dreamed to him — *I am the voice of the one crying in the wilderness, make straight the way of the Lord* — a clap of thunderous hands snapped his neck up and his eyes open to engulf him in an intense flow of energy moving between the pews and the podium. In that moment the air had thickened, so that it crackled and sizzled around him, threatening to choke him as it closed in on his throat and chest, making it difficult to breathe what was left of the oxygen in that room. His

first lungful sent his head rolling onto his chest and in his sleep
he expelled that breath of power, fear, and mortality to draw in
another that gave life to the belief: here is a force that can destroy you if you don't control it. He stood there now in his bedroom, knowing that for some mysterious reason he had simply
wanted a career in the church, never remembering the origin of
that desire.

Turning toward the mirror over his dresser, he surveyed himself intently from the neck down and reached for his Aramis
body lotion. *Put on the whole armour of God that ye may be able to stand
against the wiles of the devil.* His bronze skin was almost as even
and firm as the day he entered college, with just a few gray hairs
mixed in with the auburn on his chest. His hands smoothed the
lotion over the lean muscled arms and torso, the flat plane of the
stomach and corded thighs that had qualified him for those
three letters in all-collegiate track and field and a three-minute
introduction into most beds on campus. The man of the hour.
The man most likely to succeed in business, law, economics, politics — or pimping (depending upon whether the poll was taken
in the faculty lounge or the student center). Yes, anything that
you could parlay a liberal arts degree and the ability to be
elected the first black captain of the debating team into — anything but the ministry.

His acceptance at Harvard surprised no one, but the fact that
it was the Divinity School made front page in the campus newspaper. The caption under his handsome face was predictable:
"U of P Star Athlete Headed for a Celestial Track." And since
his latest conquest was the editor's girlfriend, the tone was predictable as well. The staff wished him the best in this new race
for a heavenly crown, but wondered if his proven and much
publicized abilities to sprint past fleshly temptations and clear
the hurdles of egocentrism might not find him at a finish line
that was a bit farther South than he intended. Whether the congratulations that circled the campus during his final semester
were sincere or not, the bewilderment certainly was. Although
he skillfully answered a multitude of questions that basically
boiled down to "why?" with a dozen clever variations of "why

not?" no one left him completely satisfied because everyone knew that in four years Michael Hollis had never even made it to chapel. He was the last person to expect there Sunday mornings because he was the first person to pass out at the parties the night before.

But he had gone a few times in his freshman year, keeping a promise made to his grandmother that he wouldn't forget his "upbringing" and go to church. It only took him a couple of services to realize that going to chapel wasn't going to church. And so on Sunday afternoons he quietly left the dorm and drove past the manicured lawn and Gothic stones of the Penn chapel into South Philadelphia to sit in the back of reconverted candy stores with stained-glass cellophane peeling at the windows. Where, more often than not, the altar was a scarred wooden table with an oilskin cloth and plastic crucifix; the battered piano missing keys if not pitch; the chairs missing leg braces if not backs. And a congregation of determined, tired faces never seeming to miss the everything they never had or never would have once they walked out that door. He always sat quietly: a slender, polite young man who seemed to want nothing more than to offer a monogrammed handkerchief to a sister weeping from the spirit, or a pair of strong arms to another who had fallen on his polished calf loafers. They didn't wonder what he was doing there. Like their faith, he was absorbed for whatever brief comfort he might bring. Every Sunday (except for the weekends the track team competed out of state) Michael made the circuit: The Tabernacle of the Saints, The Zionist Mission, The House of Divine Ascension. The names changed constantly, but the feeling didn't. Sitting in the rear of those small rooms, he could almost see the currents racing from back to front and back again. The presence of that type of raw power connected up with something in his center, where it transformed fear into fascination and mortality into meaning. All of this surfaced to tell him that he was "called." He was meant to be at the center of that energy. And now all he needed was the training.

While filling out his application for Divinity School, he hesitated a moment before the blank after *denomination*. His family had been Baptists for generations and so he finally decided to write that. But the line filled in with his second career choice was instinctual and it may have puzzled the admissions committee. Since he wasn't questioned, he didn't have to explain why, if the Divinity School turned him down, he would have become an electrical engineer.

Stand therefore, having your loins girt about with truth, and having on the breastplate of righteousness. The pima-cotton boxer shorts slid over his thighs and he fumbled in the drawer for an undershirt. The material responded like cashmere under his fingers as he pulled it over his chest and smoothed it down. Marie had never let him wear undershirts at Harvard. After cutting one of her classes at Radcliffe or standing up a prospective MBA, she was subject to showing up at his room any time of the day or night. Arms full of oranges, salami, and beer that were dropped directly on top of his open books. Her small fingers impatient at even the shirt buttons and belt buckle that took her only sec-onds — that was enough effort, she'd say. And God knows, he didn't want to tire her out. Not before the lights were off and he had to adjust his eyes to the soft, muted outlines of a body that blended so evenly with the shadows. Even in a weak afternoon light it was impossible to tell where her hairline ended and the satin of her skin began. If he didn't have light sheets, he'd never find her in the dark, he'd tease. And she'd let him know in that strange, cryptic fashion of hers that the strength and length of his *eyesight* were the least of her concerns at the moment. He could feel the tensions draining out of his body as she made him laugh, the piles of books and doubts left on his desk dissolving. His beautiful Marie. He quickly told her, although she had never asked, that a man like him shouldn't marry until fifty. But when the time came, not of imagining a life with her, but of being unable to imagine one without her, he invited her to see how he spent his Sunday afternoons.

At first he was nervous about dragging a doctor's daughter from Cambridge to Roxbury. But she sat through the service quietly, her gloved hands tapping on the silk dress and the red pillbox hat, nodding in time to the music. When it was over she simply turned to him and smiled, and without his needing to explain, she understood. But, of course, with his type of degree he wouldn't have to work in places like this. Not if he planned to support her and the three children they wanted: one for each of them and one to convince themselves that they weren't insane to begin it all in the first place. But if he simply insisted on his fondness for cramped rooms that smelled of stale cabbage, at least she could console herself with the fact that he wasn't called to the Catholic priesthood. And just to safeguard herself against that being a future possibility, she presented him with a graduation gift of a dozen of the whitest sheets he had ever seen.

Yes, it was impossible to imagine the texture of his existence if Marie had not been there to understand. She understood his frustrations over the irrelevancy of courses in Latin, Greek, and German. The eternal wading through papers on the sociological implications of the Nicene Council, Gnosticism and Early Christianity, the dialectics of Hegelian thought, all to the end of forgetting it and going about what he wanted to do in the first place. She understood his scorn about what Harvard considered a "model sermon," and she brought the champagne with which they celebrated his Th.D. and laughed with him over its real meaning: total horse dung. She followed him away from Boston, accepting that her own career would have to be put aside because there was a strange correlation between a community's increasing need for ministers and decreasing need for psychologists. She even understood that the discovery of his sterility, which deprived her of the children that could have then filled up her life, was somehow much more devastating for him than her.

But after twelve years, Marie could not understand the other women. He saw her trying. God, how he saw her do that. And he had wanted so very much to help her. But since you couldn't talk about what wasn't happening, he couldn't tell her that he respected her too much to ever have it be anyone in the church. There was no need for that hard, guarded look in her eyes when she sat on the Missionary Board or Ladies' Auxiliary. No, there was just no way to tell her the truth, that his infidelities hurt him much more than her because he had to watch the only woman he could say he ever really loved crumble inside bit by bit.

Was it the month she brought home the dark brown sheets, or

the month they moved to Linden Hills? He knew it wasn't the day she left, because he had already lost the days before and after that. He could remember saying to himself, She left last week, when the new week finally became clear. Even eight years later he could point to the very chair where he had sat for three days — completely sober — and cried. So it didn't begin then. It must have been a few years before, in the month they moved here, which was the same month she bought those sheets. Yes, his new post at Sinai Baptist, the coup of his career, the one that came complete with a home in Linden Hills — that was when. The bottom became the top.

. . . And your feet shod with the preparation of the gospel of peace. He sat on the bed and pulled on a pair of black silk socks and reached for his wing-tipped shoes. Bending over his knees caused his head to pound, and his hands trembled slightly as he looked down at his feet. With a sigh he realized that he hadn't put his trousers on and so the shoes would have to be taken off again. Maybe, if he was careful, he could slip his feet through anyway. And if he ruined the suit, that would teach him to pay attention next time. Had that been the problem? He just didn't pay attention when the line that brought him to the top of his form kept receding? At first it was a quarter, then it was half. Half of the bottle — halfway up the pews? The ratio couldn't be that exact. Then, as the churches got larger, the boards he headed more impressive, and the budgets doubled — tripled — it took much more to enable him to reach up those pews to the line where the right ones were to keep the current flowing. He was fooled for so long because the faces seemed the same out there — the various shades of brown that he knew could produce the sparks needed to refuel his efforts. But the postures in front of the church had slowly stiffened under the cashmere, silk, and beaver skins, so he had to reach over them to the others, where he felt a supple willingness to receive, be filled, and return the energy he needed to keep going. Then the line was three-fourths because they were now sitting all the way up in the back. And it was left to him to find something to help generate a circular current over the heads and bodies that threatened to absorb the flow with their plastic postures.

. . . Above all, taking the shield of faith, wherewith ye shall be able to quench all the fiery darts of the wicked. Quickly now, the oxford cloth shirt, black tie knotted without looking above the Adam's apple, initialed gold cuff links. Vest. Jacket. He began to take form, as he always did, behind the proclamative work of Tiffany, Pierre Cardin, Hart Schaffner & Marx, Shreve Crump & Lowe, Yves Saint Laurent, Cartier, and the two Brooks Brothers. They faithfully covered his front, back, fingers, wrists, and neck with the message that the Right Reverend Michael T. Hollis was ready for the outside world.

Did he really need a vest? Yes, even with his gabardine robe the church would probably be cold. Sinai Baptist had a persistent draft that defied the heating system. A cold church. After his first sermon, he remembered asking the former pastor if Sinai was always that cold and being told: Yes, but the board of trustees had just approved a new furnace. He could have gone home and laughed about that with Marie, but by then he couldn't find her at night. If those dark sheets weren't always on the bed, he could have told her why he started sponsoring those Christmas parties for Putney Wayne out of his own pocket. The board had refused, since all allocations for "foreign communities" were already tied up building mission homes in South Africa. He really didn't mind the personal cost, because if he could find a way to bring them there at Christmas, they might come back during the year. And they had at first, sitting in the back pews and the balconies, but gradually drifting away to where they could be free to worship as they believed: that the *spirit* of God meant just that. They left him alone, and he could have gone with them but he had already reached the bottom. And it took only one-fourth of the new bottle for him to believe that there still might be hope at the top. He could still stand up at the pulpit, feeling the inner warmth that meant the power was still there, and the power gave meaning to it all. Because without that — in spite of the multimillion-dollar credit union, his presidency at the Northeastern Baptist Council, his seat on the governor's planning board — somehow, he had no ministry. And his ministry was his life.

He was ready except for his hair . . . *And take the helmet of salva-*

tion. Slowly, he put his hand on the brush and brought it up toward his face. He tried to concentrate on the soft curls at his hairline, gauging the rapidly advancing gray. But there was no way not to see that a stranger was brushing his hair. The red-rimmed eyes with heavy folds under them hanging like puffed bruises. The furrowed brow that could easily hold a coin, and the slack jawline. He told himself the usual lie, it was a face that looked like death. Harsh as it was, it was better than the truth: it was a face that looked like it had no reason to live.

Heading downstairs toward the kitchen, he passed long strands of tinsel on the steps, and picked his way around smashed tree ornaments — the silvery greens, reds, and golds littering the coffee table and floor. The tall Christmas tree stood half-trimmed and leaned at a precarious thirty-degree angle. The empty ashtrays told him that he hadn't had any company last night — unless it was a nonsmoker. He found his missing bath towels mangled on the kitchen floor, lying in gummy pools of drying eggnog. That's what happened to them. But why had he gone all the way upstairs to get something to clean up this mess? He glanced over the kitchen counter crowded with egg shells, spilled sugar, open cartons of souring milk, and saw that the paper-towel rack was empty. So that was it. He would have to speak to the cleaning woman after the holidays. God knows, he paid her enough to keep his supplies in the proper place.

Stepping carefully over the mess, he opened the refrigerator door. There wasn't even time to brew a cup of coffee, and there was no point in looking for the instant; it had probably gone the way of the paper towels. Besides, the doctor told him that too much coffee would irritate his ulcer. He took out the pitcher of eggnog, the Scotch and nutmeg giving it a rich brown tint. He'd have to settle for this. At least there were eggs in it — protein. And the cream would coat his stomach. He waited a moment and felt his muscles relax after the first cup, and after the second, his hands didn't tremble as much. One more and his head would probably stop throbbing. He needed a clear head for this funeral today. Nedeed would just love to see him fall on his face. The man hated him, he knew that. Well, it was just too bad. He had been hired to straighten up affairs at Sinai and the first order of business was to examine the records of the board of trustees.

Imagine, that man had been sitting on the board for over ten years and he wasn't even baptized. And when he refused to do that — out he went. He finally saw that his money couldn't buy him everything. What kind of egomaniac was he anyway, wanting to be at the center of whatever was going on? Well, he had no say about what went on in Mount Sinai or this house. He was the only one in Linden Hills who didn't owe the Nedeeds a thing. The church gave him his mortgage. And Nedeed couldn't touch him for a thousand years and a day, not that either of them was going to live that long. Let him run around feeling high and mighty because he gave them a box to live in and a box to die in. But he needed Michael Hollis as much as the rest. Didn't he show Nedeed about the Parker funeral? It was to be held in his church and not some godforsaken funeral parlor if it was to be held at all. He had him over a barrel on that one. Just like his house number — showed him he could pull a few strings at the zoning commission as well. What did Nedeed think he was saying with an address like 999 Tupelo Drive? If the first house on First Crescent Drive was 100, and the first on Second Crescent Drive 200, then the *only* house down on the last street of Tupelo Drive should be 900 if anything. Well, if his house could be 999, the Hollis home could be 000. Luther Nedeed might see himself as the omega, but Reverend Michael T. Hollis was the alpha.

The fourth cup of eggnog started toward his mouth and he paused. This stuff was too sweet and all that sugar wasn't going to do anything but upset his stomach. He poured half of it into the sink and diluted the rest with Scotch. The heat moved from his middle, spreading out to his limbs, the tips of his fingers and making a full circuit back to the lining of his tongue. *And for me, that utterance may be given unto me that I may open my mouth boldly, to make known the mystery of the gospel* . . . Draining the cup, he went to the closet for his cashmere overcoat, searching the pockets for his mints and tinted glasses before opening the front door on the chill December morning.

For which I am an ambassador in chains.

Willie shoved the last box into the truck. "Well, we've loaded the thing now. Is he gonna drive it?"

"Naw, he told me to do it."

"Shit, you don't have a license."

"He didn't ask me if I had a license. He asked me if I knew how to drive and I told him, yeah."

"You've got no shame, you know that. Lying to a minister."

"It wasn't a lie. I just didn't volunteer any unnecessary information."

"Yeah, well it's gonna get to be real necessary if a cop stops you."

"Look, all we gotta do is follow right behind his car all the way to the church and do whatever he does. If he makes an illegal turn, we make one. He runs a red light, we run one. And if a cop shows up, we just point to that card in the windshield and say we're with the preacher. You ever heard of a minister getting hauled in for a traffic violation? They're like politicians and diplomats, with special vaccinations or something."

"The word is *immunity*. And where did the *we* come in? It's only three days till Christmas and the me part of your we ain't spending it in jail. I'll start walking and meet you over there."

"It's a long walk, White — uphill."

"It's even longer to the precinct."

"And it's cold out there."

"You don't have to worry. I hear there's central heating now, even in solitary confinement."

"Well, look, if you're dead set against coming with me, hitch a ride with Hollis. And it's probably a lot more comfortable in that chariot than this pickup truck."

"Man, how am I gonna do that? He'll wonder why I'm not with you."

"Well, tell him you want a Bible verse explained or something. You wanna turn your life around from the path of evil.

They get a big kick out of stuff like that. Chances are you won't get a word in edgewise anyway. Before he's warmed up good, you'll be over at Sinai."

They saw Hollis shut the front door and cut across the lawn toward the garage.

"Here's your chance, Willie," Lester whispered. "Tell him it's Ezakiah six eight."

"You're crazy, I never heard of no Ezakiah in the Bible."

"Neither has he, but do you think he'll admit it — just in case you're right?"

Hollis hesitated for a moment when he saw them. "Oh, I forgot you were out here. I was wondering why my garage door was up." His tinted glasses took in the tightly packed truck. "You've done a fine job, uh, Lester. Now, which one of you is Lester?"

"Me." Lester smiled.

"Yes, it's quite fine. Excuse me for not recognizing you, but we've only met over the phone, right?"

"Right. And this is my friend, Willie Mason, who really did most of the work 'cause he's heavy into church things."

"That's not true," Willie said. "I mean, about the work. But it's a real pleasure to meet you, Reverend Hollis. Face to face, that is, because we've met before but you —"

"Oh, really. Where?"

"At Mount Sinai," Willie said and Hollis relaxed noticeably. "My mother always took us to the Christmas parties you gave. And I was just telling Lester how great they were and it's really something that you're still doing it. Ya know, I was really glad when I found out you were the one we were working for today and I had a chance to help out with this now that I'm older. I guess" — Willie stalled for a moment — "I'm making a fool of myself, but I'm just trying to say that doing this gave me a small way to say thank you for giving us so much of yourself."

"Why, son, that's quite touching." Hollis went over and shook his hand. "It's moments like this that make my ministry worthwhile. And your contributions of time and labor are greatly appreciated by the church."

"No offense, Reverend," Lester said as he stared at Willie,

"but we were Episcopalians. And I never had a chance to get to those parties. So anything that Sinai can do in behalf of my time and labor would be doubly appreciated."

"Of course." Hollis laughed. "The scriptures say that a workman is worthy of his hire. As soon as the Parker funeral is over and you've unloaded these things, we'll settle accounts. You know the way to the church, don't you?"

"Yeah, but Willie was wondering if he could ride with you. There're a few things he wanted to discuss — matters of faith."

"No, that's all right, I'll ride in the truck. You're in a hurry."

"I'm never in too much of a hurry for something like that. Come on, we can talk while I drive."

Before Willie followed Hollis over to his car, he mouthed to Lester, "I'll get you for this, so help me God."

"Aw, Willie, don't mention it," Lester said loudly. "It was just a small way for me to say thank you for so much of your help this morning."

The padded car door closed behind Willie with a soft thud. The engine turned over with the same smooth power that he felt in the tufted leather at his back and the deep carpet under his feet. And the first thrust from the accelerator sent a quiet sensation through his thighs and into the base of his stomach. "This is really a nice car." The tinted glass cast a blue film onto the street as they rolled out of the garage. "Four-wheel drive, too. I can tell by the way it moves."

"Yes, it's useful in the winter, living on a steep incline like this. If we get a really bad storm, I would need chains even with my snow tires. And I hate the way they affect the smoothness of the ride once I'm on level ground." Hollis reached down to adjust the heat. "So, there were some things you wanted to ask me?" He turned and smiled at Willie, who couldn't figure out why he still needed those sunglasses on such a cloudy day and with tinted windows.

"Well, uh, not exactly. It's just that . . ." He dragged his words out to buy himself time and turned his head toward the side window to hide the panic in his face. The house number rolled by. "It's just that I was wondering about your address — the

three zeros. And everyone else's on the street is five hundred
something. I'm sure that it has some sort of spiritual meaning."

"Why, son, that's quite perceptive of you. As a matter of fact,
it does."

Willie's deep breath carried a silent prayer of gratitude to
whoever cared to listen.

"But they aren't zeros, they're *O*'s. Three eternal circles that
are quite appropriate for a home owned by the church. And
after that hint, I'm sure you can guess what they stand for."

The only thing that came to Willie's mind was a basketball
court. But that had five circles, when you counted the hoops.
That only left him the three circles that used to be on the Bal-
lantine beer commercials.

"Well, to be quite honest, I can think of a lot of things that
might fit. But I'll let you tell me."

"The Father, Son, and Holy Ghost."

"Oh, of course."

"Yes, the holy trinity. Each having no beginning and no end.
I wanted that as a reminder to the community — and myself —
that there are so many forces that govern our lives beyond the
material, the tangible. There is to be an accounting, son, for
each and every one of us. And we can't balance those books with
our stock dividends. We better pay heed to that on this side, because when we get to the other side and the body is gone, we
might just find ourselves with no soul as well."

As Hollis talked, the rapidly warming air brought the faint
scent of sour peppermint toward Willie, carried clearly by all of
the words beginning and ending with *s*. The this, is, stock, soul,
side, *Son*. Willie knew he could have hidden the alcohol more
easily if he didn't use those words. His father stumbling home,
smelling of licorice Sen-Sen and wintergreen Chiclets: "Come
here, son." If he had only called him "Willie" when he woke him
up like that at night; then there would have been a little time to
relax, a breath in which to believe that for once it was affection
or legitimate urgency that prompted what he had to say. But the
"son" told him as soon as he opened his eyes that he was going to
stand between his father's knees for hours, listening to a hundred

questions that didn't want answers even if a ten-year-old had
them. That any indication of a desire to sleep would be to risk a
slap across the ears — or worse, the sight of the man crying. If
his eldest son didn't understand, then who would? Son. Ram-
blings that made no sense, accusations that had no target beyond some mysterious "they." The same sort of double-talk that
he was obviously being handed now. Willie looked at the side of
Hollis's face and wondered what those zeros on his house really
meant, but now he knew why he needed the tinted glasses.

"It may be pressing the point to have it on my front lawn, but
as an ordained minister, the burden does fall on me. I can't just
lie back when so much is at stake. I've been around for quite a
while, son, and believe me, our people have changed. There used
to be a real concern in the church with spirituality. Now, it's get
what you can while you can, because you don't know what the
next world will bring or even if there is a next."

"No, I don't think it's pressing the point at all." Willie had already blocked Hollis out. As they stoped at the intersection of
Linden Road and Wayne Avenue, he peered up the street, hoping that someone he knew would recognize him in the car. It
wasn't often that he showed up on that corner in an LTD. "And
I'm sure people will notice your sign. We've been working in
your neighborhood all week and Fifth Crescent Drive has the
nicest homes so far, and yours is really the best one on that
street." He thought he saw Norman Anderson, but he was
wrong. "When I found out it was your place, I said to myself, 'I
bet Reverend Hollis is as rich as Luther Nedeed.' "

Hollis couldn't detect any sarcasm in his voice and he looked
at Willie sharply to see if there was any in his eyes, but his head
was turned. Hollis snorted, "That's hardly the case. My meager
salary and the upkeep of that house is a small repayment for my
services to the church and the community. Why, this car already
has fifty thousand miles on it and it's barely two years old. I'm
surprised there's not more mileage than that with all my running around to see the sick and shut-ins, getting to a dozen
neighborhood meetings a week, and God knows how many con-
ventions a year. Although you could draw a straight line from

my front door to Nedeed's down there at the bottom of that hill, there's a huge difference between how I earn my subsistence and how he does. Why, my life is devoted to the Lord and he's a . . . Well, never mind."

One of Hollis's sentences caught Willie's attention. "Is that true? Your house is in a direct line with his?"

"According to the maps at the zoning commission, and it's much larger, too. The only thing he has going for him is that his house was built before anyone else's. He may have been squatting down there since the nineteenth century, but the church has owned the acreage for my home almost as long. Do you know the Nedeeds have been lobbying for generations to revoke the property-tax exemption on my house? Now, if that's not blasphemy, what is? And I'm not telling you anything that isn't public knowledge. Sure, you could run a rope from my front door to his, but it better be fireproof when it gets to the end of Tupelo Drive." Hollis smirked.

"Do you ever see his wife?"

Hollis swung the car around a sharp turn. "Now, why would I see any man's —"

"On the street." Willie frowned at him. "Since your homes are so close, or perhaps at church. I was just wondering what she looked like."

"No, I've never seen her." His voice was clipped. "That part of Linden Hills is poorly represented at Mount Sinai. You see, that brings us right back to the problem I was talking about before. They're so concerned beyond those brick pillars about making a heaven on earth, it never dawns on them that it won't be forever in spite of those deceptive mortgages. And quite frankly, Luther Nedeed sets a bad example for the rest. He claims to be a Baptist, but he didn't even ask for a minister to bury his father and he's never brought his boy to Sunday school and the child must be four or five by now. So how can you expect the rest to do any better when he has an attitude like that? It won't do him any good, mind you, he's fighting a losing cause. Remember that old spiritual, It's so high you can't get over it, So wide you can't get around it, So deep you can't . . ." Hollis gripped the steering wheel and pressed his foot down on the accelerator as he kept chanting fiercely under his breath. ". . . you gotta come in at the door. So high you can't get . . ." The car shot up to seventy and the streets were becoming a blur. He was perspiring, the odor of moist tin coming through his after-shave. He went into a second round and the car was now up to eighty, and Willie expected him to start singing. Then they would definitely be in trouble. He wasn't worried about the police, but there was no immunity from telephone poles for anyone.

"That's a nice ring you have on." He tried to cut off the spiritual in Hollis's third round, almost shouting as he pointed to the opal stone with a diamond-studded insignia. "I recognize the symbol. My father used to belong to the Masonic lodge."

The car skidded past one red light, and Hollis jammed on the brakes at the second. "Oh, did he get fed up like me? You see, that's another one of the thousand things I have to subject myself —"

"No, he died," Willie cut him off, "four years ago."

"That's a pity. He had to be a relatively young man."

"Yeah." Willie looked out the side window. "It was cirrhosis of the liver."

"That's a slow and painful way to go. It must have been hard on your mother."

"It was a lot harder for her when he was alive. He used to beat up on her." He was watching Hollis's face. "I don't tell many people this, but you know, when I was a kid I really hated him for that, and a lot of the other things he put us through. When I got a little older, I realized it wasn't really him doing all those things, it was the booze. I guess he drank to forget, ya know? 'Cause there was a lot out there he needed to forget if he was gonna keep going. But then it got so that he started forgetting everything — like why six kids and a wife weren't speaking to him the next morning, and how all those people found a way to give him a lot of space in a little apartment. I don't really know what my dad thought the bottom of that bottle could do for him, Reverend Hollis, but it had to do something." Willie frowned and looked out the window again. "No, it had to do everything for him. Because after a while, that's all he had and it seemed like enough."

The light turned green but Hollis still sat there, staring at Willie. "You know, son —"

"Please, don't call me 'son.'" The request hung between anger and sadness.

"I'm sorry, I do remember that your name is Willie. And I make it a habit to call people by their names. I guess in the back of my mind I was thinking that you could easily be the child I never had. My wife was about your complexion, and she was sharp and sensitive like you are."

"Was? Is she dead, too?"

"You might say that." And Hollis took off quickly from the light.

Willie wondered if the alcohol was the only reason she left. He didn't think of ministers as being the type of men who would abuse a woman, but then he had never thought of them drinking before ten o'clock in the morning. Maybe he didn't have to hit her. Women were funny. He'd seen that in his mother. They could stand up under things you'd expect to keel them over, and then bruise so easily from something that shouldn't matter much. No, it had to be something besides the drinking. To leave a house like that and a man with a job like this, it had to be something else pretty awful — at least, to her.

He was relieved when Hollis finally pulled up in back of the church, and even more relieved that he had decided to ride with him: although they had done an easy seventy most of the way, Lester was already waiting there with the truck. Willie thanked Hollis for the lift and started to open the door. Hollis touched his arm and reached into his pocket for a Life Saver.

"You want one?"

"No, thanks."

"They don't help, do they?"

"Naw, and gargling doesn't either. Not if you use that syrupy stuff. Next time try rinsing with a little vinegar or straight lemon juice. My dad discovered that was the best way. Something about the acid neutralizes it."

"Let's pray there won't be a next time, Willie."

"Yeah." Willie got out and closed the door.

"Willie!" The car window slid down and Willie stopped without looking back. "Merry Christmas."

"Merry Christmas, Reverend Hollis," he answered while looking up at the huge gray stones of Mount Sinai.

Hollis sat there for a moment and then followed Willie's gaze with a deep sigh. He pulled around to the front of the church and saw that Nedeed had parked his hearse in the spot assigned for the minister. Hollis double-parked so that the hearse couldn't be moved without getting his keys. That young man had taught him one thing this morning: there are many subtle ways with which you can make one strong point.

Consciousness returned long before she opened her eyes. She lay balled up under the covers in a gentle stupor, willing herself to sleep again. The heaviness in her head and the lightness in her limbs and middle were almost pleasant. If she concentrated on either, she could float back to where there were no thoughts, just dreams that she was too tired to remember. Lying there, she could believe that she had dreamed that evening out in the mortuary. Hadn't it been pushed safely into a place that firmly locked in the unthinkable along with all the other insane nightmares that threatened to break through on reality? It had to be a dream or she couldn't have kept living with the man she saw in the mortuary that evening. She would have packed her things and taken her child away long ago, wouldn't she?

The doubts kept her there. The poor lighting. The angle of the embalming table. She had been looking for something suspicious anyway, something to explain her lonely nights in that half-empty bed. Her checking through his wallet and address book came up with nothing. She had even watched him and his male assistant closely for some telltale sign so obvious in those moments when they didn't look at each other, had no reason to touch. And so hadn't she gone out back that evening, hoping to find something? What did her mother always say — you find what you're looking for.

But she had only found him working: the white lab coat, the tubes and needles that made her shudder even when packed away. She had never witnessed this part of his work before, but obviously it had to be so. He had to undress those bodies, move his hands slowly over the skin to check for the flow of the formaldehyde. Those weren't breasts, thighs, hips; they were points of saturation. He was a technician — she knew that. He wasn't seeing ears, mouths, nostrils, and vaginas; they were openings that had to be cleared of foreign matter. And the room was cold. He trembled so because the room must be kept almost to the point of freezing. The paint. The powder. His lingering and carefulness. The success of his work depended upon it. The body had to look natural. The lipstick. Eyeshadow. Mascara. The precision made him perspire, made him bend over and concentrate that closely. It could all be explained: the utensils, the cosmetics, the care. It made her feel foolish and dirty, crouching outside in the shadows and peering under a shade at him. And that's why she turned back toward the house and ran, her heart pounding, her hand pressed against her mouth to keep from screaming or throwing up.

She ran from guilt, not from the sight of him lifting a fish head out of a plastic bag and turning it gently in his hands before inserting it in the spread body before him. She had dreamed that. And like all bad dreams, she awoke from it with a severe headache the next morning and no appetite for days. But she could thank God as she fixed him his breakfast the following day and took his shirts to the laundry, that there was a safe place for such nightmares. Then, she could keep so frantically busy with her housework and her child that at night she was just too tired to dream. And in that space of time between exhaustion and unconsciousness if her hand ever strayed to the cold place on the sheet beside her, she could sanely accept that reality; this was simply the way life was when your husband's work took him away so much at night.

Luther was draping a mesh blanket of silver fern and white roses over Lycentia Parker in her open casket when Hollis walked into the main chapel. He had been there almost at daybreak, chalking the exact location for the coffin, rearranging the positions of the floral wreaths while checking for any wilted blossoms or yellowing leaves. Then he had returned to Tupelo Drive to lead the procession to the church, and he would be the last to leave the burial site, waiting until the cemetery workers had completely filled in the grave. He turned and nodded to Hollis.

"Michael."

"Luther." Holllis went to walk past him toward his office.

"I'm glad to see that you're finally here," Luther said as he rested his hand on the coffin. "I was afraid that we would have to start without you."

"That was a needless fear," Hollis said, smiling, "since there's no way to start without me."

"Not really." Luther returned his smile. "The program calls for the choir to sing a Bach requiem after the guests file in. And then you make your entrance. Since it's a rather lengthy piece, I assumed there would be a space of at least thirty minutes in which you wouldn't be missed."

"Well, there's been a change of program, so it's a good thing you didn't embarrass yourself by being premature."

"Oh, really? Is it anything about which I should inform the family of the deceased?"

"The family of the deceased already knows what it has to. I'm responsible for this service. And you're responsible for moving the body in and out of my church. And I must say, you've done a good job so far, Luther. But then you've always had a knack of doing whatever you do thoroughly. I've never had any complaints about your performance, that's one thing I must admit."

"Or I of yours, Michael." Luther's eyes seemed to undress him. "No complaints at all."

Hollis turned abruptly, went into his office, and slammed the door. He picked up the phone and pressed the intercom for the superintendent's office.

"Ralph, good morning, Reverend Hollis. Listen, could you do me a favor and go to the choir's dressing room and have Mary Beth Wilson come here. Tell her it's important, there are some changes for the Parker funeral. Yes, yes, I know about the boys. After they've set up the tree, have them wait for me in the lobby.

And just one more thing, my throat is pretty dry so could you see if there are any lemons in the pantry. Okay, thanks."

Hollis put down the receiver and tapped his forefinger nervously against it. A Bach requiem. You'd never be missed. He'd show him just how much he'd be missed. He yanked open the bottom drawer on his desk and took out a bulky, maroon altar cloth. He quickly unwrapped the fifth of Scotch and had filled his water glass three times before shoving it back into the drawer. Popping a mint into his mouth, he went to the closet and removed his gabardine-and-velvet robe. The Santa Claus suit was hanging next to it, freshly pressed and under plastic. He forced himself to look at the mirror on the inside of his closet door, starting with his face and moving all the way down. Is this what that young man saw? A six foot, aging disappointment who had to put on a clown's outfit once a year to feel that he really counted at the pulpit. Any other time he could stand out there immobile with his mouth shut and play a tape recorder and no one would notice. If he missed a business meeting, if the credit union's dividends fell, he would probably lose his job. But what was his job? Any dictionary defined him as an agent of God, but he had never seen and would be hard-pressed to prove the existence that justified this building and the last thirty years of his life. What had drawn him was the power that was possible between people; together they created "God" — so real and electrifying you could believe that once it was a voice that shook mountains. That was what he had set out to follow. But somehow, somewhere, it was a calling that went wrong. He went back to take another drink just before there was a knock on the door.

The short, plump woman came in carrying two lemons on a saucer.

"Ralph asked me to bring these to you, Reverend. And I know what you gonna say about that music. You probably heard how lousy we sounded at choir practice, but you can't turn a sow's ear into a silk purse is all I've got to say. I can read them notes, but Lord knows, I can't make heads or tails out of that Latin. So if it sounds flat, it sounds flat."

"Believe me, criticism was the last thing on my mind, Sister Wilson. Please sit down."

She gathered her robes around her and sat on the edge of the chair.

"To be quite honest, I agree with you. And I know that you and the musical director have a history of differences about the interpretations of the hymns."

"Look, I don't know nothing about no differences of interpretation. I may not have been to some fancy conservatory in Paris like Byron has, but I've been a member of the Baptist Church all my life. And I come up knowing only one way to do things — the way we did it down home. And when I was lead soprano for the Dixie Mockingbirds I never got no complaints about my *inappropriate passion* as he puts it. But I guess there's singing and there's singing." She paused for a weighted moment. "Just like there's preaching and there's preaching."

"And there's been precious little of both at Mount Sinai, hasn't there, Sister Wilson?"

"Now, I'm calling no names and naming no particulars, Reverend Hollis. We all don't have to see eye to eye in order to see our way to the Kingdom. It's the heart condition of each man that the Lord will judge."

"Well, I want you to know that I definitely see eye to eye with you about the musical selections this morning. And they're out. I spent a lot of time in the church down home, too, Sister Wilson. And I remember that all a real funeral ever needed was a decent sermon and a decent song to put a soul away. If it was good enough for my grandmother, it should be good enough for Lycentia Parker. So what do you say? Go tell Byron and the choir that we won't be needing them this morning, and you and I can give these people a little of what they've been missing."

"Sounds good to me, Reverend. But ain't this one of Mr. Nedeed's funerals? I don't know how all this is gonna sit with those folks from Linden Hills."

"To my knowledge, Sister Wilson, neither Mr. Nedeed nor anyone else from Linden Hills is sitting up there with the Lord on his heavenly throne. And since we're hoping that's exactly where Sister Parker is heading, I think we should announce her arrival in a manner that will be heard."

The woman laughed as she got up and headed for the door. "I like your spirit, Reverend Hollis. You know, for a while I was worried about you."

Hollis just smiled and thought, For a while I was worried about myself, but that's over. Then he said aloud, "Do you know what song you'll start with?"

"Of course." She grinned. "No real funeral would be complete without 'Amazing Grace.' "

Hollis stumbled on the third step up to the pulpit and hoped no one noticed. He clasped a hand on each side of the lectern to steady himself. But perhaps it wasn't his body that was moving so crazily but the chapel. No, it was perfectly still. The faces were a blur, but he could see that at least half of the pews downstairs were filled on both sides of the aisle. If he could have focused, he would have noticed the look of dry-eyed resignation before him. The mourners sat there with the stilted patience that accompanies the beginning of a business meeting. A few even glanced at their watches. This time the agenda was death and they had simply come to pay their respects. But like all debts, if the process was too lengthy and complicated, the feelings of obligation would turn into resentment.

Hollis could feel the sweat rolling down his back under the heavy robe. The words on the sermon in front of him were totally incomprehensible, and he tried to buy his spinning head some time by making a pretense of looking with studied attention at the coffin to his left, the papers on the lectern, and then the congregation. When he had rotated full circle to his right side, where Sister Wilson sat poised at the organ, she gave him a slow wink.

"All rise for the family to enter." His voice was husky and cracked at the end, but it was covered by the first rich notes of the organ that began a winding dirge as the Parker family filed in to take their seats in the two front rows. Chester Parker led the procession, tottering on the arms of a niece. He met the intense curiosity that accompanied his entrance by pulling out his handkerchief midway down the aisle, letting it hang in his hand like a crumpled flag that said at least *he* was ready to mourn.

As soon as the family was seated, Hollis nodded to Sister Wilson and the last chords of the dirge were followed immediately by the unaccompanied chords of the human voice — "A-mazing Grace!" The first words cut through the chapel — loud, clear, and piercing. Then the rest were backed by the mellowness of the brass pipes.

> . . . How sweet the sound,
> That saved a wretch like me.

The heat was building in Hollis's body and throbbing in his temples. His blurred eyes moved past the first twenty rows and filled the empty pews with thirty-year-old ghosts. In the balcony he saw the damp bodies swaying, hands up, and heads lifted by Sister Wilson's voice. They were waiting for him. If he would give, they would receive. Just call and they would answer.

> I once was lost but now I'm found,
> Was blind but now I see.

Sister Wilson was leaning over the keyboard, turning one syllable into two, two into three. And not knowing what to do with four, she just balled them up and melted them over the walls and ceilings. Melted them over that frozen rectangle in the first twenty rows, and they began to stir uncomfortably.

The power was charging up through the floor and out of the balconies. The ends of Hollis's fingers tingled and his center was filling up. He couldn't keep this contained inside of him and survive. It was now or never. He had to preach for his life.

> 'Twas grace that taught my heart to fear
> And grace my fears relieved.
> How precious did that grace appear
> The hour — the very hour — I first believed.

When she went into the second chorus, he began to speak. And Sister Wilson knew what to do, she stroked the keys softly and hummed behind his words.

"I had a sermon prepared for today." Hollis held up the papers that he couldn't read. "But I said to myself, 'What good is a *prepared* speech when we're never prepared for death?' "

"Amen!" Sister Wilson called from behind the organ.

"Yes, I was going to take my text from John, Chapter Eleven. And you all know what John, Chapter Eleven, is about."

"I know, I know." Sister Wilson swayed.

Apparently, she was the only one. The others sat there stunned by the performance unfolding in front of them. But Hollis needed only that one voice and he could hear it echoed from the back and the balconies.

"It's about when Mary came to Jesus and said, 'Lord, my brother is dead. And if you had been there, he wouldn't have died.' And Jesus wept."

"Yes, he did."

"He wept because he loved Lazarus. Loved him like a brother — better than a brother. Loved him like you loved our dear Sister Parker."

"Oh, yes. Oh, yes." This time Sister Wilson was joined loudly by Chester Parker, who used his handkerchief to wipe his perspiring head.

"So you can see even our Lord wasn't prepared for that kind of sorrow. And I said to myself, 'Are you better than Him? Can a servant be greater than his master?' "

"Never. Never."

"So I sat in my office this morning and *I* wept. I wept like a baby because our sister was gone. And I'm coming out here now to tear up this sermon." He held the pages over his head, ripped them apart, and threw the pieces at the audience.

"I'm doing what Jesus did. I'm not prepared. Was Jesus prepared?"

"No, sir!"

"And you're not prepared either. No one is prepared for death. But death comes. Yes, it comes. It comes sneaking up — all quiet and soft. And it knows no names."

"No names."

"It knows no occupations. No rich man or poor. It knows no

Linden Hills or Putney Wayne. But it knew *her.*" His left finger
shot out toward the coffin as he leaned over the podium and
glared at the audience. "And it knows *you.*" He swung the finger
in front of him. "And it knew Lazarus. Didn't know he was the
brother of Mary and Martha. Didn't know he was a friend of
Jesus. But death knew it was time."

"Time, Lord, time."

"Are you ready for death? Are you ready?"

The veins in his neck stood out as he grasped the podium as if
to shove it over into the pews.

"Will the fancy homes, fancy clothes, and fancy cars make you
ready? Will the big bucks and big jobs make you ready?"

"No. No."

"Didn't make Lazarus ready. Didn't make Mary and Martha
ready. Even if they had had all those things, they weren't prepared."

"No, Lord."

"Not even Jesus, the son of God, was prepared. Because He
wept."

"Yes, He did."

"He wept." Hollis leaned back and took a deep breath. "But
do you know what Jesus said to Mary? He said, 'Oh, Mary,
don't you weep. And go tell Martha not to moan.' "

"Don't moan."

"Because Jesus knew that we may never be ready for death,
but we can be ready for a resurrection."

"Oh, yes."

"If your heart is right. If your heart is with God, you can be
ready. Was Lazarus ready?"

"Oh, yes."

"Yes, he was ready. Because Jesus went to the grave of Lazarus. Went to that grave and He called out — called out *three*
times."

Hollis left the podium, robes flying, and grabbed the back of
the coffin with both hands. It rocked on its stand as the audience
gasped.

"He didn't call out, 'Is your bank account big?' He didn't call
out, 'Is your mortgage paid?' He didn't call out, 'Have you im-

pressed somebody today?' No, He called his name. Three times, He called his name to see if his *heart* was ready. And his heart was ready — because Lazarus rose."

"Yes, he rose."

"Rose and started walking like a natural man."

Hollis looked down into the coffin, sweat dripping from his chin, and said softly, "So I didn't come with a sermon. I came to call." Suddenly, he screamed down into the woman's face, "Lycentia!"

Chester Parker jumped, the handkerchief balled into his fist as the coffin shook.

"Would you hear that call? Or should it be louder? Should it be louder to get through your showcase windows? Lycentia!"

Parker's hands were squeezed between his knees.

"Or should it be louder to reach all the way to the bottom of Linden Hills?"

As Hollis leaned into the coffin again, Parker leaned forward with him. "Lycentia!"

Hollis finally looked up and smiled slowly. "But she didn't hear."

"Oh God, she didn't hear." Parker collapsed into his seat.

"She didn't hear because I'm not Jesus. And Jesus isn't ready to call her now."

"No, He's not ready." Parker began to cry.

"But I want to say to her friends who are grieving — and to her family who is grieving" — his hands swept toward Parker who was almost hysterical now — "that He will one day. And I can assure you that Sister Parker will be ready then." Hollis walked back to the pulpit slowly. "Because here was a woman with her heart in the right place. And we're going to hear her eulogy now. Will the person assigned for the eulogy please come up."

He was surprised to see Luther Nedeed begin to mount the steps. Hollis held on to the pulpit with both hands, but Luther stood there calmly, waiting for him to move aside. When he finally did, Luther smiled. Turning toward the congregation, he began to read. "Lycentia Sarah Parker was born in 1915. Her union with Chester Philip Parker was blessed with no children, but she is survived by him and a host of devoted nieces and nephews who ..." There was a sigh of relief in the chapel as Luther's even monotone soothed their ears. His voice droned on and on. "She was an outstanding member of her community, giving her time and energy to serve as coordinator of the Linden Hills Beautification Project, secretary of the Tupelo Realty's Neighborhood Board, co-sponsor for ..." Their relief had become gratitude. They straightened up in the pews and leaned toward his words. And when he was through, the silent applause for this performance was deafening as he nodded to Hollis. Luther Nedeed had just placed Lycentia Parker's life into the hands of a saviour they could understand — they had saved themselves. This very building stood as a living testament to that and that was the gospel they wanted to hear under its gold-leafed ceiling.

Hollis stood back behind the pulpit. The warmth in his body was draining, leaving a chill that caused him to tremble. One by one, the ghosts faded in the back rows and the balconies, sending a breeze that drifted toward him and smelled of only his own sweat. He could see the real faces in front of him quite clearly now as they waited — some tense and others amused. He knew they weren't waiting for the Right Reverend Michael T. Hollis, because all those eyes held an edge of contempt. Slowly, he straightened his robes and his back. This was his church. He could easily top Nedeed's performance and regain their respect by doing exactly what was expected of him in that pulpit. So, quietly bowing his head, he did absolutely nothing in those final moments but intone the words: "Let us rise. And pray."

The last of the guests had filed out of the chapel, and the attendants came to remove the wreaths to the hearse. Luther stood in the empty room with his hand poised over the coffin's lid. He was pleased to see that that drunken fool's antics hadn't disarranged the body. He reached down and straightened a ruffle on the pink dress. Everything else was in place. The white cotton gloves with pearl buttons that were fixed on hands crossed at the waist. The carefully set waves in the silvery hair. Just enough

powder and blush to give the skin back its natural tones. His
women were always like this. The lips set barely parted with a
clear gloss that highlighted their original color. She was so still
lying there on her back. She had come to him that way, and he
had treated her as he'd been taught. Standing by his father's
side, being told to forget all the nonsense he had learned in
school about cosmetic techniques and procedures: female bodies
were different. With the proper touch, you could work miracles.
Their skin wouldn't remain rigid and plastic if the fluid was regulated precisely. Just the right pressure and resistant muscles in
the face, neck, arms, and legs gave themselves up completely to
your handling. Moved when you made them move, stayed
where you placed them. Attention to the smallest details —
edges of mouths, curves of wrists — could bring unbelievable life
into the body before you. But it was a power not to be abused; it
took gentleness and care to turn what was under your hands into
a woman.

His father leaving him alone that night with his first body,
everything explained but the contents of the plastic bag placed
on the table. "Son, there are a few remaining matters, but those
are best left unsaid. When the time is right, it all falls into
place." And that night, it had. Even now, in the chapel, looking
at the results of his labor sent a pleasant sensation through the
base of his stomach. She was perfect. And what was the point in
living if a man didn't love his work? Luther's hand ran along the
smooth cool surface of the coffin and, gently, he closed the top.
There was always a dull throb of remorse when he had to come
to this moment. Turning, he found himself being watched by a
pair of very young and very bewildered eyes.

Willie fought the urge to duck his head back around the door-
way when Luther turned in his direction. He forced himself to
make an exaggerated survey of the empty chapel and after what
seemed an eternity, he shrugged his shoulders and left. His face
burning, he walked back over to Lester, who was standing next
to the bulletin board in the lobby.

"Reverend Hollis isn't in there, Les. Are you sure he didn't go
by in the crowd?"

"No way, I had my eyes out for him. After all that work, he wasn't gonna slip past me. Someone said his office is on the other side of the chapel. Let's go look."

"No." Willie grabbed his arm so tightly Lester stared at him. "I mean, the funeral's not over. Nedeed is still in there with the body."

Two attendants went past them, rolling a cart for the casket.

"See what I mean?" Willie's mouth was dry. "I don't think it would be right to barge in there now."

"Willie, it's a huge room. We could go down the aisle by the wall. They'd probably never see us."

"Please, Les." Willie's voice surprised them both and he let go of Lester's arm. "Let's just wait for Reverend Hollis outside by the truck."

"But that guy said he told us to wait in the lobby." He frowned at Willie. "What's wrong with you? Don't tell me funerals spook you. There are no such things as ghosts, Willie. And, man, you look like you just seen a dozen."

Willie didn't know how to tell Lester what he had seen, because it had really been nothing. Nothing but Nedeed closing the lid of a coffin. And Nedeed certainly had a right to do that; somebody had to. But he still felt ashamed, knowing he had been caught watching. It was crazy, but he just didn't want to be in that lobby when Nedeed came out.

"I guess I'm still a little sick to my stomach from that food last night. Tell you what, you stay here and catch up with Reverend Hollis and I'll meet you by the truck."

As Willie walked toward the side door, he realized that his stomach didn't really feel right. There was a tight knot down at its base. He knew it would go away if he could forget what he'd seen. But he hadn't seen anything. Nothing but a man closing the lid of a coffin. And there was no harm in that. The cold hit his face and he breathed the clean air in deeply. A man leaning over and with his hand closing the lid of a coffin. Willie shuddered and walked quickly toward the truck. It was that right hand. It moved too slowly over the top of the lid before it clicked shut. Why, it moved as if Nedeed was . . . He shook the thought from his head as his own right hand gripped the cold metal of the truck's handle. He sat down inside, feeling safe with the door finally locked and the daylight around him. That church was so dimly lit it was possible for your eyes to play all kinds of crazy tricks on you. God, he was glad he hadn't been stupid enough to tell Lester what he had imagined. Man, he would have laughed at him from now until doomsday. Because he had seen nothing. Nothing but a man closing the lid of a coffin. And there wasn't a bit of harm in that.

She felt a growing sense of shame with each page that she read in the final section of Evelyn Creton's recipe book. She kept telling herself that nothing was wrong with what she was doing, even though this could never have been meant to be seen. It exposed such raw and personal needs that the woman herself had probably wanted to forget them. But her reading it would harm no one, least of all Evelyn Creton. Still, she glanced toward the shadows each time she turned a page as if expecting someone to jump out and demand to see what was in her hands. The rational side of her mind knew it was impossible, but there was an impulse to guard herself against being caught and she kept the book close to her body so it could be hidden quickly. If Evelyn Creton stepped out of the shadows at that moment, she would have no excuse to give for not having the decency to close the book once she realized what it finally contained. And Evelyn Creton would demand an explanation for such conduct, because this had been such a proper woman. The careful and meticulous handwriting formed the vision of quiet dignity and immaculate grooming. This woman never had a curl out of place, a ribbon knotted loosely, a stick of furniture not glowing with lemon oil. She gave the right parties at the right time for the right people. There were two sets of china and silverplate, a suit for each occasion, a set of boots for each season — and a porcelain exterior that accented whatever room it was placed in. There were probably a dozen words that the friends and enemies of the Ne-deeds used to describe her, but one of them just had to be "perfect."

They thought they knew her, didn't they? She looked at the book in her lap. They wouldn't recognize her now. After eighty years the woman was a pile of bones; the flesh on her thighs, hips,

and breasts fallen away, so that the stiff corsets, high-necked col-
lars, and heavy skirts she was buried in were no longer enough to
mask the empty cavities that had been living all along between the
covers of this book. The real Evelyn Creton. She could see her
now, turning the corner from the grocer's where she ordered her
bushels of fruit and sacks of flour. She nervously pulls her veil
tightly around her face, adjusts her wide-brimmed hat and long
gloves. She is careful to conceal every inch of exposed flesh as
she heads for one of those dingy back rooms filled with incense
and evil-smelling oils. Or maybe she's heading to the other side of
town to a railroad station where she retrieves the small packages
that can be hidden so easily. How did she feel with her precious
grams of dried bull's testicles tucked deeply in her velvet gloves?
The slivers of orchid root and ginseng wrapped in her linen handkerchiefs? What names did she use when she called for her mail at
those depot stations? Did she pretend to be on someone else's er-
rand when she sat with those grizzled old women over eyedrop-
pers that measured out the menstrual blood of virgins? She was
dressed too well to be somebody's maid. Perhaps, somebody's
daughter?

She had to be ashamed, a proud and beautiful woman like that,
to feel driven to such measures. She had to cringe at each meal,
wondering if he could taste traces of those things in his food. If
each new moon he might catch a strand of her genital hair in his
teeth. She probably lay awake in that empty canopied bed, preparing a thousand explanations in case he discovered their presence; but she would have been hard-pressed for the language to
explain their need. She had watched the twentieth century bring a
multitude of new words to Linden Hills without one to validate these
types of desires in a Mrs. Evelyn Creton Nedeed.

That must have been a bewildered woman. Driven by the need
to spend so much time in that kitchen. To be sure that she never
ran out of ingredients for the excuse to keep large round bowls
between her thighs and long wooden spoons in her hand all day.
To scrape and handle carrots, wash string beans until her skin
wrinkled from the water. To sink her fingers into soft dough so she
could knead and knead and knead until trembling from exhaustion.
And she could eat.

Twenty-nine pounds. She'd put on twenty-nine pounds since her marriage. At first, she couldn't understand it. She had always prided herself on her discipline. Three times a week at the gym. She wanted lean thighs and a taut waist. She wanted to feel the smooth line running from her rib cage to pelvis. But then slowly, the fullness on her thighs became comforting the way they would touch each other — soft, warm — as she lay in bed. The growing preference for anything sticky and sweet that took a long time to chew, filling her mouth and leaving a slick after-taste. Cinnamon buns, caramels, pecan brownies. It had taken six years for those twenty-nine pounds. The way Evelyn Creton cooked it must have taken no time at all. The woman had to be immense.

The next group of pages contained nothing but rows of pur-chase dates for household medications. There was no reason for them to be in here. She could have stood in a crowd while ordering them in a loud, clear voice at the druggist's and have them deliv-ered to her front door. The epsom salts, mustard powder, castor oil, and calomel then placed in full view on those cherrywood shelves. As she kept turning, she became conscious of her deep-ening breaths. But that delivery boy must have wondered why he had to come every two weeks.

        May 15 — Purchased: 2 quarts castor oil
                            6 pounds epsom salts
                            3 pounds calomel
        May 29th — Purchased: 1 quart castor oil
                            1 gallon ipecacuanha wine
                            3 pounds epsom salts
        June 12th — Purchased: 3 pounds magnesia
                            2 pounds calomel
                            1 quart mineral oil

Month after month, the small block letters were crammed onto the pages. Month after month, the delivery boy must have wheeled his bicycle over that lake and up that drawbridge, wondering what Mrs. Nedeed was doing with all these laxatives. She probably tipped well. She may have even given him one of the dozen cakes or casseroles she was baking that day. And even if it was the same boy all this time, he wouldn't have noticed because of the padded corset and full skirts that she was getting thinner. The year turned and turned again. But surely by now — even in that brief moment at the back door — he must have seen that her face was becoming sunken, her arm skeletal. When she reached for the packages, didn't he notice the new jeweler's brace that kept her wedding ring on? In all this time there just had to be something to cause a whisper of doubt that would have built into a cry of alarm that got this woman some help.

Her sigh was so deep it fluttered the yellowing pages. Why was she wasting her time with those kinds of thoughts? How could that boy guess that anything was terribly wrong in that house when Mrs. Nedeed always answered the door from the kitchen?

As the dates ran on and on, the amounts and nature of the purgatives mixed and changed until it was staggering. She should have been numb to the cold by now, but a heavy chill settled in her middle as she watched the relentless accuracy with which this woman measured her anguish. A personal computer.

It sat in the corner of the study upstairs, its memory discs filled with her checking balances and household accounts. Her eyes left the pages and focused on the piles of cookbooks by the wall. If it were down here now, she could match the dates in those recipe books against the dates for these laxatives. It would only take minutes to calculate the average capacity of the human stomach, then the maximum potential of calories in what she could have consumed, and subtract from that the minimum effectiveness of each of these purgatives. There was even a key on it that would let her take into account the fact that they always stripped away more vitamins and nutriments than the food could supply. So the body had to feed on the protein in the muscle tissues, eventually getting to those in the heart and lungs. It had to use up all fat, not sparing the cushion around the liver, or the lining that kept the bone joints from breaking through the skin. And leaving room for a small margin of error, the computer could still pinpoint the exact year, if not month — yes, it could probably do that. Tell her how long it took this woman to eat herself to death.

December 24th. The delivery date was given in the same clear print as the rest. It came at the bottom of the right-hand side. She sat staring at that date, her mind as blank as the pages she knew would follow it. She refused to turn them over, subjecting herself to the images they would bring of Evelyn Creton on Christmas Day. So she kept the book open to exactly where it was and imagined that delivery boy as he maneuvered his bicycle down that frozen hill and knocked at the back door. When he received his tip, he wouldn't have thought anything about the fact that it was extraordinarily generous; it was the holiday season. And he had probably spent a bit more time there than usual, listening to his customer's gratitude for the prussic acid that would save her the embarrassment of having roaches suddenly appearing while guests were in the house. Or maybe the tip was so large that he did think about it. And as he rode away, he smiled at how nice she was to appreciate the fact that he had been smart enough to hurry and make Tupelo Drive the first call on his route — since he was also bringing her a quart of vanilla ice cream.

Willie and Lester had just left Fifth Crescent Drive and were heading for the two brick pillars in front of Tupelo Drive.

"And you don't think it's kinda strange that he just up and decides that he wanted us — us of all people — to help him. And on Christmas Eve no less." Willie stuck his hands into his pockets.

"Sure, it would be strange for anybody else. But when you're talking about Nedeed, you gotta play by a different set of rules. For all we know, he may want us down there to stuff Easter baskets. Who cares? He said he'd make it worth our while."

"Well, he can make it worth *your* while, 'cause I'm not going."

"Aw, Willie, now why you going on like this when the guy just wants to give us a hand?"

"Look, you always said that the only thing Nedeed would give a burning man was a match. I don't see why you're so quick to believe that he's gotten into the charity business when it comes to us."

"It ain't about no charity. He wants something and he's willing to give something up — the old buckola, White. And he's got plenty of those."

"Yeah, Shit, I know that. But what I still don't know is what he wants with us. Why didn't you ask him?"

"In the middle of a funeral?"

"The funeral was over."

"Well, they were wheeling the body out. And even I've got enough class not to stand there arguing about who'll do what for how much when that poor woman was rotting away."

Willie sucked his teeth. "Now, how did all this go down again?"

"I've told you a hundred times. Nedeed asked me what we were doing there, and I said we were doing some work for Hollis, we'd been working for people down here all week, and then he said —"

"Wait a minute. He asked you what *we* were doing there? He didn't see us together. I was already out in the truck."

"Well, he must have seen you when you went into the chapel looking for Hollis."

"I didn't go in. I just stuck my head around the door."

"Well, whatever. Because he asked me if the darker-hued gentleman was with me. Get that — the darker-hued gentleman. What a turkey."

"Did he wanna know about me before or after he offered you the job?"

"It was after. No, I guess it was before. I can't remember that shit. The whole thing only took a coupla seconds."

"Did he wanna know my name?"

Lester stopped walking. "White, what's wrong with you? Is there something going on that I should know about? I swear to God, this sounds like one of those conversations in a grade-B detective movie. Now, I'm the first to admit that Luther Nedeed is a cold-blooded son of a bitch, who wouldn't give his own mother the time of day if he couldn't come out ahead. But, man, he's hardly in the league with the Boston Strangler or the Houston Ax-Murderer. If anything, he wants us down there to do something that would cost him twice as much for unionized labor and four times as much on Christmas Eve. Oh, he'll cut our throats — no doubt about it. But not in the way you seem to be thinking. For Christ's sake, this is Linden Hills, it isn't some back alley in — "

"Go ahead, finish it. Some back alley in Putney Wayne, huh, Shit?"

Lester's face reddened. "You've been doing that to me all day, Willie. And it's not what I meant."

"No, that's all right. But I think it is what you meant." Willie's voice was quiet and slow. "I just want to tell you something though: I've seen things done to people down here that are a lot worse than anyone would have the heart to do up in Putney Wayne. 'Cause you see, it takes a lot of honesty, Shit — honest hate or rage, whatever — to pick up a knife and really cut a man's throat. And you're right, it could never happen here in Linden Hills 'cause these people can't seem to find the guts to be honest about anything. And that's why I'm wondering about Nedeed, that's all. 'Cause of all the people down here, he seems to be the only one with enough backbone to go that far if he had to. Not that he has to with us . . ." Willie paused and frowned. "But he wants something with us, and I think he would just come out and say it."

"I swear to you, Willie, he didn't. All he said was, and I'll quote, 'I would like you gentlemen to come down to Tupelo Drive and help me on Christmas Eve. Is nine o'clock expedient?' Now, you know I couldn't make that up. I even had to think a minute about what expedient meant."

"So he deliberately didn't say what he wanted?"

Lester sighed. "No, he didn't say."

"Then I'm not going, 'cause that means it's something weird."

"Sure, it's weird. I knew from Jump Street it had to be weird. It's at Nedeed's house, isn't it? But at worst, I told ya, it's stuffing Easter baskets."

"Well, he can stuff 'em by himself."

"You've got two days to think about it."

"I've already thought about it."

The snow finally started falling as they reached the entrance to Tupelo Drive. The wind sent the flakes swirling into the red bricks of the twelve-foot pillars, and they clung there like tentacles, feathery and alive. The tall pine trees, blocking out the town cemetery on each side of the winding incline, also blocked what little light the overcast skies would have shed on the short wide streets below them. The sensation of moving from afternoon into night wasn't helped by the huge hedges and redwood fences circling the backyards that literally rose about their heads on each side of them. The snowflakes were heavy and wet, managing in moments to turn the gray air in front of them into a solid white wall. It would have been impossible to see another street below even if the road didn't drop sharply around a right curve.

The snow blew up into Willie's nose and ears, causing him to cringe. "Well, it looks like your idea is shot to hell now." He raised the collar on his pea jacket. "We can't go down there, ringing doorbells in this weather. Not that there's a whole lot we can do anyway; this stuff is gonna stick."

"Maybe we could still try. There might be something for us to do inside one of those houses."

"Les, I don't like the idea of walking around Tupelo Drive not knowing where we're going. All the other times, somebody has been expecting us. These people might not even open their doors."

"Well, if we don't do something, that's it. We're out of work because no one else has called. And the only one who wanted us down here was Nedeed, and that's not till day after tomorrow."

"Look, I wouldn't mind if it wasn't snowing. But I don't want to get lost down there in all this mess."

"Willie, there's no way to get lost. We just follow this curve around and down through the next three streets and we'll come out by Patterson Road. It just seems strange 'cause you don't travel through here often."

"I don't think you've been through here too often yourself, unless you're in the habit of visiting that cemetery, 'cause you said you don't know anybody on Tupelo Drive."

"How would I know these people? Just look at these layouts. My street is the slums as far as they're concerned."

"Well, I'm for getting back up into the slums. Besides, this place gives me the creeps. It's so damned dark and —"

"Freeze!"

They turned and saw that a police car had rolled up silently behind them. The two policemen had their guns drawn out at arm's length, both hands guiding the barrels pointed at the center of their chests. "All right! Hands against the wall, and spread 'em."

Before they could speak, one of the policemen ran over and pushed them against the brick pillars while the other kept his gun leveled at them. "I said, spread 'em."

Willie saw the pale lips pressed into a thin line, the brown stubble on the tightly set jaw, and the white knuckles strained against the gun's handle. But what frightened him the most was the reflection of his own dark face in those blue irises. That alone had the power to get his head split open or his insides blown apart — just because it was there. It wasn't a matter of innocence or guilt at that moment; it was a matter of trying to find a way to achieve the vital balance between moving too quickly, too slowly, and not at all, that would save his life until he could explain.

The bricks bit into his bare palms as he felt his body being slapped in hard, rapid succession from the left to right side of his chest, down to his legs.

"I want to know what the hell is going on!" Lester shouted. "Somebody is gonna answer for this."

"Kid, the only one who has any answering to do is you. All right, turn around."

They had put their guns back into their holsters, but the policeman standing by the car still kept his hand resting on the handle.

"We had a complaint about some prowlers in this neighborhood. And we've been following you two for the last ten minutes, and I wanna know why you ain't done nothing but stand here, casing out those backyards there?"

"Is this an official charge? I wanna know if this is an official charge? God, I hope it is, because then I'm suing for false arrest."

"All right, smart ass, you want an official charge? Loitering on private property. Linden Hills is *all* private property."

"Well, I happen to live in Linden Hills. My name is Lester-

field Walcott Montgomery Tilson, and I'm the legal owner of
the property at One Hundred First Crescent Drive."

There was a brief moment in which the blue eyes left Lester's
face and took in the sheepskin coat, suede gloves, and leather
boots.

"Well, Mr. Lesterfield whatever, you're over a mile straight
down from First Crescent Drive."

"So I can't take a walk in my own neighborhood, on a *public*
road? There's a law against standing and watching the snow
fall?"

"No, but there is a law against illegal trespassing, and you
were standing inside the entrance to Tupelo Drive, which is a
privately owned road that runs past nothing from here on in but
privately owned property. And by your own admission, you
aren't one of the residents. I can haul you in for that — and
having a big mouth." He turned to Willie. "What about you?
You live here too?"

"No, but he's with me," Lester said.

Willie desperately wanted some way to deny that and still
keep out of jail. But it looked as if he was caught between a rock
and a hard place.

"Look, officer," Willie said. "We're out here because we've
been working in this neighborhood all week, helping out some of
the people that Lester knows. You can check if you want to.
We've done jobs for the Donnells, the Parkers, and we just left a
truck up on Fifth Crescent Drive at Reverend Hollis's place.
And when you stopped us, we were about to go down on the
next street and start working there."

"So now you're telling me that you were invited down here on
Tupelo Drive?"

"Of course we were invited," Lester said. "And if you were
willing to listen, you could have heard that five minutes ago."

"All right, kid, I'm ready to listen now. Who invited you down
on the next street?"

There was silence. Then the policeman smiled for the first
time. " 'Cause if you were just going down there to knock on
doors, that's soliciting. So now we've got illegal trespassing *and*
soliciting without a license. Any way you play it, Mr. Lesterfield

whatever, you've got no business in this neck of the woods unless you can come up with a name." He paused for a moment. "Hey, I'll tell you what, let's all get out of this storm and take a ride up to the station. Maybe that'll give you time to loosen your memory." He jerked his head toward the squad car.

"I'm not going anywhere without an official charge."

"Look, kid," he said as he pointed his finger in Lester's face, "I've been patient with you. Now, I can hold you twenty-four hours for questioning, and I can do a lot more than that for resisting a peace officer. So *get going.*"

A Checker Cab was slowly coming down Linden Road as they moved toward the police car. When it stopped, the rear window rolled down and Norman Anderson stuck his head out. "Is there some problem here, officer?"

"What's it to you?"

"Well, it's nothing to me." Norman smiled pleasantly. "But Mrs. Dumont has been on the phone screeching for half an hour, wondering what's happened to these two young men. She expected them down at her house over an hour ago." Norman got out of the cab, his mincing accent and gait telling Willie and Lester that they were about to get another impersonation of what he'd often called a "Cousin Tom."

"I suppose you know Mrs. Howard Dumont, the D.A.'s wife? Well, she and my wife are old friends and since I vouched for these two, I felt that the least I could do was to come and see what was delaying them." He turned to the boys. "Well, it seems like you've gotten yourselves arrested. You know what kind of spot this puts me in? I told you she was depending on you to help out with that big party tonight for the commissioner and Chief Endicott. It's probably for the best anyway. God knows what he caught you doing." He turned back to the policeman. "Just let me know what the charges are, officer, so I can break the bad news to Mrs. Dumont."

"These clowns never said they were going to the D.A.'s house. They didn't know where they were going. And that's why they're being taken in."

"He never gave us a chance," Lester said. "I told him that I lived in Linden Hills and we were invited down here."

"Look, how long do you think I'd keep my job if I brought every cock-and-bull story some stragglers handed me in this neighborhood? I gave you plenty of time to tell me where you were going."

"Well," Norman said, "now that I've cleared all this up I guess there's no reason to take them in, is there, uh, officer . . . ?" He made a point of staring at the badge number.

"I'm going to check this story out with the Dumonts."

"Please, do. My name is Norman Anderson and I'm on my way there right now."

"All right, you two, get in." The policeman jerked open the door.

"Uh, excuse me, could I ask a small favor? Do you mind letting them ride with me? I'd hate to have Mrs. Dumont see these young men get out of a police car when the allegations against them will be unfounded." He moved a little closer and lowered his voice. "Look, we both know how funny these people down here are about their image. And even the hint of a possible arrest will put a social stigma on these two that she's bound to take personally since she'll have to let them into her home." The policeman hesitated. "The cab will be right in front of you," Norman continued, "and everybody knows it's almost impossible to turn around once you enter Tupelo Drive."

The policeman went to the cab driver's window. "I want you to take this cab straight to the Dumonts on Tupelo Drive. It's the first gray stone house on your right side. And I'll be right behind you."

When they got into the cab with Norman, Willie let out a loud sigh. "Norm, you must have been sent from the gods."

"Gods, nothing, you jokers." Norman shook his head. "You know, Ruth had a feeling that you two might get yourselves into a mess, walking around down here. Trust a woman and her intuition."

"You mean, Ruth sent you to look for us?" Willie asked.

"Naw, I really am on my way to the Dumonts. At least I wasn't lying about her and Ruth. Laurel Dumont called yesterday and they talked for hours. Ruth promised to come down today, but she wasn't feeling too well this morning so she sent me to bring her this gift. And she told me to keep an eye out for you losers because she hadn't heard anything about you since you worked for the Donnells the other day. But I didn't expect I'd have to keep you from getting thrown in the slammer."

"And you were pretty cool, too, Norm." Lester laughed. " 'The allegations against them will be unfounded . . . Social stigma.' Man, where'd you get all them Perry Mason words? You really backed those turkeys off. But they weren't about to take me to jail."

"No, they were just about to go upside your head," Willie said. "Les, you were pushing that cop pretty hard. His hand was just itching to pull out that billy club."

"I just wish he had." Lester looked through the back window. "Lousy pigs. Treating us like we were a piece of garbage. Who'd he think he was?"

"It wasn't what he thought he was, but what he thought we were," Willie said, "a couple of unidentified flying niggers. I've seen guys get their heads blown off for nothing more than that. And you were standing there, handing him all that lip. Man, I'll admit it, I was scared for you."

"If he had any sense," Norman said, "he would have been scared for himself. You're a nice guy, Les, but sometimes you fly off the handle too quickly. And this time it could have not only gotten you hurt, but Willie, too. You know he wasn't just gonna stand there and let those cops beat you up."

"Who me?" Willie said. "I would have turned state's witness quicker than you could have said 'Sapphire.' Yes, your honor, Lesterfield Walcott Montgomery Tilson got just what he deserved. I been telling the *deceased* for years that his mouth was a deadly weapon."

They all laughed as the cab turned into a long driveway, bordered on one side by an eight-foot hedge and on the other by a gently sloping lawn that stopped at the front steps of a massive, stone Tudor with a red-cobbled roof.

"Let me get up to that door real quick," Norman said. "All I need is a two-second head start on those cops and I'll fix something up for you."

They saw Norman talking to an old woman in a print housedress before the policeman joined him. Then the policeman came back to the cab and opened the door. "All right, you lucked out on this one. The Dumonts have vouched for you. But I'm warning you, next time don't be wandering around down here on foot, or someone else will call the station. Look, just write Santa Claus and tell him to bring you a Ferrari for Christmas, Mr. Lesterfield. I hear he answers that kind of letter in Linden Hills." He laughed as he slammed the door.

"Write him to bring you a personality," Lester shouted through the closed window, "but you probably couldn't spell the word."

"You see, that's just what Norman was talking about, Shit."

"Just lay off me, Willie." Lester slumped in the corner of the seat.

A few minutes later, Norman came back to the cab and tapped on the window. "Okay, now, here's the deal. Mrs. Dumont and her grandmother are in the house alone. And I figured she'd need someone to shovel the snow for them after the storm's over. So you and Lester come back tomorrow and do it. No charge. A favor for a favor."

"No charge?" Lester sat up. "Norm, did you see this place? That front and side walkway alone must cover half a city block. And it's gonna snow all night."

"It would have still snowed if you were in jail, Les," Norman said gently.

"We'll be here, Norman," Willie said. "Nine o'clock sharp — blizzard or no blizzard."

"Good boys. Okay, you take the cab and get on back home. I can call another. Her grandmother wants me to stick around for a while. It seems like Ruth's friend is in a bad way."

"What, is she sick?"

"Well, not physically, Willie — if you know what I mean. She and her old man just split up and a whole lot of other mess." Norman sighed, looking up and down the street. "You know, it's really funny. If anybody just took a quick ride through here, you'd think these people shouldn't have a care in the world."

December 23rd

She had been staring at Evelyn Creton's last page for hours. Sitting up in her cot, she would doze off with the book still in her lap and awaken to stare again, the stiffness of her neck telling her whether she had been asleep for hours or just minutes. Her mind was completely blank and her fingers lay still and calm on the edges of the cover. She now looked up at the clock on the basement wall and the westward angle of the metal hour hand told her it was nine o'clock. But nine o'clock in the morning or evening? Nine o'clock of what day? Of what season? It was cold, colder than it had been when she first came down, so it must be winter. It was nine o'clock and it was winter. It snowed in the winter. And the air got warmer when it snowed. She could feel it becoming warmer down there now. Was there snow on the ground outside? A lot of snow? Snow that would melt when the spring came, to create water that drained into the soil, nourishing the trees out there so they would produce leaves in the summer to disappear in a burst of flaming color in autumn, leaving the branches bare, bare and ready for more snow. The seasons — whatever season it was now — would change.

The book left her lap in one fierce sweeping motion and crashed against the clock, bouncing onto the floor. A jagged vertical line now cut across its circular face. She had enjoyed those changes; each one had brought some sort of beauty into the world. And that beauty had given her comfort. She wasn't like these other women; she had coped and they were crazy. They never changed. She pressed her lips together and looked at the crack on the clock. Anger began to scratch at the scars in her mind and she trembled as fresh blood seeped through the opening wounds. That's why Luther never talked about them: there wasn't a normal one in the bunch. But there was nothing wrong with her. She remembered loving the seasons, loving life. And there just couldn't have been anything wrong with what she had wanted. A home. A husband. Children. That was all, and that was so little. To ask for so little and to have it taken away. No, it wasn't wrong. It wasn't sick. If there was any sickness, it was in this house, in the air. It was left over from the breaths of those women who had come before her. The Luwana Packervilles, Evelyn Cretons, and God knows who else. Blood from the open scars dripped down behind her eyes as she looked around the basement, futile and bewildered. This didn't happen in a moment or even in a marriage. This had happened a long time ago. She could taste the anger at the back of her throat as her eyes came full circle to her son. His lace-draped arms were still spooned toward the air, the outline of her body permanently carved into the curve of his limbs. The blood's saltiness created a craving to strike out at what had happened, to destroy those beginnings. But she couldn't touch what had already escaped her long before she came to Tupelo Drive. She was left with only the ends. She grabbed up the other book and began ripping out the pages. Goddamned insane — all of them. She balled up handfuls of the delicate pages as she relentlessly tore away. She was too weak to break the heavily sewn binding, so she flung it to the floor and, swinging her legs over the cot, stepped on it savagely. Sick. Every last one, sick. The taste of blood spurred her on and she stumbled to the corner, kicking aside the cookbooks littering the floor.

She overturned boxes, pulling out dresses and scarfs, ripping easily through the rotting material. Shoes were thrown against the wall. Blouses, feathered hats, and beaded bags lost their buttons, trimmings, and sequins. Dried flowers spilled out of diaries and letters as she mutilated the pages. Shredded paper floated down around her feet in pastel heaps. She didn't have to read them. She would read nothing else. Nothing. She just didn't care anymore about their sad, twisted lives. She was surrounded by the perfumed fragments of the Nedeed women. What she couldn't tear, she stomped on, regretting that her mouth was too dry to summon up enough spit. The pleasure of her destruction mingled with the anger in her blood as one box spilled out piles of photographs and she tore at them blindly. The slick, thin paper gave way too easily so she gathered huge handfuls and dozens of women disappeared with one pull. She started on another and another until she wanted to scream from the sensation building within her. Her breathing was labored and her forehead clammy as she forced her tired arms to keep going. She pulled at the pages between the covers of a heavily padded album, but the cellophane cut into her palms, resisting destruction. She threw it on the floor and tried to mangle the pictures with her heels. Her foot skidded across the slippery surface and she lost her balance, falling to her knees. Kneeling, she slammed the album against the wall; it bounced back, fell open, and she found her frustration met by a pair of soft, compassionate eyes.

The young woman's heavy, wavy hair was parted in the middle and swept down the sides of her ivory face into a French knot that rested on her lace collar. Her upturned pug nose and narrow chin were tossed over the left shoulder, and the slender arms seemed poised to spring her body off the cushioned seat as if her full lips were caught in the act of saying *I knew you would come, and I'm so pleased to meet you.*

She knew it was the shadows cast by the light in the basement, her trembling body, and weakened vision — those lips hadn't just closed in front of her, they were never open. They sat there now on the girl's face, full and still. It's just that there seemed to be so much life in that posture. The thrust of the chin and the tilt of the waist, straining against the creamy band. But what held her were

the eyes. Large, oval wells with a bottomless capacity to absorb
any seen or unseen challenge. They slowly drained away her desire to destroy their owner, but even if she still wanted to, the finely
arched brows told her they would understand.

Almost against her will, she turned the page. The girl was posed
by an old Packard, one hand drumming the roof and the foot
propped on the running board revealing a white-stockinged leg
and T-strap shoe tapping a restless staccato while the hand on the
left hip pushed back an open fur coat over a pleated mid-calf
dress. The same thrust of the chin, this time with an impatient pout
that only managed to escape being ridiculous on the face of a
beautiful woman. The next image that shutter would capture was
so evident: a cloud of dust as she jumped in that car, gunned the
motor, and sped away. A cigarette dangling from her fingers and a
passing wave to the local bootlegger as she went to buy another
set of dancing slippers that would grow worn before they grew old.
Whoever she was, she wasn't a Nedeed.

Flipping the page, she discovered she was right. A yellowed
newspaper clipping was slipped under the cellophane:

> Mr. and Mrs. Delmore McGuire of New Canaan, Connecticut, have
> announced the engagement of their daughter, Priscilla, to Mr.
> Luther Nedeed, son of Mr. Luther Nedeed and the late Evelyn Cre-
> ton Nedeed. An April wedding is planned.

And in the next photo, Priscilla McGuire sat smiling upstairs in
the den — married to her Luther. He stood posed beside the girl
and the same leather wing chair that was still in front of the fireplace. His dark immobile face, protruding eyes, and short barreled
torso sent an immediate shock of recognition through her, defied
only by reason and the man's clothes. The spats, butterfly collar,
and pocketed vest. One hand hooked in a heavy watch chain and
the other firmly planted on the bride's shoulder. Her costume was
as formal as the announcement. Triple-tiered lace on the scooped-
neck gown, a pearl necklace and matching tiara fastened on her
thick, wavy hair. Her legs were positioned tightly together, so the
huge bouquet rested securely on her lap. But just to the right of a
white rose petal a slender pinkie finger was crooked in a salute to
the photographer as the arch of her brows and lips seemed set to
burst into laughter the moment after the flash went off.

The bride was laughing openly in the next picture. Bent dangerously over the railing of a steamship, her fur boa and loosened curls flying in the wind as she watched the arc of the bouquet flung toward the camera. But her husband's expression had never changed, with that same dark hand still firmly on her shoulder. She found her eyes riveted to his short blunt fingers. They just didn't belong there. They interfered with the effects the wind had on the loose silk coat. The light material billowed up gently, giving her shoulders the space they needed to sweep into that posture of ascending wings. But in spite of his hand, the cloth still hung on her as it would on those sea gulls near the boat's smokestack.

She saw that in the next picture his hand had finally left her shoulder. Priscilla McGuire was now held down by the child on her lap. She was again seated in the wing chair and had positioned the infant to face the camera, her hands gently supporting the arms as its spine rested under her bosom. Her shoulders and chin were bent down in a protective curve that demanded the lens capture her pride in this new extension of her flesh. With its dark oversized head, huge eyes, clenched fists, and bowlegs, only the veiled anxiety and awe in her eyes proclaimed her as the mother; but even the blindest fool could see that the man standing beside them was the father. His hand was resting contentedly on the back of the chair. And for the first time, he smiled. Lilac-colored ink had marked the bottom — *Luther: 1 month*.

Luther: 1 year. The child could now sit upright in Priscilla McGuire's lap, so her long pale fingers were only clasped around its middle. The next five photographs were exactly alike except that her hands kept getting farther and farther apart as the child's body widened and grew. At *Luther: 6 years*, the child stood up, at the other side of the chair. Priscilla McGuire's hands were now free to be placed wherever she wanted them, but they were folded completely still in her lap — as if she'd grown accustomed to them being there. She was a striking contrast to the dark figures on each side of her, the son a miniature of the man, in almost identical poses with their matching tweed suits and vests. As the years went by, they could have been three wax figures but for the determined animation in the arch of her brows and her insistence on changing the way she held her head: a little to the left, a quarter turn to the right. No one called this woman just Mrs. Nedeed; they sent cards to Priscilla. Rang up and heard a clear, bell-like voice announce that name. She decided which parties to attend, who bored or amused her, and whom she would have in that house. She was already telling the photographer that she had her own way of thinking and acting, her own definition of important or trivial, right or wrong. Twenty minutes of instruction to the housekeeper and she was off. Those rigid rooms upstairs couldn't contain her, and it was hard to imagine that she would have come back. But obviously she did each day because it was so important to sit each year and mark the progress of her child with lilac-colored ink.

There was no change — the same den, the same wing chair and the assorted beige dresses of which she seemed so fond. And the same dark fire in those eyes, matching the dark figures on each side of her. The first at the polls for the national elections in 1920. And she voted the Socialist ticket. She believed that Darwin was a fool and that Ida B. Wells should be canonized. She ran for president of the local Association of Colored Women three years in a row — and won. She urged her friends to get tickets for *A Doll's House,* and later would think *Lady Chatterley's Lover* the most important book of the decade. *Luther: 8. Luther: 9. Luther: 10.* But she cried at the club ceremony that made her Mother of the Year.

Ten years passed before she noticed the shadow. As the child grew, the height of his shoulder cast a faint shade across Priscilla McGuire's body. It had started at her lap and then slowly crawled up across her stomach, chest, and neck. What began as a slight, gray film was now deepening into a veil. She squinted in the light. It was just another illusion; the woman wasn't fading in the photographs. It was so easy for the eye to follow the dark lines from the son, across her body to the identical dark lines of the father. Her light skin, beige dresses, and prematurely graying hair could be easily dismissed if you didn't stop to catch the flashing highlights in those eyes. Why didn't she sit up in these pictures? She was leaning too closely toward the son, causing herself to be lost in his shadow.

A tight knot gripped her middle. The veil was now over her chin, drawing closer toward her mouth. The woman was not disappearing. She turned much more quickly now, forcing herself to stare only into Priscilla McGuire's eyes and fix her on that page. She knew she was losing her mind. They were nothing but family portraits taken at a time when photography wasn't sophisticated about angles and lighting. These were probably only the rejects that she kept for herself, placing them here as some sort of joke: the wedding portrait with the crooked finger, the bouquet flung into the wind. This woman loved to laugh. Look at her now, sitting there obviously amused by her position between the two grown men. Priscilla McGuire was staring straight ahead, surely laughing inside at something. But there was nothing in front of her except a round camera lens with her aging reflection caught permanently in a staid leather chair. *Luther: 20 years.* He had gotten no taller, so why was the veil now across her bottom lip? And in the next, it had finally crept up to cover her mouth. She had to know what was happening. *Luther: 21 years.* She was no longer recording the growth of a child; the only thing growing in these pictures was her absence. In the next, she would finally stand up. She would be out in the garden or strolling on the beach. She kept turning the years over and hoping.

Willie's shovel lifted another wedge of heavy snow. He had just picked up some momentum when his blade hit yet another raised flagstone that jarred his spine.

"Aw, shit!"

"You rang?" Lester looked back over his shoulder, a light spray from his shovel hitting the corner of the house.

Willie pointedly ignored him.

"I told ya, you're doing it the wrong way," Lester said. "This stuff is too deep to clear it with one stroke. You gotta take the top off first and then do another layer. At the rate you're going, you'll be tired out before we even get around to the front of this barn."

"Well, nobody can say that of you." Willie arched his sore back, turning toward the rear of the Dumonts' house. At least three inches of snow still remained on the side of the patio that Lester had cleared, while Willie's half was so clean the color of the flagstones was visible. "When I say I'm going to do a job, I do it right. And if you think I'm going back over your mess, you're crazy."

"By the time we make it to the front, nobody's gonna be able to tell the difference the way it's still snowing."

"This is nothing but flurries," Willie said as he began working again.

"But-it's-stick-ing, Wil-lie," Lester sang. "Look at what's happening already."

"So I'll go around again for good measure and when *you* go around again, you'll have twice as much to do."

"Not me." Lester shook his head. "Even if I had gone to jail, it wouldn't have been sixty days at hard labor. And anybody who can afford a set-up like that" — he nodded toward the covered Olympic-size pool with its high diving platform — "should be able to cough up for a lousy snowblower. They get one free round from me, and that's it."

Willie pressed his lips together and snow started flying from his shovel.

"I don't know what you're trying to prove, Willie. But these folks ain't worth it."

"Maybe what I'm trying to prove is that I'm not an ungrateful, self-serving bastard like some people." A huge clump flew to the side and Willie's blade dug in again. "And if it takes breaking my ass to do it, then I think it's worth it." He kept his eyes on the path in front of him, refusing to look into Lester's face. He knew he had hurt him, but being justified didn't make him any less ashamed of his words. When he finally sneaked a glance at Lester's silent back, Willie saw that his friend was fiercely clearing his section, the blade scraping the packed gravel.

"Hey look, Shit. You were right, it's coming down too hard to get this driveway clean."

"No, you were right," Lester said without turning around. "If you're going to bother to do something, then you do it like it should be done."

Willie watched him for a moment, sighed, and then anchoring his shovel, approached him. "Well, then what I was trying to do was apologize. And I should do it like a man and just come out and say I'm sorry."

Lester eyed his extended hand, letting his bottom lip tremble slightly for effect. "You're really saying you're sorry?"

"Yeah."

"I mean — really sorry. Not just half-assed sorry, or white folks' sorry. But deep down in your black balls sorry. The way someone should be who's been biting off his best friend's head every time he's opened his mouth this morning — that kind of sorry?"

Willie just stared at him, his lips pushed to the side.

" 'Cause if that's the kind of sorry it is," Lester said and smiled, "if that's really and truly the kind of sorry it is, then I just might consider —"

"Aw, go find a high roof and a slippery ledge." Willie laughed and Lester joined him.

"But seriously, White, I've been wondering what's been eating you this morning. I thought you were pissed off because me and my big mouth got us into all this in the first place."

"Naw, it's got nothing to do with you. I just . . ." Willie sucked his teeth. "I just don't sleep good at night anymore."

"Man, you should be sleeping like a stone as hard as we've worked this week. I'm gone before my head hits the pillow."

"Me, too. But then I get all these crazy dreams and when I wake up, I can't get back to sleep. I must have been up since three o'clock this morning."

"Yeah? Those must be some kind of dreams."

"No, a lot of stupid crap. Like last night. I went into this store downtown and wanted to buy my mother one of those new Disc cameras for Christmas, and the woman behind the counter wouldn't sell it to me. And so I started shaking her but she kept yelling, 'I can't sell it to you.' "

As Willie talked, he wondered why he couldn't bring himself to tell Lester the real truth about that dream. The saleswoman wasn't just shouting, she was terrified when he walked into that store and had kept screaming over and over, "You can't use my camera because you have no face." And there was no way he was going back to sleep after that. Because he knew that when she struggled free and reached for the mirror that she'd tried to get before he grabbed her, it would be true.

"And that kept you up? It doesn't sound that scary to me."

"I didn't say the dreams scared me, Les," Willie snapped. "I'm not a kid. I just said that when I wake up I have trouble sleeping again, so I'm tired in the morning."

"Tired *and* evil." Lester winked.

"Yeah. Especially when I realize I'll be stuck with you all day," Willie said, as he went back to get his shovel. A wad of wet snow hit him in the collar and he spun around.

"See, no hands." Lester held up his palms and grinned.

"I'll no hands you, turkey." He scooped up a large mound while Lester put his hands in front of his face and began to dance.

"You get one throw to square it up — just one."

"I need Spoon and the Brown Bombers right now." Willie made an exaggerated attempt to round off the ball and aim. "They wouldn't miss, and those niggers were deadly. They loaded their ammunition with boulders and aimed right between the eyes."

"They caught me once, too." Lester pointed to his forehead.

"It shows."

Willie's smile disappeared, and he dropped the snowball when he saw Luther Nedeed coming toward them. He walked slowly around the two-foot drifts, his narrow English boots leaving triangular prints along the side of the house. Wherever he had appeared from, they knew he'd been outside for quite a while because there was a layer of snowflakes on the shoulders of his worsted overcoat.

"It seems that this is my week for running into you gentlemen." He addressed them both but looked directly at Willie, who picked up his shovel and held the handle in front of his chest.

"Looks that way," Lester said, "but you sorta surprised us this time since there's no funeral going on."

"I think you tend to forget that I have interests in this community beyond that, Mr. Tilson. If everyone died, who would occupy these homes?" Luther frowned slightly. "Yes, it's important that people decide to live. But then you can't stop them from doing the other either, can you?"

"I don't know, Mr. Nedeed," Lester said. "I never thought of folks having a choice about that."

"Sometimes they do."

Willie wanted to start working again, anything to get that guy's eyes off him. Why did he keep staring at him when Lester was the one talking?

"Well, I guess you should know." Lester kicked at his shovel. "It is your business after all." He was growing visibly uncomfortable. "Well, we'll see you."

"Yes, tomorrow night, isn't it?"

Willie cringed.

"Well, uh, no, Mr. Nedeed," Lester said. "I don't think we'll be able to make it — Christmas Eve and all that."

"That's a pity," Luther said, and it seemed as if he meant it. "I know how hard you've been working this week, and why you've been doing it. I didn't plan to take up much of your time and I was willing to match every dollar that you've earned so far."

"Every dollar?"

"That shouldn't surprise you, Mr. Tilson. My family has always believed that industry should be rewarded."

Lester looked at Willie. "Why, we've already made almost two hundred and fifty dollars *each* this week."

"Then I would match it for each of you."

"One night's work?"

"A little less than two hours' work. I imagine that's the best offer you've gotten this week."

"God, I'll say. Why, sure we'll —"

"Money isn't everything, Mr. Nedeed." Willie found his voice and forced himself to look directly into Luther's face. His hands gripped the shovel as if he expected the earth to open up or lightning to strike. He didn't know why, since it was only a man — a short, well-dressed man who was standing there waiting patiently for his next sentence. But staring into those flat brown eyes, Willie felt that, somehow, those following words would be extremely important. "And I think that if you were in my place," Willie continued slowly, "your next question would be, exactly what do you want us for?"

It seemed to take a slow age for Luther's eyes to move over Willie's body. No, it was more like moving through his body, well beneath the tissues that covered his internal organs.

"I see that I've assessed you correctly, Mr. Mason. And that gives me great pleasure, since I pride myself on being a good judge of men." And then he smiled, an unhurried full curve of the lips that took another age to complete. "I want you to help me trim my Christmas tree."

"That's it? Just trim a tree?" Willie asked.

"That's all. You see, my family is away for the holidays and, unavoidably, I'll have to spend Christmas alone. Don't think I'm buying your company, it's just that old habits die hard, and it's been a tradition in my home to adorn our tree on Christmas Eve. The ornaments are quite unusual, they've been used by us for generations. And it's a beautiful sight when it's completed — but like all beauty, it's much more meaningful when it's shared, wouldn't you agree?"

Willie only nodded.

"Fine. Then I'll see you tomorrow night at nine o'clock." He turned and walked away as quietly as he'd come.

Lester blew out his breath. "Christ, what a creep show. Just when you think you've got that guy figured out, he comes up with surprises. Imagine Nedeed getting all choked up over a tree."

For a moment Willie didn't answer. He knew what it would take, Willie thought, he knew exactly what it would take to get what he wanted from each of them. He was in awe of the man. Sure, they could go there and decorate his tree, ooh and aah, then collect all that money and split. But for Nedeed there was much more to it than that. Nedeed had told them what he wanted without ever really telling them why.

"It's not about his stupid tree," Willie finally said.

"Hey look, don't start that again. You said you would go if you knew what we were going for, and now you do. Willie, I'm begging you, don't mess this up. A hundred and twenty-five bucks an hour."

"No, I'm going." Willie frowned. "I'm just saying I know it's more than just some tree."

"Yeah, right." Lester shook his head. "You forgot to ask him exactly what we're gonna hang on the tree — maybe shrunken heads. And then we'd have to find out exactly *whose* heads."

"Well, that leaves yours out 'cause he said the thing's really pretty when it's done."

Lester bent to pack a snowball and Willie picked up his shovel like a baseball bat. "Throw it on your life."

"Come on," Lester said as he brushed off his hands, "let's stop jacking around so we can get out of here."

They worked steadily for the next half hour, clearing the left side of the house and the front walkway. They had just started up the right side, moving toward the back again, when they heard a woman's voice calling, "Laurel." It was much softer than the other sounds of life around them. It blended with the scraping of their shovels, the clinking of tire chains on a car driving slowly up Tupelo Drive, the distant whir of a snow-blower on the next street.

"Laurel."

Now they could tell it was coming from the rear of the house. The woman's voice had increased only slightly in volume, registering the image of someone being summoned to take a forgotten package or a set of keys. At first Willie thought that the footprints leading from the back patio to the street belonged to that person. But they would have seen her pass long before, and no one would wait until now to call. He glanced over his shoulder, expecting the person to emerge through the front door, and then he could tell her that someone back there wanted her. But the door remained closed and the street vacant as the woman called again, a bit louder and insistent — "Laurel."

Willie saw his own question reflected in Lester's face. Why was the voice in the rear of the house? There was no passage back there. No one could walk through those eight-foot hedges.

"*Law*-rail," it sounded to their ear, "*Law*-rail."

They frowned at each other and took their shovels with a silent accord and returned up the path they had just cleared, moving toward the patio and the long-drawn call. It now held an edge of impatience that might be used to summon disobedient children. Looking up, they saw the old woman they had met in the house. She was leaning over the windowsill, the printed housedress open at the throat, and snow flurries blowing into her face. "*Law*-rail." Her impatience now turning into mild anger at being ignored as she shifted her numb hands on the ledge, wisps of gray hair collecting snowflakes like soft lint. It could have been a child with her mittens off, books dragging, and boots filled with snow. It could have been a bowl of soup growing cold, or a sandwich going stale. They followed the direction of the woman's voice and saw that it was a tall, slender body in a silver bathing suit crushed into the bottom of the empty pool — "Laurel" — but it remained the cry of an old woman, calling a little girl home.

"I heard you the first time, Grandma." The child ran into the house, her dress and socks splattered with muddy water.

"So why didn't you answer the first time, miss? A hard head makes a soft behind."

Roberta Johnson closed the screen but hesitated before shutting the peeling wooden door. The wind was sending damp gravel spinning down the Georgia dirt road, and the tops of the sycamores and pecan trees were already bending over. It was going to be a blowing rain, no doubt about it. But it might not reach past the porch, and she would welcome the breeze.

"You still standing there in them wet clothes? The last thing I need is a case of pneumonia on my hands."

She got a towel and sat the child on a kitchen chair, kneeling to remove the damp shoes.

"You're determined to be a trial today." The towel dabbed gently at the feet and legs dangling from the chair. "Determined to wear me out — as if this heat isn't doing a good enough job as it is. You think I got nothing better to do than chase up and down these roads after you? Well, I'll tell you, miss, I got a whole lot of things more than you on my mind." She spied a tiny scratch just above the calf and bent to examine it closely, satisfied it was the same one she'd seen yesterday. "Heartaches. Children ain't nothing but a mess of heartaches. And ain't this red mud?" She frowned at the towel and then picked up the discarded socks. "You been in that ditch! Laurel, I have told you and told you more times than you —"

"I know" — Laurel nodded, her thick braids swinging over each shoulder — "more times than I have fingers and toes. And guess what, Grandma? I know how many times that is — it's twenty. I can count up to twenty now." Her full, round eyes were triumphant and only a shade less proud than the ones she smiled into.

"Well, ain't you something," Roberta said as she took in the coffee skin and thick, bushy brows. "Hardly five and doing that." She might be the spitting image of her poor mama, but she always knew the child would take her brains from their side of the family.

She stood Laurel on the chair to pull off her dress. "But I'm warning you, miss — stay out that ditch or you won't live to count past much more than that. All I need is a drowned child to show your daddy when the summer's over. Yes, Lord, that's all I need."

"Oh, I can't drown, Grandma."

"You'll drown fast as the next one, miss."

Not that your father's new girlfriend would mourn much, Roberta thought. She had never seen a clutchier, more mean-spirited woman. And her son couldn't see through it. He actually thought there was something behind all that head-patting and cheek-pecking that barracuda rained on Laurel when they brought her down in the summer. Why, the only sincere thing that woman ever did was wave good-bye to the child through the window of that car: just like his daddy, God rest his soul, soft in the head and loose in the pocket when it came to a pretty face.

"But Daddy told me I can't drown."

"Now, why you making up tales on your daddy? I know he never told you any such foolishness."

"Uh huh." Laurel's face was serious. "He told me I was his brown sugar baby. And sugar don't drown, Grandma, it melts in the water and makes it sweet."

Roberta laughed in spite of herself. "Well, I'll tell you what. I don't want all this brown sugar melting away in a nasty old ditch, 'cause then I couldn't do this." And she gave her a hug.

Laurel's small arms wrapped around the woman's neck, and she whispered in her ear, "Oh, but, Grandma, you should hear what pretty music the water makes."

Roberta released the child slowly, stared into her face for a moment, and set her firmly on the ground.

"It's time for your nap."

Then she sat alone in the quiet house, listening to the rain drum on the tin roof. When it finally stopped, she put on a pair of her husband's old overalls and fishing boots, and dragging a pick and shovel to the road, she began to fill up the ditch. Since the ground was soft and she worked steadily, Laurel was still asleep when she came back into the house.

Music and water. Laurel brought both in abundance to that five-room cottage each summer. There was a constant chorus of glasses breaking mezzo-soprano, chairs scraping baritone, doors slamming in measured time to the shrill notes of her laughter mixing with those of the neighborhood children. The only silence came from dripping bathing suits and towels thrown over the shower rod and back-porch railing. When Roberta had realized that it was impossible to keep Laurel away from the water, she made sure that she learned to swim. Standing by the edge of the sandy pond with her arms folded, she had watched five summers ago as a neighbor's boy taught Laurel to float. He had a difficult job because the eight-year-old kept struggling against his hands. She didn't want him holding her up, she wanted to be free. Now Roberta shook her head and cursed that day as she maneuvered around the pools of water left by the dripping clothes. No one needed this many bathing suits. Whoever heard of such nonsense: freshwater suits for the pond, and saltwater suits for the lake. And when you multiplied that by three times a day, it added up to a whole lot of aggravation. And she knew Laurel was lying about not going out to the far end of that lake, 'cause she was hardheaded.

Once Roberta had walked those three miles behind Laurel's bicycle tracks and stood in the lake's high weeds among the maidenhair fern and sea roses, watching her slender arms cut through the glassy surface, well past her friends, until she could have been some sort of silver fish way out on the waves that Roberta, arms crossed, willed to hold her up. She knew that if they didn't and Laurel went under, no power on earth could have kept her on that shore, and she didn't swim a lick. She waited and argued with the girl all the way home, contented now that there was no need to worry. But she still asked the same question each time her long-limbed granddaughter bounded through the door.

"You been out to the deep end of that lake?"

"No, ma'am."

"Liar!"

Laurel laughed and sat spread-legged at the kitchen table.

"Get your wet bottom off my chairs, miss. It ain't enough I hardly got one dry spot in this house already? Go change into something."

"It's too hot." Laurel folded her towel over the chair seat.

Roberta stopped chopping her turnip greens and went to the refrigerator. "The Morgan boy came by looking for you today. Seemed mighty disappointed that you weren't around."

"Aw, who cares about him? I don't even like boys."

"Yeah, and a kitten don't like cream." She set the glass of lemonade on the table and went back to the sink. "But it does my heart good to hear you say that, 'cause it's just what I told him."

"Oh God, what did you say, Grandma?"

"Just about what you just got through expressing."

"No, I mean what *exactly* did you say?"

Roberta never turned around. "For somebody who don't give two hoots about a somebody else, you sure seem awful interested in what went on this afternoon."

"I just hope you didn't hurt his feelings, that's all. You know how you can talk sometimes, and everybody might not understand you like I do."

"Now, I like that." She turned her head toward the table. "I talk the way I've talked all my life, miss — plain and clear. And the folks around here don't have any trouble understanding me.

That little peanut-headed boy got my message right off that you were only thirteen years old in spite of them long legs and whatever lies you been telling him about your age, and you didn't care to be keeping company. *And* I said that if that's the reason he keeps hauling his little greasy behind over to this side of the road, he just better haul it back the other way."

"I can't believe you did that." Laurel rolled her head in her hands.

"Well, believe it," Roberta said, " 'cause I did. And his feelings didn't seem to be hurt one bit. No, as a matter of fact," she continued slowly, "his feelings seemed right healthy when I invited him to supper tonight as long as he was willing to sit at my table and behave himself like a proper gentleman."

She took Laurel's kiss stoically and glanced at her back as she ran toward the bathroom. "Yeah, I thought that would get your butt out of that wet suit."

Later that evening they sat on the porch together, Laurel's head resting in Roberta's lap, the crickets and bullfrogs competing as hard to give them sound as the fireflies and stars did to give the light.

"You know, you getting too big for this," Roberta said as she stroked the thick, wavy hair.

"I wish I didn't have to leave you." Laurel sighed and buried her head deeper into Roberta's lap.

"It ain't me you don't want to leave, it's Mr. Yes, Ma'am–No Ma'am over there."

They laughed again as they had while washing the dishes about the Morgan boy who had come to supper with his tie so tight he could hardly swallow, and so nervous he had answered each of Roberta's offers of food with both Yes, Ma'am and No, Ma'am.

"No, really, Grandma. You don't know how awful it is at home."

"I seen your awful — nice big room to yourself, color TV, record player, and all kinds of gadgets. I should have it so bad."

When Roberta's son had announced his sudden marriage last

year to a woman she had never met, she made it her business to take a twenty-eight-hour bus trip and do just that. She arrived on their doorstep with four suitcases, two packed with her clothes and two that were empty. She stayed just long enough to find out what she wanted to know: whether or not she would have to fill those two other bags and use the extra one-way ticket safely tucked away in her pocketbook.

"Well, I hate it there now."

She felt the slender shoulders tense as the words hissed through the girl's clenched teeth.

"Your daddy should hear you talking like that, it would break his heart. He's worked real hard for you, Laurel. You know, some men wouldn'ta saddled themselves with a baby all alone, and you weren't much more than that when your mama passed. I tried to get him to leave you down here with me then, but he felt that you were his responsibility. And he's done right well by you. I know it ain't easy for you to share him now. You've never really had to share anything, have you? But I think you're old enough to understand that grown men have needs, Laurel. Needs that can't all be satisfied by a little girl. And I got to give him credit; he coulda married a long time ago, but he was wait-ing for the right one — not so much for himself, but for you. And your new mama seems right nice."

"She's not my mother. My real mother would never treat me the way she does."

The hand that was stroking Laurel's hair became as still and glacial as the next words: "What has she done to you?"

"She won't let me cut my hair."

Roberta expelled a burst of air that burned her lungs as it left. "Lord have mercy! You been laying here whining 'cause of that? I oughta cut your throat." She shoved Laurel's head from her lap.

"No, really, Grandma." Laurel sat up and leaned over. "I have a chance to swim in the city-wide competitions, but all this hair slows my official time."

"So braid it up and pin it to your head, like you do here."

"I do, and that's just it. It's too bulky to fit under a cap and these braids are added surface friction. And in the water that can make a lot of difference."

"I don't see what difference a few ounces of hair can make. And she's right not wanting you walking around looking like a scalped Indian. Besides, the Good Book says that a woman's hair is her crowning glory."

"See that, you're taking her side — just like Daddy. He's always taking her side about everything. I thought at least you would understand. But no one understands."

And her eyes burned with that strange intensity that always bewildered Roberta. The child was too high-strung. She would wrap her soul around the most trivial things: the slant of sun on a rock, the curve of a wildflower. And they had to be pried gently from her hands because the need for them came from some mysterious valley that opened without warning inside of her. Roberta could tell when that was happening; her voice took on the plaintive echoes that it did at that moment. She was down there now, and Roberta would have to coax her back.

"Laurel, remember the story of Brer Fox and Brer Bear." It was halfway between a question and a command. "They had stolen Farmer Brown's chicken, plucked it, and put it in an old gunny sack. And then they met him on the road and he had his huge, double-barreled shotgun over his shoulder and wanted to know what they had in the bag. So they told him it was nothing but an old tomcat they had found and skinned. And when Farmer Brown went to untie the sack, Brer Bear whispered to Brer Fox, 'What we gonna do when he finds out it ain't no cat?' And Brer Fox said — 'Me, you, and that chicken is gonna improvise.' "

She didn't get the smile she was used to, but she went on anyway. "So you see, sometimes when things ain't going quite your way and you gotta deal with just what's on hand, two people can put their heads together and maybe come up with a way to turn what could be a bad situation into a tolerable one."

Laurel listened, but her eyes were far away and filled with tears. She put her head back on Roberta's lap.

"What I was thinking," Roberta said, "is that if we go into

town Saturday and get Miss Lucinda to put one of them new relaxers in your head, you could still keep peace at home and your
hair would flatten out enough to fit under a cap so you could
swim. How does that sound?"

Her only answer was Laurel's soft breath and the tears she
could feel hot and acidic through the thin summer cotton. "I
want my mother. I want my mother."

It wasn't petulant or whining, but it echoed such an emptiness
that Roberta shuddered as she cupped the thick hair in her
hands.

"Well, I'm the closest thing to a natural mother you got," she
whispered through the screen and out into the night, "so God
help us both."

Music and water. The two became one for Laurel the next and
final summer she would spend in her grandmother's house. Roberta stood on the edge of the pond, holding a tape player like it
was some unpredictable animal.

"Now when I'm in the water, you count to five and push the
button I showed you," Laurel called from the rocks. Wildflowers
had been pinned into the two thick braids crossed over the top of
her head. And the body that had rounded and filled was curved
gracefully over the boulders as she moved into an arabesque that
propelled her into the water.

Roberta gasped when she disappeared under a surface that
gave almost no evidence it had been disturbed. The five seconds
seemed a lifetime and when she pushed in the concave button,
the recorder came alive in her hands with the vibration of violin
strings that she could feel all the way up to the top of her skull.
Simultaneously, the strings pulled Laurel's arched form out of
the water, into a backstroke that hit the surface each time a full
note was played. It was difficult to tell whether her body was
making the music or the music her body, as she turned, plunged,
and lifted to each change in tempo. She'd disappear with each
roll of the bass drums to be resurrected by a clash of cymbals
and sent spiraling toward each edge of the shore by the wind
from the clarinets. It seemed effortless, as if she'd changed the

water into another element. It was liquid air that rewarded every perfect twist and turn by keeping her afloat, keeping her moving, and keeping her free.

She came dripping up on the gravelly dirt, laughing through her heaving chest. "What do you think? I was a little off during the second movement, but I'm working on it."

Roberta handed her a towel. "I didn't know you was gonna jump from them rocks. My heart almost fell out of me."

"Aw, that's nothing." She waved her hand backward, not even granting the ledge the dignity of a glance. "When I work with my group, I come off a ten-foot platform and I hold form all the way down. Just imagine, Grandma . . ." She sectioned the horizon with her hands. "There's Cheryl, Renée, Connie, and then me — all on these ascending platforms. First strings, Cheryl goes. Second strings, Renée. Third, Connie. And then, crescendo — *me*. Right through this flowered hoop. It's wild."

"It's insanity." Roberta thrust the recorder at her. "I don't know what's gotten into your father, letting you do something like that. You could break your neck."

"Oh no, not in the water." She stared out over the pond. "It can be a little scary when you're first up there. But it's all in the balance and how you hit the surface. And it's the greatest feeling in the world when you do it right, Grandma. It's like there's no difference between the air and the water except that the water is safer. Once you get down there and hold still, it lifts you right up, sorta like it was a pair of warm hands or arms. And you come up to all this beautiful music that was really there anyway if you knew how to listen. And then you just move and move and move." She began to do arabesques, jetés, and pirouettes around Roberta.

"Well, if you wanna dance to all them fiddles, why don't you go take up regular ballet?"

"Because it's not the same. It's —" Laurel stopped as if the need for that question would make any answer futile. "It just isn't." Then she smiled. "I'm hungry now. Let's go home."

But Roberta wasn't fooled by that smile. She saw Laurel drawing her thoughts into that private valley that she visited so much that summer while offering everyone else the tokens of her eyes, ears, and mouth.

Roberta touched her shoulder. "I must say you looked right pretty in that water. And with all them flowers in your hair. I guess you're glad you didn't hack it all off last year."

"Uh huh," Laurel said as she pulled the columbines and daisies out of her braids, crushing them before they were thrown in the dirt.

Roberta knew she had made another mistake. Even a passing reference to Laurel's stepmother sent her into one of those "moods," where she picked at her food or settled in the porch swing, staring into space for hours.

That summer she grew especially quiet when it rained. She played one tape over and over. Chopin's Fifteenth Prelude, she told Roberta, who still called it the one where the man kept plunking off-key. It was just her womanhood coming down, Roberta thought, the insides got to catch up the outsides. And knowing how exhausting that race could be, she would bring her a glass of milk, a slice of peach pie, or some biscuits and jam. "Keep your strength up," she'd command before going back inside to her ironing.

It was music and water that kept Laurel away the next year. But the phone brought her voice into the house. Summer was the only time she and her group could really practice together. And she wanted a job this year, but she would try to come for a visit before school started. If not, Roberta was still coming up for Christmas, right? No, she didn't have her eye on some fast-tailed boy up in Cleveland. They sure eyed her enough; but didn't Roberta always say that looking wasn't having, and having wasn't keeping? Well, no boy was going to keep her tied down. Kisses, hugs, and loads of love but it was time to go now. So Roberta didn't hold her, and she put the phone in its cradle with only a twinge of regret, accepting that it was indeed time for Laurel to do that.

The telephone became an important presence in Roberta's house. She knew it would ring at the end of each school year, on

her birthday, Easter, and the second Sunday in May. It gave her
ordered and aging years a predictability that was pleasant, but
when it rang at sporadic times because Laurel couldn't complete
the cycle of some triumph or crisis without sharing it with her, it
gave those remaining years meaning.

It rang now, insistent and shrill because she couldn't reach it
quickly enough. The act of getting up from over the washtub
had to be performed in small increments, making sure the back
would unbend, the knees would support the body, and the legs
would get her across the room. There was no need to come to
graduation because she was going to kill herself, the voice announced dramatically and was told that Roberta would save her
the trouble if she didn't shut up and stop all that crying. She had
been accepted at Berkeley and she couldn't go. That woman had
decided to get pregnant and now her father could only afford
the state university. No, she wasn't being selfish. They knew she
had wanted to go to California for ages. Hadn't she worked for
the last three summers, saving all her money for this? Yes, the
state university had business administration but they didn't
have a decent swimming coach. If she went to Berkeley, she
might get a shot at the Olympics. No, California was not full of
freaks and mass murderers. She didn't care what the *National
Geographic* special said, it wasn't going to fall into the ocean. Why
was she bothering to talk to her anyway? This whole conversation was a waste of time. And a waste of money, Roberta reminded her before slamming down the phone — Laurel had
called collect.

Roberta went to that high school graduation, and Laurel
went to Berkeley. But even if Roberta had been invited to her
college commencement, she wouldn't have gone. She had
learned to become truly suspicious of anything associated with
the state of California. She stopped watching its game shows,
and predicted well in advance for her residents the national ills
that would come from putting two of its citizens in the White
House. And it even reached the point where she refused to buy
its oranges and raisins. It wasn't paranoia or senility; it was just
extreme caution. Because all Roberta knew was that she had

cashed in her life insurance to send a child she had named Laurel Johnson to the state of California, and it sent her back a stranger.

Laurel Dumont got out of the silver Mercedes and stood in front of the weather-beaten house. The scant material of her halter top clung to her back and she ran her hands over her damp throat. Already she could feel the sweat rising through the pores in her scalp, her closely cropped hair forming tight ringlets at the base of her neck. She was glad that Howard had decided to stay back at the Sheraton, he was finally right about one thing: Atlanta was the only civilized section of Georgia. This place was ungodly hot. But he was wrong about the car; renting the Mercedes didn't make her seem more at home. Sitting in that heavy, air-conditioned box and trying to maneuver it over these winding, bumpy roads had given her a fierce headache because she had to concentrate in order not to lose her bearings. Landmarks that should have been familiar took on a different shape and size through the tinted glass and over the circular hood ornament. The only way to tell when Clover Road changed into Bennett's Pass was the texture of the ground, when gravel became clay. But the cushioned springs made it all seem the same, and she'd almost missed turning right at the crucial third pine. As the tires screeched to a halt and she had to do the impossible, back up with a dusty rear window, she might have cursed Howard for leasing the car or cursed herself for making the trip, but that would have taken some clarity about exactly who was to blame, and she didn't have that. There was just the pervasive feeling that she in that car on that road was wrong.

Wrong. The word slipped out of the mouth, forming an invisible circle of air that quickly solidified to join a similar chain of steel links tightening around her chest. Wrong — she and that man back at the Sheraton who could walk into any court and prove their legal right to sign the register "Mr. and Mrs. Howard Dumont" as long as no evidence beyond a ten-year-old marriage license was required. Wrong — she and the house on Tupelo Drive that defied all their efforts to transform it into that nebulous creation called a home. Wrong — she and the career at IBM that she clung to with a desperation mistaken for pride, ambition, or contentment; mistaken for everything but what it was — a mistake. But if she let go of it, what else was left? There would be nothing to cling to except another link in a long chain that contained only totally circular, totally evasive wrongs.

She hadn't seen them building up behind her because she'd spent so much time captivated by the images in front of her: the Phi Beta Kappa pictures in her yearbook, front page of the *New York Times* business section, the bridal pictures in the Dumont family album. All before her twenty-fifth birthday, and in all of them she had been smiling. No wonder the world pronounced her happy, and like a fool she had believed them. Perhaps, just once, if she had failed a course, missed a plane connection, or glittered less at Howard's parties, she might have had time to think about who she was and what she really wanted, but it never happened. And when she finally took a good look around, she found herself imprisoned within a chain of photographs and a life that had no point. She had kept driving because memory told her that there was a point at the clearing of those pine trees. And wedged into it was a house, an old woman, and a beginning.

She stood in front of it now, the house at the end of the road, with its parched lawn and withering borders of marigolds and geraniums. Reddish dust had coated her leather sandals by the time she reached the picket fence. The rusty latch grated against the wooden post, stripping away tiny flecks of white paint. It was amazing how large this yard had seemed once, but she had definitely grown no taller in the last seventeen years, and thank God for that. At eighteen she was already over five-ten and had shuddered to think that she would reach six feet. Now she felt sixty feet tall as she covered the narrow walkway in three quick swings, bending lower than necessary to clear the screened porch door. She was conditioned by years of striding into boardrooms on five-inch heels that gave her the speed and height to announce that she and whatever she had to say were to be taken seriously or not at all. An Amazon. That's what she'd become. The biggest woman at IBM; she'd allow them that one joke as she sank into the chair next to the executive director and crossed the shapely pillars they had learned to respect. Those feet had kicked down doors, caving in the few faces that were foolish enough to be braced against them.

But the closed door that was now in front of Laurel shocked her. Roberta knew she was coming, she had called and told her, so this was obviously some sort of statement that she wasn't welcome. Laurel stared at the door. Wasn't welcomed or wasn't believed? How many other times had she called and not come? Or come and not stayed? Laurel couldn't count the uneaten dinners kept warm on the back burners, the freshly made beds not slept in because her business plans had changed and she was just "passing through." Her hand reached for the latch to push open the door and hesitated. How many times had there been just no time for the woman in this house? The answer made her release the latch: just one time too many. And so she would have to knock like any unexpected visitor and hope to be invited inside.

Her jeweled hand balled into a fist and she struck the wood so forcefully the door rattled on its hinges. The silence that followed threatened to suffocate her as she grasped the door frame and pounded again. She forgot that her long wait could be credited to the dawn of Roberta's eightieth birthday, and that the stoic lines of the face she finally saw were the result of most of those years spent rarely smiling about anything. Roberta's pleasure was usually registered in her eyes, but they were covered now with the gray film of age and were shaded by the drawn blinds in the house.

"I ain't deaf, but I would be if everybody who came here banged on this door like you," she greeted Laurel.

"Well, can I come in?" Laurel massaged her knuckles as she moved past the widening door into the front room. The shadows made it seem small and dingy as she tried to adjust her vision to the shapes around her. "And can I give you a hug?" She could feel the bones' fragile outlines as she wrapped her arms around the woman's shoulders. "Aren't you glad to see me?" She leaned back and smiled into Roberta's stony face. "You don't seem to have much to say."

"Because you done asked three stupid questions in just as

many seconds." Roberta released herself. "And when you get to be my age, you learn not to waste your breath answering them."

Laurel watched as she shuffled back to her easy chair, the sound of the felt house slippers blending with the shadows in the room. She faded into the corner behind the side of the chair, leaving Laurel standing helplessly in the center of the floor. She looked around the house with a growing despondency — the old gas stove with totally empty burners, the wooden kitchenette, the braided rugs separating the kitchen from the sitting room. Behind those closed doors would be two closet-sized bedrooms and a bath. It was little more than a shack. And the place had the smell of old age about it — that inexplicable mixture of dry sweat and moist saliva. But what had she expected? What in God's name had she hoped to find here?

"If you standing there thinking about lemonade, it's in the icebox. And bring me a glass while you at it."

The voice came out of the past, melting the distance between them. She rushed to obey and do her part in recapturing the magic. Inside the refrigerator, the thick discs of lemon floated in the cut-glass pitcher with a clarity that made her want to cry. It would be sweet, sticky sweet, the way Roberta never drank it. The ice cubes were still blocked and solid, put in and timed so they wouldn't dilute the syrupy liquid before she came. The room was dark, and as long as there were no mirrors, she might be able to believe that it was made for the little girl who had just ridden up that road on a bicycle. The little girl with two thick braids who dreamed of swimming in the Olympics. As she turned to swing open the cabinets and grab some glasses, the rows of canned food hit her between the eyes like a sledgehammer. Moving quickly to the next set of doors, she found sacks of flour and rice.

"You've changed the cabinets," she cried out to the darkness and slammed the door shut.

"Miss, my cups and glasses are where they been for the last thirty years. If anything's changed, it ain't them."

Laurel gripped the counter and concentrated — the far left, that's where they were. Why did she think the right? "I don't know why you have it so dark in here, it would confuse anyone," she said aloud to cover her growing panic as she banged through the cabinets. "And don't tell me it's because it's cooler that way, because it's not. I sent you an air conditioner years ago *which,* Daddy told me, you gave away. That's not fair, and you know it. You give away my air conditioner and then keep this place pitch-black and expect people to find things." Her voice was an octave higher when she finally discovered the glasses. "And you had the door shut when you knew I was coming. You never shut the door. But what do you care if it would hurt my feelings."

Her hands trembled as she gave Roberta the lemonade.

"I ain't got to sweep your feelings off my floor like I do the dust that would blow in here on a dry day like today."

Roberta watched her as she sat down in the chair, crossed her legs and began to swing them like the short ticks of a clock. Laurel took two long swallows and turned the wet glass in her hand repeatedly.

"But you ain't come here to talk about my cleaning habits, or the way I keep cool in the summer." She leaned over toward the young woman. "Why did you come, Laurel?"

There was a long pause, and then her voice was barely a whisper. "When people are in trouble, don't they go home?"

Roberta covered her clenched hands gently. "But this ain't your home, child."

"I know." She nodded as her tears further distorted the strange shapes in the darkened room. "But, Grandma, when people are in trouble, don't they go home?"

So Laurel went home. And home was Linden Hills. If she had any doubt, she could look at her driver's license, or call up the post office just to be sure — 722 Tupelo Drive was where her mail had been sent for the last ten years. Not that the carrier needed the house number: everyone knew that the twelve-room stone Tudor had belonged to the Dumonts for over sixty years. The four bedrooms and three and a half baths could boast of nothing but the sweaty backs of lawyers on their sheets and the grime of government officials swirling down their drains. Laurel's husband had kept the tradition going by combining both of those professions: the first black D.A. in Wayne County, hand-picked to be the next state attorney general. And he had chosen the only type of woman his family would have accepted. Laurel came with the Dumonts' ingrained prerequisities: she was sepia, stunning, and successful. She walked into a house that was com-plete, and could think of no major changes to make. The couple had everything; she had to believe that because everyone told her so. And with so much in that house, they didn't miss each other as they both stumbled on their way up, not realizing that their stairways weren't strictly parallel. Slowly, deceptively, the steps slanted until the couple's fingertips could just barely meet across the chasm. They might have discovered it sooner, but for years they could still see each other clearly as one packed the other's bags to catch a plane or Metroliner, listened to the other's speeches for that crucial meeting that always seemed to overlap a birthday, a vacation, or an anniversary. And since their hands were grasped so tightly on their respective set of stairs, it wasn't until they had nearly reached the summit and had time to pause that they realized they had been moving to-gether but away from each other. The gap wasn't large, but it was enough to keep their one free hand from touching, regard-less of how they strained.

Some women would have filled that space with children. Then each could have grasped the infant's hand and let it mas-querade for the flesh of the other. But Laurel filled it with the only two things she could honestly associate with home. After seven years, she had made her first changes in the Dumont prop-erty: she turned the den into a music room and installed a diving pool. Howard didn't protest the carpenters tearing down walls and ceilings to put in shelves and speakers for her hundreds of classical albums and tapes. And seeing that she had purposely designed it to leave room for only one chaise lounge didn't bother him much because he knew how she liked to be alone with her music. But the garage had to be moved and the entire backyard excavated for the style of pool she wanted. If they built a normal-size pool, there would be space for landscaping, garden parties, and barbecues. That sort of an arrangement would be a business asset for both of them, but few people were trained like her to use a thirty-foot diving platform. And when they had children, wouldn't it be better — and safer — for them to be in shallower water at first? But he knew by then that his words were spoken across a void that would preclude any children. So if there was a pool, there might be a chance for a family; and if there was a family, there might be a home. When they both happened to be at 722 Tupelo Drive, they would make love on the chaise to her string quartets, and in the summer he would watch her swim. Too late, they both realized that music and water just weren't solid enough to bridge their gap permanently. Laurel's pool and music room hadn't turned 722 into a home; they only gave her an excuse to return there.

She returned to Tupelo Drive that summer after leaving Roberta. And she stayed. Dressed in either a silk Japanese robe or a terry-cloth wrap, she spent the late summer and early autumn on the chaise lounge or diving platform. She began by telling the office that she needed an extra week off and then an extra month. Finally, she let her answering service intercept all their calls. Her decision not to move a step outside that property grew into inertia and, ultimately, fear. She became terrified that new words or new places would be lurking traps to keep her away from what she was seeking. Georgia wasn't her home, nor Cleveland or California. They had been only way stations that she had passed through. The thought of her dislocation was stifling; the number of places she couldn't claim, dizzying. She had stopped at them all only long enough to get her picture taken. And just maybe if she could freeze reality around her now, she'd know where she belonged. And with that reference point — with any point at all — she could discover what had gone wrong. So she desperately clung to the two things that had felt right for most of her life. When it became too cold to swim, the music got so loud it was deafening.

She thought she heard Howard say that he was leaving to think things over, that he had tried to reach her, but she just

didn't seem to care anymore about him or their home. Yes, he
had definitely mouthed the word "home," because she remembered that it fit so well with the rounded tones coming from the
oboes. The piccolos then kept time with his trembling bottom
lip. She had just let herself go all to pieces. What did she plan to
do about her job, her career? How long did she think she could
stay away and not be replaced? If she needed professional help,
he could get it for her. She couldn't keep herself locked away like
this forever. Look at him, dammit. Something had gone terribly
wrong. Her laughter reached the pitch of the violins. Had he
disturbed her for that? For that illuminating piece of information? If he couldn't come up with any sharper observations, he'd
never make attorney general.

She couldn't hear the doors slam, to the music room, bedroom
closets, or front hall, but she assumed they must have because his
clothes and books were gone. And she couldn't hear the file of
visitors who came all through the late autumn: her father, half-
sister, and stepmother. The neighbors from Tupelo Drive
mouthing concern or curiosity above the volume of her music
until they tired of the competition and went away. She didn't
have to worry about hearing Roberta.

Roberta came in mid-December and just stared.

Laurel looked across the room from her chaise and there she
was, sitting in a straight-backed chair she had dragged in from
the dining room. Laurel said nothing but didn't have the pleasure of feeling that she was ignoring Roberta. Hands folded in
her lap, she calmly allowed the crashing cymbals and thunderous piano chords to wash over the printed housedress and worn-
down slippers. She only moved when the doorbell rang, quietly
disappearing to return again and take up her vigil. They spent
the entire day like that together. Finally, Laurel rolled over and
switched off the system.

"Well, have you heard enough?" She spoke without looking at
the woman. "I'll run down the program for you. The morning
began with Rachmaninoff's Prelude in C-sharp Minor. Then
there was Beethoven's Fourth Concerto in G Major followed by
Brahms's First Symphony. We started the afternoon with Cho-

pin's Fourth, Twenty-second, and Twenty-fourth preludes. Then moved into Tchaikovsky — his Fifth and Sixth symphonies, I played the Sixth twice. And for the last three hours it's been Mahler — I especially like his work. Did you notice that I've spliced the tapes, so there's absolutely no break between the last and first notes of his Eighth and Ninth symphonies?" She continued to talk into the ceiling. "I hope you've come to discuss what you've just heard, because beyond that I've nothing to say to you or anyone else."

"I heard enough the first five minutes I sat here. And the rest of the time was spent trying to make sense out of what I was seeing." Roberta's voice was even and slow.

"I don't care what you were seeing. You saw what all the others have seen: a woman who just doesn't want to be bothered. Can't everyone understand that? I just want to be left alone."

"You said you was willing to talk about that music. Well, what I was seeing was what I was hearing. I can't pronounce them names like you, but that last man — the one you say you like so much?"

"Mahler. Gustav Mahler."

"Yeah, him." Roberta nodded. "It's a might bit different from Bessie Smith, Billie Holliday, or even Muddy Waters."

"I'll say."

"I can hear them starting from the same place, though."

"The same place? They're worlds apart."

"No, they in the same world." Roberta shook her head. "They all trying to say something with music that you can't say with plain talk. There ain't really no words for love or pain. And the way I see it, only fools go around trying to talk their love or talk their pain. So the smart people make music and you can kinda hear about it without them saying anything. You can hear the hurt in Bessie or Billie and I just kinda wish that I'd come here and found you playing their stuff, 'cause that man you seem to like so much — that Mahler — his music says that he ain't made peace with his pain, child. And if you gonna go on, that's what you gotta do."

"So running out and buying the records of women who were

drug addicts and alcoholics would help me, right? Women who got their identities through a crop of worthless men they let drag them down? All that moaning about Jim Crow, unpaid bills, and being hungry has nothing to do with me or what I'm going through."

"You ain't going through nothing much more different than what they went through."

"It's a lot different. But how would you understand?"

Roberta narrowed her eyes. "I guess what folks say is true then. It's lonely at the top."

"It's damned lonely."

"Well, Bessie and Billie are telling you that it ain't so crowded at the bottom, either," Roberta snapped. "You think you done found a special music to match your misery. A misery you got somewhere in the head. No, you ain't never had to worry, like a lot of us did, about Jim Crow or finding your next meal, but if that's all you hear in them songs, then you don't know as much about music as you think you do. What they *say* is one thing, but what you supposed to hear is, 'I can.' " Roberta came and stood over her. " 'I can,' Laurel, that's what you supposed to hear. It ain't a music that speaks to your head like some of this stuff you been playing, or to your body like that rock music of these kids. But it speaks to a place they ain't got no name for yet, where you supposed to be at home. Open up that place, child. 'Cause if you don't, there ain't never gonna be no peace — with the love in your life or the hurt.

"Remember what you asked me this summer? When people are in trouble, don't they go home? You came looking for it back there, but Georgia wasn't really home for you. It was just a shack where you had learned to be at home with yourself. And I had prayed that when you grew up, you would carry that away with you. If you feel you've lost that, Laurel, you didn't lose it in Georgia and so there weren't no point in coming back there trying to find it."

Laurel's face was closed and stony as she kept it turned away from the woman.

"Yeah, I forgot. You said you only wanted to talk about this

here music, and I got a little off the track, didn't I?" Roberta
sighed. "Well, I done exhausted myself on that subject."

She returned to the hard chair with a slight limp, and grimaced as she sat down, grabbing her back. "I'm plain folk, and I
ain't educated. I'd be the last to deny that. But I'm willing to
learn, and I'm ready to sit here — today, tomorrow, for as long
as it takes. Baby, get up and put something else on by that
Mahler man. Maybe this time it'll get a bit more clear, and I can
find something else to say to you."

Laurel did get up. She wrapped the robe around her and went
and kneeled in front of Roberta, taking her hands. But she felt
even that didn't place her low enough, so she sat back on her
thighs and looked up into the woman's face.

"Where do I begin, Grandma?"

"The beginnings are gone, Laurel. But we can start with
today and what you got around you."

"What day is it anyway?"

"It's December sixteenth. And there's nine more days till
Christmas. If we start now, we can have us some kind of holiday — surprise everybody. Get us a tree, and the fixings for a big
dinner. You can cook for an army in that kitchen of yours, but I
brought my own candied fruit and spices."

Laurel laughed and the vibrations hurt her in the middle.

"Oh yes, I did." Roberta nodded. "Christmas wouldn't be
Christmas without a decent fruitcake and I been soaking them
things in brandy for months. It was too much to haul up my own
sweet potatoes, but I figured that even these old frostbitten
northern potatoes would turn out a respectable pie with my secret mixture of cinnamon and nutmeg."

"Grandma, the sweet potatoes in these stores probably came
from Georgia."

"Yeah, but they lose something with all that traveling, believe
me."

"Oh, I believe you." Her eyes clouded over. "You can lose a
lot when you travel too much."

"But anyway" — Roberta's voice got louder — "first thing we
gotta do is set to cleaning this house. Get them floors and win-

dows shining again and the sinks scoured. When I first walked in here, the dust looked at me like I was the one that didn't belong."

"You don't have to worry about that, I've just been lax. There's a woman I can call."

"No, ma'am. I don't trust nobody else to be cleaning where I have to eat and sleep. People just don't take the same care when it ain't their home."

"This is my home, isn't it, Grandma?" The question could have easily come from a dazed and lost child.

"Of course, it's yours — and right smart at that."

"And I can make it, I mean make it into something nice and warm for Christmas like homes should be." Laurel's eyes burned inward as her fevered hands gripped Roberta's. "And I can have Daddy and the family over for the holidays. I know I've been awful to Claudia all these years and she's really made him such a good wife, she's been a better wife than . . . And Howard, I can try to make it up to Howard, too. I haven't been too kind to him either. And he's really not such a bad man, Grandma. But I can do something about that now, can't I?"

Roberta's nod was as slow as it was sad.

"Yes, I can." Laurel pressed her lips together. "I can do it."

She tried. She tried unbelievably hard — until the day that the snow began to fall. Opening up that "place where she was supposed to be at home" was terrifying when she discovered the weight of its emptiness. But she stayed close to Roberta, hoping to fill it with her presence. She followed the stooped and withered shoulders closely around the house, polishing mirrors and tables, vacuuming upholstery and changing draperies. She ignored the fact that the cleaner the house became, the emptier it felt. The discarded magazines and newspapers, the layers of dust and disarrayed rugs had at least taken up extra space, space she now covered with hanging wreaths, bunches of mistletoe, and huge trays of hard candy and nuts. She ordered the largest Christmas tree she could, and it groaned under the weight of Fiberglas balls, oversized doves and stars, yards of silver tinsel. She bought presents for people she hadn't seen in years and piled them under the tree. She plugged in the phone again and it began ringing, shrill persistent music that accompanied the sound of whisks against metal bowls, the opening and closing of the oven door, the new Christmas albums. No Mahler, no Bessie or Billie, she told Roberta, they were too sad. But songs for this season, songs to mix with the aroma of ginger, mace, and burnt sugar that filled the downstairs. She played the music — loud. She laughed — loud. And she sat up in bed at night in the silent house and wondered why it wasn't enough. The weight pressed down on her noticeably then, growing heavier each evening as she paced her room, hoping to relieve it so she could breathe. If she lay down with it, she knew she would suffocate and she feared dying in her sleep.

She begged Roberta for stories. Tell her again about the way she had met Grandpa, the only boy who dared come to church without a tie. Tell her about Brer Fox and Brer Bear stealing the farmer's chickens, about the time she had spanked her for selling her tricycle for a nickel; tell her anything that she could throw into this gaping hole that threatened to crush her to death at night. With a growing horror, Laurel began to realize that all she had been doing that week only added to the weight. Roberta's presence, the decorated rooms, the endless chatter about childhood friends weren't filllng the void, but feeding it. She was taking in the sight of an old woman, the sound of old stories, and the smells of an old tradition with nothing inside her to connect up to them. The woman-child just wasn't in there and neither was the woman.

It soon became too painful to laugh with that heaviness on her chest, so she smiled a lot for Roberta's sake. Then even the slightest noise, the lightest touch began to irritate her. She wanted more than anything else to be left alone, but it was too late. In a few days the house would be crowded with people and talk. Just the thought of the rustling paper and grating laughter exhausted her. She stayed in her room during the day, trying to sleep since she couldn't at night. She told Roberta that an old knee injury made it too difficult to keep baking and cleaning.

The ease with which her lies were accepted brought tears to her eyes. She ached to tell Roberta how much she cared about her, but she knew she'd start crying. And Roberta was right: only fools tried to talk their love to someone else. So Laurel sought an alternative route to allow her to meet her grandmother halfway. In desperation, she thought about the two people who had come the closest to being called friends. The three of them formed a strange triangle where she was in the middle between a woman who admired her and a woman she admired.

First she tried calling Luther's wife, who had always thought her so strong, so self-assured. Why, Laurel had found a way to keep a career and a home going. Laurel actually headed a whole division of men at IBM and didn't take any flak. She needed to hear the special awe and deference in that voice when she picked up the phone and realized it was her. Laurel needed that open pride for what she had become before she called Ruth Anderson to hear hidden pity for the exact same thing. The phone at the Nedeeds rang with a dull hum, ending in sharp clicks that reverberated in Laurel's middle. She kept the receiver to her ear for at least twenty rings, dreading the moment she must put it down and add the burden of yet another empty. Now, where could she be? There was one woman who never went anywhere. She seemed so content nested down there at the end of Tupelo Drive. No, it was more than contentment, a certain smugness as if it were a privilege to wait hand and foot on that prude, Luther. She didn't want a life of her own. She was so willing to live vicariously through Laurel's life, to call at least twice a month and listen patiently to her complaints about her job.

Laurel frowned at the receiver and put it down. But then, her friend hadn't called in quite a while, had she? No, not since the summer, and Laurel had been so out of it, it never dawned on her. It didn't make much difference, she never had anything worthwhile to say.

But, then, was that what Ruth Anderson thought of her? She also hadn't spoken to Ruth since the summer and Ruth *never* phoned her, but she was so willing to listen whenever Laurel rang up on Wayne Avenue. Strange, she had started calling out of pity for Ruth: a broken marriage and losing that house on Fifth Crescent Drive. And then remarrying a man who was a mental patient and worked in factories — when he could work. But slowly, very slowly, she began to sense that Ruth was actually pitying her — as if Laurel were mired down there on Tupelo Drive and the best thing that could have happened to Ruth was that divorce and moving back to Wayne Avenue. Laurel kept calling because she admired that in the woman: the ability to pretend with such ease. No, she kept calling because she admired *that* woman, *that* ease. And she became the pretender. The phone stopped after the second ring. "Ruth? It's Laurel, darling. Merry Christmas!"

She remembered hanging up the phone and taking advantage of the relief on her chest to fly downstairs and tell Roberta that an old girlfriend was dropping by the next day. They were going to exchange gifts. No, not something you could buy but something made with your own hands. This particular woman was in pretty bad straits right now, and so they had agreed to bake each other something. Laurel prided herself on the novel idea; she had saved Ruth embarrassment. But hadn't Ruth been the one to suggest it? Hadn't Ruth said, "Why don't you get up out of that bed and let's make each other a Christmas gift?" Hadn't there even been a tremor of urgency in Ruth's voice? She didn't know why, there had been none in hers. She had just called to say Merry Christmas. Her grandmother was spending the holidays with her, and she and Howard weren't together right now. There was nothing so terribly tragic in that. Ruth had gone through a separation herself, even a divorce. She now vaguely recalled the coaxing, the soothing in Ruth's voice. Why, Ruth had been trying to calm her down, and Laurel just couldn't remember why she felt she had to. It couldn't have been anything that she said: problems, yes there were problems but nothing Ruth hadn't heard before. Was it the way she heard it now? Laurel just couldn't remember that, but she set about making a rum pound cake with frantic energy, chattering to Roberta that she felt so much better now. Why, she was going to make a dozen pound cakes, and rearrange all the furniture in the living room for the party Christmas Eve. She thanked God that Ruth had been home, that she had this reprieve — she could try again for Roberta. And see how Roberta was watching her. Every time she turned around, Roberta was looking at her — and always smiling. She was even too excited to be disappointed when Ruth got sick and sent her husband instead with a box of ginger cookies. She badgered Roberta to show her how to string them up on the already overburdened tree. Yes, she was doing her best to make the most of that reprieve. Then the snow began to fall.

It started to come down heavily just as Ruth's husband left, his arms full of cake and six bottles of Howard's best wine. She looked out the window and saw it sticking firmly to the tree branches and lawn. She lay in bed, shades drawn, and felt, rather than heard, it covering the world outside. It emptied into her as she stayed awake all night, arms across her forehead. She was still in that position when Roberta tapped lightly on her door the next morning.

"Laurel, there's a man downstairs to see you, a Mr. Nedeed. I told him you might not be up to seeing nobody. But he was right polite and said it was important if you could just spare him a few minutes."

"Is his wife with him?"

"Ain't nobody down there but him. When he first rang the bell, I thought it was them boys that's out back, shoveling the snow. Did you see how much it done snowed out there? A regular blizzard, and it ain't stopped yet."

She didn't have to see; she could feel that it hadn't stopped. Inside of her, it was building on roofs and the steep slope of that hill, mantling the naked trees and dull hedges with a shimmering coat of crystals. Soon the sun would be bright and sparkling across its glassy surface, dripping tiny diamonds from the tips of branches, the landscape quickly turning into a perfect, storybook picture. The sight spilled its full weight into her middle, and she finally caved in under the inevitable. There was absolutely nothing she could do after this. She got out of bed, moving like a crippled bird. She had tried her best, but — despite all of her efforts and on top of everything else — it was going to be a White Christmas.

Luther stood up when she entered the living room and offered his hand.

"Good morning, Mrs. Dumont. I apologize for disturbing you so early."

"It's all right, Luther." She sank laconically into a deep-cushioned chair, wrapping her robe around her legs. "And since when have we been so formal?"

"Well, this is a formal call."

"Oh, I see." She sighed. "I was wondering why you came alone."

"My wife's away for the holidays, visiting relatives."

"Oh, really, where?"

"San Francisco."

"I don't remember her telling me that she had relatives in that city. In fact, I didn't think that she had any living relatives."

Luther narrowed his eyes just a flicker. "She has *distant* relations in several places, but I didn't come here to discuss my in-laws." He cleared his throat. "I assume that you didn't receive the letter from the Tupelo Realty Corporation."

"It may have come, I don't know." She glanced toward the front foyer. "There's been a lot of mail lately. People send a lot of cards, and I got tired of opening them."

"I understand. So then I suppose it's safe to assume that you haven't been in contact with your husband."

"You don't have to *assume* that, Luther. I'm sure by now the whole neighborhood knows that Howard and I are separated. His Mercedes is gone, isn't it?"

"Well." He cleared his throat again. "If you open the mail that you've received lately, I believe you'll discover that he's decided to file for a divorce. I'm truly sorry that you had to hear it from me first, Mrs. Dumont, but he sent notice of such intentions to the Tupelo Realty Corporation earlier this week."

"I don't understand why I had to hear it from you at all." Laurel straightened up in her chair. "Not that I care one way or the other. But it's none of your corporation's business what goes on in this house."

"You're perfectly right. But this house, itself, is my business. And since your husband has informed us — as he's legally bound to — that he no longer plans to reside in these premises, I came to find out when you plan to vacate as well."

"Oh. I don't plan to vacate at all. If Howard doesn't want to live here anymore with me, that's his affair. And my lawyers will have to get in touch with him — by mail, I assume — since he's kept his whereabouts such a secret. But I'm sure he knows that I'm more than able to buy him out of whatever rights he feels are his."

"I don't think you understand, Mrs. Dumont. This land was only *leased* to the Dumonts in 1903, and subsequently the Tupelo Realty Corporation underwrote the mortgage for the house that was built on it. Now, that gave them the right to live here for a thousand years and a day, which in effect is a small eternity, but it's *still* a lease. And under our stipulations, if the Dumonts no longer wish to reside here and there are no children to inherit the lease, the property reverts back to the original owners: my family — the Nedeeds. That decision has been made, Mrs. Dumont. And, believe me, I was quite pained to hear it, because the Dumonts are one of the oldest and finest families in Tupelo Drive, and I had hoped to have them here forever. But, unavoidably, things do happen, and I'm inquiring about your personal plans to vacate."

"No, let's back up a minute, Luther. Howard Dumont made that decision, not Laurel Dumont — not *me*. And this Dumont is telling you that she's going to stay here."

"The decision isn't yours, Mrs. Dumont."

"You're damned right it's mine." Laurel leaned over. "Don't come in here, bringing any of that crap from the Middle Ages. You see, I *know* how it is in your house, Luther. But Howard speaks for Howard, and I speak for me. We're in the twentieth century up here at Seven Twenty-Two Tupelo Drive. And I have as much say about the future of this property as he does."

"You're in Linden Hills, Mrs. Dumont. Read your lease. And this property belongs to the Tupelo Realty Corporation. Whatever is *in* this house and whatever you've added *to* this house is between you and your husband to divide by whatever laws of whatever century you choose. But Howard Dumont has decided that there are to be no more Dumonts at Seven Twenty-Two Tupelo Drive, and according to the original terms of the lease, that's how things must stand."

"I'll see you in court, Luther."

"Unfortunately, you won't be the first."

"But I'll be the first to drag your ass all the way to Washington, D.C."

"There's no need for that sort of language, Mrs. Dumont. When you think about it, what would you do alone in a house this size? You would probably come to the conclusion that it was best to move anyway."

"Daniel Braithwaite didn't move, and his wife has been dead for years. I didn't see you running down there to kick him out — when you should have. That crazy old Peeping Tom with his decayed willow trees is a disgrace to this neighborhood."

"Daniel Braithwaite has the right to that property for as long as he lives. And there was always the chance that he might remarry."

"Well, I might remarry, too. Did you ever think about that?"

"Of course, a young woman like you should. But if you did, the lease would still be invalid unless we decided to negotiate with your new husband — if he qualified."

"This conversation isn't taking place." Laurel shook her head. "There is no way that this conversation is taking place in my living room, with this man looking me straight in the face and telling me that I don't exist. That *I* don't live in this house."

She began to laugh, shrill bursts of air with her head thrown back. It went on and on.

"I'm truly sorry, Mrs. Dumont. But that's the way things have always been here."

"Don't look so distressed, Luther." Her hand went to her heaving chest. "You see, this has never been home, and you've just added a new dimension to it for me. Thank you, and Merry Christmas." Now her laughter couldn't be differentiated from a scream.

"Please, do you want me to call someone for you?"

"No, why?" She took deep breaths and then tightened her

lips. "I'm fine. I just want you to get the fuck out of my house. But don't worry, we'll meet again in court."

"I don't think so, Mrs. Dumont." He stood up, his eyes penetrating and a bit sad. "I truly don't think so."

If it had been honest anger, it might have helped. Or just simple indignation would have carried her through. But she watched his retreating back and felt nothing. If the house had burned down the moment he closed the door, she wouldn't have cared. She had fought him only through reflex, a reflex triggered by a history of firing against ingrained male assumptions that she didn't count. But now that the practice session was over and the target gone, Laurel took in the full weight of his words: she had never lived in a house in which she had never lived. He thought he was bringing bad news and he had looked so comical sitting there, trying to be compassionate when he'd actually come with no news at all. Yes, Luther had brought her absolutely nothing.

She wanted to laugh again, but the lips that curled up to smile were trembling. The emptiness of all he had said finally expanded the waiting void to the top of her skull. It pressed her mind up against the rigid cranial bones, so that the shapes and textures in the room could only filter through its vacuous light, and it gave them a clarity that was monstrous. The reds, greens, and yellows exploded around her. The sharp points of each Christmas-tree needle, the curve of the sofa arm, the fine print in the wallpaper, were standing disembodied and torn from any meaning or sense that her compressed mind could have given them. Dear God, she was going insane. She clung to the fragment of reason that had voiced the thought. Pressing her fingers against her temples and squeezing her eyes shut, she tried to push back the tremendous weight crushing her brains. There had to be something left to save her. A tiny blue bubble formed by the pressure of the void against the soft brain tissue began to balloon at the remaining tip of her mind. She concentrated as it grew round, translucent, and shimmering: *Oh, but, Grandma, you should hear what pretty music the water makes.* It inflated in smooth, undulating ripples, lightening her head and lifting her body out of the chair. Of course. What could she have been thinking of to let things get this far? Where was Roberta?

She sped past the textures and shapes that now took form and meaning through the waves of blue light. This table once held a bathing cap, that coatrack a terry-cloth robe. These steps led up to a bathroom where swimming suits could be draped across shower rods. The diamond tiles in the kitchen pointed toward the patio door, whose metal tracks slid open to a flagstone path. And at the end of the path was the pool. She must find Roberta, tell her that although things hadn't worked out her way, it was still going to be all right.

Roberta wasn't downstairs, but Laurel found her up in the guest room, eyes fluttering and breath rattling with light sleep. A flood of tenderness came over her. She had put this woman through so much this past week. She had made her carry the load for both of them, and it showed. Roberta rarely took naps during the day. Laurel started to awaken her and share her happiness over the tiny blue sparkles cascading down the walls of the room, but she hesitated. For once in her life she wouldn't be selfish, she'd let the old woman get her rest. Laurel smiled, kissed the wrinkled forehead, and gently closed the door.

Running into her bedroom, she quickly stripped down and stretched the silver bathing suit over her lean body, feeling it become one with her skin. She glanced at her bare feet and frowned: there was so much snow outside. The doubt threatened to overwhelm her, but going to the back window, she saw that the path was miraculously clear. Slipping on a terry-cloth robe and a pair of thongs, she headed for the patio door.

The cold air might have stopped her as it numbed her exposed body, or the metal tarpaulin rings that resisted her efforts to release their frozen hooks. But she made it because she thought music. Clenching her trembling jaws, she pulled and rolled, pulled and rolled, until the pure aquamarine of the pool's high walls and floor jumped up to engulf her eyes. The color vibrated the blue bubble, filling her middle with fluid sound as she shed small, icy tears of relief.

She hurried back to the base of the platform because flurries were already trying to speckle the pool's bottom. Her limbs were stiff so she ran in place and did several deep knee bends. Feeling the blood circulating and warming her, she dropped the robe, kicked off the thongs, and began to climb. One hand over the other, grasping the aluminum rungs, she stopped every ten feet to massage her fingers and flex her knees. On finally reaching the top, she breathed deeply. The platform was covered with snow, so she held on to the side railings and pushed it away with her bare feet. She had to be careful or she would slip and go crashing onto the cement siding. She knew this was dangerous even in the best of weather. The body weight had to be evenly distributed on each foot, the arms and torso held at an angle that provided the vital balance as you moved toward the end of the platform. And it was much more difficult because the cold was numbing her extremities and distorting her sense of weight. Lining her toes up evenly an inch from the platform's edge, she began to swing her arms over her head in a 180-degree arc. She knew it by heart: it was going to be a straight, thirty-foot dive at the twenty-foot end of the pool, but each time you must judge the point of descent. A slight dark movement at the far corner of her eye didn't break her concentration: she was used to spectators. Choosing an area where it was still totally blue, she began to talk herself through the part that never came naturally. Legs straight, body forward, toes thrust. She sprang. Chin close to her chest, that familiar grip of terror in her stomach — anything could go wrong up in the air. But once she got down, there would be nothing to fear. Once she got down, she'd be free.

"Laurel, Laurel."

The old woman hung dangerously out of the upstairs window, the name on the verge of becoming a hysterical chant.

"Oh my God." Willie was immobilized, his head swinging between the pool and the window.

"We better get to her," Lester said, and at first Willie couldn't figure out which woman he meant. "She might fall out of that window." Lester ran toward the open patio door, his motion snapping Willie back.

"Call the cops," he yelled to Lester as he headed for the pool. "No, call an ambulance — call somebody."

He swung himself down the ladder at the far end, the high aquamarine walls looming over him as he ran. Pink and beige stains were slowly spreading from Laurel's body into the surrounding snow. From the angle of her neck, she couldn't possibly be alive, but he had the irrational fear that she might be suffocating with her nose pressed so firmly into the bottom of the pool. Without thinking, he turned her over.

Her face was gone. The photo album trembled in her cold hands as she realized there was no mistaking what she now saw: Priscilla McGuire ended at the neck — and without her features, she was only a flattened outline pressed beneath cellophane. The narrow chin, upturned nose, and deep fiery eyes were a beige blur between the shadows cast by the two grown men on each side of her. The entire face, the size of a large thumbprint, had been removed. This had been done on purpose. There was no way this wasn't done on purpose. Cleaning fluid. Bleach. A drop of hot grease. Over and over, page after page, the smeared hole gaped out into the dim light. The sight of it sickened her as she kept slamming through the album, feeling her empty stomach heave. She had been tricked into this . . . *I knew you would come, and I'm so pleased* . . . into another twisted life. What other kind of woman would have kept something like this? A healthy mind would have never . . . She came to the last photograph. And scrawled across the empty hole in lilac-colored ink was the word *me.*

The bile moved up into Willie's throat and he quickly turned his back to the crowd in the yard. He had been trying to keep his stomach muscles tightened against it for the last half hour, but the sight of Laurel's covered body being lifted from the pool on a stretcher brought back the image he had blocked from his mind. Running to the unshoveled side of the house, he retched into the snow. Lumps of yellowish-green mucus slid into a set of deep footprints. Ashamed, he tried to cover it up by pushing snow over it with his feet, but his body acting with a will of its own emptied his stomach again. He tried to muffle the sound as if he could be heard above the squawking police radios and the loud murmurs of neighbors brought out by the sirens. They stood in puzzled and horrified clusters around the pool's edge, a few still trudging up the path he had shoveled what seemed a decade ago. Willie reached for a handful of snow to clean his sour mouth, but the moment it touched his fingers he got flashes of the colored stains that had surrounded Laurel's body. Dropping it, he brushed off his hands and rummaged in his pocket and found a piece of stale licorice.

Turning, he saw that Lester was still talking to the policemen. He should go back over there and say he was leaving if they didn't need him anymore, but his legs weren't steady and his limbs kept vibrating from the weakness inside him and the frigid temperature outside. He jammed his hands into his coat pockets and tried to stop shaking. He refused to look at the pool, afraid that his stomach would let go again. He avoided any eye contact with the occasional glances that the neighbors threw his way. He didn't want to be asked any more questions. So he stared at the snow banked between the hedges and the house, at the double path of footprints now focusing clearly. The strange, triangular-shaped crevices appeared vividly in two determined sets of lines, leading up and then away from the backyard. This was the path she had taken? No, she might have come up that way, but it was certain that she didn't go back. She had gone out wrapped in white canvas. She had gone out without a ... Willie's insides began to cramp again. God, please let his legs work — he had to get out of here.

"Son, are you all right?"

He hadn't seen the old man approach, so he almost screamed when his shoulder was touched. The man's light-brown skin carried an ashen tint from the cold air, but the gray eyes were gentle through the steel-rimmed glasses. There was something reassuring, almost calming, about the slightly stooped back as he leaned over Willie.

"No, I'm not." Willie's jaws trembled as he spoke. "I don't feel too good. I've gotta get out of here. I mean, I'm cold and we've been out here so long and —" He pressed his lips together and jammed his hands deeper into his pockets.

"Of course." The voice was smooth, soft. "You're one of the young men who found her. I saw you talking to the police. You've probably been out in this weather for hours, and no one's given a thought to your comfort. You must excuse us, we've all been overwhelmed by this. But wait a moment, please."

Before Willie could respond, he left and returned as quietly as the first time. "I believe the police have all the information they need from you. If there are any further questions, I told them they could reach you at my house."

"Hey look, I just wanna go to my own place, ya know?"

"Of course. But I assume that you live some distance from here, and you can't walk back up this hill the way you are now. And if you're willing to accept my hospitality, you'll get a little rest and some warmth while I call you a cab."

"I'm sorry, I didn't mean for it to sound like that. It's just that . . . Oh Christ, I don't know what I mean anymore."

"I understand, believe me, I do." The gray eyes never left Willie's face. "My name is Daniel Braithwaite, and my home is just one street down. Once we're there, you can collect yourself and be on your way."

"Thank you." Willie was growing uncomfortable under the man's bland stare. "But I have to wait for my friend."

"I'll go see what's keeping him. Why don't you meet us by the front steps? Go this way." He pointed Willie toward the side of the hedge. "It's a bit snowy, but you won't have to work your way through the crowd."

Willie plowed through the snow, following the set of triangular footprints toward the front of the house. He knew exactly what they were now, but he refused to think about what they meant. He didn't want to think again for a year. He let his mind go blank as he sighed and stared at the front of the Tudor.

"Christ!" Lester shook his head as he came around the corner. "The way those cops were going on, you woulda thought we pushed her off that diving board."

"Maybe somebody did," Willie said almost to himself.

Lester stared at him and started to speak but changed his mind. "She was just nuts, that's all." His face was pale in spite of the cold. "But what a way to die."

They stood there in silence until Braithwaite joined them.

"A pity, a true pity." He spoke while looking up at the windows. "They had to sedate the grandmother, and the authorities are going to have to locate her husband. This will be a crushing blow for Howard." His long sigh formed a double tube of condensed air from his nose. "I would hate to be in his shoes when he finds out. Of all people, for it to be his wife." He sighed again. "His wife."

"Her name was Laurel." Willie was staring into space.

"What?" Braithwaite turned to him.

"I said, her name was Laurel." Willie's voice got louder. "Laurel."

Lester looked at him strangely. "You okay, Willie?"

"No, of course he's not." Braithwaite touched Willie's arm. "This whole affair has been a shock to all of us. And standing out in this weather won't help matters any. Well, come along."

The noisy hum of activity around the Dumont home was swallowed up as they followed Braithwaite down the gently sloping road that curved to the right, bringing them into the back of the third and final set of houses on Tupelo Drive. They walked in complete silence, each seemingly intent on the crunch of snow underfoot. Willie's head was tucked into his collar as he guided himself by the impressions of Braithwaite's round-toed boots, so he didn't notice that headstones from the cemetery flanking the streets were now quite visible through the low-hanging pine tree branches. Braithwaite's house was the only one in a widely spaced crescent of four that didn't have a huge wall of hedges in the back. The split-level ranch house was surrounded on three sides by gnarled willows, their branches trailing the ground like bleached skeletal fingers. They approached the house between low stone benches and the dwarfed bonzai trees of a Japanese garden holding intricate patterns of rocks and boulders that pushed up through the snow-covered dirt.

"It's difficult to keep up a lawn on this sandy incline, so I decided on this arrangement. It's really quite pleasant in the summer. I stock those pools with goldfish."

Willie could easily imagine the old man sitting under his pale-green willows on those stone benches next to the small marble ponds. His whole manner seemed to fit that type of setting.

"We can go in through the side door. I rarely use the front."

The steps were brushed clean, exposing a grass welcome mat. And over the bell was a brass plaque engraved *Dr. Daniel Braithwaite*.

"The nameplate is new." He ran his fingers over the surface. "I used to have one with my wife's name on it as well, but I've been a widower for almost twenty years and I don't know why I hung on to the old plate. I suppose keeping Anita's name up there somehow kept her close to me. But there comes a time when we have to accept the reality of things, don't we?"

"But if you're a doctor, why didn't you help?" Willie said. "I remember that you were one of the first ones who got there right after the police. Why didn't you see if —"

"You've mistaken that sign." Braithwaite opened the door. "I'm a history professor, or at least I used to be."

"I'm sorry, I thought you were a real doctor."

Braithwaite laughed soundlessly. "You just might have a point, young man. Maybe I shouldn't have that up on there. If I accept that I'm no longer married, I should accept the fact that I'm not associated with the university anymore. But I'm still doing research and so I guess that justifies it. Besides, I've lived longer as Dr. Braithwaite than I've lived as anything else."

"It looks like I'm gonna spend the whole day apologizing to you. But I didn't mean anything, Dr. Braithwaite, really. I wasn't trying to insult you."

"Yes, I know." Braithwaite led them into a large, dark room. "It's strange, but even in academic circles nowadays young people prefer not to be addressed that way. They think it old-fashioned. But when I got my degree from Fisk, it was something to be proud of. There were so few of us at the time, and we wanted it to be known. Why, with the Civil War just being over . . ." He winked at them and seeing their blank faces, burst into laughter.

"My God, I guess you really do think I'm old enough to have been around then."

"Of course not," Lester hurried to say, "but maybe World War One or something."

"Yes." Braithwaite smiled. "I was alive during that war. But believe it or not, I was just a bit too young to fight."

He turned on the overhead light and motioned for their coats, but for a moment they forgot him as they stood in stunned amazement. The room had to be over half the size of the house, and at first, they thought it didn't have any walls. The ten-foot ceiling must have been held up by the stacks of books starting down at the very floor. But the oak shelves were custom-built to fit every available inch of wall space, even lining the door frame and the fireplace. Crammed in above the leather-and-gold bindings and loose, dusty spines were manila folders and newspapers. Three-foot stacks of papers and files surrounded a scarred desk, facing the only unshelved wall; instead there was a heavy purple drapery hanging from ceiling to floor — next to it, a high-powered telescope.

Willie finally spoke. "This is amazing."

"No, it's a mess." Braithwaite motioned them toward the couch in front of the fireplace. "But I wasn't expecting any visitors today." He removed an empty soda bottle, soiled paper napkins, and a greasy plastic plate from the coffee table. "Make yourselves comfortable. I'll be right back."

The patchwork quilt draped over the sofa's back smelled of fresh sweat and old dust. The sofa's arms were slick, and the cushions had been mashed down and bore the imprint of a human body.

"Did you ever?" Lester ran his hands along one wall of books. "This place reads like a *Who's Who in American History* — Paine, Franklin, Henry Adams. Willie, look at this. The entire set of the Federal Works Project's slave narratives. And he's gotta have every *Crisis* in existence — his start from 1910. *Journal of Negro Education, Journal of Negro History, Black Enterprise* — all of them, Willie." Lester kept going down the line, "Booker T. Washington's *The Negro in Business*, Carter G. Woodson's *The Negro Profes-*

sional and the Community, Frazier's *Black Bourgeoisie.* I don't believe this — every one of the *Atlanta University Studies* and, oh my God — Du Bois's *The Philadelphia Negro.*" He took the volume out. "And it's a signed first edition. I bet these are all first editions. This room is worth a fortune."

"I know," Willie said. "He's got more books than the library over on Wayne Avenue. There's got to be at least five hundred just over this fireplace." He looked at a thick volume entitled *Poetry of the Negro.* Imagine, he had thought it was a big deal because he'd memorized 665 poems, and there was more in this one book than in his entire head. There was something awesome about one man owning all this knowledge.

Braithwaite came in with a silver tray, holding a crystal decanter and three sherry glasses. "I hope you don't mind sitting in here — there's not much to the rest of the house. After my wife passed, I kept it closed off to save on fuel. Don't look surprised, we're not all well off down here on Tupelo Drive."

There was a quiet dignity and deliberateness in the way he poured their sherry and handed the glasses to them, his long fingers cracked and ashen in the joints. It made it easy to overlook the crumpled pants bagging in the seat and knees, and the frayed shirt collar with gravy stains.

"I thought of heating some soup. But this will set you right."

As the effects of the alcohol spread through his body, Willie realized how tired he had been. His insides began to loosen up, and all the feelings and questions he had suppressed that morning rose toward the surface. If he drank enough of this stuff, it would deaden them, and that's exactly what he wanted. He knew he couldn't do it here, but he ached to be home so he could really get drunk.

Braithwaite leaned back in his chair and stared at them with his opaque gray eyes. "World War One, eh?" He seemed to be enjoying a private joke. "Yes, I was just a bit too young to be drafted for that one, and as luck would have it, when the second one came I was just a bit too old. So I've seen no combat — on the battlefields at least. But wars are fought in many ways, my young friends, many ways." He sipped his drink and his mind seemed to drift off. "We saw such a battle today. She fought valiantly, but she lost. I knew it was going to happen, it was just a matter of time."

"You mean you knew she was crazy?" Lester asked.

"She wasn't insane," Braithwaite said. "True insanity, as frightening as it might be, gives a sort of obliviousness to the chaos in a life. People who commit suicide are struggling to order their existence, and when they see it's a losing battle, they will finalize it rather than have it wrenched from them. Insanity wouldn't permit that type of clarity. Laurel Dumont died as deliberately as she lived, believe me. And I could tell she was on that path months ago."

"But if she was a neighbor of yours," Lester said, "and you could see she was disturbed, why didn't you do something?"

"What would you suggest I do?" Braithwaite's voice was mild.

"I don't know — talk to her old man. Get her to see a shrink. Something." Lester leaned over. "If she had been a friend of mine, I —"

"But think now. She was the daughter of someone. The wife of someone. And even the granddaughter of someone right there in the house with her. Could they stop her? So how do you suggest that a mere outsider would have been any more effective?"

Willie shook his head. "I'm sorry, Dr. Braithwaite, but I can't buy that. I can't believe that someone would know what was happening and just stand there." He shuddered. "That's not being human, that's being a . . . a I don't know what."

Braithwaite looked at him fixedly. "Weren't those very human footprints that you saw in the snow?" He nodded at the shock on Willie's face. "Yes, I know you saw them and I saw them, too."

"What footprints?" Lester's head swung between the two of them while Willie just stared in his glass.

"The footprints of someone who came up along the side of that house, stood there, watched, and then went away. Right, son?"

"Willie, what's he talking about?"

"I don't know what he's talking about." Willie gripped his glass.

"I'm talking about not being able to stop the course of human history, a collective history or an individual one. You can delay the inevitable, set up roadblocks and detours if you will, but that personal tragedy today was just a minute part of a greater tragedy that has afflicted this community for decades. And the person who watched it unfold understood that. He understood that to try and stop her would be like trying to ward off a flood with a teacup."

"I don't have a tenth of your education, Dr. Braithwaite," Willie said, looking slowly around the room. "You've probably forgotten more than I'll even live to know." Now he looked straight at Braithwaite. "You see, I'm from across Wayne Avenue. And two guys on a Saturday night will often get into a real ugly argument. Everybody knows they're not mad at each other, they're mad about the lousy paychecks in their pocket — or no paycheck. And then they're mad because they're in that bar anyway, or at that poker table, when they should be home 'cause there's kids to feed and rent to be paid. But they can't face that 'cause they know those paychecks ain't gonna do it, and they're even madder that they'll do it even less once they leave that bar. So they're aching for a fight, ya know? And if they start a fight, someone will probably get killed. And everyone else in the room knows that 'cause they're feeling the same way, too — that it would take just a little to push them over the edge. So you make a joke, you buy one of them a drink — you do *something* to keep the steam down. Even though you know that next week the same thing will probably happen again — different faces maybe, but the same damned thing. And it's gonna keep going on, 'cause Putney Wayne won't change and those paychecks won't change. But you still say to yourself, 'It would be a crime to let this happen.' And I don't care how you want to break it down, there was a crime committed out there today. As sure as I'm sitting here, there was a crime."

"Holy shit, you mean someone killed her?"

"They might as well have." Willie looked down into his glass.

"But who?"

"That's not the point, Lester."

"I believe it is." Braithwaite nodded. "Tell him who saw it."

"Yeah, who, Willie?"

Willie hesitated. "Nedeed saw her, Lester. And he just stood there. He didn't lift a finger."

"Christ, that figures. But how did you know?"

"His footprints. Remember how he seemed to appear from nowhere? Well, those pointy-toe shoes were all on the side of the house that we didn't shovel."

"And you think that's a crime?" Braithwaite asked.

"I know it is," Willie whispered.

"You're damned right," Lester said.

"There was a time when I would have thought so," Braithwaite said very gently, "when I was young like you. But I've seen too much over too many years." He went over and drew the draperies on the far wall. "You see, I've had the privilege of this."

Brilliant light flooded the room because the entire wall was made of double Plexiglas. And in front of his desk, Linden Hills stretched up in its snow-covered awesomeness. Through the naked willow trees, they could clearly see the police car pull out of the Dumonts' driveway, the shrubbed meridian running up Tupelo Drive to the brick pillars, sections of Linden Road, and even the very housetops on First Crescent Drive.

"You didn't think you could see that far up from here, did you? It's a strange topography. When you're up there, you can't see all the way down, but if you're situated at just the right point on Tupelo Drive, you have a view all the way up. No one's ever thought about that here, because these homes were designed to face down — except, of course, for the Nedeeds." He caressed his desk, a full, measured stroking. "I've spent many years having the privilege of seeing what Luther Nedeed has seen. Yes, I even watched him enter and leave that backyard. And I understand his futility."

The light gleamed on his steel-rimmed glasses as he turned around to them. "Do you know what this area was like once, when Luther's grandfather was around and your grandmother, young man, Mamie Tilson? Oh, yes, I knew who you were. I've watched you both all this week, slowly making your way down this hill. Well, the road you took was unpaved once and most of the homes there little more than shacks. And the Nedeeds changed that almost single-handedly. A lot of families up there owe their educations to the Nedeeds. I know I do. My family's biggest dream was for me to become foreman at the turpentine factory that was once on the other side of town. But Luther's grandfather set up a scholarship fund that made it possible for me to attend Fisk. He said, 'Daniel, go out there and learn all you can and then bring it right back to your community. Whatever field you decide on, we can use it here in Linden Hills.' He didn't think he'd wasted his money when I came back as a historian instead of a lawyer, engineer, or a *real* doctor. He put me down here and let me work. I've built a reputation from my studies about Linden Hills. The Nedeeds have given me exclusive access to all of their family records: survey reports, official papers from the Tupelo Realty Corporation, even the original bills of sale that date back to 1820. Priceless information that wouldn't have been appreciated at the time anywhere but here and by anyone but them. When I first started my studies, no one in the outside world cared about the fate of a ragged sod hill. But look at it now. Sure, researchers come from all over the country and even Europe, trying to get access to the records about this community. But Luther has assured me that they will be mine exclusively for as long as I live."

"Then you know everything about the Nedeeds." Willie could feel his heart pounding as he leaned toward Braithwaite. "I mean the wives and children and all? You've got their lives all in your books?"

"The family is right out there." Braithwaite pointed up the slope. "You see Linden Hills and you see them. The first Luther Nedeed lived for this community, and he passed that spirit on to his children. That there was something to strive for, something to believe in, that we could make it in spite of what the world said. Believe me, he wasn't terribly happy, always having to fight the Wayne County city board, the white realtors, and sadly enough, the folks right here to turn this place into something to be proud of. The Nedeeds kept going because they felt our people needed a role model. It wasn't easy, but they did it. And that was real black pride.

"I watched them build this place up from practically nothing. A handful of illiterate and unskilled people came here and prospered because of them. I've seen families grow up and grow out from being under the heel of Wayne County. Those families owe all that to the Nedeeds, but somehow they've forgotten that. Now, moving in here has simply become the thing to do, the place to be. But to be *what?* They don't see that clapboard house at the bottom of this hill anymore. At the foot of this hill are colored men with a sense of purpose about their history and their being. If Laurel Dumont had had that, she wouldn't have been so tormented that she felt the need to throw her life away."

"If you really knew my grandmother, then you knew that she despised the Nedeeds," Lester said. "They caused this mess that you're talking about. They built the homes and they set the price tags, Dr. Braithwaite. They wanted a bunch of puppets who would give anything to be here. And that's just what they've got. My grandmother used to tell me and anyone else who would listen, 'You wanna make it in Linden Hills? You just gotta sell —' "

" 'That silver mirror God propped up in your soul,' " Braithwaite interrupted him. "Yes, I can almost hear my old friend now. And I remember her well, sitting up there on that porch chewing her tobacco. Your grandmother was a very shrewd woman, young man. But she was wrong about that. You see, she'd only come down here on occasion to fish with Luther Nedeed, and passing by these houses as you've done this week, she thought that the people in them were selling little bits of themselves to make it. If she'd had my vantage point all of these years, she would have known that they've sold nothing; pieces of themselves were *taken* away. And if anyone was more disturbed about that, it was the Nedeeds. They slowly began to realize that people could live here, but with a few exceptions like myself, it was inevitable that they couldn't work here. So they had to keep going out and coming back with the resources to move down, but with less and less of themselves. You see, Mamie Tilson mistook the ends for the means. And that wasn't the fault of the Nedeeds. If you must fault them for anything, fault them for wanting power. But it was *black* power they wanted. These were to be black homes with black aspirations and histories — for good or evil. But that's not what Luther inherited. Put yourself in the place of a man who must reign over a community as broken and disjointed — as faceless — as Laurel Dumont's body. If he could have stopped her, he would have. But what he saw diving off that platform was already a shattered dream."

"So what you're saying is that what he did was right?" Willie asked.

"Now, think back, I never said it was right. And I'm not saying it was wrong either."

"But it's got to be one or the other," Willie said.

"Why? Why should it be other than from some personal need that the young, like yourself, or the intellectually sluggish have to want their worlds neatly boxed? Was slavery wrong? It would depend upon who you were talking to and when — black or white. The rise of Hitler? The fall of the Aztec empire? There are no absolute truths, and the best historians know that. You strive to capture a moment of time, and if your work is done properly, history becomes a written photograph. Put your subject too much in the shade, too much in the light, dare to have even a fingernail touch the lens or any evidence of your personal presence, and you've invalidated it." He went to a shelf and pulled out a huge tome. "Look at this — the work of a lifetime. It's one of my eleven volumes about the history of Linden Hills. By the time I had only completed volume six I was being seriously considered for a Nobel Prize. It was with this volume that I detected that there was a drastic change in the goals of this community, that what my studies were actually amounting to was the record of a people who are lost. I didn't bemoan that fact and I didn't applaud it; I did nothing but continue to compile the data that Luther brought me and to crystallize my own observations. I'm now into the twelfth volume, and I've heard that I'm being considered again, because no one else has been privy to these documents, and since the turnover here is tremendous, there's a mass of data almost each year." He stepped over to the window and tapped the telescope. "I miss nothing; I record it all in its minutest detail. As long as they keep coming — and they will do that — I'll finally get that ultimate recognition."

"Did you ever stop to think that you could use your work to help save people?" Lester asked. "If you admit it's a terrible situation and you have all the evidence to prove it, why not come out and say so? You're in the position to have people listen to you."

"I don't believe you've heard a word I've said. People are going to come and live in Linden Hills regardless of what I or anyone else does. Do you know that when that crucial sixth volume brought me international acclaim, Luther's father threw a huge party and made gifts of the entire set to everyone who lived here? Did they sit down and take the time to read it? Did they trace themselves as I'd traced them, making that headlong rush into damnation? If they did, it hasn't stopped them. Because it's inevitable, don't you see? And I would have been foolish to try and hold back that flood. And since that's the case, I would have been a greater fool not to take advantage of the access the Nedeeds have afforded me to this priceless information. Luther knows and I know that I can only hope to record that knowledge, not rectify it."

After such knowledge, what forgiveness?

Willie was startled when they both looked at him, and he realized he had thought aloud. "I wasn't asking that question. It's just a line that popped into my head from some poem. I really don't know why," he lied as he glanced around the room involuntarily. "It doesn't have a thing to do with what we've been talking about."

"You know, I'm quite fond of poetry and I've quite a few interesting collections here. There's even a signed copy of that wonderful Mr. Cullen's *The Black Christ* somewhere in this jungle. I've always felt that creative artists and historians are somewhat in the same business, the task of capturing life. Who was the poet you were thinking of?"

"You know, it's really funny but I can't remember." Willie

felt rather than saw Lester's shock, and he prayed he wouldn't say anything. The linen napkins carefully folded for them, the silver tray and crystal decanter obviously held back for special company and offered with the long, delicate fingers that had spent a lifetime scribbling what would do people no good — or a little worse than no good. You don't repay kindness with needless cruelty.

"That's a pity," Braithwaite said, "but it's one of the reflections of our times. Young minds today are dulled by television and other visual sensations. When reading was one of the few pleasures available, we could recite whole passages to each other."

"Yeah, that must have been something," Willie said.

> *Here I am, an old man in a dry month*
> *Being read to by a boy, waiting for rain.*
> *I was neither at the hot gates*
> *Nor fought in the warm rain*
> *Nor knee-deep in the salt marsh, heaving a cutlass*
> *Bitten by flies fought.*
> *My house is a decayed house.*

Lester turned to Braithwaite. "I wanted to get back to something you mentioned before. Since all your work about Linden Hills comes from the records and information that the Nedeeds have given you, no matter how objective you try to be, you're still only getting one side of the story — their side."

"That would be true if I relied solely on their documents. But that's not how a reputable historian works. You take the family records and then you must view them in light of material from other sources: county court transcripts, the minutes of the state realty board, personal interviews with the residents here, et cetera. It becomes a whole series of checks and balances from numerous sources before you come up with the whole story, the real story if you will."

> *After such knowledge, what forgiveness? Think now*
> *History has many cunning passages, contrived corridors*
> *And issues, deceives with whispering ambitions,*

Guides us by vanities. Think now
She gives when our attention is distracted
And what she gives, gives with such subtle confusions
That the giving famishes the craving. Gives too late
What's not believed in, or is still believed,
In memory only, reconsidered passion. Gives too soon
Into weak hands, what's thought can be dispensed with
Till the refusal propagates a fear. Think
Neither fear nor courage saves us. Unnatural vices
Are fathered by heroism. Virtues
Are forced upon us by our impudent crimes.
These tears are shaken from the wrath-bearing tree.

"But the greatest test of all is what I've seen with my own eyes. I have *studied* these people. Yes, I've moved among them, eaten with them, laughed with them, but I've known my purpose here from the beginning and I've never let myself get too involved. I was placed on this very spot as soon as I graduated from school, so there was no way for me to get caught up in the mad rush down this hill and have my work tainted. I'm already sitting on the last street of Tupelo Drive, and no one will ever live in that house at the very bottom but the Nedeeds. Remember, this whole wall is a window that faces *up,* and it always will."

"Those willow trees block your view for over half the year," Lester said. "And Nedeed might be counting on that."

"My trees are dead. I killed them when I realized that they might interfere with my work. I didn't cut them down because I was so terribly fond of them. Willows are the most elegant of all trees. And, you see, in the fall and winter I can still imagine that they will bud again in the spring, and my sense of loss isn't so great. Yes, I had often thought about what you just said, and yes, I am certain that the information they give me can be verified."

To lose beauty in terror, terror in inquisition
I have lost my passion: why should I keep it
Since what is kept must be adulterated?
I have lost my sight, smell, hearing, taste and touch:
How should I use them for your closer contact?

"No, son, these are photographs," Braithwaite said as he weighed the volume and frowned, "taken with extreme care and immeasurable accuracy." He took off his glasses and pointed to his eyes: "And this is the camera." He turned to Willie. "You see, I knew you didn't have the whole story of what went on today. How could you? You were too close to it. So I made a special effort to bring you here to explain — not Luther's side or my side, but all of it. And for you especially, it's important at this stage in your life to guard against hasty conclusions."

"Well, sir." Willie cleared his throat. "I've seen a lot these last few days and I'll admit that I haven't sorted it all out yet. But I can say one thing, and I hope you won't take this the wrong way — I wouldn't live in Linden Hills if it was the last place on earth."

The even voice that answered was as soft as it was sad: "Then you must read the twelfth volume of my work when it's completed, because everything you've done this week is in there. I've watched you, and I've made inquiries. You're bright. Ambitious. And now, up close, I can smell the potential about you. You might think you're only passing through, but for someone like you, young man, this probably will be the last place on earth."

"Hey, how about that, Willie?" Lester winked. "The professor's predicted that we're gonna be neighbors."

Willie didn't smile. He wanted to punch Lester. He always went on like everything in life was a joke. But some things were deadly serious.

"Excuse me, Dr. Braithwaite, this has all been nice of you, but I'd really like to go home now and lie down. Could you call that cab for us?"

"Surely. Forgive me. I suppose you've figured out that I don't get much company, but I didn't mean to bend your ears."

"No, this has been great," Lester said. "I wanted to ask you about that copy of *The Philadelphia Negro.* Did you really know Du Bois? — because it's signed."

"Why yes, we met once at a dinner party at the Nedeeds. Now, that's an interesting story . . ." he began, and then glanced at Willie. "But unfortunately, it's quite a long one and —"

"No, you can tell him," Willie said. "If you don't mind showing me where the phone is, I'll call the cab myself. It might take
a while to get through with all this snow."

Willie had gotten three busy signals in a row when he put
down the receiver and sighed. He could hear Braithwaite's
laughter through the open door in the hallway. To his left, the
darkened front room had dust covers on the furniture. So he
really didn't use this part of his house. Quietly, Willie moved
into the living room and saw the closed drapes on the front bay
window. That was probably the one that looked down the hill.
Feeling like a thief, he walked over and pulled one edge of the
drapery, the bright light making him jump as if an alarm had
gone off. He glanced back over his shoulder before pressing his
nose to the glass.

The white clapboard house at the bottom of the slope sat
quietly behind the snowbanks and its frozen lake. There was no
sign of life in or around it. It was difficult to imagine children ice
skating down there or women hanging wreaths in those windows, sweeping the porch, drying laundry, but in almost two
hundred years it must have happened sometime. *History is a
written photograph.* Closing the drape, Willie wondered if Braithwaite would have gotten a much different picture all these years
by keeping his desk up against this window.

She knew she was dying. Sitting back on her heels with the album
in her lap, she could feel it happening: the passage of air through
lung tissues that disintegrated a little with each breath; heart muscles that pumped and weakened, pumped and weakened with
each surge of blood through the body; blood moving through each
loosening vein, each tightening artery, nourishing cells that split
and divided toward a finite end hidden by her skin. The cold that
settled around her and the emptiness within her helped to give the
process a clarity that would have been lost if she'd had the free-
dom of the outside world. In the normal rush of affairs, it was so
easy to forget that she was born dying. And being deprived of the
infinite expanse of the stars or the sound of waves from a bottomless ocean, she had to anchor the questions and answers for her

limited existence to the material enclosed within those four walls.

It had all come to this. She curled her fingers around the cellophane pages, the past dissolving into the present and bringing with it the meaninglessness of whatever had gone before. Everything else, every other word or action had been only a bizarre temper tantrum against fate. Because after all that, here it finally was: a dying body, the ticking of a cracked clock and a smeared photo album marked *me*.

Staring at the gaping hole that was once Priscilla McGuire, she reached her hand up and began to touch her own face, her fingers running tentatively across the cheeks and mouth, up the bridge of the nose, and spanning out over the eyes and forehead. She tried to place the curves and planes, the shape of the jutting cheekbones and texture of the hair into the hollow of the hand that she brought back and held before her. The fingers returned again under the parted lips, in the holes of the nostrils, over the arch of the brows, and under the hair to the bone of the scalp. She brought her fingers back again and again with a new shape and form to place in the air before her.

But it was difficult to keep it all in position. When she returned with the curve of her ear, the chin had shifted and melted up toward the mouth; the nose dissolved before she could bring back the lips. She started all over, pressing a bit harder into the hollows of her cheeks, under the chin, moving quickly to return with a new shape in her fingers before the image vanished. She now closed her eyes and used both hands, trying to form a mirror between her fingers, the darkness, and memory. What formed in her mind might be it, but she needed to be sure. She looked at the small light bulb overhead — if she only had a shiny surface. The plastic cereal bowls were too dull and crusted, the silver spoons too small. Her head turned toward the sink and the aluminum pot she had used for catching water.

The pot was tilted against the sink, its handle lodged in the drain. Water had collected there, so she lifted it carefully and brought it back under the light. Holding the pot as still as she could, she found that an image would form if she brought it down to her waist. As the water came to rest, a dim silhouette appeared in front of her. Rimmed by light, there was the outline of her hair, the shape of the chin, and if she turned her head slowly — very slowly — there was the profile of her nose and lips. It was impossible to determine the shape of her eyes, even from the side, but this was enough. No doubt remained — she was there.

She took the water and began to walk back toward the cot. She moved slowly past the metal shelves, the empty cereal and milk cartons, the scattered and torn remnants from the boxes and trunks, the shrouded body of her child. In that small space, she passed the ghosts from every spectrum of human emotion she'd released in that room. But when she finally sat down to cry, the tears belonged to none of them. The gentle drops were falling from her bowed head into the pot because this was the first time she had known peace. Raising the rim to her lips, she began to drink the cold, rusty water. So it had all come to this. She would take small sips, very small sips — and think. Now that she had actually seen and accepted reality, and reality brought such a healing calm. For whatever it was worth, she could rebuild.

December
24th

T he final credits for *Miracle on 34th Street* rolled onto the screen of Willie's secondhand black-and-white set. He reached for his *TV Guide* and sighed. That was it for the night. There was only the sermonette and then "The Star-Spangled Banner." As much as he hated losing those last ten minutes before he was forced to be alone in the quiet room, he wasn't going to put himself through that: whoever the band was, they always played the damned thing off-key. There was absolutely nothing left to do. The tiny kitchenette was immaculate. Every scrap of ribbon and colored paper had been slowly folded and put away. The presents for his family, Lester, and the Andersons were stacked up neatly in the corner. Wrapping them had taken hours because he had made sure the paper was cut evenly and tightly molded to the shape of each box. The ends were glued instead of taped so that there would be a smooth, continuous surface. Ribbons were matched to the various colored prints, each crisscrossed with a different design before being looped and shredded to form stars, flowers, and butterflies. And this year he was going to admit to his family that he had wrapped them himself instead of lying about having it done at the department store. He would risk having his brothers ridicule him because it looked like something a woman would do. This was his way of doing things; it had always been his way. And they would just have to accept that or give him back his damned ties, shavers, and gloves. He could keep them for himself since he hadn't bought himself anything anyway. Or he would return them to the store and get a down payment for the new coat he needed so badly. But he was planning to use the money that he got from Nedeed to buy a coat. Willie wanted to forget that he had to go back down into Linden Hills. When he thought about Christmas Eve, he imagined himself walking up the steps to his mother's apartment building, loaded down with shopping bags full of gifts. Grinning and banging on the door with his foot because he had a quart of Chivas Regal under each arm for their party. Still, the money for those presents had come from Linden Hills, and the two bottles of Scotch would have to be bought from what Nedeed gave them tonight. He tried to pass over all that and just concentrate on what it would be like spending Christmas with his family. Going down to Nedeed's was just something to get through without thinking, like he had to get through this night without sleeping.

He got up, shut off the television, and looked down at his clothes. He was so tired that if he undressed, he might be tempted to lie down on the bed. And since the room was cool, he might pull the covers over him and, once he was warm, he might fall asleep. And if he fell asleep, there was no doubt about one thing: he would dream. Willie made a wide circle around the bed and sat on the windowsill, one foot on the floor and the other leg propped up against the pane with his elbow on his knee. The cold of the glass penetrated his shirt and pants, chilling his shoulder and the side of his thigh. Good, this was exactly where he'd spend the rest of the night. There was no danger of falling asleep here. He saw that the snow had already been trampled into a gray mush, lumped with garbage, exhaust fumes, and cinders. The calendar said that there should be a full moon, but it wasn't visible from his window. Willie could see only a small patch of sky between the buildings that surrounded his one back room. The same snow, the same sky, would be different just a few blocks away in Linden Hills. The snow was still clean down there, and under a full moon that had nothing to block it but bare tree branches, it was probably glistening on those long slopes and wide streets.

Why was he always thinking about Linden Hills? Wasn't it enough that he spent his days down there? He didn't have to spend his nights there as well, but it seemed as if he wasn't allowed to leave it; he even brought it home in his dreams. A tremor went through Willie's spine. Now, why had he thought that? He didn't mean to say that; he had meant to say that he even brought it home in his *thoughts.* He was always thinking about Linden Hills, that was all. So when you think about a place all the time, it's like you never leave it. He glanced at the bed, frowned, and then sighed very deeply. He was too tired to lie to himself anymore. No, he brought that place home in his dreams. All those dreams this week were about Linden Hills. But you were supposed to dream about things after they happened, not before. Yet it had happened with that woman who killed herself. He had dreamed that she would have no face. No, he was the one who had had no face, but it was still about her. In fact, all those dreams had been about women and none of them had had names until now. He knew her name was Laurel. God, how could he ever forget that name after yesterday?

Now there was nothing left to dream about but Nedeed. What was that woman like down there in Nedeed's house? He had never heard her name. A whole week in Linden Hills and he had never heard her name. But she was waiting for him, he felt that in his guts; he just had to fall asleep. Willie shuddered. Christ, now he really was turning into a woman — he sounded like somebody's superstitious old aunt. Wake up, man. This is the twentieth century, and that's Putney Wayne outside your window. You're free, black, and twenty. And that's the way you're gonna stay. Free to move anywhere in this neighborhood, or in this world that your pocket change allows you. Free to stay as

black as you are today unless you decide to fill your bathtub
with Clorox. The only thing that's gonna change is your age.
Yes, he would turn twenty-one next year. He had no say about
that, but that's the only thing he couldn't control. There was no
such thing as fate or predestination. He wasn't too certain about
there being a god, but if there was one, he wasn't up there pulling any strings. People pulled their own strings, made their own
fate. If some clown down there in the alley on a holiday drunk
came by right now with a gun, shooting up into the air, the bul-
let would go through his brain. But *he* had decided to sit at this
window. He had turned off the TV, gotten up, and placed himself right here. An inch to the right or left would make all the
difference in the world. Life was chance. And dreams were bullshit. It was time to grow up. He wasn't being drawn into anything. He was going down to Nedeed's because he needed the
money. He could change his mind anytime he wanted to, even
up to the last second if need be. And so what? The world would
keep turning, the moon would keep rising. And the only difference his going or not going would make would be in his pocket.
So the guy was weird. So he'd lied about his wife. That was Nedeed's problem, not his.

All those people in Linden Hills had problems, which only
proved one thing to him: they were part of the human race.
Name him one man without a problem, and he'd name the day
that the funeral would be held. Willie's laugh was dry and
soundless. He had seen a funeral this week. When that poor slob
got married, it was like a death march and Willie was the only
one who seemed to know it. And then the real funeral hadn't
been that at all, at least not to that guy Parker. He couldn't put
his wife away fast enough. A wedding that was like a funeral,
and a funeral that was already a wedding. If anything was the
problem with Linden Hills, it was that nothing seemed to be
what it really was. Everything was turned upside down in that
place. And he was tired of thinking about it, tired of trying to
put all those pieces together as if it were some great big puzzle
whose solution was just beyond his fingers. If life was chance,
and it could all change with someone moving just an inch to the

left or right, there were no answers. Then where was he going? And what had he been doing with his own life until now? He wasn't going to stay in Putney Wayne, that much he knew. And he wasn't going to keep bagging groceries until he was fifty years old. There was better for him than that. So was that professor right? Linden Hills would be the place where he'd end up? Where he *had* to end up?

Willie's head began to throb. He was wrong. If he could ask those questions, then there had to be an answer. But there had been no new poems this week. His poetry had always helped him sort things out. He had asked a hundred questions and he had a hundred answers in his head. He remembered his very first poem. He couldn't have been more than five years old. He had asked himself one day in school, how can my mother love my father when he makes her cry? And the poem just came while he was tossing that blue alphabet block. A little nothing of a rhyme that he still carried around, but that had been the beginning. He grew up believing that there was a poem somewhere to fit everything. But this past week he couldn't put it all together. Over and over he had asked himself when the day was through, What does it mean? And there was nothing. Images, snatches of phrases, he had loads of those but nothing to order them. Other people's work had kept cramming itself into his mind. But where was his? Maybe it was just overload. He had already memorized 665 poems and this last one just wasn't working out. Would he have to start writing them down? He couldn't imagine that. Poetry wrote itself for him. If he had to pick up a pen and paper, he just knew there would be nothing to say. And even if he forced himself to jot something down, those strange curves and loops in front of him would be as unreadable as Chinese. His poems only made sense in his ears and mouth. His fingers, eyes, and nose. Something about Linden Hills was blocking that. And to unstop it, he would have to put Linden Hills into a poem. But first he needed the right question, didn't he? Perhaps he hadn't been asking the wrong questions all week, just ones that were too big. It would take an epic to deal with something like What has this whole week meant? He'd leave that to guys like Milton. No, just

find something small and work from there. Find something immediate, and it would write itself out. Okay, you can't separate
Linden Hills from Luther Nedeed, who seemed to be in the
middle of almost everything this week. So what is the question
about Nedeed?

Willie knew how to do it. Just close his eyes and let the images
swirl about as he emptied his mind. The first line would always
come that way. Just close his eyes, relax his mouth, and it would
create itself. And once it was there, the first line, the next and the
next would be as inevitable as his breath. The process always
frightened him a little. The way it would come from nowhere,
push itself up from some space inside him, full-blown and de-
manding to spread. In a way, it was like playing God. The first
seeds for everything in the world must have followed a blueprint
like this. Fractured roofs and sloping lawns, broken tree
branches and wedding cakes swirled in his mind. Crystal chandeliers splintered, doorbells chimed and chimed, sending up
echoes that made him shudder. But he kept himself suspended,
feeling it grow up from his center, threatening to make him lose
his balance and go tumbling to the floor or crashing out through
the closed window. Christmas trees of all shapes and sizes.
Ruth's face melting into Lester's face into Nedeed's face. Nedeed's face tightening into a ball and then bursting into liquid
circles that curled into fingers, shooting out at him and encir-
cling his brain. Nedeed's face dripping from the housetops,
moving like dark volcanic lava down the slope of Tupelo Drive.

He was almost there. At that terrifying place where his groin
contracted and release was demanded before his mind went over
the edge. He kept pushing himself toward that dangerous point.
He couldn't stay awake forever. And those dreams would never
end until he had the first line. And if he had just that one, he
could sleep. He would have made peace with those night images.
If they were anything, they were that: the first line unborn. It
came with an expulsion, a relief that always felt like ejaculation
and, more often than not, brought tears to his eyes. And once it
was out of his mouth to be heard by his ears, he knew he was
committed.

Willie's sigh misted the cold windowpane — a round, iridescent fog. He got down from the ledge, the chill stiffening his
joints, and he moved like an old man as he undressed. Twenty
syllables. Later, they could be arranged to form any pattern he
wanted. Usually, the poems ran in a series of stress on the fourth
and third, fourth and third. But it wasn't always necessary and
he was too tired to care. The first lines were there, so he could
sleep now. Willie pulled the blankets over himself without fear,
welcoming the drowsiness he didn't have to fight anymore.
There would be no dreams tonight. Before he drifted off to sleep,
he followed a childhood habit, repeating the lines in a soft chant
that assured they would be remembered in the morning. "There
is a man in a house at the bottom of a hill. And his wife has no
name."

Her name was Willa Prescott Nedeed. After thinking about it for
hours, she knew she was safe starting from there. She had owned
that first name for as long as she had the face she was now certain
that she possessed. The aluminum pot was held firmly on her lap.
Thirty-seven years ago she had been born and given the name
Willa. It wasn't thirty-eight years yet, because her birthday was
June 14 and that was in late spring. It wasn't spring yet. It was winter because it was cold down there. She didn't know how her
mother decided upon the name Willa. She remembered asking her
once and being told that she just liked the rhythm; it was lyrical and
delicate.

She took her first steps to the sound of those two syllables. Pink
ruffled dress, matching hair ribbons, and soft-bottom shoes with
bells on the laces. "Come, Willa, Willa." Yes, when she first got off
her knees with the exhilarating discovery that her feet could take
her anywhere in the world, she directed them toward outstretched
arms calling that name and telling her that her final choice of that
destination made her a "good girl, good girl." The shoes kept
changing. Saddle oxfords in grade school, maroon loafers in high
school, platform heels in college. Her feet were the only part of her
body she didn't grow up despising and she regretted that they had
to be covered. So she had always loved beautiful shoes. When no
one ever picked her to be partners in Double Dutch, she could

stand in the corner of the school yard and stare at her polished toes. The penny loafers that never took her on a date at the drive-in were still rubbed with oil every Saturday night. The French heels that never danced at the senior prom carried her up to the stage where she received her graduation certificates for perfect attendance and civic duty. The applause then was good and loud. Fine, but the name Prescott had come from her father. It had belonged to his father and the father before that. So there was little choice on his part about her last name.

Both of those people were now dead. The people who made Willa Prescott. But Willa Prescott Nedeed was alive, and she had made herself that. She imported the white satin pumps that took Willa Prescott down the aisle six years ago and brought her back up as Willa Prescott Nedeed. Her marriage to Luther Nedeed was her choice, and she took his name by choice. She knew then and now that there were no laws anywhere in this country that forced her to assume that name; she took it because she wanted to. That was important. She must be clear about that before she went on to anything else: she wanted to be a Nedeed. After all, every literate person in the Western world knew it was a good name.

A thousand images now sprang up and threatened to fracture themselves, blurring Willa's resolve to reach a clear answer to a simple question: How did she come to be exactly where she was? She pushed away what had happened or why it happened. If there was any hope for her at all, it rested solely on the how: How did she get down in that basement? Okay, so far she had the facts that thirty-seven years ago she had been born Willa Prescott and six years ago Willa Prescott married Luther Nedeed, became Willa Nedeed, and Willa Nedeed in a pair of suede boots walked into a white clapboard house in a place called Linden Hills. Yes, keep it simple. Keep on the track, and there just might be hope. She took another small sip from the pot, concentrated, and went on.

Now, she wanted the name Willa Nedeed. She wanted to walk around and feel that she had a perfect right to respond to a phone call, a letter, an invitation — any verbal or written request directed toward that singular identity. And she did that. She became a wife and less than a year later she walked into Hyacinth Memorial, this time with leather moccasins on, and became a mother. She gave birth to a son. The doctor said it was a good, clean delivery. She almost lost control then, but she pressed the pot into her middle and took a deep breath. Yes, she had given birth to a son. That made her a mother. The child was fed and bathed, and kept from harming himself before he understood the danger of sharp objects and hot stoves. He was clothed properly for the weather. He had toys and, later, books — alphabet books because he was just learning to read. She gave him her attention and her time, so he learned to speak and then form sentences. And he began to learn the difference between right and wrong. He was guided and corrected. Now, with that evidence she could be tried by any court in this galaxy or the next and be acquitted as a good mother.

And while she was doing all that, she was also being a wife. She cleaned his home, cooked his meals. His clothes were arranged, his social engagements organized. When he chose to talk about his work, she listened. And she was careful not to bring him petty household problems that might overburden him more than he already was. She accepted without complaint their separate bedrooms and the fact that she spent all those nights alone, that he could be distant and distracted at times, that so much of his life just couldn't include her. Once again, with that evidence, she could be tried by any court in this galaxy or the next and be acquitted as a good wife.

All right, she was still safe. But now she had to be extremely careful when she took it from there. Willa Nedeed was a good mother and a good wife. For six years, she could claim that identity without any reservations. But now Willa Nedeed sat on a cot in a basement, no longer anyone's mother or anyone's wife. So how did that happen? She stared at the concrete steps leading up to the kitchen door. It happened because she walked down into this basement. That was simple enough; that was clear. In a pair of canvas espadrilles, she walked down twelve concrete steps away from her home and into a room that was cold and damp. Willa had to squeeze her eyes tightly so she would see only those steps. It was so easy at this point to see the cots and shelves of food, the clothes and blankets that awaited her. So very easy to recall the

bitter argument that was planned up to the final outburst that ma-
nipulated her down those steps. The sound of the bolt as it slid into
place. The intercom that kept clicking on and off with insane messages about adultery, the complexion of the child, and lessons to
be learned. As important as it was, none of that was really at the
center of exactly *how* it happened. It happened because, taking
one step at a time, she descended those basement steps. And
since the Prescotts conceived a baby girl with healthy leg muscles
and tendons, she had started walking down them from the second
she was born.

If she took it a millimeter beyond that, her thoughts would smash
the fragility of that singular germ of truth. Its amber surface quiv-
ered in her mind, a microscopic dot of pure gelatin, free from the
contamination of doubt or blame. That action was hers and hers
alone. The responsibility did not lie with her mother or father — or
Luther. No, she could no longer blame Luther. Willa now marveled
at the beauty and simplicity of something so small it had lived
unrecognized within her for most of her life. She gained strength
and a sense of power from its possession. Her back straightened
and she looked around the basement, replaying each moment
spent there through this new and awesome reality. There was regret — oh God, there was that — lying in the shrouded body of
her son. But that too became her sole possession as the soft
amber cell began to spread on its way to setting up roots in the
center of her being.

Upstairs, she had left an identity that was rightfully hers, that
she had worked hard to achieve. Many women wouldn't have chosen it, but she did. With all of its problems, it had given her a measure of security and contentment. And she owed no damned
apologies to anyone for the last six years of her life. She was sitting
there now, filthy, cold, and hungry, because she, Willa Prescott
Nedeed, had walked down twelve concrete steps. And since that
was the truth — the pure, irreducible truth — whenever she was
good and ready, she could walk back up.

A full winter moon, hanging low in the sky, illuminated the
curving road in front of Willie and Lester as they made their

way down the final slope of Linden Hills. They were leaving the high walls and hedges of Tupelo Drive behind them, and the tall pines that blocked the view of the cemetery disappeared. A short wooden fence allowed the moonlight to shine on the even rows of lime headstones that ran to the bottom of the hill on both sides of the Nedeed home. The white clapboard house seemed ringed by light as the moon washed over the frozen circle of water surrounding it. The wind was strong at their backs, and they had to lean against it and lock their legs to keep from sliding down the icy road.

"I don't blame that guy for not wanting to tackle this last turn," Lester said. "With those lousy tires that gypsy cab woulda been stuck here till spring."

"It sure is quiet down here." Willie pulled his neck deeper into his collar. "And did you notice, there are no more streetlights. If the moon wasn't out, we could never find this place."

"Well, it's not like there are a whole lot of choices," Lester said. "The road ends here and eventually even a blind man would have to stumble onto that house since it's the only one down here."

"Yeah, and you'd think they'd want an easier way to leave home than driving all the way back up this hill. Tupelo Drive could have kept right on into Patterson Road. I know that's what runs behind Nedeed's house. And with him having a business and all . . ."

"His business is right at his front door." Lester pointed to the cemetery as they passed. "See how low he built that fence? He probably just hauls the bodies over."

"Aw, come on." Willie laughed.

"Naw, I guess not having the roads intersect just gives him privacy. Nobody's got any reason to come down here unless it's to see him. And he doesn't need hedges or anything 'cause of that lake." Lester shook his head. "A strange dude."

"To say the least."

They walked in silence for a few moments.

"You know, Willie . . ." Lester watched where he placed his feet. "I get the feeling that you know a lot more about Nedeed than you're letting on. I mean, all that crazy business yesterday about him seeing that woman who killed herself. And then the day before that, your freaking out about coming here tonight. Remember, I'm in this with you, too. And if there's something I should know, why don't you just come out with it?"

"Look, you know a lot more about Nedeed than I do. I never laid eyes on the man before this week. I didn't want to say nothing about those footprints 'cause I wasn't really sure. And even on an outside chance they were what I thought they were, I didn't even know what it all meant."

"Yeah, but why did I have to find out from Braithwaite? I mean, if he didn't say anything, I really believe you never would have told me."

"That's not true, Les. It's just that everything got a little wild yesterday — with the cops and people and all. And when you think about it, what have I seen that you haven't this week? I haven't been anyplace you haven't been. God, we might as well have been married, as much time as we've spent together."

"That's no lie. The only thing we didn't do is sleep together."

Willie cringed, and Lester noticed it. "How have you been sleeping lately, Willie? Still get those dreams?"

"Naw, I slept like a baby last night — honestly. And I finally figured out what it was. I haven't been able to make up any new poems this week and it was bothering me."

"Are you kidding me? How'd you expect to find the time to do that? I'd get home and be too tired to even eat, some nights. Ya know, it even got to the point where my mom asked me if I was working too hard. I must have looked pretty bad for *her* to tell me to slack up. And yet people wonder why black folks ain't produced a Shakespeare."

"Well, I don't have any hopes of being that. But I think I can come pretty close."

"Then you better find an easier way to make a living. Or come up with some scheme to hit it big quick so you can sit up in one of these cushy pads on Tupelo Drive and compose your masterpieces."

"Yeah, but do you remember us meeting any poets down

here? You'd think of all the places in the world, this neighborhood had a chance of giving us at least one black Shakespeare."

"But Linden Hills ain't about that, Willie. You should know that by now."

"So where's the answer for someone like me, Shit?"

Even as Willie asked, he knew there would be silence. He glanced back over his shoulder and the sight almost made him stop walking. Infinite rows of rectangular and round windows were sending a mellow glow out into the night. All of Linden Hills stretched up in a magnificent array of colors. The snowy incline was blazing with reds, blues, and greens forming designs everywhere, from circles to each pattern of the constellations. Tiny electrical stars flickered in the bare tree branches and outlined the driveways and roofs. A lump formed in Willie's throat. God, it was so beautiful it could break your heart.

"Maybe," Lester said softly, "maybe there's a middle ground somewhere. For me as well as you. I know I can't keep living off my mother forever. And it costs money to keep up a house even if there's no mortgage. There's repairs and property taxes. But . . ." He sighed. "But I don't know why it must be one or the other — ya know, ditchdigger or duke. But people always think that way: it's Linden Hills or nothing. But it doesn't have to be Linden Hills and it doesn't have to be nothing — ya know, Willie? I mean, in spite of all the propaganda and those ads and crap that Nedeed floods the world with, there *are* other places to live. But it's sorta easy to forget that. I mean, what's so special about this place? Just look at it. This is the end of Linden Hills and look at it."

They were now at the edge of Nedeed's lake and Willie did look, long and hard. The house was unbelievably simple compared to the ones farther up. The only thing that gave it an aura of distinction was the huge frozen lake it seemed to be built on. The moon showed up the plain, boxed lines of the wooden planks immaculately preserved under white paint. The three-sided open porch held a double swing and that was the only decorative feature besides the long shutters on each of its windows. Even with its three stories, it could have been dwarfed easily by any home on Tupelo Drive. It sat there quiet and unlit, almost shrinking under the expansive wash of moonlight.

"There are no lights on. Do you think he's home?"

"Oh, he's home," Lester said. "He always struck me as the type who likes to sit in the dark."

The side view was as unspectacular as the front, even though they could now see the funeral home and chapel across the drawbridge that let them over the lake. Up close, Willie searched in vain for any sign that might set the house apart as belonging to a legend. And there definitely wasn't a shred of evidence that it sheltered a monster. Why, it was nothing but a house. But then what had he expected, since Luther Nedeed was nothing but a man.

Luther stood at his den window, watching the lights smolder and glow up the slope of Linden Hills. That window had given him a view of his land in the spring when the trees took on a pastel powdering of green; in the summer when the leaves were deep and glossy just before autumn turned them into bursts of red and gold. But there was nothing to compare to this beauty. The bright lights forming intricate patterns in the naked branches were the work of human hands, decisive not capricious, so it would be assured of always looking that way. There was a deep sense of comfort for him in that certainty. He wished that he could stand there all night and not have to turn and face the upheaval within his own home. This was the one season he looked forward to all year. A time to rest and tie up all the loose ends. To do nothing from now until January 6 but read all the books he had neglected, sleep until noon, and take long quiet walks away from the Tupelo Realty Corporation and the funeral home. His assistants dared not call him about anything short of an earthquake or flood during this time.

In his mind's eye the darkened rooms came alive with mellow candlelight and gleaming crystal. Swags of berried juniper draped the banisters and doors, their velvet bows sprinkled with rosewater and glitter. Tubs of small decorated cedars lined each side of the hallway. And there were wreaths everywhere: holly entwined with golden tansy from the front door, rings of purple-leaf sage and lavender for the windows, the punch bowl sitting in a crown of pennyroyal and rue. His father giving him small sips and later a whole cup of the brandy punch as the smell of roast goose and baked ham drifted from the back kitchen. Mountainous platters of molasses cookies and sweet potato buns, warm and moist from the oven. And once, even a molasses-cake house, whose roof lifted off to reveal cut rock- and ribbon candy. Long, unhurried talks with his father before the fireplace, knowing he wasn't going to leave the house for days. There was nothing but a feast of time to work out the questions that puzzled him while the man was relaxed and the embers slowly burned down.

Luther sighed and turned away from the window. The burning logs in his den seemed to highlight every empty space and corner that should have been filled with anything except darkness. The silent and shadowed room threatened to rise up and condemn him. But how could that be? He ran his eyes along the mahogany wainscoting, down the plastered walls, over the hardwood floor. The deep, open hearth of the fireplace, the blackened andirons. He knew every plane of that room, every irregular surface, each crack and stain in the wood. It would have been easier to separate the elements in his breath than to separate his soul from the material in that house, than to separate that house from that hill.

He walked over to the rolltop desk and removed a folded gold case. The four portraits unhinged in his hands. This man had come to Linden Hills with only a cardboard suitcase and a dream. No one helped him to haul or smooth the logs for the shack that stood on this very ground. He ate nothing but wild turnips and cornmeal biscuits for six years — six long years — because the price of a brood hen was also the price of a load of bricks. And this man poured the cement for so many of the foundations up there with his own hands. And this one gambled every dime he had to keep this community afloat during the Depression. And this one personally hauled coal for his tenants during the worst blizzard in forty years, losing two toes from frostbite. Yes, they had hauled wood and coal, hauled every official of Wayne County into court, received no thanks, and asked for none.

Luther's blood pounded in his temples as he stared at his face again and again. He couldn't imagine where he would be, or what he would do, if he wasn't here. But he didn't have to, because he was — again and again. So what was he to have done? To accept her child was to deny himself. He snapped the case shut as the past week reeled out in front of him. He truly didn't know how much longer he could go on. If he could just touch what was wrong up there, crystallize it so it would be fought, he wouldn't be afraid — regardless of how immense the opponent turned out to be. But he felt himself flailing at the wind. He couldn't control this chaos forever by himself, and there was no son this Christmas Eve. No comfort. He felt old and tired. He was so very tired of the people up there. What good had he actually done this week? Winston Alcott was coming to Tupelo Drive and he would leave the same way Laurel Dumont had; Luther could already see it. Give Winston four or five years and he'd break down. So what had he accomplished by forcing that marriage? He had bought himself a little time, that's all. He had temporarily filled another home. They didn't understand the importance of a family, of life. All of those sacrifices to build them houses and they refused to build a history. Father, forgive me, Luther almost whispered aloud, but sometimes I wish you had left me another dream.

The tall balsam fir stood naked and alone in the center of the room. The sharp pungent smell of its needles scratched at the back of his throat and he swallowed hard. At least he would have his tree for the holidays. He had driven fifty miles to get it. He couldn't understand why people substituted those hateful plastic imitations for this. Christmas began with a trip to the woods in search of just the right balsam: symmetrical branches, a healthy bark, and firm needles, his father always said. But times had changed. He had gone to a tree farm, which was the closest he could get to a patch of woods. He had fixed his purchase into the iron, three-legged stand he'd brought down from the storage room along with the wooden boxes of ornaments. Yes, they were the same as he remembered so his tree would be exactly as he remembered. And there would be three pairs of hands to decorate it, two dark and one fair. When it was finished, he could sit back in his chair and not have to think about whose hands they really should have been. That wouldn't come to him unless he allowed himself to think about the lack of aromas from the kitchen, the lack of a child's voice and his own answering in return. He could spend the holidays in his chair and know that at least one thing hadn't changed.

Luther brought in the bowl of brandy punch and arranged three cups around it. This one recipe he knew by heart: one part lemon and orange juice, one part cognac, two parts dark Jamaican rum, three parts peach brandy. He had doubled all the ingredients and added apple and pear slices. He would have this and cheese and crackers for dinner. He paused before drinking his third cup. Cheese and crackers for Christmas Eve. Did she know what she had done? He took the fourth cupful back to his chair, sat down, and stared at the fire. Cheese and crackers for Christmas Eve. And strangers in his home. Strangers handling ornaments that belonged to his family. He wanted to go down those stairs and just shake her. Did she know what she had given up? His blood was warming rapidly. They were the fifth generation of Nedeeds in this house, the fifth, and the first not to have a Christmas Eve together. There was no reason for this, none. She could have come up long ago. He had forgiven her. It was his fault anyway; he had chosen that woman and was willing to accept the responsibility of that choice. It was an error in judgment, one that his father would never have made, but unfortunately, he had. But it wasn't irretrievable; it's just that the child had died. Luther frowned and sipped slowly. He had truly never meant for it all to get so out of hand. This compounded feeling of futility was new to him as he wavered between self-pity and anger. Anger won out. He was not going to sit there brooding; the past was gone. And if he had to do it all again, he would do nothing differently. He had every reason in the world to act as he did, and under the circumstances, he had been more than just. The boy wasn't a Nedeed, that's all there was to it. And there's only so much a man can be expected to take.

But it was cold down there. The thought came from nowhere as Luther drained his cup and ran his fingers along the rim. And she was just as alone as he was. There was something so terribly wrong about people being alone on Christmas Eve. But he just couldn't let her up now. It was too soon after the child's death. By the new year, yes, definitely by then, she would have fully understood how very precious life was. He wouldn't have his family ending up like the Dumonts, who were totally lost to Linden Hills. Her husband could never be persuaded to come back, to start again, after such tragedy. The thought depressed him. If his own wife died, could he start again? He would have to — the whole laborious process — because there must always be Nedeeds. There must always be Christmas and celebration. There must . . . Luther got up from his chair and headed for the kitchen. He turned the water valves on under the sink full force before pressing the intercom: "It's Christmas Eve, Mrs. Nedeed." He sighed, and then went to answer the doorbell.

Willa's sleep was deep and dreamless. Arms folded under her head, face muscles relaxed, she breathed in. In, past the brain cells, where memory mingles with desire and night images are formed. In, past the heart tissues that beat out the rhythms of human limitation. Well past the bottom of the lungs that are only involuntary slaves for continuing existence. She breathed in to touch the very elements that at the beginning of time sparked to produce the miracle some called divine creation and others the force of life. An unconscious journey in toward the power of will that had crept alone in primordial muck eons before being clothed with fins, scales, wings, or flesh. Then she breathed out. Out, past cells that divided to form ovaries, wombs, and glands. Out, past the crumbling planetary matter that formed the concrete for that room. Out, toward the edge of the universe with its infinite possibility to make space for the volume of her breath. She breathed in and out, her body a mere shelter for the mating of unfathomable will to unfathomable possibility. And in that union, the amber germ of truth she went to sleep with conceived and reconceived itself, splitting and multiplying to take over every atom attached to her being. That nucleus of self-determination held the tyrannical blueprint for all divisions of labor assigned to its multiplying cells. Like other emerging life, her brain, heart, hands, and feet were being programmed to a purpose.

It was a birth accompanied by the sound of thunder from the metal sink in the corner. She stretched her arms and arched her back while fluttering her eyelids to awaken full grown into a sphere defined by the words *It's Christmas Eve, Mrs. Nedeed.* Not dissimilar from the bursting of other larvae that are immediately affirmed into a season and a direction: moths uncurl and begin to fly, tree crickets to chirp, army ants to march. Willa rose from those stained and rancid bedcovers to begin keeping house.

She stripped the sheets and blankets from the cot, shook them out for a quick airing, and then remade her bed. She smoothed the sheets and tightly folded and tucked the blankets into the corner. Gently, she lifted the child from his cot and placed him on hers, careful not to wrinkle the surface. Then she started on his bed. Yes, she was Willa Nedeed and so this was the end of the month. It wasn't the most perfect existence to begin with, or even the best time of the year. But it was all she had. She held the cereal bowls and spoons under the running water until the crusted food was soft and then scraped them clean with her fingernails, drying them on the hem of her dress before stacking them on the metal shelves. She moved without hesitation or any sign of stumbling, her mind locking into the point of the universe she was positioned in. She awoke Willa Prescott Nedeed on Christmas Eve. And after she straightened the basement, she was going to start on the rooms upstairs.

"Gentlemen, come in."

As they stepped over the threshold and Luther closed the door against the freezing wind, Willie breathed in the heated air of the long hallway. The walls were unadorned, the hardwood floor shellacked and covered by a simple runner that led straight ahead toward the staircase. Their coats and knitted hats were hung on a petaled coatrack, the dark mahogany matching a small tea table in the corner. No wreaths, no flowers, no pictures. He had hoped there might be family portraits on the wall, but they were probably upstairs or in the darkened rooms to his right.

"I appreciate your coming in spite of the weather. I believe the temperature has dropped terribly outside."

"It sure has," Lester said, his face red and lips trembling, "and there's a mean wind."

"I anticipated that, so there's something in here to warm you before we begin. You don't have to worry about getting back, I'll drive you both home."

"That's real nice of you, Mr. Nedeed."

As they walked down the hall toward the den, Willie was certain that no matter what Nedeed said, his family had been gone for a long time. He didn't miss perfume or cooking odors, but the scents that are carried from the sparks of light switches going off and on, the oil from fingerprints left on door frames, the friction of leather soles against wood, static electricity on a comb, breath on a mirror. Those things brought living smells to a house that took months to fade. And this hallway and those darkened rooms smelled empty.

Luther's den was another matter. The high stone fireplace, the heavy walnut tables, the fringed Oriental rug, the leather furniture. The air definitely came alive, but Willie felt out of place. Not because of any excessive luxury — the furnishings, while meticulously preserved, were still scarred and worn, but they seemed to suspend him in another time. Why, it was like walking into a movie set for *Wuthering Heights.*

"Gentlemen, please." Luther handed them each a small cup of the brandy punch, enunciating each syllable of the address as if he meant just that: gentle men. And this was a room for heavy murmured voices, tweed cloth, and aged tobacco. Even the huge aquarium with those strange ugly fish couldn't dispel that.

"I suppose you plan to spend the rest of the evening with your families. You, Mr. Tilson?" Luther sat down and sipped his drink.

"Yeah, and it's gonna be good to rest after this week. I worked my . . . I mean, I've really worked quite hard."

"And you, Mr. Mason?"

"You can call me Willie."

"Fine," Luther said. "And you can call me Mr. Nedeed." He waited, and they supposed he wanted them to laugh, so they did.

"Yeah," Willie said, "I'm going to my mother's place. We have a big family. I guess you'll be alone for the holidays, huh?"

"Yes, I will."

"That's too bad. Will your wife be back for New Year's Eve?"

"I'm hoping so."

That was the second question, and Willie realized that Nedeed wasn't going to volunteer any information beyond exactly what he was asked. This was a man you just didn't get personal with, and a third question on the same subject would be considered rude and followed by a pointed evasion, letting him know that it was none of his business. And if he couldn't bring himself to say, Hey, Luther, old boy, exactly where is your wife? — how could he find out what he wanted to know most of all, her name? Lester would be the one to ask that right out if it ever occurred to him, but he was sitting there busily slurping his punch.

"Hey, this stuff is pretty good," Lester said. "Mind if I have another? Your cups are kinda small."

"Please help yourself."

While Lester went to the sideboard, Luther seemed quite content to sit and watch Willie.

"Your fireplace is nice." Willie got up to avoid Luther's eyes. "You don't often see them this big."

"It was built along with this house. At that time carpenters were still allowing for the fact that some families actually cooked in them."

"Yeah, I've seen that in magazines." Willie put his hand on the mantel and stared at the burning embers. A log crackled and broke, sending up blue and orange sparks. There was a hollow hum to the pulsating air as it spiraled up the chimney; it sounded like the beating of a human heart. *There is a man in a house at the bottom of a hill. And his wife has no name.* When he took his hand from the mantel there was a light film of dust on his fingers. Willie rubbed his thumb slowly over his index finger to remove it. For some reason, the texture made him want to cry.

"Now, this one is truly a prize." Luther gently held up a gilded cornucopia. The gold paper cone was netted with silver threads and trimmed with lace. Incredibly tiny glass-blown fruit and nuts filled the center. He extracted an apple on the tips of his fingers. "I'll have to hang this one myself."

It was about the twelfth time he'd said that in an hour and Lester winked at Willie. Luther had handled most of the glass figurines that now adorned the tree, only trusting them with the tin snowflakes and papier-mâché peacocks. Even then he told them exactly where to position the ornaments on the branches, often going over to move something a fraction of an inch forward or back.

Willie held one of the exquisite birds in his hand. The brilliant colors were finely drawn and the spun-glass tail fanned out over his palm. "Where do you want this one, Mr. Nedeed?"

"Oh, anywhere, anywhere." Luther intently unfolded a miniature steamship from tissue. "You have a good eye for balance, Mr. Mason. I trust you." He looked up and smiled. "What do you think of this?" The embossed cardboard boat was an exact replica of the original. Tiny silver chains, strung from the deck to the stacks, had silk flags attached to them, and he fluffed out the cotton simulating smoke.

"It's unbelievable." Willie shook his head. "I've never seen a tree like this."

"That's because the world is in love with plastic today." Luther hooked the steamship on a branch. "Through no fault of your own, you were born into an existence of the cheap and pre-fabricated. Each one of these ornaments took hours to create and a lifetime of craftsmanship to perfect. So of course, it's extraordinary."

"My tree at home doesn't look too bad," Lester said, "and we've got green balls just like this." He bounced the globe on his palm.

Luther quickly snatched it from him and gave him a paper bell. "Here, put this up. This ornament was hand-blown in Germany and hand-dipped in lacquer to achieve this unique color. My great-grandfather bought them, so I doubt that you have anything quite like this."

"Hey, look, I didn't mean to offend you. I'm just saying that there are all kinds of ways to decorate a tree."

"Why don't you help yourself to some more punch?" Luther nodded curtly toward the sideboard. "And would you please bring me a cup while you're at it."

Lester winked at Willie again as he passed him. It was Nedeed's third drink since they'd been there, and he'd obviously been drinking before they came in. Willie wished that Lester would stop trying to irritate the man. The sooner they got done, the sooner they could leave. There was something a little eerie about the way Nedeed kept going on about that tree. The way his eyes changed when he looked at it. And he kept staring at their hands, almost timing his so the three of them reached for the branches together. Maybe he did miss his family. Willie had to admit that Nedeed was right: this tree was going to be beautiful. But as it began to take form, it only added to his sense of frozen time. The glass icicles and beads, the wooden and paper toys. Yeah, those things meant a lot because they were passed down, but shouldn't there be at least a few things bought this year, if not this century?

"No, not there, Mr. Mason." Luther stopped him from hanging a crocheted stocking. "We have to leave sufficient space for the candles, and I prefer to have the metal trinkets near them."

"You mean there's gonna be candles on this tree?" Lester asked.

"There have always been candles on our trees. I couldn't imagine Christmas without them. And just wait until you see what that type of light does to some of these ornaments." He spun a mirrored diamond on its string.

Willie frowned. "But isn't that dangerous, Mr. Nedeed?"

"Not if you know what you're doing. And I plan to position them all myself."

"You're gonna string popcorn and that kind of stuff, too?" Lester asked.

"When I was a child we would some years. Or there would be

sugared fruit and nuts." Luther sighed and sipped his drink. "But not this time. No, for now this will have to be enough."

Willie pried the lid off the last wooden box. Tiny houses were layered in cotton.

"Ah, yes." Luther brightened. "I had almost forgotten about those." He picked up a log cabin complete with a stone chimney. "Did you know, gentlemen, that there's a story behind each of these? My great-great-grandfather lived in just such a . . ." And he began to tell them as they filled up the rest of the tree.

Meticulously, Willa Prescott Nedeed folded and packed away the torn books and clothes. She buttoned each blouse, snapped each purse, and arranged the scarves and hats in neat layers. When she had filled one trunk, she closed it securely and began with another. She recovered what pages were left whole from the cookbooks and diaries, smoothed them out, and stacked them away. Tiny shreds of paper left the floor, ripped photographs. She had worked steadily and mechanically for an hour, so it was almost done. She pressed Priscilla McGuire's album on top of the last box, folded the cardboard lid slowly, and took one final look around. Everything down here was in place. Beds made, dishes washed, the metal shelves dusted, the floor picked clean.

She went over to her child, bent down, and lifted him up. The stiffened limbs fit snugly into the curve of her body. The chin rested on her shoulder, cushioned by the lace veiling that dangled onto the floor between her knees. For a brief moment she squeezed the small back. She was so sorry for what she had done. He had barely had a chance to live. He was just learning to write his name. His father had said that he didn't care what she called him, so she had taught him to spell Sinclair. Willa headed for the concrete steps. The kitchen was next.

Luther was placing the final candles on the tree, their dull creaminess a pleasing contrast to the metallic snowflakes and stars. He used just enough to provide a perfect counterbalance to the array of birds, fruit, flowers, and toy houses. The deep green balsam had become a fragrant haven for his cardboard paradise.

He stood back from it and nodded his head. "Now for the crowning touch, gentlemen. We position the top globe, light the candles, and our night is done." He glanced around the floor at the scattered boxes. "Where did you put my tree top?"

"We haven't moved anything," Lester said. "We've only handed you what was here."

Luther began to rummage through the cotton and tissue paper. "Well, it must be around. It was packed with all the rest. A round globe with webbed edges — the thing is huge. You must have seen it."

They helped him search through the clutter.

"See, Mr. Nedeed, it's not here," Willie said.

"Well, then where is it?" He glared at them as if they'd hidden it.

"Look, Mr. Nedeed," Lester said, "we haven't left your sight since we've been here. Maybe you just forgot it when you brought in this other stuff."

"I brought seven boxes down from the storage room. Each year everything is packed away in exactly seven boxes."

"Well, there's only six boxes here." Willie's eyes scanned the floor again.

Luther counted behind him, and then searched under the sofa and wing chair. "Yes, you're right. How could I have made an error like that?"

Lester smirked. "Too much punch."

"It better be upstairs." Luther spoke while staring at the top of the tree. "It just better be upstairs." He headed for the door to the kitchen. "Wait here."

Lester whispered, "Ya know, Willie, I think you were right. That guy had murder in his eyes. Did you see the way he looked at us? Who'd wanna steal any of this old-fashioned junk? And if he's cooked this up just to get out of paying us, I've got news for him."

"No." Willie sighed. "It's just that those things mean the world to him."

"Damnation!" They heard Luther rattling around loudly in the kitchen.

"Just listen to that." Lester shook his head. "He doesn't even curse like other people."

Luther hurried back into the den. "The bulb's blown up in the storage room and I can't find my flashlight. I'm going to need your help. You, sir," he said, pointing at Willie, "bring two candles."

As he followed Luther through the door into the kitchen, Willie shrugged his shoulders at Lester, who pointed to his head. At the end of the room were two adjacent matching doors. The right one was bolted and the left was flung open.

"Hand me one candle," Luther said, "and then you follow behind me with the other. Hold it high so there will be enough light."

The narrow, twisting stairwell was only wide enough for one adult body. There wasn't even space to form shadows as Willie tried to maneuver up the steep wooden steps, each one high enough to reach his kneecap. When they reached the top, as short as Luther was, he had to stoop in order to move around in the storage area. Willie's candle sent quivering shadows across the dusty overcoats, work boots, fishing gear, and boxes. Luther finally found what he was looking for.

"Yes, here it is. I had forgotten how large this packing case was. This will take a little strategy."

He told Willie to blow out his candle and back up a few steps. Then Luther inched the box down the staircase toward him, and each of them lifted one end. "Now, if we coordinate ourselves, we can get this down. Each time I move, you move back one."

Tightly clutching his end of the crate, Willie began to descend the steps slowly.

Willa's foot touched the bottom of the concrete stairs. She began to climb, feeling each joint in her knees as they lifted her closer to the door. She held on to the child tightly as each step took her farther above the stale air in the basement. There was no doubt about her path. It was coded into her being: twelve steps to the door, then into the kitchen. After cleaning that room, she would start on the den. Then up the hall toward the staircase to the bedrooms. She would begin with hers, move to Luther's, and then on to the child's.

But first each step was bringing her closer to the kitchen and the disorder whose oblivion was now inextricably tied to her continuing existence. Each step, repeated a million times and millions of feet away on much lusher ground as the wingless queen amidst a horde of army ants trudged on, watching the deadly tarantula, the sleeping crocodile, the rifle-bearing hunter eaten away in front of her eyes. While the only thing stopping Willa was simply a bolted wooden door.

Willie stumbled on the next to last step and felt his body flying through the door into the kitchen. "Oh God!" Instinctively, he grabbed onto the box and it was snatched from Luther's hands and went down the steps with him. He tried to turn and cushion the crate with his body, but its sharp edge jammed into his sides as he rolled and hit his head against the sink. When his eyes cleared, Luther was standing over him.

"You fool." The evident pain in Luther's voice softened his words as he knelt over the crate, tearing away at the cover.

"Oh, my God, I'm so sorry, Mr. Nedeed. I'm really sorry."

Willie was totally unheard as Luther, perspiring and his breathing labored, unwrapped the globe.

"Mr. Nedeed, really, I'm so —" Willie grimaced, holding his side as he got to his knees.

Luther was visibly trembling. "It's all right," he whispered as he slowly turned the globe. "It's all right." Then he focused on Willie. "Forgive me." He stood up. "But you have no idea what you almost did."

"Oh, I do." Willie was trembling as well. "And I'm so sorry. But those steps are so steep and —"

"Let's forget it. Bring the box." Luther's eyes never left the globe as he headed for the den.

Quickly, Willie picked up the crate and cotton, his bruised head pounding. He shut the storage door with his foot. Since his arms were full, he braced the crate against the two doors. Reaching under it, he felt the metal bolt slide toward the left as he turned, rushing to follow Luther. A slow chill breeze trailed behind him from the basement door as it crept open.

* * *

Miraculously, the bolt slid back when Willa reached for the knob, saving her from crushing her face into the door. She shifted the child in her arms and pushed it open. The brightness of the kitchen was blinding and she leaned against the sink, squeezing her eyes shut to ease the pain. Red and yellow sparks burst under her lids, and she waited patiently for them to subside. She took deep breaths so her lungs could become accustomed to the air, feeling the warmth seep as far down as her trembling stomach muscles. Slowly the shapes became clear to her watery eyes as she batted them rapidly, bringing in the smeared cherrywood cabinets, the greasy, porcelain double-sink, the chrome faucets, the crumbs and dirty dishes on the countertops and kitchen table. By the time the room had focused down to the spotted tiles on the floor, the crumbs on the table had already vanished under a wet sponge. One arm was wrapped securely around the child, while the other methodically attacked all the grease and dirt within its reach. Plates and cutlery slid into the racks of the dishwasher; the damp mop, wedged up into one armpit, snaked over the tiles. Accustomed to working quietly so she wouldn't disturb any activity in the next room, she moved through the kitchen, leaving every surface wiped clean. Finally, satisfied that there was nothing else to do there, she straightened up and headed for the den.

"Now you gentlemen can turn around." Luther's globe was in place and lit on the tree. A short fat candle sat in its center, the light radiating through the webbed spokes in dazzling bursts of color. Surrounded now by candles, the tin snowflakes and stars rotated on their silver threads in the heated air as the golden edges of the cardboard ornaments melted into their lacy trims. "And you will finally see what I meant." Luther's eyes shone under the light.

But when Willie turned around, he saw what Willa saw. There in the mirror next to the open kitchen door was a woman, her hair tangled and matted, her sunken cheeks streaked with dirt. Her breasts and stomach were hidden behind a small body wrapped in sheer white lace. The wrinkled dress was caked under the arms with dried perspiration, the sagging pantyhose torn at the knees and spotted with urine.

"Luther" — her voice was cracked and husky as Willie's hand went toward his tightening throat — "your son is dead."

Luther spun around to the kitchen door. As the woman crossed the threshold, dragging the lace between her legs, Willie wanted to scream. It wasn't terror or shock; he just needed desperately to open his suffocating windpipes and scream so he could breathe again. Reality is based solely on the senses. And he could feel the tissues in his mouth and nasal passages drying up from a lack of air, depriving him of taste and smell while, in that split second, he was also being forced to surrender faith in his eyes. And when Luther turned back to them, face muscles immobile, voice incredibly even, "Gentlemen, thank you for your help. Your checks will be in the mail," he lost total faith in his ears as well.

Suspended in a world where reality caved in, Willie now stood out on the front porch, the raw wind biting into his body, with no memory of how he had left that house.

That same blankness was reflected in Lester's bewildered face. They neither touched nor spoke as the wind shrieked between them, carrying the silent questions behind their widening eyes. Even if they felt they could now trust their voices, there would have been nothing to say. Where were the guidelines with which to judge what they had left behind that door? They stood there frozen in a space of time without a formula that lost innocence or future wisdom could have given them. There would have been no question of smashing in that door if their world were still governed by the rules of cowboys and Indians, knights and dragons — black and white. But their twenty years immobilized them in a place where they were much more than boys, but a long way from being men. There was no way of telling exactly how long they might have stood still in that cutting wind if they hadn't heard the crash.

Luther Nedeed made two mistakes that cost him his life: he thought Willa was leaving the house, and he read the determination in her eyes as madness. She was heading for the piles of boxes and loose paper in the corner by the hall door. But she kept walking when he called her, walking when he touched her, so he blocked her path with his body. That brought them face-to-face. He had never encountered the eyes of a lone army ant, marching in defiance of falling rocks and rushing water along the great Amazon, the wingless queen who cannot fly from danger, blindly dragging her bloated egg sac as long as at least one leg is left uncrushed; so the dilated pupils in front of him registered insanity. Her fist lashed out and caught him across the Adam's apple, making him bend and choke. As she brushed past him, he sprang up, grabbed her tightly behind the shoulders, pulling her away from the door. He was trying to force her down into the chair. But that leather chair was back toward the kitchen, and the kitchen led to the basement door, and the door opened on twelve concrete steps leading to the morgue. She had cleaned those rooms. Every cell in her body strained against his hands and he found himself being pulled toward the hall.

Then he reached for the child. The moment his fingers touched the wrapped body, making a fraction of space between it and Willa, her arms loosened for one to shoot around his neck, the other his waist, and the three were welded togther. Luther tried to wrench free, but they breathed as one, moved as one, and one body lurched against the fireplace. The trailing veil brushed an ember, the material curling and shrinking as orange sparks raced up its fine weave. There was no place in her universe to make sense out of the words, "My God, we're on fire." No meaning to his struggle except that it was pushing her back into the kitchen. And now no path to the clutter by the door except through the lighted tree. They went hurling against it, the top smashed a side window, and the December wind howled in.

"Something's happening in there." Willie grabbed Lester's arm. "We've gotta do something."

"What are we gonna do, Willie?" Lester snatched his arm away. "Just tell me that, huh?" His whole body was trembling, and the tears in his eyes didn't come from the wind. "He's not gonna let us back in there." Lester turned and kicked the door viciously. "Son of a bitch!"

"We could call the cops."

"And tell them what? Who'd believe us? Christ, I don't believe it myself."

"But she's in there, Les." Willie took him by both shoulders. "Don't you understand? She's in there."

"I know, Willie, I know," he whispered, not knowing anything except that the look on Willie's face had turned him into a stranger.

"Come on, we can tell them that Nedeed killed the kid." Willie jumped over the banister and down onto the lake.

"But he didn't kill him." Lester swung over after him. "You know that."

"I don't know nothing, but we've gotta do something."

They ran, skidding and sliding across the frozen water. They had just reached the edge when they heard a dull roar and, glancing back, saw smoke billowing from the side of the house as the den draperies went up in flames.

"Oh my God, the place is on fire!"

"That fucking tree. There's no fire alarm down here. We've gotta get up to Tupelo Drive."

But Willie had already started back across the lake.

"No, White!" Lester pulled him back.

"What do you mean, no?" Willie shoved him in the chest. "She's in there."

As he ran toward the house, the den window shattered and flames shot out, crawling up to the porch roof. An arm grabbed him around the neck and he fell to his knees. He smashed his elbow back into Lester's stomach, twisted around, and threw him against the ice. "Get your hands off of me!" When he was tackled from the front, he beat at Lester's jaw and mouth. A blow to the side of Lester's nose split it open, but the next one slid across his cheek because it was now covered with blood. It took a knee up into his stomach to send Lester flat on his back. Willie was free and he charged toward a porch that was totally consumed in flames. A weight slammed against his spine and he

spun crazily across the ice with Lester riding him. Willie's right
arm was wrenched up and his chin forced back into a hammer-
lock.

"For God's sake, White, look at it!" Warm blood and tears ran
down Willie's ear.

The front door burned through, sending flames fed by the relentless wind curling all the way up to the third-floor windows.
With his chest forced against the ice, his chin jammed into the
air, Willie listened as the roar of hot and cold blasts caved in the
porch roof. It fell as if moving through solidified air, charred
ashes fanning out on the snow in loops and curves that matched
the arc of red embers against the smoke. The air kept beating in
a dull hum, a deliberate rhythm and pattern that branded itself
on his mind. Something inside of him ended there, but the
nightmare was still to begin.

Racing up that steep incline, his lungs burning. Falling and
tearing his coat and trousers, his palms and knees seared by the
icy concrete. Tasting blood in his throat, feeling it wet on his
blistered knuckles as he yelled and banged at the lighted houses
along Tupelo Drive. Faces appearing and disappearing — the
unopened doors. The lights going off, the draperies parting. The
lights going off, the shades going up. The lights going off . . .
going off . . . going off . . .

"They hear us," Lester's breath was coming in short, painful
heaves through his bruised nose.

"But they're not opening the doors."

"They're scared, White. Don't worry. Somebody will call."

"They're at those windows, Shit. Look at them, they're at
those windows."

Willie stumbled up and down the middle of Tupelo Drive,
confused and dazed.

"Tell me I'm dreaming, Shit. Please, tell me I'm dreaming —
they're watching it burn."

But as Lester anchored his hands on both sides of his friend's
neck, the white clapboard house blazing in front of him, those
darkened windows looming at his back like gutted eyes, he knew
that only real life could be this insane.

"No, White. Somebody will call."

"Yeah, they'll call." Willie backed away from him. "You bet your ass they'll call." He bent and picked up a huge rock, ran to a picture window and shattered it. He grabbed up another and was headed for the next house when Lester wrestled it from him.

A shade went down and a light on.

"Yeah, you see? They'll call now, lousy bastards!"

They heard sirens up on Linden Road. "White, I told you they were coming." But it was two police cars, racing at a dangerous speed down the icy slope. Lester took Willie's arm. "We've gotta get out of here." They ran back toward the burning house. With nowhere to hide, they jumped the low fence and crouched behind the gravestones.

Lester didn't own a watch, so he couldn't tell how much time had elapsed before the fire trucks actually got there, and he didn't know how long it took them to extinguish the blaze. But he was certain that Willie had cried through the whole thing. Excited voices had carried into the cemetery, mingling with the muffled sound of Willie's, as the firemen cursed the lake that sent their tires skidding, cursed the wind and the frozen hydrant caps, while the men scattered about breaking what few windows were left in the back, ice caked on their eyelashes, beards, and gloves as tons of water poured over the house. Lester had expected to see three bodies brought out, but one massive bulk was covered and carried to the ambulance. He couldn't feel the ends of his toes or fingers any longer but he stayed bent over in the snow, waiting for Willie to get done. Lester kept his back turned away, not daring to move or speak; this was something Willie had to complete, feeling that he was totally alone.

When the trucks finally left, the Nedeed home was a pile of charred wood, one side completely gone and the others only represented by high pointed spikes. The water was freezing over them, so that under the moonlight, tiny droplets glistened as they rolled down the three jagged shafts. But Willie still kept his forehead pressed against the crumbling gravestone. He gripped the ancient monument, crying as only a man-child could. Tight, defiant tears that fought each touch of the night air for the validity to exist in such number and depth.

Finally, a hand touched Lester's shoulder. "Are you ready to go?"

"Yeah." He got up and beat his knees to circulate the blood as sharp pains shot through his joints.

They stepped over the fence and, without looking at the ruins, headed for the rear of the yard.

"We better go this way and just climb the chain fence in the back," Lester said. "We'll be out on Patterson Road."

"Yeah."

There was silence until Willie told the biting wind, "They let it burn, Shit."

"Yeah."

Silence again. Suddenly, Lester stopped walking. "But they let it burn, White."

"Yeah."

"No, don't you see — they let it burn."

A deep sob caught in Willie's throat as he told the wind once again, "They let it burn, Shit."

"Yeah."

They let it burn

Each with his own thoughts, they approached the chain fence, illuminated by a full moon just slipping toward the point over the horizon that signaled midnight. Hand anchored to hand, one helped the other to scale the open links. Then, they walked out of Tupelo Drive into the last days of the year.

Also available in the
Methuen Modern Fiction series

NTOZAKE SHANGE

Betsey Brown

Betsey Brown is a black girl aged thirteen, poised at the still point between the enchanted world of childhood and the passionate promises – romantic and political – of the adult world. The time is 1957, the place is the black community of St Louis, and Betsey's private drama takes place against the cultural upheaval of the school integration programme and the Civil Rights movement.

Into this beguiling portrait of an extended black family confronting racism and court-ordered integration, as well as the stresses within the black community itself, Ntozake Shange weaves a magical story of adolescent awakening. Betsey's impulsive first romance, her impatience to be grown and her intimations of approaching adulthood are counterpointed by her mother's and grandmother's story, and all are combined into one magnificent song of a black family at a specific and decisive point in American history.

'Writing in the vibrant, lyrical vernacular familiar to readers of her *Sassafrass, Cypress & Indigo*, Shange stirringly evokes the love and respect that finally reunite this uneasy family. By depicting and personalizing the racial tensions of the 1950s through the lives of appealing characters, Shange has produced a memorable, quietly powerful book.'   *Publishers Weekly*

NTOZAKE SHANGE

Sassafrass, Cypress & Indigo

Sassafrass, Cypress & Indigo is the story of three coloured girls, three sisters and their mama from Charleston, South Carolina: Sassafrass, the eldest, a poet and a weaver like her mother, gone north to college, living among Bohemians in Los Angeles and trying to weave a life out of her work, her man, her memories and hopes; Cypress, the dancer who leaves home to find new ways of moving and easing the contractions of her soul; Indigo, the youngest, still a child of Charleston – 'too much of the South in her' – who lives in poetry, can talk with her dolls, and has the great gift of *seeing* the obvious magic of the world.

In a book of astonishing immediacy and beauty Ntozake Shange has created a dazzling evocation of black American culture, rich with recipes and letters, choreography and magic spells, music and poetry. As in her hugely successful stage play *for colored girls who have considered suicide when the rainbow is enuf*, her themes are black women's lives, their conflicts, dreams, souls. This, her first novel, reveals her magical command of the storyteller's art.

'This marvellous first novel from Shange . . . may well take the readers by storm. Shange's tale is poignant, surprising, deep, as she looks at the different worlds of women and their special places therein.'

Publishers Weekly

NTOZAKE SHANGE
A Daughter's Geography

In her book of poetry, Ntozake Shange maps the expand-
ing horizons of the black imagination today, from the
indigo moods of Harlem streets to the sun-drenched
colours of the Caribbean, from passionate songs of pain
and outrage to the tipsy cakewalks of love's exhilaration.
Out of the music of black speech she creates poems that
fall over your day like a wash of azure, words that dance,
strut, cruise, weep, and shout with life and power; songs
to declare her visions and map the geography of life and
beauty she would claim for her daughter.

for colored girls who have considered suicide when the rainbow is enuf

This is a series of poems, distilled over time and interac-
tion into a work of prose poetry that became an
enormously successful Broadway show.

In language that flashes with wit, passion and simple
truth, we hear, from the mouths of seven women, mono-
logues telling of the double oppression – of being black
and a woman. We are told of Harlem and St Louis, rape
and abortion, alienation and dreams. But whether she is
recounting an episode of bleak exploitation, or evoking a
mood of resignation and quiet strength, Ms Shange's
voice is always lyrical, honest and deeply-felt. With the
joy that comes from daring to sing of her own experience,
she has created a work of art that will be welcomed and
cherished.

LOUISE MERIWETHER

Daddy was a Number Runner

The unforgettable story of a black girl in Harlem, poised on the edge of a terrifying womanhood.

Francie Coffin, twelve years old, lives in a run-down tenement in Harlem, daughter of a proud father and a God-fearing mother. Darting around the streets of Harlem with the number slips for her father, Francie's manner is tough and resourceful. Yet she is still a child, naïve and innocent, and for a time her concerns are the urgent concerns of childhood – avoiding a fight with her best friend Suki, attracting the attention of Justin, the boy from out of town.

But Francie's Harlem is a world full of danger – drunks, riots, prostitutes and pimps – and the more she sees the more she understands about her future. Her story is a moving account of a young woman's rite of passage, of the journey from childhood to adulthood and the inescapable knowledge that transition brings.

'The measure of Miss Meriwether's art is that she has been able to capture a community as complex as Harlem and to render in depth such a wide range of characters while remaining faithful to the perceptions of a 12-year-old ... her deft characterization lifts her people off the page and makes them live ... honestly told and carefully crafted, it is a most important novel.'

The New York Times Book Review

MICHÈLE ROBERTS

The Wild Girl

In the parched soil of Provence, a fifth gospel has been discovered, Mary Magdalene's account of Jesus' teaching and her relationship with him. It is a book of revelation, for it unveils a new Christianity, one which embraces the female equally with the male and acknowledges and celebrates women's spirituality. It is also a passionate story of love and search, of separation and rebirth, centred on Mary as the wellspring of womanhood.

Michèle Roberts' new novel, following *A Piece of the Night* and *The Visitation*, offers a brilliant and moving vision that is also startlingly modern in its conclusions. It confirms her stature as one of Britain's most talented and exciting new writers.

'Michèle Roberts is intelligent and passionate; by her rich use of symbols and metaphor she transforms feminist cliché into something alive and moving.'
                                        Times Literary Supplement

SHEILA MACLEOD

Axioms

After sixteen years of marriage, Claudia Hughes has finally faced up to the deceits and infidelities of her husband, a once-famous pop star. Now abandoned in the family home with her two adolescent children, Josh and Matilda, she is confronted simultaneously with her own identity crisis and the children's destructive response.

Worse is to follow, but for Claudia survival must be endured, and the bitter fruit of the experience might even, eventually, begin to offer her some nourishment.

Sheila MacLeod, prize-winning author of *The Art of Starvation*, has written an angry, irrefutable and unforgettable novel of broken marriages and what it feels like to be left holding the pieces.

'[What] makes it very difficult to put down is the memorable bitterness of Claudia's version of the events and the sober intelligence and sadness with which Sheila MacLeod carries her thesis through. Her prose is strong, her style pure . . . quite excellent writing.'
Anita Brookner, *Evening Standard*

JEANETTE WINTERSON

Boating For Beginners

Was there pizza before the Flood? Were there secretaries? Or designer-cut suede cat suits? Was there a fixed minimum wage in the catering industry? Should we believe everything we read in the Bible? The answers are all in *Boating for Beginners*, Jeanette Winterson's hilarious new novel.

Meet Mrs Munde, an Astrologer Without Telescope, who cooks for the Noah Household. Meet her daughter Gloria, whose elephant Trebor is not house-trained. Meet Noah himself, not just a religious leader but a family man with a penchant for home-inventing. Meet Bunny Mix, the most successful romantic novelist this side of Ur of the Chaldees. What terrible fate do they all have in common and what was *really* found on Mount Ararat?

Illustrated by Paula Youens and inspired by Northrop Frye and the Orange Demon, *Boating for Beginners* is even more bizarre than most of the Old Testament and certainly a lot funnier. It may not be the authorised version, but will we ever know?

These and other Methuen Paperbacks are available at your bookshop or newsagent. In case of difficulties orders may be sent to:

Methuen Paperbacks
Cash Sales Department
PO Box 11
Falmouth
Cornwall TR10 109EN

Please send cheque or postal order, no currency, for purchase price quoted and allow the following for postage and packing:

UK   55p for the first book, 22p for the second book and 14p for each additional book ordered to a maximum of £1.75.

BFPO   55p for the first book, 22p for the second
& Eire   book plus 14p for the next seven books, thereafter 8p per book.

Overseas   £1.00 for the first book plus 25p per copy for
Customers   each additional book.

While every effort is made to keep prices low, it is sometimes necessary to increase prices at short notice. Methuen Paperbacks reserves the right to show new retail prices on covers which may differ from those previously advertised in the text or elsewhere.